⁺⁺ Praise for ⁺⁺
⁺ HOPELESSLY
Teavoted ⁺

"A witchy romance with cozy vibes, a cursed heroine, and just the right amount of spice. What more could you ask for?"

—Kami Garcia, #1 *New York Times*
bestselling coauthor of *Beautiful Creatures*

"The perfect magical read, *Hopelessly Teavoted* is full of charm and yearning and so much witchy fun! Audrey Goldberg Ruoff's debut belongs on everyone's TBR!"

—Brigid Kemmerer, *New York Times*
bestselling author of *Warrior Princess Assassin*

"*Hopelessly Teavoted* is a romantic, devilish delight. With wit, flair, and a quirky friends-to-lovers couple, this book is just the right mix of sweet, steamy, and swoony."

—Gwenda Bond, *New York Times*
bestselling author of *The Frame-Up*

"*Hopelessly Teavoted* is a colorful, sweet, and swoony debut that makes you feel like it's spooky season all year round! This tender friends-to-lovers romance scorches with yearning and sexual tension, with a unique, paranormal twist. Audrey Goldberg Ruoff writes with all the whimsy, sparkles, and heart to create a magical world readers will want to sink into with a warm cup of tea of their own. I can't wait for everyone to fall under its spell!"

—Mallory Marlowe, *USA Today*
bestselling author of *Love and Other Conspiracies*

HOPELESSLY
Teavoted

A NOVEL

AUDREY GOLDBERG RUOFF

ATRIA PAPERBACK

New York Amsterdam/Antwerp London
Toronto Sydney/Melbourne New Delhi

ATRIA
PAPERBACK

An Imprint of Simon & Schuster, LLC
1230 Avenue of the Americas
New York, NY 10020

This book is a work of fiction. Any references to historical events, real people, or
real places are used fictitiously. Other names, characters, places, and events are
products of the author's imagination, and any resemblance to actual events or
places or persons, living or dead, is entirely coincidental.

Simon & Schuster strongly believes in freedom of expression and stands against
censorship in all its forms. For more information, visit BooksBelong.com.

For information about special discounts for bulk purchases,
please contact Simon & Schuster Special Sales at 1-866-506-1949
or business@simonandschuster.com.

The Simon & Schuster Speakers Bureau can bring authors to your live event. For
more information or to book an event, contact the Simon & Schuster Speakers
Bureau at 1-866-248-3049 or visit our website at www.simonspeakers.com.

Manufactured in the United States of America

1 3 5 7 9 10 8 6 4 2

Library of Congress Cataloging-in-Publication Data has been applied for.

ISBN 978-1-6680-6832-8
ISBN 978-1-6680-6833-5 (ebook)

To Alex, who has always made me feel as though stumbling across a town house floor is really dancing a tango in a grand, creepy ballroom. What bliss. This one is for you, my love.

Content Warning

This book contains off-page death of a character's parents due to the COVID-19 pandemic. It includes depression and anxiety, a brief fight sequence, and a reference to off-page relationship violence happening to a minor character, discussion of drug overdose, mention of gun violence, and toxic, misogynistic behavior. This book includes on-page sex, all of which centers clear consent. If you are sensitive to any of these things, please take care while reading.

CHAPTER 1

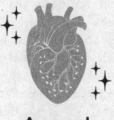

Azrael

Eight Years Ago

Azrael Hart had missed his chance.

Again.

Victoria's freckled nose pressed up against the glass of the car door as the engine started, and for a moment, they were kids again. As though she weren't driving the few hours to college, and he weren't catching a ride to the airport to fly three thousand miles away from the girl he'd loved since he was six years old.

"Devil dammit," he swore. He shoved his hands in his pockets and replayed the speech he had planned. In his head, he'd given her the note, which he folded now, and shoved in his wallet, crushing the heavy weighted paper he used for his most treasured compositions against the sweaty, useless palm and tingling fingers that had failed him. His fingers were supposed to push a strand of hair behind her ear. To tuck it gently there, and ask her, in a voice that would have come out low and velvety, if he could kiss her. That perspiring palm was supposed to have been cool and collected and to have pressed against her soft cheek. He wanted to have pulled her face toward his own like he did in his best daydreams.

Instead, his hand had flapped, an awkward bird in the wind, wet with anticipation, as he told her good luck and then gave her a handshake.

An honest-to-devil handshake, like he was his uncle Larry, the funeral director, doing grim business and sealing a deal for a discounted casket and viewing package.

He was a fucking mess.

Vickie was sunshine and daisies and happiness. The echoes of their childhood friendship were everywhere, even when he turned to face his house, which sat on the grounds next to hers, the property marked off by a white picket fence on her family's side and a wrought-iron one on his. Running a useless hand through dark brown curls, he looked up at the winding spires of the gothic mansion that was the Hart family home.

Now his hair was sweaty, and his hands steamed with angst and unused spells. He would need to at least magic a shower before he left, or risk alarming everyone on the airplane even more than he would if they caught a glimpse of his morbid parents in all their attire.

He looked up to the sweeping window from where his parents watched him.

A familiar clatter of combat boots on the stone walkway told him his sister was nearby.

Good. That crushed the longing in his chest.

Azrael swallowed and wondered if his family suspected how he felt about Victoria.

His mother stood there, straight dark hair hanging over her snug, high-necked, black velvet gown, the lace of the sleeves stretching over her fingers as she raised them in acknowledgment. Concern flickered across her face, pale as a sheet above bloodred lips. The way his mother glided across the ground made him shudder with embarrassment. Years of revulsion from adults and peers alike taught him that, good intentions or not, his parents caused scenes simply by existing.

Victoria's parents were an exception, but only because the Starnbergers primarily spoke the language of black American Express cards and chauffeurs like the one who was about to squire Vickie away before Az could tell her of his hidden heart. The Hart family might be known for their proximity anytime something unusual happened in town, but they were wealthy enough to purchase the respect of their posh neighbors. Though the grounds surrounding both houses were vast enough to require a car, and there was no way to see if the Starnbergers stood watch from their window, Az knew the answer.

They never bothered.

"Did you at least kiss her farewell? You should do that. Like, now." His sister's mouth pulled into a smirk, and he knew he was blushing. Priscilla was his *younger* sister. How was it that she knew precisely the right way to boss him around?

Goddess, he hoped Vickie hadn't heard that.

Vickie rolled down the window one last time. This was his moment.

Prissy looked at him and shook her head. "Weirdo," she murmured, patting his arm so he knew that even if she was judging him, she did at least also care.

"If you decide this sulky, sad boy isn't good enough to be your long-distance bestie, you can always pick me instead." She pointed toward her face, nodding solemnly.

Vickie smiled, and Azrael's heart seemed to stand still. He was never going to have the courage to tell her.

"I pick you already. You're already my friend."

His sister's smile stretched wide now. "Damn right," she said, waving one last time, and running back toward the door, but not before giving him a stern look. "Have fun at college! Be safe, but not too safe!" she called over her shoulder.

It was just the two of them now, and the insurmountable distance between his hand and the rolled-down window. He willed himself to move toward it.

His feet did nothing.

"Text me when you get there," he murmured, weakly, instead. He held up his hand a final time, hoping she couldn't see the glistening sweat.

She looked at him for a moment. Bit her lip.

"Bye, Az," she said. "Miss you already."

All he had to offer her in return was a weak smile.

He should have run to her then, but the window was rolling up, the car away, and then it was over. She was gone.

Vickie's stop here was the real goodbye, and his parents and sister had said farewell the night before in an embarrassingly overaffectionate dinner in their family dining room.

He checked his watch.

Az had a plane to catch. There was nothing he could do besides trudge reluctantly up the sweeping cobblestone path toward the gated entrance of Hart Manor.

Twisting the gleaming silver doorknob in his hand, Az grimaced at the chill that ran through him upon touching it. Carved like a church door, the mahogany behemoth was so imposing that at times in his childhood, his sister teased him about the way it made him jump. But he swore it was more animated than the rest of the house; the moaning noises the door made did little to dispel the suggestion of something supernatural inside. The door grumbled now as he advanced but made no louder groans that might promise ghoulish behavior afoot.

The tingling sensation in his hands alerted him to the trap before the door swung completely open. It took no more than a lazy snap of his fingers—the Hart family signature magic—to turn the pile of gravedirt rigged to fall on him to harmless soap bubbles, which shone purple and popped, like his dreams of running off into the sunset with Victoria.

A titter of teenage laughter followed, and he sighed, rubbing his temples.

"I take it you didn't tell the beautiful Vic-to-ree-aahhh how you feel?" Prissy sang it like the Kinks, and to retaliate, he snapped, shooting a volley of the soap bubbles at her, this time filled with rose-gold glitter dust. When they burst, she frowned, shaking the festive sparkles off her braid and her black vest.

"Fuck you, Azrael. I'll look like a devil-damned My Little Pony for the rest of the week. You know how hard it is to get rid of glitter."

He smiled wickedly now. "I do, sister dearest. Just as you

know how hard it is to shake the truth curse of gravedirt. Imagine going off to your first week of college being literally forced to answer everything truthfully for seven days."

She crossed her arms, blowing black bangs out of her eyes, which glowed golden brown like their father's. "It would have eased up after a day or two," she retorted. "By day three, you would have been able to swallow the truth back down. At least, some of the time."

"Still. Prissy," he said. "Not cool."

Even in a family of witches, Azrael was the odd one out. His curly hair and hazel eyes came from his maternal grandmother. The siblings differed in more than appearance; at two years younger, Priscilla was always willing to give her opinion. Or pull a prank. Azrael kept to himself, mostly. He loved his family, even though he would never fit in with them completely.

Maybe he had no place in the magical or the mundane world.

"It would have been funny in hindsight," she said, sulking.

Ironically, had she pranked him just a few hours earlier, the gravedirt could have worked out perfectly for him to finally be honest with the one person he *might* fit with.

Either that or it would have forced Azrael to bare his entire soul to the girl he worshiped, only to have her reject him. All the moments over the past few years when he'd mustered the courage, only to stop short when he finally got his chance. All the poems he'd written and burned. All the daisies he'd magicked into existence and then quickly pushed away before she could see them.

Rubbing his temples, he decided it was better this way. To pine desperately for what might possibly be rather than deal with the crushing reality if she didn't love him too.

Which she didn't. He was almost entirely sure.

Priscilla studied him, and he must have looked more wrecked than he realized because she didn't attempt another prank, but patted his shoulder instead, leaving a few trace specks of glitter.

"Come on," she said. "I'll help you finish packing." She snapped her fingers, and his suitcases appeared on the landing, undoubtedly packed with the precision of Prissy's magic.

On their way upstairs, Azrael spotted the guillotine, but Prissy didn't make a move toward it, and she casually pulled him out of the way of a swinging axe that sliced the air above the staircase. The under-stairs apparition cackled at her caution, but they both knew better than to engage with it, for neither of them could see ghosts, and it was harmless, other than scaring the occasional visitor.

"Thanks, Priss."

"Don't mention it. You get a reprieve since you're both heartbroken and leaving for college, possibly forever, to become some kind of sunshiny, strange normie."

He grimaced. "I'm not heartbroken," he insisted. "And California's not *that* far away from Vermont. Some witches go international, you know."

"Azrael Ashmedai Hart!" The rasping voice echoed across the upstairs hallway like sandpaper against wood. His father stood, as always, in a three-piece suit with a starched white dress shirt and a bow tie, in a deep shade of merlot today. Benedict Hart ran a hand through snow-colored, shoulder-length hair in a nervous tic that Az recognized all too well. With his golden-rimmed eyes, he was the family member who was most obviously a witch, at least to a trained magical eye, though his mother and sister certainly dressed the part enough to leave the townsfolk speculating that the Harts were the weird kind of wealthy.

It was a wonder the mundanes didn't figure them out immediately. And yet, here Az was, nineteen and about to leave for college, and no one in all of Hallowcross, save Vickie, knew that the Hart family didn't just dress like they belonged in his mother's eclectically witchy tea shop in the middle of downtown, they *were* magical.

Pausing for a moment at the top of the stairs, Az looked down at his father expectantly.

Benedict cleared his throat, waiting. When his son did not say anything, he went on.

"Did you see Vickie off properly?"

"Yeah, Dad. It was fine."

Arms crossed, his father grunted, as though he wanted to say more, but beside him, Az's mother rested her hand on Benedict's arm. The simple intimacy of the gesture was like an exhale, and his father relaxed. He nodded almost imperceptibly, letting the line of interrogation go. It was always like this; though Az's father sat on the North American Council of Witchery, his mother ran both his father's life and the shop.

Hopelessly Teavoted had an ornate sign with the name carved across it in shiny letters. Inside, it smelled like vintage books and incense, freshly ground coffee, and the tea of the day. They had a small side business trading in magical equipment with the odd witch traveling through, but those were so few and far between that it had been months since his mother had served anything other than antique cups full of surprisingly delicious beverages, sometimes magicked gently to wear away at worries or soothe a deserving soul.

Persephone Hart was as kind as she was committed to the pallor of her deathly white skin. That was saying something. Once, when he was a small boy, Az had held a sun-bleached bone he'd confiscated from his dog, Cerberus, up to her and noted no real difference in color. She must have powdered it to achieve the shade.

Az loved his parents, and even his annoying sister, but he couldn't handle being seen at the airport with them today nor taking any of the ignominy of the Hart name with him to the Golden State. Not after everything that had happened with his classmates calling him odd, and everything that had *not* happened to Az in Hallowcross with Victoria.

California was a fresh start. A chance to be normal. He just wished that he didn't see a heart-shaped face with enchanting green eyes and slightly frizzy brown hair whenever he shut his eyes. That he wasn't haunted by swirls of freckles and the almost of loving her.

"Are you certain you don't want us to take you to the airport?" His mother tapped her long crimson nails together. "Uncle Larry said we can take the hearse if you have a lot of luggage."

Azrael blanched. The very last thing he wanted was to roll up to the airport in the hearse, of all things. He'd had enough of the teasing and staring in high school, and if he had it his way, he'd never set foot in the halls of Hallowcross High again in his life.

"I'm fine," he said.

He repeated it to himself when the rideshare pulled up and he rolled a single, sleek black suitcase down the cobblestone drive, trying not to notice the way the driver stared up at the sharp spikes of the gates and the general gloom of the grounds.

I'm fine.

The refrain pounded through his brain as he watched the familiar haunts of Hallowcross drift by through the car window: his mother's tea shop, Hopelessly Teavoted; the local salon, Blade Runner; and the twenty-four-hour diner, Don't Go Bacon My Heart. All the absurdly punny shops on Main Street faded into a winding stretch of highway. When he got to the airport, and the driver paused for the cars whipping in and out of the departure zone, he reminded himself once again.

I'm fine.

The Zoloft kept him from panicking; even witches believed in better living through chemistry. And he remembered what his mother had told him: *When the weight of the world seems awful, we look for the ways that we can make it better.*

Small magics to fix the world.

He focused on moving through the security line, speeding it up with the snap of his fingers and a pinch of simple magic to relieve the head and foot aches of the agents standing all day. When they visibly relaxed, Az smiled as the line became more pleasant for everyone.

I'm fine, he reminded himself as he boarded the enormous plane, the sun creeping through the windows. A mother a few rows back wiped sweat from her brow while she wrangled two small children into their seats. All it took was a subtle snap of his fingers to lower the cabin temperature, and she exhaled relief. The children settled, and Az smiled to himself. The world had a history of burning witches, but magic could heal the world in so many small ways. It was beautiful, really, when he could let go of his shame over his eccentric family long enough to remember all the good they had to offer.

Azrael slid into his seat and gave the flight attendant a wave. She winked, whispering to the attendant next to her, who also smiled and raised his eyebrows at Azrael.

They were both attractive, and they couldn't be too much older than he was. He would enjoy kissing either, but it was no matter, because that all-too-revealing note was burning a hole in his wallet, and his heart was stuck on the impossible dream of the girl next door. And of course, because they were not Vickie, it was easy enough to wave again, and to smile at the resulting blushes. He had this effect on strangers, so why couldn't he ever find the same bravado when he was with her?

He stretched out, wishing he had opted for comfortable clothing instead of fitted jeans and a pressed white T-shirt, a gray bomber jacket completing the look, which he hoped screamed *normal*.

I'm fine, he insisted as the plane lifted off and his stomach flipped for a moment as it rose into the air. He closed his eyes. He'd do a pass of the plane on the way back to the bathroom and magic away small inconveniences as much as he could without being noticed.

His father said they had an obligation to help mundanes. That magic meant compassion. And it calmed him to walk the plane and tap his fingers against each other.

Snap. A cord connected fully for a kid's tablet.

A few more snaps, and the airflow increased on a sweating older woman.

A quick snap and the man struggling with a crossword puzzle suddenly remembered that five down was *kumquat*.

By the time he reached the bathroom, the mood had shifted. Sun streamed through the windows, and a little boy raised a daisy-print blanket in front of it, casting pink and yellow tones on the tray table in front of him. It reminded Azrael of Vickie, and his heart twisted.

I'm fine, he told himself.

The assertion was undone as he returned to his seat, and the plane dipped through turbulence. The queasy feeling reminded him of how he felt sometimes when *she* came into a room, smelling like strawberries and lavender, and humming to herself. Usually, it was something he wanted to fuck her to softly, like Edward Sharpe. Oasis.

He was fine. And even if he wasn't, Azrael Hart was a witch, going to his top choice of schools to study screenwriting and live his dream. What more could he ask for? There were plenty of men and women in California he could serve his heart to on a platter.

He hoped.

CHAPTER 2

Victoria

Now

Robbie had picked the worst possible day to dump her.

Not that there was ever a particularly good time to be dumped, but she had convinced herself that it would work out and she would become effortlessly cool and composed. This was supposed to be the only exception to her string of romantic bad luck.

He was her second serious, long-term relationship. Even though she had jumped from dating Natalie to that unfortunate incident of hope and then heartache, and then right into Robbie, she had told herself it would work out. It was normal for him to be gone for long stretches of time. Dating Robbie gave her space. She knew she should be heartbroken, but good goddess, she couldn't care enough to pay attention to his dumping. Maybe there was such a thing as too much space?

He was still talking, head hanging out of the side of that ridiculous convertible that compensated for things she was all too familiar with, the top up to keep the hot July wind from messing with the blond hair she had watched him blow-dry to perfection that morning, increasingly irritated at the way he rummaged through her hair products without asking.

"...two ships passing in the night, and sticking around and

letting you get more and more clingy will honestly only hurt you in the end, Vicks."

Clingy. She had gone days without talking to him sometimes, but he still used the same word Natalie had so many years earlier, and it glinted off his professionally whitened teeth. From far away, he looked like an album cover, but up close, he was the kind of unnaturally tanned that would leave him leathery in a decade or two. She should have known something was off when he packed up silently. Robbie was never quiet when there was an opportunity to talk about himself.

The prick.

He'd played along with the trip back to Hallowcross, even played house with her in her childhood bedroom, fucking her with wild abandon last night against poofy pink throw pillows, which was awfully unbecoming now that she knew he had intended to break up with her from the rolled-down window of his absurd sports car.

"Fuck you, Robbie," she bit out.

"Hey. Don't be like that, Vicky Vale." The nickname, once a cute symbol of their new love, was now a slap in the face. "Wasn't it nice that we had a final week together?" He was giving her that lopsided grin that made his fans go wild. "Babe, we went out on a high note of you screaming my name. Like the good times, before you got all serious." That million-watt smile was a death wish now.

Murderous intention clear on her face, she stalked toward the car, ready to smack the gloating look off his face. She wouldn't *actually* kill him, but she was going to hit this smug motherfucker as hard as she possibly could.

Robbie's face dropped at her scowl, and he sped off into the sunlight, hair ruffling as he rolled up his window. She was left seething in a cloud of dust and fumes with nothing to do but keep her appointments.

Under the heat at Blade Runner, the upscale spa in downtown Hallowcross, she unpacked her feelings, half expecting to be shattered. But all she felt was tired and relieved. Things with Robbie had been over for a long time before that morning. She emerged blonder, peppier, and smoother than the version of herself who had just been dumped.

An hour later, that veneer was a much-needed armor against the world of Amelie and Maximillian Starnberger. She sat on a white sofa in the middle of an absurdly plush taupe shag carpet in her parents' sterile home. She fiddled with her manicure, which matched her yellow top, and gingerly poked at the unfamiliar shape of her glossy, voluminous hair. She knew her parents, though. The effort to polish herself for their world *would* persuade them. Even if it meant she had to set things on fire, literally, she was willing to do it. What had happened to the Harts was a fucking tragedy, and she couldn't stand by while a big chain company bought up the shop. Not when she had dipped in and out of school for twice the recommended amount of time and reluctantly earned three-quarters of an MBA after a bachelor's degree in business at her parents' insistence while nursing a hankering for a quirky business of her own.

She was going to convince her parents to buy Hopelessly Teavoted. Vickie knew that the Harts had both been witches. But not even magic could protect them from a virus that had preyed on magical and mundane folks alike.

The universe had done wrong to take a couple so enamored with each other. Not to mention how terrible it must have been for Priscilla. And for Azrael, who she hadn't spoken to since the incident. A little twist of that old rejection wrung out in her chest when she thought of him. She pushed it out of her mind in favor of the fonder earlier memories. The friendship she'd sworn never to blemish with romantic complications, though a lot of good that vow had done. The little boy who had danced with her in their childhood bedrooms to Fleetwood Mac and Frank Ocean. Sure, she missed him, and she had considered texting, or even calling when his parents died, but he had made his feelings clear all those years ago.

He was better off without her. No need to *cling* to the memory of a relationship that was never going to work out.

She'd kept in touch with Priscilla and spoken to the younger Hart sibling when her parents first died, so she knew the restrictions on air travel were enough that Azrael couldn't leave California. Prissy had mentioned the magical council she worked for halting interdimensional portal travel to stop viral transmission, but that bit had gone over Vickie's head. She grasped the concept of craft magic, but she didn't know it the way she knew her own gift.

Or, as her parents called it, her curse. She despised that word. Ghosts were less of a curse than a frigid family.

"Victoria Elaine." Her mother's voice pierced the air with the confidence only socialites and sociopaths could pull off. Vickie wilted. This never got easier. Around her parents, Vickie felt every one of her imperfections like a thousand tiny paper cuts to her soul. And her parents were always so indifferent toward her.

Until they needed a favor.

"Your father requires some important information from Mr. George."

Vickie sighed. There was no way Kyle George, a man with two first names, was going to be an interesting ghost. Her father's business associates were never friendly. She suspected that there were sinister aspects to the Starnberger empire, though she wasn't privy to the details. Maximillian Starnberger strode in, aware of his commanding presence in any room he entered. Her mother smiled, and he swept down to kiss her cheek.

"Amelie, my darling." The greeting was transactional and cold. It suited them.

Maximillian held up a pair of gold cuff links with a suspicious red splatter about their edges. Vickie hoped it was tomato sauce as he set them on the ornate end table next to her.

It was *not* tomato sauce.

"Poor fellow was killed in a car crash. I managed to take these off the corpse; told his wife that they were a company gift and that they meant the world to me to remember him by."

"That's nice, at least," Vickie offered. Her father was never sentimental, and who was she to question it? "I guess you can't take all the wealth or fancy cuff links with you, huh, Dad?"

Maximillian shook his head, frowning at her informality. "He loved them because they were a gift from his mistress. Kyle loved few things, but she was one of them. She has these—"

Vickie held her hand up, cutting him off. This made more sense, but she was still unwilling to hear what the dead man's mistress had.

"Go on, then," Maximillian said. "We will speak more after you're done. I need the passcode for his platinum clients."

She rolled her shoulders back, ignoring the creeping wave of guilt over using her gift for profit. She had a vague understanding that they owed something to someone in exchange for her powers, but she didn't know the details. Once she had turned twenty-one, they'd contacted her once or twice a year to deal with clients of the unalive sort. Best to get it over with and then convince them of what she'd come here for.

It wasn't enough that the Starnbergers owned half the town. It wasn't enough that they had both reached a pinnacle of success that could have kept them living like royalty for ten lifetimes over. No, they had to go and arrange for Vickie to talk to ghosts. The catch, of course, was that she could only do it with an object the deceased had loved with their whole heart. And spirits, like time, were fleeting. Gone forever once the objects they loved burst into flames.

Coming back here and asking her parents for the money was big enough to barter with them in the only trade they valued.

She closed her eyes and picked up the cuff links, hoping that the deceased had loved the objects enough.

From the way the gold grew hot in her hands—a flame springing up, but not burning her—she knew he had. Once objects heated, there was no stopping the fire.

Within seconds, the silver shimmer coalesced into a semi-translucent form, and a moment later, a short man in a sharp-looking suit with a wispy, regrettable mustache stood in front of her.

"That truck came out of nowhere. I swear I only had a single bump, not enough to put me at fault."

"Mr. George," she said flatly. Realizing that she wasn't any sort of authority, he heaved a breath of relief. Except nothing came out. He noticed, holding his hands up and startling.

"Mr. George, you're dead, and we have five minutes here before you're gone for good."

"Shit," said the specter, still staring at his hands and the pristine floor shining through them. "Is this Hell? It seems cold enough to be hell, but it smells good for an afterlife."

Newly dead, then, if his corporeal senses were lingering. He'd lose those in a few days. She sighed. It had taken her a while to figure that one out. The gift didn't come with instructions.

But unlike Kyle George, she was a quick study. For a person who presumably had not known about the existence of magic, he was taking this pretty well. Some ghosts, usually those more in touch with the occult in life, realized at once that they were dead. Others protested and had to be calmed down before they could be helpful. But he didn't strike her as caring about anything enough to panic about his sudden state of unalive. In fact, it was hard to tell if men like him were actually ever human to begin with. She had a goal, though. If she wanted her parents' support, she needed to get Kyle George's password. Favors were the way to win their fleeting approval. Her chest ached with the emptiness of what she'd never had, but she pushed that aside to focus. She didn't know the precise terms of the arrangement they had made for her to speak to the dead, but that didn't stop them from insinuating that because they owed someone *something* for her powers, she owed them everything, in turn.

"My father would like you to tell him about the passcode for the platinum client files."

The ghost smirked. "I bet you would, old boy," he said, turning to her father, who was now glancing around the room, eyes falling on objects, but never on the spirit.

"He can't see you," she explained. Kyle was a bit dimmer than most ghosts. Usually, they picked up on the gist of what was happening, but this particular shade seemed impervious to logic. Kyle huffed, but she ignored it. "It would be helpful if you could tell me the passcode."

"Fine. It's KyleDog."

"Seriously?" It was her turn to cross her arms. "That's your top secret passcode for your most important accounts?"

"Yes, who are you to judge me? Some sort of ghost psychic? I knew Max's kid would be a little off." She shook her head, surprised that he even knew her father had a daughter.

It was often enough that people didn't.

She turned to her father and told him the devil-damned passcode.

"Anything else?"

Her father looked eager, but the ghost spoke, and she held up a hand. Maximillian's shoulders tensed. He glared at her, and then at the space next to her, though unable to see the man. His scorn was about six inches too low and to the left. This, at least, made her chuckle.

"Those fucking cuff links are the only thing I truly loved, you know."

"Yes, you'll pass on after this. To wherever you're headed."

Vickie paused. She'd be the last soul this man spoke to before that. Looking at his narrow, ratlike face and limp blond hair, she couldn't bring herself to care much for the loss.

He looked at her, determination glinting in his eyes.

"Listen, Veronika."

"It's Victoria."

"Right. Do two things for me."

She sighed, rubbing the cuff links, now scalding as the flame in her fist licked higher. They didn't have much time.

"Sure," she agreed. Who was she to deny a dead man his last request?

"Have your father tell Candie I would have left. She was worth it."

Vickie bit down on the impulse to tell him that if he was going to leave, he would have.

"And second. They really should know, all things considered. It's on them. There's shady stuff going on at Brethren of One Love."

"The megachurch?"

"Yeah. I'm not sure what, but I kept seeing one of the college kids from my neighborhood headed in there. He's a fine upstanding fellow. Straight As, captain of his lacrosse team. His mom is—well, she's a close friend." The ghost winked, and Vickie shuddered. "She was worried about him. I told her it was probably over a girl, but the night I died, I saw him go in there again. After hours. I almost told his mom about it, but he's just about a grown person. Still, no reason for him to be around that insufferable group at Brethren."

Her eyebrows furrowed, Vickie puzzled at that. There could be a thousand reasons for a student to check out a different church. A girl. A boy. Hell, maybe a religious conversion. Kyle was trying to buy time in his last moments. She shook off the nagging feeling at the back of her mind that this was consequential.

"It felt important," said Kyle. He looked desperate enough to lie. "The school might be involved. I mean, just because I told some kid's smoking-hot mom I love her in the heat of a moment doesn't mean he was *my* kid. But still I saw—"

But Kyle George's time had run out, and Vickie was tired of listening to his tales of philandering. She stepped back, dropping the crumbling cuff links. The ash of them flamed orange, red, and finally gold, and within seconds was gone, along with the last remains of Kyle George's immortal soul, on this plane, anyway.

"What was that about a church?" Her father adjusted his tie, not looking as surprised as one might expect for a man who had just heard a one-sided conversation that made Vickie look like a person in need of medical assistance.

Which made sense, since her parents, upon learning there was magic in the world, had arranged a deal with a devil for their only daughter to see dead people. Obviously, they wouldn't stoop so low as to bargain for death powers for themselves.

She picked at her bright yellow nail polish.

"He said there's something shady going on at the mega-church."

"Well, that's certainly always the case with religious organizations wringing money from the poor and handing out platitudes about how they'll go to Heaven if they simply vote to remove rights from women and give those rights to demagogues."

"Don't you and Dad also wring money from people?"

"My darling, we are stockbrokers; we at least don't try to hide what we are doing by masquerading it as the work of the Lord. Ours is an honest sort of robbery." Amelie tilted her head, and bleached blond hair shifted like a silken waterfall. Even with the blowout, Vickie's didn't look that flawless, and she was sure her mother had noticed.

"We never should have brought that megachurch to town," Maximillian muttered.

"You did what?" Vickie blanched.

Her father shrugged. "We thought it would be good for business. It's one of those clever multilevel marketing–modeled organizations. It's good business. Your mother had this idea that we could join and use it for weekly Sunday networking."

Amelie shrugged. "It turns out they were too despicable for us to tolerate, and stingy to boot." She examined her perfect French manicure.

Unbelievable. Her parents were unbelievable.

"So you brought an actively recruiting church to town to try to turn a profit, and then abandoned it to wreak havoc on Hallowcross?"

"Victoria, we aren't responsible for other people's decisions." Her mother sighed, and shook her head, as though Vickie were the unreasonable one.

"What else did Kyle say?" Her father's eyes bored into her, commanding.

"Ah, Dad, Kyle also wanted you to tell Candie he was going to leave his wife."

Her mother gave her father a sharp glare.

"Well, obviously I won't, Amelie. He was an insipid little man."

"Just know that *I* am no Charlotte George, and I am not above murder should your eyes wander." Her words were ice. Not for the first time, Vickie shuddered at her parents' cruelty.

Her father dropped down to the couch next to her mother, and whispered words that made Amelie's lips twitch upward in the closest assimilation Vickie had seen to a smile. This would be a perfect time to slip out, but she had additional business here today.

She cleared her throat, and her mother shook off the haze of lust.

"Yes, darling?"

"I need to talk to you about school."

Her father focused his attention, sharp and suspicious now, on Vickie.

She sunk into the chair, wishing the upholstery could swallow her whole.

"I'm not going back. I want my own business."

"Is this about Robert?"

"Robbie," she corrected. As always.

"You're well aware I don't care to partake in juvenile nicknames." Her mother's eyes sharpened. "That boy is talented and handsome, and from such a good family, but honestly, Victoria, do you really want to be a permanent groupie?"

"We broke up." She avoided the razor-sharp blue eyes digging into her, and bit back the correction that a person in their late twenties was more of a man than a boy.

"Oh, thank goodness," said Amelie. "Groupies are so clingy and gauche. Even if he *had* ever married you, you would have been either a headline or a punch line. Maybe both."

The chair was haloed by yellow nail polish chips now.

"I want to buy Hopelessly Teavoted. I want to run the tea shop, and tinker with magic."

"No," said her mother.

"Absolutely not," said her father. "You return to school and finish, and then we can talk about your options."

Vickie shook her head. It would have been easier if they had agreed, but she was willing to do things the hard way.

"I already talked to Priscilla Hart. She's too busy at the Council of Witchery to take over. A buyer is lined up to put in a chain coffee shop otherwise."

Her mother's glare intensified. How was that even possible? Vickie had the magical gift, and yet here she was, a butterfly skewered by a sharp sliver on a board for examination.

"We won't pay for it." Amelie shook out her hair again, chin lifted. "And you have no idea how disastrous it would be to have to pay for *everything* we have provided for you."

Vickie shrugged, ignoring the threat. It was typical of her mother to play dramatic. "I'll take out a loan."

"You'll finish school, or we will formally cut you out of the will. I'll have our lawyers on the phone as soon as you step out of here." There was no arguing with Maximillian.

Vickie sighed. She had suspected it would come to this. It was part of the reason she had stowed two suitcases in her yellow Volkswagen this morning. The car had barely made it back here from school, but it would do. There was an apartment above the shop, and she had already put in an inquiry at the bank. Prissy could be ready today, she said.

The Starnberger name would help her with getting what she needed. If she hurried.

"Call your lawyer," she said, her voice as cold as her mother's eyes. Her father stood up.

"Victoria," he began, but she held a hand up.

"Don't bother. Cut me off. I'll do this on my own."

She walked before she caught any reaction. If she knew her parents, their first move would be to make good on the threat with their family lawyer, and it would take him some time to draw up the documents, even for his wealthiest clients on retainer.

Vickie was counting on it, because it would give her enough time to sign the paperwork at the bank before anyone caught wind that she was no longer a wealthy heiress. She hadn't been raised by sharks for nothing. When she pulled up to the Loanly Officers' Club, the town bank, and the teller ran out to greet her, she knew she had made it.

She would save the tea shop that had meant so much to her as a child. And if she ran into Azrael Hart, she would get to see an old friend again.

She would *not* think about that one time at college. She would not think about the brief moment where she'd recognized that her body against his body was the closest she'd ever come to religion. It had been a blip. A one-off six years ago. A strange convergence by a meddlesome universe with a perverse sense of humor.

She was absolutely not thinking about Azrael Hart at all several hours later, as she stood with the little bronze key to his mother's shop in her hand, staring at the bells above the door. This was her dream, and it was the closest thing to coming home that she would ever have. Shaped like tiny silver skulls, those doorbells reminded her of her old neighbors in a way that made her heart twist. Benedict and Persephone were really gone.

Vickie was about to turn the key when a voice startled her enough to drop it.

"Hello, Victoria," he purred.

She turned around, but the man who stood in the doorway was unfamiliar to her. Yet there was something about his face that said she knew him. That she *wanted* to know him.

"Can I help you?" Vickie kept her tone neutral and stooped to pick up the key.

The man shook wavy black hair out of his eyes, which were quite unfairly violet blue. He cracked a breathtaking smile that she was willing to bet had destroyed its fair share of people.

"I believe you can, but it might be better if we went into this quaint little establishment first." His smile was insouciant, and she scowled at him.

"Just what exactly makes you think I'd invite a man I've never met before inside?"

"Ah, pet, that's not precisely true, though, now is it?"

Victoria prickled at the nickname, and at the sense that he was not lying.

"What could you possibly say to me that would make me change my mind?" She crossed her arms. People were out in the bright morning sunlight, and the street was crowded enough that she had nothing to be afraid of so long as she didn't go in the store with him.

Which she most definitely was not going to do.

"I regret to inform you that as of 11:05 this morning, your parents, Maximillian and Amelie Starnberger, have cut you off legally, severing all financial and otherworldly ties."

"Otherworldly? What are you, the world's most macabre lawyer?"

He smiled wider now, and she cursed her stomach for betraying her by flipping over the beauty of the expression.

"You *could* call me that. I've been called worse. Demon. Scoundrel. Fallen angel."

He winked at her, looked around, and waved his hand.

Flame jumped from his fingertips, in a hue she recognized precisely as that which consumed the objects she touched when the ghosts were gone.

"Fuck," spat Vickie. "You're an actual devil, aren't you? *My* devil?"

He shrugged. "Some people call me that, but I find the term a bit judgmental, don't you?"

"Lucifer," she breathed, the hairs on the back of her neck rising.

Frowning, he shook his head. "No, but that guy *is* a piece of work. The greater devils had wings and lost them. As a lesser devil, I've never even had wings at all." He sounded wistful.

"I'm Olexandre," he continued, shaking perfect, glossy hair out of his face. "But you can call me Lex. Now, are you going to let me in, or shall I smite everyone here on the street to give us a wee bit of privacy?" His voice was smooth. Cold. She couldn't tell if he was bluffing.

Vickie dug her nails into her palms. She had prepared to talk to a ghost today. To outwit her parents and to be cut off if it came to that. To find the nerve to purchase her dream. To grapple, even, with the memory of the incident and what it might mean to run into Azrael again. But she had not, in fact, prepared to deal with the actual devil responsible for her unusual ability.

Fucking Robbie really had picked the absolute *worst* time to break up with her.

Gritting her teeth, she opened the door and gestured for him to go in, following him and doing her best to ignore the view that his strut provided. It was no wonder he was magical; she figured he would have to be to get into pants that snug.

She squashed an indecent impulse to step closer, to run a hand along the pants to see if they were really leather. He was dangerous. It wasn't her fault she found that a tiny bit hot.

"I'll be quick, pet," he murmured, turning to her, and raising his eyebrows, as though reading her unease. Hopefully not her mind. Devils couldn't read minds, she reassured herself.

"The cocky ones so often are," she said, crossing her arms.

"My, my. We're skipping right to claws, I see. I'm game, though we do have a bit of business to square away first." He stepped closer to her. A wicked smile cracked wide across his face, slightly crooked. She was absolutely certain that stronger people than her must have fallen for it in the past.

And yet she wasn't unseasoned. She didn't have to trust a devil.

"What do you want?"

"It's not what I want, but what I need, dearest one."

Vickie rolled her eyes at that.

"Fine, what do you *need*?"

"There's the small matter of your parents' debt. There's no way to put this delicately, but now that they have disowned you, you'll need, of course, to pay the remaining balance. In exchange for your gift."

Hot or not, she was going to strangle him, to wrap her hands around his lean neck and pull him closer. No. Her nerves were too frayed in the wake of her breakup with Robbie, and, if she was honest, with the agony of knowing she might eventually run into Azrael again.

The mere thought of that threatened to open an old, un-yielding wound.

Better to push it aside and focus on the anger.

"Excuse me, but I did not make a deal with a devil. I was a child."

"Of course not. I would never collect on a child, which is why their repayment plan did not begin until your twenty-first birthday. Standard child labor law."

"Standard child labor law in a deal with the devil?" Vickie pursed her lips, exhaling through her nose in frustration.

"Perhaps you had better sit while I explain."

"I don't care how arrogant and good-looking you are, and how used to getting your way you might be. This is my shop and I'll sit if I want to."

The devil's torturously pretty eyes lit up. "You think I'm handsome, do you, pet?" His voice was a purr. A trap.

"That was your takeaway?" Vickie gestured up and down. "I think you're using an entire arsenal of charms to distract from delivering terrible news."

Lex frowned and slid into a seat.

Vickie crossed her arms. Her legs were tired, but she abso-lutely could not cede the verbal battle now, not when it was so clear that he had an advantage.

He gestured, and a shimmering parchment appeared in the air, unfurling gracefully. She could make out teeny-tiny text—no one took the words *fine print* more seriously than devils—and her parents' signatures at the end of the paper, which stretched almost as tall as she was.

At the bottom, under the signatures, was an addendum. He pointed, and the text at the bottom magnified as he read.

"Pursuant to the severing of all ties, mortal and other-worldly, of one Victoria Elaine Starnberger from her parents..." He skimmed over their names when she tensed, pausing.

"Don't stop on my account," she ground out. She might have to reestablish contact with her parents for the sole purpose of cutting them off again, the absolute bastards.

"The aforementioned owes payment in full of the remaining balance of souls, to be collected by the next thinning of the veil. Should the debtor fail to repay, the interest would be compounded, calculated at a rate of 100 percent, and ten souls, two per year, with the possibility of early collection rolling over to the following year, to be paid in full over the course of ten years."

"You're saying . . ." Her nails were digging into her palms now, the pain tethering her enough to stop from screaming or throwing something in rage. "You're saying that I owe you ten souls by, what, Halloween? Or I'm in your debt for another decade?"

Lex put his hand to his chest, as though offended. "Why not at all, sweetness, that would be quite cruel. You only owe me the remaining balance, and your parents did collect seven as promised. But ah, yes, the bit about the next thinning of the veil, on Halloween, is correct. As is the consequence. Can't be helped."

"You're saying I owe you three *souls*?"

"Don't worry, pet. They're absolutely dreadful souls. And most definitely already dead, so you won't be killing anyone, just reaping." He must have seen the look on her face, because he continued, too brightly, "And just think, your powers will be paid in full, and you'll be free to pursue whatever little fortune-telling grift you have set up here."

"Tea shop," she bit out. "It's a tea shop, you absolute ass."

His brow furrowed. "I could have sworn there was something

about a fake psychic. Well. No matter. Clearly, this is a café," he said, winking. "And now that you say so, it's quite charming. Care to serve me a cuppa?"

Her glare was answer enough, and he stood up, smiling at her in a way that made her hair stand up and sparks run down her spine. The lilt of his voice was ageless, an accent born of centuries of bargaining across lands and languages. It was, regrettably, incredibly seductive.

"Is there anything else I should know about what I owe you?"

He flashed her a dazzling smile. "Just that if you behold any of the remaining objects in progress after the terms of your contract, they shall be incinerated per the terms of your contract on October 31 at sunset should you fail to fulfill your obligations. So, you know. Be careful what you touch if you happen to have an object with particular sentimental value; may be best to wait until after Halloween to lay hands on it. All standard stuff."

"Incinerating my belongings is standard?" She stared at him. He was too good-looking to be so difficult. Or maybe just good-looking enough? She wasn't sure.

"Not all your belongings, pet, that would be dreadful. Only objects that anchor a ghost, of course."

"Of course." She frowned, eyebrows knitting together.

"Is that a firm no on the tea, then?" The curve of his smile beckoned.

"It's a *very* firm no." She ignored the way his eyes smoldered. Magical creatures could be so thirsty.

"Very well, then. I'll be in touch about the first soul soon, Victoria."

He vanished in a dramatic pufff of smoke that she was quite sure was unnecessary, and only after he had gone did she realize that part of the draw she'd felt toward him was natural.

In many ways, magical, at least, he had made her what she was.

CHAPTER 3

Azrael

Azrael Hart had returned weak and weary from his flight and the taxi back to Hart Manor. He was broke, his screenwriting career had stalled, and his parents were dead. He had left behind California and the damp basement apartment in a house full of more cats than were ideal for an allergic person, especially because cats flocked to witches. Even the mundane ones had a sense for magic.

Which is precisely how he'd ended up bringing Emily Lickinson home with him. His former landlady had insisted that Emily could not be parted from him, and Az found himself flying home with a yowling cat, impervious to his snapping magic as cats so often were, who only curled into a corner of her carrier and settled once he had snuck his hand in to pet her.

Azrael found himself staying back in his old bedroom, at the mercy once more of both the house and his younger sister, who lived down the hall from him, just as she had in their childhood. He needed to pick up cat food, and he needed to talk to Priscilla when she got home from the Council meeting. But most of all, he needed time to clear his head. It had been years since he had seen the looming spires of Hart Manor, and he was surprised at how much he loved them again, even returning in grief.

The other things were too complicated, so he grabbed the

key and set out into the August night for the task that he *could* manage.

The part of his heart that he had tried to carve out and throw away lingered here in Hallowcross, and his body felt physical relief at returning to it. Being here now, he was closer to feeling whole, and it had absolutely nothing to do with Victoria Starnberger, who he hadn't seen in years, unless you counted that spectacular and then horrible time in her college dorm.

Which he most certainly did not.

Azrael had tried for years not to wish that a specific someone loved him. He had been so alone that it could have been anyone, as long as it was *someone*. But if he was honest, when he shut his eyes at night, a familiar constellation of freckles haunted him, and specified quite a bit more than *just* anyone.

Fortunately, there was a good chance Vickie wasn't even in town. He stopped himself from looking her up when he could, and in the hectic haze of losing his parents and moving, it had been a while since he'd scried to make sure she was alive.

And when he did check in, it was out of friendship alone, of course.

He didn't even deserve to search for her on the internet, let alone with magic, and he knew he should have worked harder to repair the friendship after that one time. But it had been too painful, and he had been too young. And too hurt to reach out.

Even the feel of her name across his brain made his chest ache and his wrists throb. Absentmindedly, he rubbed a hand over his heart. He looked up and saw that his feet had taken him back to the place his mother had loved so much instead of to the grocer he'd meant to visit first for the Friskies shredded chicken in gravy that Emily liked best.

Tea shop first, then. Priscilla had said he would love the new owner.

When he opened the door, the small skull bells tinkled in a way that reminded him of his mother enough to make him want to cry. Thank goddess the new owner had kept them. The windows were polished to a high shine, and the cozy assortment of mismatched coffee tables of different heights and high-tops scattered among high-back chairs and couches were the same. The scent of coffee and the tea of the day—it must have been mint—hit his senses with a flood of memories laced with a third scent—one that made him think of warm summers and soft grass.

Strawberries.

His head snapped up as his heart recognized, before he saw her, what he would behold. Azrael was not a witch for nothing. He could sense the smell of her and the feeling of being close that he had forced himself to forget even after six years. The way his magic whispered in his ears and wound around his fingertips in response. *Home.* Her back was to him, her messy brown hair streaked with blond piled on top of her head, which she shook at the sound of his footsteps.

Priscilla would pay for this. He would have to prank her mercilessly for neglecting to mention that Vickie worked here now. Yes, he'd at the very least hex her favorite thriller novels so that knives shot out when she opened them. He'd spell them not to hit anything vital, but he might even enlist the help of the under-stairs haunt to serve her retribution for this omission.

Vickie hadn't turned yet.

"Go away. I told you I'd do it, but it's only been a few weeks. There's no need to come gloat. I'll help you collect when it's time."

"I— What?" Az didn't know what to make of her reaction. Vickie froze, and spun around, her face going white as a sheet under her freckles.

Fuck me. He'd thought he'd gotten her out of his system, but all he could focus on now was how he wanted to kiss every one of those freckles, especially the smattering under her lip in that place he remembered so precisely. It was the completely wrong reaction to seeing Vickie. The last time he'd been that close—well, it was best not to dwell on that.

"Az," she breathed, and for a moment they were back there, standing in the rain outside her dorm building, about to make terrible choices. If he could just get to her in this moment of softness, and figure out what she was doing in the shop, it would all be fine. Everything was fine. He opened his mouth, preparing to stay casual. Aloof. Perfect.

He was *fine*.

"What the hell are you doing in my parents' shop?"

Fuck. Fuck. *Fucking* goddess, that had come out so poorly that he might be willing to try just a teensy little memory wipe, just for a second, even if it was ill-advised. And illegal.

Her eyes narrowed and she watched his fingers come together.

"Azrael Hart, don't you dare even think about hexing me to forget right now."

Her stony green eyes said she meant it. Memory wipes were prohibited for so many reasons: to keep magic secret, to protect consent, and to avoid being a jackass. It had been a terrible idea to even think of violating international human rights laws just to regain her good opinion.

Which he'd pretty much already lost forever, anyway.

He'd have to go about this the old-fashioned, mundane way, then.

"Sorry. I, uh, haven't been myself lately. Since my parents died, really." The honesty was a peace offering, one that spilled out more easily than it ought to around her. He couldn't help himself; he had always needed her to *know* him, for better or for worse. "Maybe before that too."

Her eyebrows furrowed.

Slapping his errant, tempted fingers on his leg, he looked away from her. He'd been moments away from fading her memory. And he already hated himself enough for the time in her dorm that had sullied their friendship.

She eyed his palm carefully, and bit her lip.

"I'm sorry about your parents, Az. You know I loved them."

She had. Much more openly than he had ever allowed himself to, and now they were gone, and he was a bloody monster. A devil in more than just two names.

He swallowed, trying for some semblance of normal. "It's good to see you, Vickie. The last I heard you were still in business school. Are you home for break?"

She shook her head and stepped back an inch. As far as she could go against the counter. Blinking, he tried not to imagine what it would be like to brace her against it, their bodies aligned, the softness of her against all his sharp angles.

"No. I'm taking a permanent hiatus from school at the moment." He snapped out of his inappropriate reverie. He could feel color rising to his cheeks, the shame of his body's unbidden reaction to her, even after all this time.

"That doesn't really—" he began, but stopped, seeing her face.

Vickie stared for a moment, and cocked her head, before smiling.

"Fine. I dropped out. I bought your mom's shop. As a little early birthday present to myself. I'm taking a big leap, following my dreams, all of that stuff."

"You WHAT?" He paused for a moment, dumbfounded. "You're telling me that Maximillian and Amelie Starnberger—the town's founding family—agreed to buy a campy little tea shop?"

Vickie bit her lip hard enough that it was distracting. He shoved his hands into the pockets of his jeans to stop them from magically snapping mood-setting music into existence, or even worse, from tracing the constellation of freckles on her cheek next to those pink lips. The bottom one was just a little bit poutier than the top . . . and now he was staring at her mouth like a fucking pervert.

When he looked up, she was looking out the window, nibbling that bottom lip. Devil dammit, to be those teeth.

"Not exactly, Az. They disowned me. Formally and legally. But I took a loan. I've got it completely under control."

He glanced around at the empty tables. Not a single soul,

though she'd set out pastries and the accompaniments for tea as carefully as Persephone Hart ever had. This was all that was left of his mother, and now here he was, making an absolute ass of himself.

"I have to get out of here," he mumbled, dragging a hand through his hair, and snapping his fingers quietly behind his head to send the warm scents of the shop drifting through the air outside.

"What? Are you in town for a few days?" she asked.

"No," he muttered, the strawberry scent of his childhood love reminding him of too much loss. "I'm back home. For good."

He ought to have been here. Ought to have rented a car and driven the weeklong trip across the country as fast as he could. The least he could do now was help save the shop that had meant so much to his parents. With another snap of his fingers, the scent of mint tea and nutty lattes drifted a few blocks farther.

He was already a failure as a son, as a screenwriter, and as a friend. And now he was even failing the cat, which needed food.

"I have to go feed Emily Lickinson," he muttered.

"Who the *fuck*," she said, hitting the last word angrily, "is Emily Lickinson?" Her eyes sliced into him. Her hands were at her waist. He had to be misreading it; he was nothing to her now, and she couldn't possibly be jealous of a cat.

Dragging a hand over his face, he felt sweaty and nineteen again.

"My cat."

"I thought you were allergic." Her face softened.

"I am. Emily Lickinson doesn't care, though. They make pills for that."

"That's an incredible name for a cat," said Vickie. She smiled. "I'm glad it won't be just you alone writing all day."

He cleared his throat, flattered she remembered, and uncertain of why he found this next declaration embarrassing. He'd sworn to himself not to give a bat's ass about it when he took the job. But Vickie was different. The remnants of friendship made him desperate for her approval.

"I am actually living back at Hart Manor. With my sister."

"She failed to mention that." Vickie cocked her head to one side.

Oh, he was going to make his sister pay for this later. He ran a hand through his hair, pretty sure he could figure out what Priscilla was up to. "Yeah. I took a job teaching English at Hallowcross High. I start in a few weeks." He said it softly enough that he wasn't sure she would catch it, but her face lit up immediately.

"That's amazing, Az! You're going to be a teacher. Can I call you Mr. Hart?"

"No." He hated that idea, for uncomfortable reasons pertaining to the bow of her mouth again.

"Fine, fine. Azrael it is, as always. The witch named twice for the devil."

He shook his head, unsure what to do now, and looked around, but the shop was empty. She had loomed so long in his mind after the last time they had seen each other that he saw her everywhere, in anything that smelled like strawberries. In between the lines of songs they had loved as children, anytime they came on the radio.

Those times he had occasionally given in and scried—just out of friendship, of course—she was always laughing, and in the past few years, often with a heartthrob that he recognized as an up-and-coming musician. He hated that guy enough to change the station if his songs came on, even if the bitterness did make him an ass. An ass who was staring now, looking guilty as sin, and needed to say something.

But when he opened his mouth, they both spoke at once.

"Speaking of the devil," she said, while his words rushed out in a jumble as he asked, "How's the famous Robbie?"

Outside the shop, people were starting to gather. The spell was working.

"What?" Her eyebrows furrowed. "Oh. We broke up last

month. But honestly, it was over long before then." She looked murderous, and he thought he ought to change the subject.

It had absolutely nothing to do with the sudden uptick in his heartbeat, and the way his fingers wanted to magic her flowers, or a playlist. One full of old, obscure love songs.

"What were you saying about a devil?" he asked, willing his mischievous digits still.

"Oh, nothing. We can talk later. I'll text you. I better get ready to win the hearts of these customers," she said, looking at the door, which someone was pulling open. He watched through the wide glass window front as people flocked toward the entrance, illuminated by the setting sun.

"I can't believe we are finally getting busy this late in the day," she said, beaming. "Same number as before?"

"Yeah. Same number. Always."

Azrael smiled. He hadn't drowned in unrequited love for this woman for years without learning when to take a hint. And he most certainly did not love her anymore. He couldn't. It would be too embarrassing, too pathetic, to hang on after discovering years ago that he'd never been more than an itch for her to scratch. He'd be damned if he stood here awkwardly waiting for her to ask him to leave.

"Happy early birthday," he said, hoping it came across casual, and like the date wasn't seared into his brain. "I have to go." He turned away from her. "Emily Lickinson, you know."

"It was good to see you." She gave him a smile that he felt deep in his chest as he held the door open for people filing in, suddenly eager for an evening tea and snack.

He should have been charming, but his tongue felt incapable, so he raised a hand, waving. He walked away toward the corner store for the cat food and then toward home and the giant, fluffy monster that was probably murdering all of his mother's best upholstery.

The least he could do was stay away from Hopelessly Teavoted and Victoria for a respectable amount of time.

CHAPTER 4

Victoria

She didn't want him to leave, even if he did have a cat, of all things, to get back to. But like he had after the unfortunate happenstance in college, Az turned away too soon and left her wanting. He was not the accomplice she had counted on in childhood. The friend she had valued so much in high school. He was just the man she'd made a mistake with in college.

Pushing the thought out of her mind, she told herself that it had been years, several flings, and an entire asshole boyfriend since that incident. It certainly did not deserve to occupy this much real estate in her mind, however titillating it was to sometimes turn it over.

No. She would not keep thinking about this.

She closed the shop, ready to give Priscilla a piece of her mind for failing to mention Azrael's return. The last she'd heard, he was still in California, probably relaxing on sandy beaches with a lover on his arm. Perfect and mundane and totally magicless, the way he'd wanted it when he fled as far as he could get from Hallowcross, Vermont, as fast as possible.

She set her phone on the counter and pressed Priscilla Hart's number, switching it to speaker.

"Priscilla Hart, reluctant devotee of an electronic device with too much control over my life."

"It's just a cell phone, Prissy."

"Victoria! How's the leak in the shower ceiling?"

"You fixed it perfectly—thanks for that. You failed to mention, though, that Azrael was back in town."

"Did I? That's odd. Must have slipped my mind. He's here to stay, you know. Has he been by the shop?"

The flat brightness of her tone was not fooling Vickie; her old friend had been scheming.

Priscilla barreled on, "Prickly and suspicious, Azrael. And always so worried. I'm sure it was nice for you two to run into each other again organically."

Wiping down a counter, Vickie rolled her eyes, glad she had not opted for a video chat.

It was true that Azrael took a while to warm up to people, but once he did, he bloomed like the roses his mother used to grow in her garden in shades of crimson, scarlet, and black. Gorgeous and fragrant with a loyalty worth waiting for.

Azrael had once been witch roses to her, magical and blossoming in colors uncanny to the human world. The angles of his face were obscenely sharp, breathtaking to some and distasteful to others, but she had thought that she could see him, really see him. The way that long ago, in his mother's gardens, she had seen that the thorn beneath the shiny flesh of the bloodred flower was as delicate and lovely as any mundane thing.

"Victoria? Are you still there?"

"Yes," she said. "Just cleaning up here, lost in thought. Anything else major you need to tell me? Another sibling I don't know about? Did you call my disastrous college girlfriend too? Maybe you could dig up an old high school flame to show up next week and embarrass me."

She picked up the teacups that had been drying in a rack and began to stack them in the cabinet. Priscilla's mother had such charming and eclectic taste in the servingware here.

"Actually, if you must know, I do have other news. I'm seeing someone delicious and delightful."

"All right, joking aside, tell me everything," said Vickie,

careful not to drop any of Persephone's legacy of bat and cat and witch mugs.

"Hold on, let me get comfortable. This is a great story." The sound of rustling over the phone must have been Prissy settling into one of the plush armchairs at Hart Manor. The memory twisted, just a little bit sharp. It was the cozy furniture she missed so much. Not him. "So," said Prissy. "Her name is Evelyn Vishwakumar, and she lives in the most gorgeous condo, temporarily of course; she's here for Witchery Council business. She has the dreamiest Disney princess eyes, and I am just fucking obsessed with her."

Vickie smiled as she swept the floors.

"Go on."

"She could be the heroine in a romance novel, Victoria. I went to an honest-to-goddess film festival with her. I wore an outfit that wasn't black."

"Sounds serious."

"I burn for her," said Priscilla, her voice grave. Good for her. Prissy Hart deserved some happiness after all that tragedy. "Listen, about Azrael."

"The devil I will. Let's not."

"I don't know exactly what happened, but he misses you. The two of you were so close. He would never want to hurt you."

Vickie's lips pressed tightly together at the memory of quite the opposite of that sentiment, but she said nothing, and focused on cleaning up. Priscilla had tried making a case for him a few times before, usually after a few drinks, via text message.

Once it had led to Vickie awkwardly texting back and forth with Az, but things between them had stayed strange.

"Az has always had a thing for you, really. Since we were kids." Vickie's mouth opened and then closed again.

She shook her head. "I don't need a pity setup." Her eyes narrowed. "Or an excuse for you to get him out of the house, if that's what this is."

Prissy went on. "Seriously, Victoria, he's lonely. I'm worried about him."

The thought of that loneliness softened her feelings toward Az, who had been her friend before that incident, and all the subsequent self-loathing. Not just a friend, but her best one.

She missed him too. As a friend.

"It's weird to pimp out your own brother," she mumbled.

Priscilla laughed. "It's weirder to totally ignore your childhood best friend for whatever dramatic reason the two of you might have. You're both adults."

They were. And there was no reason they couldn't be friends again now, especially as he was grieving. But she wouldn't be foolish enough to think she could handle another no-strings situation with him.

As long as she could keep things in the friend zone, the way he was so clearly desperate to do, they could be solid. Like they were as kids. The thing in college had been a blip on the radar. A momentary, lustful mistake. She could move past it.

"I'm sorry, Priss, I have to mop up. I'll talk to you later."

"How about a drink tonight? You can meet Evelyn and gloat into my wine with me about how hot she is."

Vickie paused, running through her prep schedule for the next day's baking in her head. "Yeah, that would be fine. As long as there's food."

"Meet me at Kessel Run at eight?"

"You would be willing to go to a nerd bar for me? What about Free Spirits?" Vickie knew Priscilla preferred the upscale cocktail bar, where they'd met last month for Hopelessly Teavoted business.

"You sound like you need it more," said Priscilla.

She wasn't going to argue, if only for the sake of the Less Than Twelve Parsecs Nachos, which were absolutely the best bar snack north of Manchester. "See you at eight, Priscilla."

"Talk soon!" Prissy's voice was suspiciously enthusiastic, and between that and the concession in meeting places, Vickie didn't doubt for one second that she was up to something.

She tapped the phone to hang up, and shook her head. Priscilla was mistaken; Vickie remembered what Az had said to her in college. There'd been a time when she'd thought he had feelings for her. But after what happened, she knew exactly where she stood with Azrael Hart.

Alone, in the pouring rain, crying her fucking eyes out and hoping he would come back.

In the end, he never did.

Enough years had passed that it shouldn't matter, but the *almost* of the whole thing made her want to run out into the night to find him now and demand he tell her why.

She consoled herself by mopping the floors vigorously.

Her heart felt cracked and empty, but the floor sparkled by the time she was ready to swipe on some mascara, change her shirt, and head out to meet the second Hart sibling of the day.

The lighting was dim at Kessel Run, but she would have known her old friend anywhere.

Priscilla Hart sat at Vickie's favorite table, the two-top all the way at the back, farthest from the bar, and yet, Vickie was unsurprised to note that at five past the time they were supposed to meet, she had already commanded a drink.

Like in high school, and the few times Vickie had seen her since, Prissy was clad in all black, hair sleek and shiny and brushing the lapels of a satin blazer with intricate dark green leaves patterned on the breast pocket. Her black slacks were perfectly tailored, and she had traded her combat boots for Louboutins. Vickie couldn't help but think she was the goth garden version of Andy from *The Devil Wears Prada*, post–Miranda makeover.

Goodness knew there were enough actual devils in Vickie's life to make such comparisons.

"Vickie," Prissy said, holding up a hand, her expression inscrutable. "Welcome to my lair."

"Prissy! It's so good to see you!" The other woman got up to accept a hug, still holding a tumbler full of amber liquid. "What are you drinking?"

"An alcohol," Priscilla deadpanned.

"Charming as ever," said Vickie, picking up the menu off the table and sliding onto the tall chair across from her.

A smile flickered across Prissy's face. "I ordered you those nachos with the stupid name. They look terrible, like heartburn in a starship-shaped pan, but I love you, so I ordered them anyway." She took a long drink from her tumbler. The corners of her mouth ticked upward. "Also, it's good to see you on non-tea shop and apartment business."

Vickie sighed with relief at the thought of the food. It would be nice to eat something that wasn't from a package or baked in her shop. Even if she really ought to save money.

"It's good to see you, too, Prissy. Where's your girl?"

Prissy's eyebrows furrowed for a moment. "Council business. She's very serious."

"Yeah?" Victoria wasn't sure if this was a good thing.

"She is extremely dedicated to her job," said Priscilla, her face breaking into a smile. A good thing, then. "But she's also hot and posh, and devil damn me, that British accent."

"You love to hear a British accent."

"Goddess, you really do," sighed Priscilla, looking a bit wistful.

"Are you ready to order?" A man in a Wookiee T-shirt and an apron approached their table with tremendous caution, giving Prissy a wide berth, as though she might bite.

"I'll have a Greedo Mojito." Vickie scanned the menu. "And a Burger Fett."

"And you?" He didn't quite make eye contact with Priscilla.

"I'll have another whiskey lemonade," she said.

"Do you mean a Ha—"

"I most certainly do not, *Daniel*." She glared at him, cat eyes sharp enough to kill.

"Sure, sure thing," he said, half running back to the computer at the bar.

Vickie laughed. "What did you do to him?"

"I was perfectly nice; I just told him that I would not be calling my drink a Han Solo What a Man Solo all night. I have dignity, you know." As if to emphasize it, she checked her lipstick in the camera of her phone, nodding satisfactorily when she saw that the dark red had not smudged. "Never could get Mom's lipstick spell right," she said, and the undertone of it made Vickie reach for her hand.

"Hey. I'm so sorry."

Prissy shrugged, her face dropping for a moment. "It's not as bad anymore. I mean, it's still bad, but it's tolerable. The grief. The lipstick, on the other hand, even if it's not exactly the way she did it, is damn near perfect."

"I miss them too." Vickie's heart ached for the loss of Benedict and Persephone. The parents she'd never had and the pain over the parents she did have swam together, and for a moment, she was lost in thought. The scent of mint reminded her of the conservatory.

"Greedo Mojito and Less Than Twelve Parsecs Nachos," Daniel said brightly. He turned to Prissy and added apologetically, "It just means twelve toppings."

"It's okay. I won't bite."

He looked unconvinced but somewhat relieved, and returned with Prissy's drink before heading back to the increasingly busy bar.

Prissy leaned into Victoria. "I *do* actually bite, just not him."

Vickie giggled into her mojito. She had missed this. Hallowcross. Prissy. All the Harts.

"You know," said Priscilla, "don't think I don't remember that my brother also loves space shit. I saw him digging out his old posters to decorate his classroom."

The thought made her chest twinge, remembering how earnest Azrael was with his love of, well, everything.

"I don't pretend to know what happened between you two, but you should talk to him. He was so excited to see you."

"He said that?"

Prissy winked. "He didn't have to; it was all over his face."

Vickie shut her eyes. She'd forgotten how much of a meddler Priscilla Hart could be. "I need to talk to him about something a ghost said, anyway."

Priscilla sat up straighter, setting her drink down. "What did a ghost say?"

"My parents were up to their usual shit. I meant to mention it, but I've been swamped. I think Amelie and Maximillian made another mess luring that megachurch into town, and then walked away from it." She sipped at her drink. "They're good at walking away."

The table jiggled ever so slightly, and Vickie remembered that Priscilla, like her brother, was also prone to the weight of anxiety. She was just a lot better at hiding it.

"Hey," Vickie said softly. "At least we know what to expect from them."

Her friend sighed, and for a moment, Vickie recognized the same little girl who had cried when her favorite toad died. From the moment she'd stepped foot in Hallowcross again and met with her old friend to arrange for the shop, she'd noted the marble exterior occasionally encasing that tenderness, shielding the world from it, or her from the world.

Vickie wasn't sure which one, but the mask was back up on Priscilla's face. The one that had won her reputation on the Council as no-nonsense.

"I'd be lying if I said we weren't trying to keep tabs on them," Priscilla admitted, and though her breezy tone said she didn't care, her careful stare suggested otherwise.

"You'd be a fool not to," Vickie said dryly. Her friend's face relaxed ever so slightly, and it was small enough that a stranger might never know, but they hadn't grown up together for nothing. "Did you know they were responsible for bringing the church here?"

Prissy shook her head. "No. The church was on our watch list, but your parents only went once or twice, so while it had initially crossed my mind that they might be cutting more deals"—she paused, waving a hand toward Vickie—"ultimately, they became a low priority in the rush of the pandemic and all. And then..."

Her voice trailed off, and Vickie knew what she didn't

want to say. And then Benedict and Persephone died, and Prissy's world turned upside down, and Azrael couldn't make it back in time for any of it, not for sitting shiva, not for the funeral service, handling the estate, and figuring out that they couldn't afford to float both property taxes on Hart Manor and the cost of running the shop. The timing had been awful, but disease knew nothing of death and mourning rituals. The world spun on, blissfully oblivious to human folly.

Vickie swallowed, shaking off the dark thought. She had an image, too, and hers was made of sunshine. And, like Priscilla, she could use a façade to make it through.

"Well, they definitely invited the megachurch here, thought about cutting a deal, but decided that kind of bullshit was too much even for them." She paused. "Which, honestly, is bad news, if it's too much for people who would bargain with their own child."

Priscilla scowled. "That *is* bad news. I'll run it by Evelyn, see if she's heard anything." She gestured to the bar. "I was actually glad to see things busy here tonight. I've heard rumbling about pressure on churchgoers to stop drinking. And apparently, they tried to organize a review of the romance section of the bookstore. Got shot down by the local librarian group, but still. It's scary that they tried."

"What. The. Fuck."

"Exactly. Hallowcross is wonderful *because* people are open-minded here, with the exception of the occasional asshat. We should be able to have a good time without the puritanical bullshit that plagues some other places."

"That megachurch has bad vibes," said Vickie. She'd be damned if she let some ultraconservative religious movement run anything or anyone out of town. She'd gone away, but she was back now, and that had to count for something.

Her friend was giving her that look, the one that said she had something to say and she was going to say it whether Vickie liked it or not.

Goddess, she remembered that look. It had gotten the three of them into no small amount of trouble in childhood.

"Whatever it is you have to say, just say it."

"You said they bargained with you." Priscilla's eyes narrowed, and her mouth turned down. She was going to make Vickie say it.

"Yes."

The look on her face was too close to the one her father had given them the time they'd used his most rare shadow craft materials to make a magical dollhouse.

It had taken *ages* to get rid of the creepy little wooden doll that kept popping up, but how were they to know how potent Hawthorne wood was?

Just as she had to her father decades ago, Vickie caved to Priscilla Hart.

"Fine, the consequence for my gift is that they owed souls, to be collected for a lesser devil. When they legally disowned me, that debt transferred automatically. I have to collect three souls for him."

To her credit, Priscilla only nodded. She didn't bother with any reassurance; they had both been around such magic long enough to know it simply was what it was. But when a wicked smile crept up her friend's face, Vickie knew she was in trouble.

"I've got a good idea," Priscilla announced. "I'll talk to Evelyn if you talk to Azrael."

Her eyebrows waggled, and this? The matchmaking tendency? She came by that honestly, too, and it was all Persephone.

"Priscilla, you live with your brother. Can't you just talk to him?"

"He's been so different since our parents died. He needs a friend who isn't a relative, Vickie," Prissy wheedled. "Besides, the consequences of that kind of debt could be serious. He'd want to know. As your childhood best friend. Who has fewer and fewer people in his life."

The dead parents card was too much to ignore, and Priscilla knew it.

"I'll think about it," Vickie said.

Shaking her head, Priscilla reached for the nachos and took a large, sour-cream-laden bite.

"Damn. I was wrong about these. I want to hate this kind of gimmick, but I love them." She stared at the chip as though the remaining shredded chicken and guacamole on top of it might hold the secrets to the universe. "I will always need these terrible nachos with my glass of alcohol from now on. It's awful. Awful, I tell you." She shoveled another into her mouth, managing to look glamorous even when dabbing shredded cheese and salsa off her cheek. That kind of composure had to be an art form of some sort.

"About Azrael," Vickie reminded her. So what if a part of her wanted more details? They had been friends for ages, and it had absolutely nothing to do with the incident.

"Sorry," said Priscilla, "those are the terms of the deal. Hey, I just remembered." She sat up straight, lifting her glass. "Isn't it your birthday soon? We could have a little catch-up the day of. You. Me. Evelyn. Azrael."

Vickie swallowed, shaking her head.

"I, uh, have plans."

The plans were inventory-related work tasks, but Priscilla didn't have to know that.

Prissy shrugged. "Some other time, then. I bet Az would want to wish you a happy birthday too." She waggled her eyebrows, and Vickie shot her a look.

"It's a busy month," she deflected. It wasn't untrue.

Priscilla gave her a hard look, but let it go. She shoved another bite of nachos into her mouth, and that was that.

Vickie sighed. It looked like she had no choice but to let Priscilla think she could insist her way into Vickie and Azrael being something again.

They could be friends, she decided, watching the server make his way over with her burger. Friends were nice.

CHAPTER 5

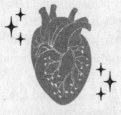

Azrael

Three days after his first visit, Azrael was back at the shop, unable to help himself. But in his return, he'd forgotten Sultry Sundays, his mother's old weekly tradition where people dressed up as the strange, the seductive, and the sensual. Some drew inspiration from music videos and movies, and some from whatever whim struck them. When he pushed open the door and strode into Hopelessly Teavoted, he was unprepared to find Vickie scantily clad and forcing him to admit the foothold she had in his memories.

For a brief moment, Az was an awkward nineteen-year-old again, frozen before leaving for college eight years ago, pining for his best friend. Today, he had actual business with her, and for that, he could put aside the guilty longing and the volatile cocktail of hormones that was not helping his eyes, those betrayers, stay above her neckline and out of trouble.

He needed to stay centered. To keep his mind from wandering. Coffee, maybe. Tearing his eyes away from Vickie, he made his way to the counter.

"Hello there," said the girl at the register dressed as Frodo Baggins, of all things. His Tolkien-obsessed father would have loved that, and the thought made his heart twist. She was just a kid, and she smiled briefly beneath the sort of piercing that went through her nose and out both nostrils. He thought that maybe this was in style, but he wasn't sure. He'd always been afraid of needles, a fact his sister had exploited endlessly with illusion hexes in their childhood. "What can I getcha?" The chirp of her voice was a friendly little sound to match the polite bob of her pink Afro as she nodded her head in greeting. Vickie was out of eyesight now, which made things easier.

"A coffee, please."

She smiled, swiped his card, and then handed him a mug. Lost in thought, he walked to the self-serve area.

At the coffee counter, he filled it up, sprinkling in a little bit of sugar, then walked over to the wine-colored wooden chair he had always loved best.

From his seat, he watched Victoria bus tables, trying, but unable, to resist her gravitational pull. She was different. This was no longer the gangly, freckled girl from his childhood. This was a woman in a sexy robe, the sleeves tapering into red lace over her curves, the weight of the years in her arms, her thighs, her breasts. Her ass. Devil damn him, he was kind of a creeper, staring at her like that while she reached up to grab a canister of tea off a tall shelf, hem creeping halfway up the backs of her thick thighs and threatening him with oblivion if she reached any farther.

The memory of Vickie hurt more than seeing what he would never touch again, now in red lingerie and a silky robe under a ridiculous skull-patterned apron.

He tapped his fingers against the tabletop and concentrated on not thinking about what was under the robe. Tried not to imagine gently circling her wrists with his hands and brushing that edge of crimson lace on the long sleeves. He forced himself not to consider the way it would slide across his fingers if he asked her to go upstairs with him. He was not imagining the way the fabric might feel against his hand if he placed it on the small of her back, or the even softer slip of what her skin would be like against his fingers if he skimmed them lower to dip beneath the edge of the robe.

Az was definitely *not* picturing kissing her through the robe until she screamed his name the way—well, no. He was definitely *not* thinking that. At all. Just because his body held some residual wanting didn't mean he cared for her as anything more than friends.

Vickie turned her head and smiled at him in a way that made him wonder if his thoughts were written all over his face. The glitter sparkled in her hair, which was set in rollers, just like in the "You Need to Calm Down" video. He half expected her to pull out a blender and start making a cocktail.

Azrael swallowed.

Sultry Sunday was about embracing yourself for who you were, his mother used to say, but he never had participated, not really. He had always just dreamed of feeling normal.

"Az!" Vickie called from across the shop, waving. "Where's your Sultry Sunday outfit?"

He shrugged and raised a hand in greeting. It was muscle memory. She asked him this every time. Always had. Vickie had gone all out for it since childhood, and he knew what it was like to come with her, usually dressed as one of her favorite musicians, while he lingered next to her, a dark star in the orbit of a bright sun.

Today, just like all those other days, he was clad in designer jeans and a solid gray T-shirt, always unwrinkled. What good was magic if it couldn't at least iron your clothes and fix your hair from time to time?

And devil damn him, Vickie was beautiful, Az thought, taking note of the bright blue eye shadow and red lipstick, so different from her usual makeup. Azrael needed to concentrate hard on why he shouldn't be thinking of her this way. But as that silk dressing gown slid across her smooth skin, hard was quite possibly the worst and most tempting word choice. Vickie was so soft, and she was handing a plate of croissants to Hank Dewey, who was in a sheer pink bathrobe with hot pants underneath. Hank was a sort of grandfather figure in town, and so seeing him now *did* help Azrael get a hold on his suddenly unpredictable libido.

Well. He was calm now. That was something.

"Morning, Hank," he said, admiring, as always, the bravado of a man in his sixties willing to live that authentically. Az wished for that kind of freedom, but the shackles of his self-doubt weighed as heavily on him as the memory of everything he had ever ruined with Victoria.

"Azrael Hart!" Hank's jolly face lit up in a smile. "Back in Hallowcross at last! It's good to see you, son. This year has been a tough one." Hank teared up a bit here and looked like he might stand, cross the distance between the tables, and lean in for a hug. Vickie's fine eyes darted over him, calculating. Az hated hugging people he didn't know well, though he didn't mind physical contact from those he was closest to. But so many times as a child he had poured his insecurities in Vickie's ears about how a high five or a handshake from an acquaintance or a stranger could unsettle him.

It would be hard for the retired postman to understand the bubble of personal space Azrael enjoyed and preferred left undisturbed. Hank's comfort at hanging belly-out in a sheer robe did not make Azrael any less nervous about extraneous physical contact, to say the least. His parents had him tested as a child, for he was *so* different from pranking, audacious Priscilla. His pediatrician and psychologist, as well as his mother's plant craft spells, had all reported clinical depression and anxiety. It was to be expected, they all said, for him to not want to be touched much. The Harts had concluded that Azrael simply required a larger bubble of personal space than most. And Zoloft, which, frankly, allowed him to function close to something like a human.

But surely adult Victoria would leave him to battle his deepest fears. It had been so long since she had been the girl next door that he loved.

Vickie stepped closer to Hank for a moment, defusing Azrael's tension by placing her body between them. "More tea, Hank?" She smiled at Azrael, raising an eyebrow. She was blocking Hank for him. Intercepting potential hugs as though she cared about what he needed.

Like his parents, Hank's husband had died in the pandemic, though much earlier on than the Harts. He didn't want to refuse the hug, but he also didn't want the hug.

She remembered. Fuck if that didn't tug at his heartstrings. Az snapped his fingers, and some of the tension loosened from Hank's shoulders. He couldn't cure grief and wouldn't want to, for pain like that had purpose, but he could nudge Hank in the direction of fond memories of his husband that might ease the pain of it all. Azrael could help him to feel the love persevering in that grief, and to find comfort in the knowledge that memory was a blessing.

"Ah, no thanks, Victoria," Hank was saying, pulling Azrael out of the spiraling misery of realizing that perhaps he wasn't quite as over his childhood flame as he wanted to imagine. "I have plenty, and I'm focused now on these beauties." Hank gestured at the pastries on his plate.

"I'll let you enjoy, then." Vickie walked toward Azrael's table, and his face flushed hot.

"Can we talk while you're closing?" Az hoped he sounded cooler than he felt. "Prissy said you needed something."

A week back in town and already he was as much a mess over her as he ever had been. He raked his eyes across her face, hoping it was not obvious. Reassuring himself that he was only here because of that nagging feeling that there was something magical she wasn't telling him. Because of the whispered tip from his sister, that meddler, that he should check in with her as the shop's new owner. Nothing else.

And now here he was, already memorizing, or rather realizing how much the memory had imprinted directly on his brain, the swirls of her freckles and the tilt of her smile.

Fuck, he was a mess.

Victoria was calm and collected, though. There was a daisy tucked behind her ear in between the curlers and spray-on glitter that rounded out the ensemble.

"Sure. We close in twenty, and Hazel's off then. It's just me cleaning up."

Hazel must have been the teenager at the counter with the bright pink hair who was now looking with great interest between him and Vickie. A grin crept up her face, mischief glinting in her brown eyes.

This made him smile; it was one of the things that he was looking forward to about returning to a classroom after substitute teaching to make ends meet in California. Teenagers were not always subtle, but they were much cleverer than most adults gave them credit for. The astute observation when she caught his eye, looked at her boss, and raised her eyebrows was both embarrassing and amusing.

"Are you all right, Az?" Vickie's voice was gentle and quieter than usual, tucking around him. This was a private question.

Victoria paused. An emotion flashed across her face that Az hoped was not pity. The corners of her mouth tugged down, and her eyebrows furrowed. He knew he looked bad. He hadn't been sleeping since his parents died. The guilt of not having been there weighed on him, and he felt lost. Listless. Magic thrummed sometimes at his fingertips, aching to be let out, and wasted away in whispers in other moments, like it threatened to disappear. Like he could never get the closure to properly grieve, and his body didn't know if it should mourn his lost family in fireworks of power or in low depths of despair.

The grieving was endless.

Now that he was back here, when he closed his eyes at night, if it wasn't his dead parents he missed, it was *her*. In a different way, of course, and the juxtaposition of the grief and the lust, the two disparate types of longing, was maddening. He felt like an asshole half the time, waking up hard and uncomfortable after dreaming about what he had no right to dream about. Struggling with the depravity of what he pictured while trying not to think of her in the shower. Languishing in an emotional pile of rubble the other half of the time. Knowing, as he did, that he had let his parents down and had missed his chance to say goodbye.

Grief was a strange bedfellow that rolled over him in waves, sometimes wasting days in gray numbness and other times just spurts of disenchantment between twisting, bright memories of the girl he couldn't get out of his mind now that he was back here, where he had loved her once.

Az hadn't answered, his eyes fixed on the black tablecloth and the candelabra-shaped sugar holder that topped his table, avoiding looking up and trying not stare at the curve of her bottom lip, slightly redder than the top, just as he remembered, or the alluring, plump dip of her neckline below her apron.

"How are you, Azrael?" Vickie's voice quieted as she asked after him again. He didn't want to open that topic, but when he opened his mouth, words tumbled out, unbidden.

"I'm fine. I've been better, but I'm fine. Being in my mom's shop, I mean your shop, but you know it makes me think, and all."

He bit back a groan of embarrassment. He did words for a living. How was it possible for him to ramble this badly?

Reaching for the coffee cup at the edge of the table, Az meant to snap again to cool the air, in an attempt to pacify the man at the counter who appeared to be arguing with the kid at the register about his change. He vaguely recognized the man's face from his Zoom interview as his new department chair, and hoped the man didn't recognize him. Vickie was looking at the interaction, too, probably deciding if she needed to step in. Azrael snapped under the table, and then frowned.

It *should* have calmed the man down, but nothing happened. If anything, his glare had sharpened.

That was strange; his magic didn't run out unless he'd exerted tremendous amounts of power, or, as he discovered once in college, indulged in any sort of hallucinogenic drugs, in which case it was prone to wild explosions followed by droughts. He wouldn't repeat that mistake; it had taken weeks to get the spaghetti off the ceiling while his powers returned, and he wasn't friends with that former roommate anymore.

Maybe it was the grief, muting his abilities.

"Sorry, Mr. Thornington. Here, enjoy a donut on the house," said Hazel, handing him a bag.

Hazel flipped off Mr. Thornington as soon as he turned around and stormed out of the shop, and Azrael smiled at this, the magical misfire forgotten. He was willing to bet that curmudgeon had earned a floor donut. His fingers grazed the coffee cup, missing it, and then scrambled for purchase.

Trying to catch it proved ruinous, and the remains of his coffee spilled over the table and onto his lap, the cup shattering into shards on the floor.

People turned to look, but Vickie smiled reassuringly. "It's just a cup, Az. It's fine."

He cursed his awkwardness.

"I'm so sorry. I'll pay for it."

Vickie pulled a towel from her apron and mopped the table off with one hand, passing him napkins for his pants with the other. Dammit, now he was imagining her rubbing his pants.

He was such a mess, and she was literally picking up the pieces.

"It's fine, Az. Don't worry about it. I know you've been going through it."

"Can't put a broken mug back together—or a broken heart," he muttered, blushing. He'd meant over his parents, but what if she thought he meant her? His cheeks burned now. "I am so sorry. And I have been having a rough time of it. Still, I should have called you. Many times. I'm sorry." He was striking out here, without even another bad joke to fall back on.

"I get it. I should have called, too, when . . . well, when everything . . ." She bit her bottom lip, cradling the shards of mug carefully in her hands. Goddess, he wanted to be those teeth. "Can I get you something to eat? We have donuts with music-themed names today. I can get you a Raspberry Beignet or a Caramel Me Maybe."

"Did you make them?"

She beamed a little. "Yeah, I did. I've been doing all the baking."

"Then yes. One of each." Finally, his words were coming out normal, as though he didn't feel the echo of being awkwardly in love with her more than a decade earlier, and then having that one horrible, glorious misunderstanding six years ago, when he'd thought for a moment that everything was finally falling into place.

"I'll bring them over." She paused, pursing her lips a little bit, and leaning in. "There's something I need to talk to you about. Something, *you know*, not mundane."

Well, now it made more sense that she agreed to talk to him after closing. Maybe Priscilla was being serious about her needing his help, and not just a meddling little match-maker emulating their mom. Vickie needed help with a magical problem, that was all. And she had no idea what Az felt for her, after all these years, and clearly not even a smidge of similar feelings. That was fine; he'd lock away his thoughts down deep, as always, as if, if he pretended they didn't exist for long enough, he could make them disappear. He would focus on the tea shop, familiar once more with throngs of people eager for beverages and pastries with a side of occult servingware.

"Of course. We can talk about it when you're done here." Azrael snapped his fingers, adding just a smidge of happy memories to Hank's tea.

He'd done his part to make Hank a little happier, and now, if he could, he'd make Vickie's day a little better too. He snapped twice to send the glorious donut smell farther into town. After all, it was what Persephone would have done.

Vickie bounced over to the counter—a feat in the heels she was wearing—and spoke to Hazel, who looked over at him, grinned, and nodded.

Within a minute, Vickie was bustling about, delivering the last pastries and placing a little cup with a black cat and a matching saucer on his table. She set the plate of donuts next to the cup, which he recognized well.

It had been his mother's favorite, and he watched Vickie's short red fingernails against it as she put it on the tabletop.

"I thought you might like to use this one instead." She smiled at him, and he nodded, tracing the familiar design.

"Let me know if you need anything else, Az." Vickie's voice was like a cloud, a dream, and he almost groaned, knowing that refrain would take days to leave him now.

He ached for her desperately. Again.

She had no idea how much else he needed.

CHAPTER 6

Victoria

Business was picking up.

She tried to reassure herself that it was good news, both to keep the store afloat and to keep her distracted from thinking about how badly she missed the idea of maybe one day working it out with Azrael. How much she had been lying to herself for years now, shoving away the memories of dancing in his bedroom to her favorite music as a kid, the occasionally haunted armchair rocking back and forth along with her.

How she had pictured, even then, what it would be like, to live in Hart Manor with him. Embraced by his family and his house, where she felt much more alive and welcome than next door in her parents' cold, modern monstrosity.

How she had loved Benedict and Persephone, and how they had been so much warmer than her own parents, despite what the town often said about their macabre and morbid ways. There was love, real love, in Hart Manor, in the very beams of the house, which creaked and yawned and lived with the family that loved there.

It had always been her and Azrael, and Vickie had told herself for too long that they were just friends. And now, when he was back in front of her, she remembered how hard it was to be just friends with him. She saw his tentative smile and curly hair, and felt the same way she felt walking into Hopelessly

Teavoted. Like she was home. Seeing Azrael felt like really, truly coming home.

"He likes you, you know," Hazel whispered conspiratorially, running a finger over her pink hair.

Vickie rolled her eyes. She loved Hazel, but her teenage insight was failing her in this moment. Azrael sat there, shifting his coffee cup from hand to hand. The way Vickie clutched the tray of donuts she was putting away had nothing to do with her feelings for Azrael. Not a thing.

"He—no, he's my old neighbor. We had a weird moment once in college, but trust me, it ended badly enough to avoid. You'll get it when you're older. Some people seem like a great idea on paper but just never really click in reality."

Hazel smirked. "I knew it. You totally love him. Oh my god, and look at him just sitting there for this long. He *totally* loves you too."

"Hazel. He will *hear* you."

Vickie really didn't know why the idea of Hazel thinking Az liked her bothered her so much. Maybe because she knew how far it was from the truth. It had been so many years since he had walked out of her dorm after the rain, his wet shoes and clothes pooling tears of regret on the linoleum floor behind him. The remaining dampness had soaked into the fancy striped throw rug her parents had bought for the room after scoffing at what they considered to be slumming it in the dormitories.

Freedom was what she had called it. Freedom to make her own choices, like the disastrous one she made with Azrael her sophomore year.

It had been a disappointment then, but she was old enough now to know that this was not unusual for matters of the heart. People either disappointed you or they didn't, and she wasn't going to let Azrael Hart's rejection six years ago drag her down. She'd had plenty of great sex and even a sort of love with Robbie in between. *Clingy*, both he and Natalie had called her. But neither of those relationships defined her.

If Robbie breaking up with her hadn't been devastating, Azrael's behavior after one brief lapse in judgment shouldn't be either after all this time.

Vickie returned to the pastries and checked her watch. People were starting to leave, the little set of skull bells jingling pleasantly with each departure. She smiled, thinking of Persephone Hart and how people so often misjudged her because she looked the part of a gothic vampire in a house guarded by wicked iron spikes. It had always struck her as ironic that the tidy white colonial mansion with its pristine blue shutters was inhabited by her awful, calculating parents, and the haunted, perpetually foggy grounds of Hart Manor hosted so much earnest affection.

In the corner, even Hank was starting to finish his crossword and his muffin.

From across the room, Vickie saw that asshole regular who always gave Hazel grief. He was eyeing Hank. Chet something. He was a teacher at Hallowcross High, too, and Hazel had told her he was famous for making a student and her parent cry at a back-to-school night once. Vickie glared at him, daring him to try anything in her shop. He made eye contact and raised his eyes suggestively, of all things.

With a flourish, Vickie walked over to the Hex Bigotry, Witches sign that hung over the wall display of stickers with the same slogan, and adjusted it, giving him a pointed look. He rolled his eyes and returned to his coffee and pretentious reading selection. Hank, walking over, presumably to use the restroom, but also quite possibly simply to gossip, stopped at the counter.

"He's been reading that same page of *Moby Dick* for thirty minutes, and I saw him open it to a random place when he got here." Hank smiled at her knowingly, leaning in.

"I guess the whale isn't the only dick in that book," he said, chuckling with glee, and made his way to the bathroom.

Vickie was feeling cross this morning, but in her defense, she had seen Chet do the same thing with *Oliver Twist* the last time he was in here. It seemed that there was no limit to the dickish behavior of this particular customer.

Something nagged at the corner of her mind as she watched him, the cruel set of his mouth souring a face that might otherwise be nice to look at.

Vickie almost took her phone out to text Azrael, who would have appreciated Hank's joke. But that was silly, to text him from across the room, like they were in high school again. And besides, he was snapping under the table, doing some sort of magic. Better not to disturb him.

She looked up, surprised to see that despite the late hour, a line had formed, and soon she was ringing up people and handing out coffee cups and muffins and filling carafes with iced coffee and juices so quickly that an hour flew by. The next thing she knew, Hazel was next to her, taking orders and making things move twice as fast. During a brief lull, they switched places, and then it was Vickie serving muffins and walking around to refill sugar packets and creamers. They rarely did this kind of business so close to closing.

She checked the coffee makers, trying not to look at Az too much. When her wandering eyes did land on him, he was looking anywhere but at her. The last of the customers trickled out, and when Hank left, Vickie took the carafes to the sink in the back.

Azrael must have still been wary of Sultry Sunday attire. Persephone and Benedict had been so comfortable with who they were. Witchy and weird and sexy. So openly in love with each other that he called her "my darling" and she called him "handsome" in casual conversation. So obviously attracted to each other and so handsy in public that people in town had speculated that the Harts had some sort of kinky sex dungeon.

Which they *definitely* did; she and Az had awkwardly stumbled upon it once as teenagers, empty of any witchy or human occupants at the time of their discovery, thank goddess. But the chains and toys had been exciting nonetheless, and had led to a tensely whispered conversation about the benefits and drawbacks of spanking and whips afterward, and some feelings that she had not yet understood at thirteen.

She tried not to remember those particular thoughts as she scrubbed out the coffeepots, rinsing them and setting them to dry before returning to the front, where Hazel was packing up the remaining pastries to take home.

Azrael still sat at the same table, of course, looking half-miserable and half-eager. So different from Persephone's certainty, though Vickie remembered her telling them as teenagers that she, too, had struggled once to figure her life out.

Now that the shop was empty, Hazel was raising her eyebrows and clearing her throat while leaning her head so far over that it looked like she could be auditioning for a role in *The Exorcist*.

"I'll leave you two alone, then," the girl announced almost in a yell, and Vickie winced. There was no way Azrael hadn't heard. Or seen the overly enthusiastic gestures.

"Yes, thank you, Hazel. See you tomorrow night." She took off her apron, hanging it on the hook, adjusting her robe, and trying not to check to see if Azrael's eyes followed. She forced herself to wave and smile at her lone employee instead of looking at her former friend.

"Have fun, boss." Hazel winked, and Azrael looked at the ground.

Like he probably wanted to melt into it. Like the idea of any extracurricular fun with her, even now, was a burden too great to risk looking her in the eyes for. Goddess, how she had missed those hazel eyes. She thought that maybe his face was a little bit flushed. This made her smile; after all this time, he was still uptight about lingerie.

But now Vickie was staring, and Az would think she had been sitting around moping after him. He probably had some beautiful person back in California that he pined for. With very tasteful, full-coverage underthings. Probably still silky and sexy as hell, but, like, demure and shit.

"You want to wait until I'm done cleaning and prepping in

the back?" she offered. The only way out of this awkwardness was through it, and she was determined to stick to her normal routine for both her depleting bank account and hopeful business sense. But it didn't seem right to make him work for free in his dead mom's shop when he had come here to talk.

"I'll help," he said. "I missed it here, anyway. It's been too long since—"

His voice cracked. His wrecked face pulled into a furrow as his eyes darted from the little skull bells to the cat cup in front of him. Then to the sign over the counter with a rainbow Black Lives Matter fist wearing a pointed hat. The stickers with the words Hex Bigotry, Witches. All little relics of Persephone, her shop, and her vibe, had to be overwhelming for him. There was so much loveliness lost in the death of his parents, so much magic, real and imagined, in the town of Hallowcross, now gone forever with them.

Without thinking about how it might make her look, Victoria walked over to Azrael and threaded her fingers through his. For a moment, she felt naked, as though the lace and silk had evaporated. She hoped he didn't notice the way her breasts tightened, nipples hardening under the delicate fabric. The traitors. His hand was warm, and she concentrated on that feeling as her nerves tingled with the magic that rested in his palms. She shut her eyes, unwilling to see if revulsion flashed across his face.

She only opened them once he exhaled loudly enough for her to feel the whoosh of air, which sent tremors down her spine. "I forgot about that," he whispered. Azrael was a witch and Vickie was devil-kissed, and when they touched their magics recognized each other, fire and insight, sparks and might. Their hands knew each other.

Probably the rest of their bodies would, too, but she sure as hell would never get a chance to test that out again.

She hadn't forgotten, though, what it had been like to trace his tingling skin.

He sighed again for a moment, and she wanted to capture

it, to swallow it whole. His eyes were shut, and both their hands rested now on top of the table before he stood up, not breaking the link, and she was reminded of how tall he was. That much she had forgotten. Had he always been this tall up close? It was the closest they had been since that moment six years ago, and he seemed larger. Taller, broader. Even the air around him felt thicker with grief, she realized.

But when Azrael opened his eyes, the startling greenish strands in the brown, his pupils blown wide, it was no longer sadness she saw there, and she stepped forward without another thought. The heel of one of her precarious shoes slipped, and she fell directly into him, losing her balance and mourning ahead of time the indignity of falling flat on her face.

Which never happened. Instead, a strong arm wrapped around her waist, holding her upright against him while the other, still entwined in her own, pulled upward and, for a moment, held her in a pose as though they were tangoing here on the floor of the tea shop. It felt like time froze with the inhale she held for a few agonizing seconds, their bodies aligned with the stars, the thrum of magic rippling warmly across all of her.

She breathed deeply, hoping he didn't notice her heartbeat sped up. Praying simultaneously that the incessant pounding of his own wasn't just the adrenaline of avoiding a near fall. Perhaps there was lust left yet in Azrael Hart for her, though she wasn't kidding herself into thinking it was meaningful.

All those years gone by, and her stomach still swooped low, looping as though she were about to board a particularly dangerous and thrilling roller coaster. He tipped her back, and for a brief series of seconds, she thought he might kiss her. Her heart pounded. They had been few enough that she *had* forgotten how breathless the times before Az had kissed her were. How momentous.

Evidence of a somber thought danced across his face, and he winced and set her upright, moving away.

"I'm sorry," she started, the cold of his absence noticeable all over.

Oh goddess. She was so off. She'd read it wrong. Shit. What if he thought she had lunged into him and tripped on purpose? Shit.

"No. I am," he began. His voice sounded shattered again. Tense. "I got carried away. My dad always used to sweep my mom like that, and for a moment, when I went to catch you, I lost myself. I didn't mean anything by it, and I'm sorry."

He didn't mean anything by it. Sure. That made sense.

She'd even heard it before. From him.

It doesn't mean anything. The words echoed, hollow across the stretch of time, but the hurt in her chest felt recent. Raw.

Victoria couldn't fathom why it would make her feel so gapingly empty, but she could forgive him a mistake in a moment of grief.

His parents were a great love story, and it was fair to mourn them. If part of her wished he felt even a little bit of that intensity toward her, she could push that to the side. Pretend it away.

She was good at ignoring sobering things. It had been necessary to survive growing up in the cold Starnberger mansion, and she had polished the skill over the decades, sharpening sunshine and joy into weapons against the abyss of cruel riches.

"Don't worry, Az. Here, come with me to the back, and I'll change into more sensible clothing." Heading through the door without turning around, she didn't want to see whatever honesty his face would betray. "I was hoping you might be able to help me with an odd thing that a ghost told me."

If the declaration startled him, he didn't say so.

"Was it 'long time, no see'?" he called from the other room. "You know, because you can't see a ghost—well, most of the time, anyway?"

Shaking her head, Vickie laughed awkwardly. The hinges protested as he pushed through the swinging door behind her. She could feel his longing for things to be normal between them. Friendly. It mirrored her own. Well, almost.

"Hey, Vickie, why are ghosts so lonely?"

"Why?" She sat down in front of the desk to unbuckle her heels, propping them one at a time on the surface and rubbing at her ankles a little after removing the snug straps. One of them had dug an awkward line through the flowers tattooed on the inside of her leg, and she spent a few extra moments kneading the skin there.

Azrael looked away, a muscle in his jaw twitching.

Great. Now she'd made him uncomfortable. She didn't allow herself to entertain the possibility that the look on his face was something else.

"Why are ghosts lonely, Az?" she tried again.

He cleared his throat.

"Because they, well, they've got no *body* to lean on." His voice had cracked a little. A crooked smile snuck up the side of his serious face as she groaned at the joke. A nervous hand scrubbed through his hair. She wanted to act normal. To put him at ease, the way he was clearly trying to do for her with ghastly wordplay.

"That was awful." Vickie pulled tie-dye sweatpants out of a bag under her desk and shrugged them on, still seated, and slid her feet into green Chucks. Slipping the silky robe off, she folded it and placed it in the bag, taking out her favorite T-shirt, faded yellow with pink roses and a cartoon beaver on it. She stood up and tugged the shirt over her head.

Azrael was studying a spot on the wall as though it held the secrets to the universe, his throat working. If he had any more ghost puns, they were dead on his lips at the idea of her changing.

So he was just as tightly wound about nakedness and bodies as ever.

That tracked.

"Listen, Az," she said, washing her hands and moving to measure out tea into containers for tomorrow morning. He moved, without instruction, to do the same for the pastry dry ingredients, following the little laminated signs Persephone had kept taped on the cabinets without even needing to read them. "Thanks for doing that," she said, and he nodded.

"It's like second nature, really, Victoria. It's nothing." Azrael's voice was rough, and she wondered if it was the memories of his mother filling it with ragged emotion.

Vickie tensed. "Don't. I know things haven't been the same, but don't use my full name like we aren't even anything anymore. We're friends, however distant. Full names are for, like, weighty confessions. Breakups. Vows of eternal devotion. Please."

Az's face softened. "Vickie. Sorry. I thought it might help with, you know . . ." He finished with the flour and ran a nervous hand through his hair, leaving traces of white in its wake. "With making it feel normal between the two of us."

"Az, you're a witch and I see dead people. We won't ever be normal." It was unfair, really, because normal men couldn't even look like that: cheekbones chiseled from marble, peppered with a five-o'clock shadow, and hair tossed into a smooth perfection of curls that his fingers twitched over, again. If only Azrael had ever been a little less pretty, this all could have been easier.

"I'm a high school English teacher," he corrected. "And you run a tea and pastry shop. We're normal," he insisted.

"Sure," she said. "There's that. Though, truth be told, it's kind of magical on its own without the powers. Okay. We can play normie if you want. What *do* you want, by the way?"

"I wanted to ask you a favor," he said. Vickie's heart fluttered traitorously. "I know you don't like to use the flames without good reason, but I never got to say goodbye."

Ah. That made more sense than the romantic declaration she had, for a moment, expected. Hoped for? But she was soon distracted, looking at him. Misery wrote itself in lines across his forehead, and she ached for the depth of his sadness. Kicked herself for her errant, inappropriate thoughts when he'd clearly matured enough not to make every hour sexy time in his mind.

"Of course. I'd be happy to help you say goodbye." Vickie would do it for his parents' sake alone, and in penance for the inappropriate attention she'd paid to that stubbled jawline that a raw, impulsive part of her begged to sit on. The offense of six years ago notwithstanding.

"I wanted to try to find some way to wrap my mind around it before school starts." He paused, shutting his eyes and rubbing his left arm with his right before he opened them. "Sometimes it feels like my heart is actually breaking. Did you know grief can do that? Cause actual chest pain? I went and got it checked and everything."

"Oh, Az," she said softly. "I'm so sorry. I know they would be so proud of you, and this new job."

He ran a hand through his hair, leaving it disheveled in a way that she tried to ignore. This wasn't the moment to lose her mind over how good he looked a little bit messy.

"I start in two weeks. It feels like both an eternity and not enough time."

"I get that," she said, rubbing a hand over her own heart for a moment. "Tell me what you need."

He nodded and swallowed, twisting a ring on his pinky that she recognized now. It was silver, and engraved with thorns, moons, and roses.

It had been his mother's.

"I have this." Az's voice cracked. He wouldn't want to part with the gift his father had given his mother in love. Maybe the last thing that he had.

"No," she said firmly. "There must be objects around the apartment we can use before it comes to that. Is there a special gift that Benedict gave her? An heirloom they would have shared?"

Az swallowed, and his mouth tensed. "Sorry," she said softly. "I didn't mean to rub salt in the wound. I just know how much your parents meant to each other, and it's a pretty safe bet that there's something else."

His brownish eyes lit up, and she studied the greenish speckles around the edges. It was as though his father's gold and his mother's brown had fought and each had won out, in their own ways. It was just like his parents. Passionate. Together. Wonderfully odd. She saw so much of Benedict and Persephone in him. So much of what she had once thought would be her true home.

"Salt and pepper shakers. She collected salt and pepper shakers. He bought her a little skull and raven set with an Edgar Allan Poe quote." He smiled and rubbed at the crook of his left elbow. There was a small raven tattooed there that she hadn't noticed before. The ink was crisp and fresh, either recent or well moisturized. Possibly both. "They were gray and black, a few inches tall. Damn, my parents were weird, but they loved each other so hard." He paused. "I miss them," he admitted.

Friends could hold hands in grief. She threaded hers through his again and squeezed, ignoring the tingling sensation of touching him.

Vickie's fingers had more ideas than just hand-holding, though, and her other hand moved to trace the little bird.

"Is this new?"

"Yeah," he said. His voice was quiet. Thick. "I got it right after they died. When I couldn't go. I wanted a way to remember them."

"It's perfect," she said, forcing her hand away from his inked skin. It was totally inappropriate to feel all sorts of tempting sensations for her friend while he described the depths of his grief. The winding of longing thrumming through her veins was as unyielding as her pulse. Goddess, she was an asshole. She needed to focus.

"Think she would have stored them upstairs in the apartment?" Vickie couldn't bring herself to release the hand that held his, but she did step back, putting distance between them. For safety.

"Probably, yes. Is it empty?" His eyes clouded with emotion. Grief, probably.

"No. I haven't had a chance to clean it out; I just kind of put everything in the den to clear out the bedroom."

His mouth ticked up into a smile. "You've been living in the teeny upstairs apartment? The heiress to the Starnberger fortune in a one-bedroom walk-up with creaky floorboards and a leaky shower?"

She smiled, forced now.

"Hey. The leak is fixed now, thanks to a bit of clever home improvement magic by your sister. Also, I'm a *former* heiress. My parents cut me off, remember?"

He squeezed her hand before dropping it and nodding in the direction of the door.

"Priscilla made you go to Free Spirits, did she? The one with a dress code?"

Vickie smiled. "I made her meet me at Kessel Run, that *Star Wars* bar, last week to make up for it. I introduced her to the nachos there, and the best table in the back corner. It's my favorite."

Azrael smiled wide now, and the crinkles at the corners of his eyes made her shoulders relax again until he frowned.

"I've been meaning to check that one out." He cleared his throat. "About your parents. Sorry. That's fucked up. You deserve better." He paused, and then continued, softer. "You've always deserved better than them, Vickie."

Shrugging, she studied his face. He looked earnest.

"It's fine. They're selfish. They never wanted me to cling too tightly. It was just a matter of time before I crossed their lines."

He bit his lip.

"If you don't mind, and if it's not too much to ask, when you look around, see if you can find the shakers." His voice was all gentle apology rubbing against her, and the traitorous veins in her wrists pulsed for him, achy with memory. She swallowed.

"Sure," she said, uncertain about whether she'd cleaned up the banner of hanging underwear that wasn't supposed to go into the dryer.

She could make sure he didn't go into the bedroom. How hard could that be, really?

He looked at his watch. "I don't want to take up any more

of your time. Maybe text me if you can find them, and that will give me some time to think about what I want to say to my parents."

Her heart dropped. Azrael Hart didn't want to go upstairs. There was too much between them. They had too much history and too much baggage, but they could be friends. She could pretend the flame was extinguished, that he didn't make her want to cradle his head in her hands, run her fingers through his messy hair.

"Sure, Az. I'll look for them."

"Thank you," he said. "It means a lot. What did you need to tell me about ghosts?"

"It's no big deal. Your sister has Evelyn looking into it, but one of them mentioned that new megachurch."

He frowned. "If Evelyn's already on it . . ." He trailed off, shrugging his shoulders. "Let's see what happens before we interfere with Council affairs." She nodded, and he went on. "Thanks again for looking for the shakers."

She avoided his eyes. "It's what friends do, Azrael."

"Friends. Right." A muscle in his jaw twitched, and for a moment she thought he was going to say something else. "Good night, Vickie. Enjoy that last week of twenty-five."

Vickie swallowed. Of course he remembered her birthday. Of course.

She spent the better part of the next hour scouring her apartment for the salt and pepper shakers, and by the time she found them, wrapped carefully in a box in the closet of the spare bedroom, it was late enough that she thought twice about texting him.

Before she could think better of it, she snapped a picture, careful not to touch them, and sent it to him.

Vickie: These have to be the ones. Think they'll work?

Bubbles popped up right away, and she smiled, awaiting his response.

The bubbles disappeared. She waited a moment before tossing the phone on the couch and scowling.

Purple smoke drifted from under her kitchen counter, rising upward until Lex appeared.

"Is this all really necessary?" She gestured to the smoke.

"Not at all, but it's just so pretty, don't you think?"

He wasn't wrong, but he was awfully dramatic. Dramatic and arrogant and the opposite of Azrael. Which piqued her curiosity, if she was honest.

She smiled, and stepped toward him, watching his violet eyes dance with amusement. Lex towered over her, wearing a fitted suit that looked like it cost more than the entirety of her new apartment.

"It is pretty," she said, poking a finger through a remaining wisp of it. "But it doesn't feel like anything."

"Would you like it to feel like something?" His smile was crooked, and he stepped toward her.

What she would *like* is for Azrael to have come up to the apartment himself. Or not to have left her on read. But what she had was a handsome devil. Who was she to be choosy?

"Maybe." Vickie crossed over to the countertop, casually closing the box with the salt and pepper shakers. She wasn't entirely sure that Lex was trustworthy, and Azrael might be just her friend, but that didn't mean she wanted Lex or anything else to get in the way of what Az needed.

"Aren't you supposed to be doing the opposite of that?" He chuckled and gestured to her repacked box.

"Don't worry about it." She shoved the box to the back of her countertop. "What brings you here with no notice?"

"Just a list, pet. A list of souls." Lex flicked a finger lazily, sending more of that purple smoke into the air.

Vickie tensed. "You brought me a hit list."

"Now, now. These folks are already dead. And to be clear, they're dreadful people. It's angelic, really, that I've identified them for this. It will make the world a bit better, not having them."

She crossed her arms.

"How can I be sure of that?"

"I'll walk you through it. Here, the first one. In life, he lobbied for less gun control. Part of the group that prevents digital records of any gun ownership so that it's hard to cross-check when people have a history of violence or some other good reason not to have a weapon of human body destruction."

Uncrossing her arms, she nodded. "Okay, yes, I can get behind that."

Lex ran a hand along her countertop, and then rolled up the sleeves of his suit jacket, casually, as though he knew exactly what his muscular forearms did to people.

She tried not to notice too much, but she only saw the dead; she wasn't dead herself. And damn, those forearms.

"Shall I go on?" He smirked, watching her closely.

"Yes," she said.

"The next soul is a woman who runs a drug ring. A witch, but not a good one. You'll know as soon as you meet her spirit, I'd warrant. She'll feel *off*; it's the repercussion of a lifetime using magic for evil. She's responsible for many terrible things. Nothing plant-based or harmless, either: she's about the big-league drugs. The kinds that beget assault."

Vickie frowned, and he did too. "See, pet? I'm not a monster, unless you count being a monstrously good lover." He winked.

"The third soul?"

"To be determined." His brow creased. "I can't put my finger on who yet, but there's someone meddling in Hallowcross, someone I don't know, but I'll know them when I smell them." He frowned. "I'll substitute someone else if we can't find out who in time. It's someone tricky. Someone who's bargained with a creature stronger than me, if you can believe it. They're shielded. But there have been signs." He grinned wickedly. "Don't worry, dearest. I'll find them."

She ignored the sharpening of his smile, and the way it made the hairs on her arms rise. "Signs? How can you not know?"

"Talk to your witch friends. They're investigating. There

have been magical disturbances. And it's not my deal, so I can't track it the way whoever is behind it could. But I will, and you'll help me, because the alternative is too awful."

Vickie swallowed. "What's the alternative?"

"Well, you could renew your contract with me." She frowned at that. "Fine, fine," he continued. "We can find a different soul to reap if we must. But I don't like to reap who we don't have to reap. Your gift, when used for good, sends a spirit to its final plane of existence. Reaping is only for special occasions. Souls who deserve torture or terrible accidents."

"Accidents?"

He grinned. "They do happen. Still, don't worry. This is why I don't make bargains like the one I made with your parents more than once a century. You're my only girl with death powers."

"I bet you say that to all the girls."

Lex stepped closer. "I most certainly do not. But I can arrange for other types of deals, with less . . . permanent bonding. Or other types of bonds, if you're interested."

She bit her lip. She wasn't *not* interested.

"What types of deals would those be?"

He smirked, violet eyes flaring.

"Why don't we start with telling me what you can imagine?"

It was normal to imagine it, and she was free to tie herself, figuratively or literally, to anyone, and yet, she wasn't ready to close the door on the man who still haunted her, years later. Maybe later, but not yet.

"What I imagine is you getting back to business, me repaying my debt, and you moving on to torture the next unsuspecting mortal." She said it as firmly as she could, and Lex pouted.

For a moment, hurt flickered across his face, but he shook his head.

"You think on that, pet. It doesn't make a difference to me." His voice was cool, but there was an edge to it. "I can't say I get many rejections, though, in the end." It was downright icy now.

She crossed her arms. "A little rejection will be good for

you, then. Something new and exciting." She smiled, leaning toward him ever so slightly before catching it and correcting her posture.

He cocked his head for a moment, narrowing his eyes and nodding. "I'll be back when it's time to collect." He ran a finger down the side of her cheek, then disappeared into a cloud of the same purple smoke, leaving behind a trail of dark glitter and the faint scent of bergamot and ginger.

CHAPTER 7

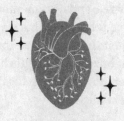

Azrael

Azrael had thought he might lose his mind when Victoria unbuckled those strappy, bright pink heels with her feet up on the desk. He'd lost the punch line to his best ghost joke, that was for sure. He'd traveled across a country and yet somehow found himself back here, as though looped around in time. Since he'd seen her ankle in the back of the shop, he could still close his eyes and feel it, the longing. He was basically a Victorian slut, thirsting over the little strip of skin above her foot.

Her scarlet toenail polish had matched her fingernails, and the thought of running his finger along her ankles and the tattoo she must have gotten sometime between now and then, of shaded roses winding higher as the expanse of her legs glistened, had been so tempting. He had memorized the wall to prevent his gaze from slipping up her calves and thighs. It was an instinct, the remembering, like it had been yesterday and not years ago, what it had been like to touch those legs, hands shaking in disbelief that it was really, actually, *finally* happening. The little gasps he had treasured so much from her mouth. The scent of summer and his wildest dreams. The way he thought about her all the time and hadn't been able to believe in those stolen hours that she was there, next to him—and on top of him and below him.

There had been plenty of beautiful people since then, but

no one could drown out the memory of Vickie. There in the back office of the tea shop it had been too real to process. She smelled like strawberries, and he remembered how impossibly soft her skin had once felt against his fingers. How she made him feel magic, not just the kind that came with his bloodline but also the kind that burrowed into his heart and clung there refusing to let go, even now, after all this time. Always.

He stared at the text message.

Vickie: These have to be the ones. Think they'll work?

He'd typed and deleted, and then thought about it for hours, until the night had slipped away into the early morning hours, and no amount of Netflix or Hozier records could soothe the ache of not responding. How could he respond? How could he possibly blend his feelings for his parents and his feelings for Vickie and come out looking something like human and normal?

The sun was already rising by the time he finally drifted to sleep, mad at himself for staying up so late. The curtains of his room drew themselves shut, and the light dimmed. The temperature dropped slightly as the house remembered exactly how he liked to sleep. He curled up under a comforter, phone next to him.

When he woke up, it was mid-Monday, and he realized with a jolt that he had never responded.

Asshole behavior. All he wanted to do was repair whatever was between them—safer to focus on the friendship—and all he'd managed was asshole behavior.

He grabbed his phone and typed out a message.

Azrael: Sorry. I really appreciate you looking for those. I got more emotional at the sight of them than I expected.

He plugged the phone in, went to brush his teeth, and by the time he had returned, he had a reply.

Vickie: I get it. I'm working most of the week, but the shop is closed on Wednesdays, if you want to come over then.

Azrael: Let me just double-check that I don't have anything for work. The first staff day isn't for two weeks, but there's a tour of the school this week

Azrael: Don't take this as I'm not eager, I just really want to make sure I don't double-book.

Azrael: I appreciate you doing this, btw.

Vickie: I'm DEAD. Azrael Ashmedai Hart taking a TOUR of Hallowcross High?

Azrael: I know, I know. I work there now.

Vickie: Azrael Hart?? THE Azrael Hart who said he'd never set foot in that place again, like, every day the summer after senior year?

Azrael: Haha. Laugh it up.

Azrael: You're sleeping in a bed my parents definitely fooled around on.

Vickie: AZ. First of all, good for them. Second, this is a new bed. I sold that one. I may not be rich anymore, but even on a shoestring budget, I sprung for a new mattress.

Azrael: Probably for the best.

Azrael: And now I've grossed myself out thinking about that.

Vickie: Sorrryyy

Azrael: It's ok. It's actually kind of comforting to remember how much they loved each other.

Azrael: I'm trying to focus on that. We have to do a grief counseling training after the tour.

Vickie: oh shit, I'm sorry. What happened?

Azrael: not a current student, thankfully. A college kid. He graduated three years ago so there are quite a few kids who knew him, and we just want to be ready to help.

Vickie: That's so awful, Az. I'm sorry.

Azrael: I'm just glad they have a training for it. I think we're also going to get lessons on preventing overdoses.

Azrael: Tell me something happy, though. Distract me for a moment?

Vickie: Can do. Remember the time Mrs. Kingfisher in the front office actually clutched a pearl necklace when your parents got you for early dismissal? I thought that was just an expression.

Azrael: Yeah, well, she was pretty uptight.

Vickie: Probably didn't help that your dad thwacked your mom's ass on the way in.

Azrael: I imagine not.

Vickie: Or that your mom did likewise on the way out.

Azrael: The horrors, really.

Vickie: I'm glad I knew them, Az.

Azrael: Me too. Their memories really are a blessing.

Azrael: Hey Vickie?

Vickie: Yeah?

Azrael: Thanks. For the saltshakers, and for talking me through this.

Vickie: That's what friends do. Let me know about Wednesday.

He didn't want to end it there, but he also didn't want to bother her at work, so he opted to feed Emily Lickinson, who was meowing plaintively at his ankles. He needed coffee, and then he needed to check his email.

CHAPTER 8

Victoria

She tried not to take it personally that Azrael was taking a tour of their old high school instead of hanging out on her day off, but it did mean that she had finally tackled organizing and cleaning the apartment for a few hours, and then catching up on laundry.

Around noon, her phone buzzed, and she was glad no one was around to see how widely she grinned when it was him.

Azrael: Mrs. Kingfisher still works here.
Azrael: She was in charge of getting me a parking pass and staff badges.
Azrael: I was just sad not to have anybody's ass to smack
Vickie: All you had to do was ask
Vickie: Kidding

She wasn't, not entirely, but it was too easy to fall back into this, to pretend that what had happened in college hadn't happened, and that they were still friends with potential the way they had once been.

They were still friends, though.

Azrael: That's OK, probably best not to anger the person in charge of helping me if I lose my badge

Azrael: Which I don't plan on doing. I'm still terrified of her.

Vickie: Any of the teachers we had there still?

Azrael: I think only Hammonds in science.

Vickie: Aww I loved her

Azrael: Yeah she seems great, still.

Azrael: You love to see your heroes live up to the hype

Azrael: My department chair is kind of an ass, though

Vickie: He comes into the shop, I'm pretty sure. Want me to poison his coffee?

Azrael: He unfortunately is on the list of people I ought not to anger. But I will keep it in mind.

Azrael: I'm trying to give him a chance. Maybe he's just having a bad day. When we stopped by his office on the new teacher tour, he looked at me like I personally tried to turn in homework late to him.

Vickie: The offer for accidental coffee tampering still stands. Even if this text message chain would make me culpable.

Azrael: I'd magic away the evidence, international Witchery Council text law or not.

Vickie: That's the Azrael I know and love

Dammit. Why did she have to say *love*? Why was this friendship launching itself right back into her heart? That foolish organ should be working hard to forget all the catastrophe that had stretched between them.

Azrael: hah

Azrael: I bet you say that to all the people offering to commit crimes to clear your name.

Vickie: You caught me.

Azrael: Hey, would you maybe want to grab a drink with me? We could call it an early birthday toast. Just between friends.

Now she was grinning embarrassingly. The laundry buzzed, and she put the phone down for a moment. She could let him sweat while she switched it to the dryer.

Azrael: Just casual. It's a casual drink invite.

Vickie: I'd love to. We can do the saltshakers, too, if you want

Azrael: Let's keep this one about your birthday. Prissy said you're busy this weekend, so Thursday might be better?

Fuck. She'd been trapped by Priscilla Hart. At least there was no glitter in it; when they were growing up Prissy's traps almost *always* included glitter. Some weeks she and Azrael would come to school doused in it after a barrage of pranking back and forth, which was how someone started the rumor that Azrael was secretly a stripper.

She smiled. She would have been too shy to tell him that in high school, but he would make an absolutely fantastic stripper. He could have a whole broody, grumpy character going. And he would definitely look amazing in eyeliner.

Azrael: Kessel Run at 5:30, so we can catch happy hour?

After she closed the shop on Thursday, Vickie would have been embarrassed if anyone had seen how many outfits she tried on before leaving. It was her birthday celebration, if a few days early, and she told herself that was why she opted for her best pair of jeans and a pink crop top, that it was totally casual to put on makeup and fix her hair for a birthday drink with a friend.

When she walked in, he was sitting at her favorite table, the one in the back. There was a plate of nachos waiting in the middle of it. If seeing him again was a death sentence for her resolve not to catch more feelings, well, this detail, him remembering that she'd mentioned this, and ordering snacks, was a final nail in the coffin. She couldn't help the goofy grin spreading across her face, or the enthusiasm in her steps toward him.

"I thought you might like these," he said, the corners of his mouth sliding upward.

She leaned over and hugged him. It was a friendly thing, just a few seconds, but the feel of his arms immediately wrapping her, of knowing his response was to keep her closer, was enough to make everything hazy. Touching him was too confusing. He smelled like he always did, like amber wood and lemon, and just like at the shop, he felt big. More filled out than she remembered him being in college. It was a strange sensation of the familiar and the unknown.

"What was that for?" he asked, his cheeks slightly flushed.

"For getting me nachos. And my favorite table."

"Oh." He smiled, relaxing. "Well, happy early birthday. I'd like to buy you a drink, too, but I wasn't sure what you're drinking these days, and I didn't want to assume."

The consideration of it was enough to make her want to hug him again. To climb him like a tree, really. She resisted and sat down instead.

The same server from before came back, this time dressed in a shirt that said Han Shot First. The beauty of small towns was that it was fairly easy to become a regular in a place like this.

"What can I get you? Greedo Mojito?" She smiled at his memory.

"Let's do a Wretched Hive. I've always wanted to look into beekeeping. It seems kind of cool."

"We locally source the honey for it, and buy the lemons from the same farm. It's run by a wonderfully eclectic pair of sisters, who are shut-ins, and big cheese afficionados, too. The maple gin is local, too, so you might as well call it a Vermont Hive."

"That would be slightly less on brand," said Azrael, smiling. The waiter blushed, and Vickie wondered if there was anything there.

And why the thought stoked a tiny flare of jealousy in her gut.

Azrael put his hand on her shoulder, running his thumb down an inch for a second and biting his lip.

"It's her birthday this weekend," he said. "She'll be twenty-six on Sunday."

Daniel looked overjoyed. "Oooooh! I love birthdays. We have a whole birthday thing."

"Oh," said Azrael, looking at her nervously. "Oh no, I don't know if she wants a whole thing—"

"Fuck yes, I do," she said. "I love a birthday thing."

The waiter nodded and hurried off to the bar. They could see him mixing the drink and then fiddling around with something underneath the counter.

He returned with Vickie's drink and what looked like the top half of a Darth Vader helmet.

"We don't do the mask bit anymore, but if you want, you can wear the birthday helmet."

She plunked it on her head, hoping that Daniel was the sort to disinfect this thing between special occasions. He was already back behind the bar, wiping it down fastidiously, which was a good sign.

"That looks nothing like Darth Vader," he said.

"I guess you really do need the mask, but I can appreciate, from both a selling beverages and a cleanliness standpoint, not handing one out to customer after customer in this particular scenario." She wrinkled her nose.

"It's giving the guy from *Spaceballs*," said Azrael, laughing in earnest. His eyes crinkled, and she felt that smile all the way to her toes.

Goddess, she loved it when he smiled.

"Use the Schwartz, Azrael," she said, in her best Rick Moranis voice.

"I mean, I'm game for using Force in consenting situations between adults if you are." His face was bright red now. His hands gripped the table, knuckles white, and her breath caught in her throat.

"Exactly what kind of 'force' would that be?" She leaned forward, chin on her hand, trying not to think of the sex dungeon they'd found in Hart Manor as kids.

He paused, eyes darkening, pupils wide, and ran a thumb across his jaw for a moment before answering. "Using the force of friendship, obviously."

Vickie bit her lip, shaking off a slight disappointment. That was better, though. Easier. A much safer idea than what she'd momentarily envisioned.

"Speaking of friendship, how do Monday or Tuesday night sound? For the contacting, you know." Telling herself this was for friendship alone wasn't entirely a lie; while it might be a little romantic to meet her former, well, whatever he had been to her, so late, she was always up at such hours already after work weekend nights prepping pastry and the like for the weekend rush. Her birthday wouldn't make her any less in debt to the bank.

"Yeah," said Az, swallowing the last of what looked like a cider. "Let's do Tuesday. That works better for me." He glanced at the menu. That little crease between his brows was back, and she wanted to smooth it away with her thumb. "Hey, want to split the ice cream sundae they have here? They call it a Hoth Planet Explosion."

"Is that even a question?" She had missed this. The friendship, the easiness between them. Maybe they could just not talk about what had happened. Pretend it away.

Pretending could work. It had to.

CHAPTER 9

Azrael

He'd insisted on Tuesday. For his schedule, he had told her, but it was really because he didn't want her to have a late night unless it lined up with the day the shop was closed. He had arrived a little before closing to help her, a few snaps here and there to clean counters and restock.

Az was trying not to be a pervert now, walking behind her up the stairs to the apartment above the shop. He focused on the hardwood of the stairs, and the bat-patterned coffee cup he'd swiped from downstairs, almost empty. It was hard for him to be near Vickie without touching her. The brightly printed sweatpants were flattering, and he had always had a soft spot for that beaver T-shirt.

Az loved her enough to have done her the favor, years ago, of making sure she wasn't burdened by any strings. By the weight of his useless, unrequited love. Hadn't someone brilliant once written that it was like bitter almonds? Vickie was tart berries bursting on his tongue, and the knowledge that she would never love him turned the sweetness to dry dust. The bitterness had always been the feeling, not the flavor, he realized, finally understanding one of his favorite books a little better.

When they walked in, he saw that she had not been lying about only organizing in small chunks. He had the sudden urge to ask if he could stay over, since the shop was closed Wednesdays. Spend the night and help her sort things out.

He'd be lying to himself if he pretended not to be interested in more than just home arrangement. But lying to himself had worked out before.

Though less dusty than it had once been, the apartment looked like it hadn't been rearranged, other than the bedroom and an overflowing bookshelf. A gray couch with a few cardigans thrown haphazardly across it sagged comfortably against the wall facing a television. Her shut laptop on the coffee table suggested that she curled up like a cat in the corner of that couch streaming things rather than watching them on the bigger screen. Az smiled, ran his fingers over a fleecy throw, and glanced over to the kitchen and the door to the bedroom. Her eyes followed his, and then widened.

Vickie sprinted across the living room to pull the blue door shut, but not before he caught a glimpse of a clothesline spanning the bedroom and drying out some very sexy underthings. Pinks and yellows and purples, reds in many shades, all festooned in a way that made him bite back a groan just thinking about her hands slipping those delicate lace monstrosities on and off.

Az tried not to be jealous of whoever was lucky enough to see those.

He tried, even less successfully, to banish the lust from curling, warm and fog-like, in his stomach, and seeping lower into regions that could cause physical consequences.

One ought not to sport a raging erection in the midst of an important conversation with someone who was very decidedly just a friend.

He dragged the hand aching to touch her down his own face instead, trying to think of anything sobering. His awful former boss. His old landlady's litter box. The time he'd accidentally trod on Emily Lickinson's tail and she'd clawed his foot viciously in return.

He drained the last of his coffee, as though he needed the

additional caffeine coursing through his veins along with lust and the magic of her closeness. He set the empty cup down on her counter.

"Hey, Vickie. What do you call it when you steal someone's coffee?"

The corners of her mouth twitched. She had always laughed at his jokes. Even the bad ones. "What?"

"Mugging," he deadpanned.

She threw her head back and laughed, a tinkling, familiar sound that made his chest ache. "Your humor still sucks, but I missed that." Her green eyes relaxed now, looking at him. "I missed you. When you were gone, I missed you." His heart beat louder, so loud he was pretty sure she could hear it.

"I missed you too," he said, swallowing. Reminding himself not to get lost. Not daring to hope, but wanting to, a little; the joke was bad enough that he wanted to believe her laughter was *for* him. "The shakers," he said, swallowing down his wishes.

"I have them," she said, walking over to the cream-colored island and setting down her bag before rummaging through the navy cabinets. "Go on and look. I don't have anything embarrassing in the kitchen," she said.

Azrael wondered what embarrassing things were tucked away elsewhere that he could convince himself not to fantasize about. But opening one of the cabinets, all he found was a blue box of macaroni and cheese and a family package of ramen noodles next to a sleeve of crackers. "Healthy eating over here, huh?"

"Shut up. It's like college again, opening a business, but without a meal plan or my parents' credit card. I haven't even had time to go through all the kitchen things here, and I mostly eat the pastries downstairs."

Smiling, he could picture her existing on nothing but dessert and instant noodles. She didn't seem upset about it, so he wouldn't be either. But he *did* want to clear the air of any lingering weirdness. He might still have feelings for her, every so often, but there was no way she ever had to know about them.

This way, they could at least be friends, and, hell, he would take the agony of her closeness over never seeing her again.

"About college," he began. They'd both been direct enough in that moment, but letting it sit for years, unaddressed, made it feel unresolved.

Turning around, she held up the box with the small black raven and a white skull. "Found them," she said, avoiding his eyes. "We'll talk about the college thing later. First, your parents."

He needed to talk to his parents, and it sounded like she also had more pressing matters than rehashing their dramatic past. He sighed. What were his midtwenties if not an unresolved checklist of parts of his life that had almost, but not quite, fallen into place?

"Ready?" She was looking at him now, her bright green eyes earnest and worried under the loud eye shadow. He wanted to wipe the slate clean so that no awkward memories lingered, but he also couldn't bear to lose even the sliver of happiness that had been that night.

And besides, memory magic wasn't just illegal, it was wrong, and he should *never* fuck with magic around Vickie without her express permission.

Well, never again.

He needed to focus. He reminded himself of his father's ridiculous three-piece suits, and the coordinating pocket squares the man had loved so much.

"It's just five minutes," warned Vickie. "They can see and hear you, but you won't see or hear them, and then the object burns, and they disappear. We can probably find other objects, but still. Think about what I could tell you later, to make the most of it."

Part of him wanted to tell her he had changed his mind. To avoid his emotions. It was the same tactic he had tried to use years ago for the sex talk, but Benedict had been clever. Speeding car, on a freeway, fast enough that Azrael couldn't duck and roll out even with magic. This time, Az was behind the wheel. He could stop her from summoning them, and run away from his issues like a child, or he could accept and address the grief weighing on his mind.

"Do you want to do this?" Vickie's voice was gentle.

Fuck. He did *not*. He wanted to get in his car and drive away into the woods, or pull her down into its spacious back seat, and convince her to make him forget everything. But he couldn't, because they had just started to be friends again, and because he couldn't run from his grief forever.

And, also, he *did* want to talk to his parents. He missed them. His mom with her eccentric, dramatic flair, and ridiculous, loving heart. His father with his three-piece suit and his wordless grunt, as though Henry Cavill's Geralt of Rivia had been crossed in personality with the style and comportment of Gomez Addams. He missed his father's staunch, unfailing support of his children. Like the time that Viola Ravenscrow claimed it was unnatural for Priscilla to date women. Benedict had shadow-hexed the woman so quickly that the invisible stitches holding in her words lasted weeks. She had to go around writing out requests without her voice and magicking her food, premashed, into her esophagus. When her ability to open her mouth and speak finally returned, he had a stern talk with her, and she ended up writing a check directly to the town's shelter for displaced LGBTQIA+ youth every year since.

Azrael knew he had his father's reserve and shyness. He hoped he had his mother's heart. But after leaving, he had struggled in his career as much as he had with witchcraft in his youth. Except this time, he didn't have Benedict to patiently help him with shadow craft until his witchery was smooth and powerful. This time he didn't have Persephone to take him aside for private lessons on herbs and plants and flowers. He needed his parents. This was the only way to reach them.

"You're sure?" Vickie repeated it gently. She was not going to force him, and she would understand if he backed out.

Swallowing, he nodded again. He'd been preparing since he first asked her. Since before that, really. His throat felt like it was made of sandpaper, and he wasn't sure he could talk, but he'd have to find the words. It had been a long time since he'd watched her speak to the dead.

"Please. I need to talk to them."

She nodded, and reached for the salt and pepper shakers, bird in one hand and skull in the other. Traces of flame licked around her fingers, though the objects were not yet consumed, and from memory he knew the flame would not hurt her. She just had to keep contact.

Vickie blinked. Her face relaxed, and her eyes filled with tears, listening to voices he couldn't hear but wanted to so desperately.

He wished for a different world where his parents had survived.

Vickie could see them one last time, but he couldn't.

Tugging a hand through his hair, Az focused on inhaling. Exhaling. The pain was still there, but he could breathe through it. He ran his hand down his face, and he could feel her concern.

Their concern, really.

"They want you to know that they love you so much, and they're so proud of you and Priscilla."

Hot tears ran down the face partially covered by his hand, and he couldn't bear to see her, standing there in sweatpants, glitter from her hair escaping to her cheeks and hands as the flame worshiped her palms like his lips had, once. When she put on glitter for Sultry Sundays, it always lasted, and something about that reminded him of his childhood. Of being really, truly happy.

It was too much to have lost Vickie, to have never really had her at all, and then to be without half his family as well. The universe had bestowed a brutal pounding on his soul, and rivers of sorrow traced patterns on his face, leaking into the collar of his shirt. He cried with abandon for all the losing. For the heaviness of all the wanting.

It was both overwhelming and a relief to cry like that, finally.

Shutting his eyes tight, he spoke.

"Mom. Dad. I love you. I'm so sorry I wasn't here. I tried—" His voice broke, and a small sob racked through him again.

"Az," Vickie was saying softly. "Az." He knew that with a shaker in each hand, she couldn't touch him without breaking the connection, and he shook his head. The sensation that she was standing close was enough, and he needed to get this out while the shades of his parents were still around to hear it.

"I tried to make it in California. I really wanted to. It just wasn't happening, and then by the time I tried to go home it was too late and flights and portaling were suspended, and I just want you to know that I love you both so much. I am sorry. For being so embarrassed and so standoffish and never realizing how wonderful you both were. For everything."

He opened his eyes, and Vickie was crying too. She still clutched the shakers in her hands, and he walked toward her, thumbing the wet, dark tears away from her cheeks. Allowing himself the small moment of tracing her freckles and swiping away trails of her mascara as she sniffled, leaning her face into his hand for a moment.

"Az," she began, voice heavy with emotion. "Your mother said you have nothing to apologize for. She said she's so proud of you, no matter what. That they've always carried your love in their hearts and that they will no matter what, just like you will carry theirs, and their magic, even when all the objects are gone."

"Mom," he began. "I . . ." Vickie shook her head, staring behind him, and he turned to match her view and face the ghosts, which no amount of hopeful longing would let him see.

"Hold on, Az, your dad has something." Vickie bit her lip, and he could feel, standing close as he was, that the objects were heating up.

They were running out of time. Her eyes widened, and her grip on each trinket tight enough that both edges of her palms went white with pressure.

"We need to warn the Council about the Brethren of One Love."

She was worrying her bottom lip and nodding, clearly listening to his father.

"The megachurch?"

"Yes. They're not the first shades to warn me about them. I actually wanted to talk to you about that." She blinked, and her face tensed. "Another ghost mentioned something off there. Your father is not sure what they're doing precisely, and he doesn't know who is to blame, but he said to start with what happened to Madam Cleopatra. He said there are consequences to what they tried to do to her," she said. Her brows drew together, and hairs raised on his arms. It was a bad sign that two sets of ghosts had warned Vickie about this church. He stepped toward her as the flames increased.

She frowned. "I don't see what that has to do with anything, but fine. I'll tell him."

"Madam Cleopatra, the fake psychic? And tell me what?"

"Yes, her. Tell you that I, ah, ran into the devil who made the bargain with my parents. Olexandre. They cut me off, like I said, formally with a lawyer. Your mom says he's a lesser devil, and his gift should be harmless, but still. I owe him. Three souls." She wasn't quite meeting his eyes, and he noticed that she was *blushing*, of all things.

"I've heard about Olexandre, the heartbreaker. When you told me your parents disowned you, you left out the part where you met a handsome devil to whom you are now legally bound," growled Azrael. He pressed his lips together, feeling a muscle in his cheek jump. "Are you all right?"

"I'm *fine*, Az. He's just a lesser devil. They give out nice gifts, really. As I'm sure you know. Like talking to ghosts. Charm. Persuasion. Dream walking. That would have been a cool one, actually. And who says he's handsome?"

Azrael ran a hand through his hair anxiously. "They are *always* handsome, Vick. It's never a deal with an ugly devil. Come on now."

She shook her head.

"I'm sorry, Az, it's about to be over." The heat next to him was scorching, and he gasped at it, reminding himself that it couldn't harm her. "Az, they said to be careful. To stay away from the church until we know more about it. To find Madam Cleopatra. To alert the Council. Anything else you want to tell them?"

The burning licked up toward her elbows now.

"I love you," he said once more, to the air over her shoulder. Hoping it would land on his parents' ears as the salt and pepper shakers went up into flames and he stepped back, watching the fire shoot up from her palms and eventually flicker out. The ash remaining fell to the floor.

A small, stubborn part of him that refused to give up also hoped the three words landed in Vickie's ears.

Even if he had given up on honesty some years ago.

CHAPTER 10

Victoria

Azrael looked like his heart was breaking, and it made sense. It was tragic not to see them himself to say goodbye.

Goddess, why couldn't she and Az have just let go and loved each other the way the Harts did? Like an old-fashioned movie or slow music that wound its way around the table of a record player, pumping out blood and passion and sensations. She was caught in a memory, the temptation to want that with him. To dance a tango in the grand ballroom of Hart Manor under the moonlight. To share passionate kisses like the ones she'd witnessed between Benedict and Persephone from inside a claw-foot soaking tub when she and Az would sneak around the house as kids.

All that and more.

Her words had fallen short in showing how his mom had reached for his tearstained face, or how his dad looked both formal and welcoming in a suit as always, white hair brushed back and clean in death. If only she had real magic to show him how much his parents cared. If only she and Azrael hadn't been so perfect and so awful together for that one day. Then she could at least touch him and distract him from the grief and loss winding into his soul.

But he had been absolutely clear. After two years of late-night clumsy phone calls, confusing texts, and summer internships keeping them on their respective coasts, one day, he had just shown up. She had been dreaming of him, and in the dreams, she ran through flames and called his name. The next thing she knew, he was on a red-eye flight. He walked from the train station near her school in the rain. Said he'd used what was left in his bank account on the round-trip ticket. Told her he had just needed to be there. That he had to see her in that moment, even just for the weekend. That he'd heard her calling to him in the universe. Summoning him. She had thought, for a foolish instant, that it was the soulmate-level love that his parents had.

When she asked why Benedict and Persephone didn't pay for the ticket, he laughed. Thunder booming overhead, he told her that when you finally decide to seize your destiny and go for what you want, it ought to be on your own terms and with your own money.

It had been so perfect then.

Before he'd changed his mind.

They had stood in the rain awkwardly for a few moments, six years ago, chests heaving in a tense pause while they decided. Droplets gathered and fell from his long lashes. She remembered all too well how his lips had pressed against hers, gentle at first. How he had cradled her face, how desperate she had been to give in to the inevitability of the moment. Kisses turned harder. Hands wove into soggy hair. The feel of his mouth against hers had been like coming up for fresh air after breathing smog for her entire life. His hands had traced her sides, his fingers warm, stable, and unwieldy all at once. She had wanted him to touch her everywhere. The imprints of his thumbs felt tattooed into her hips. His fingers slipped under her shirt to the dimples where her back met her ass. Venus dimples, he'd called them, kissing them reverently in her room later and then moving lower, while she thanked her lucky stars her roommate had agreed to clear out for the weekend. She wished she didn't remember the slick drawl of those moments quite so accurately.

Somehow, on the creaky and uncomfortable twin bed of her dorm room, Azrael had touched her like they were more than two brash twenty-year-olds hooking up in a dormitory. It had been a homecoming, his lips on hers and the taste of his name on her tongue, and then the way she came undone when he moved that lush, magical mouth lower and lower.

Afterward, she had thought this was it. That this would be forever. She woke up to the smell of him, woods and tart lemonade, and she had wanted to tell him she loved him. To make him scream her name and beg and profess his love for her.

But he got up to go get them coffee, promised that he could never let her want for anything, and he came back an hour later, with two cups gone cold and a strange expression on his face as he explained that this was just one time, just to get it out of his system, and that they had no obligation to each other.

We're just friends, he had said.

I don't think of you that way.

It doesn't mean anything.

She'd have to be pretty fucking desperate to start the heartache up again after they had confused lust and a lifetime of building physical attraction with actual feelings. She had forgiven him for misunderstanding, but she might never forgive herself completely for loving him. And she had resolved to pretend that it was just friendship between them now.

They had been doing so well.

Clingy Vickie, almost latching on where she didn't belong again, but this time to the one person she had ever truly fit in with. The one person she couldn't stand to lose again.

Still, Azrael was grieving, and she told herself that was why she stepped closer, letting the ash fall from her fingertips to the floor. They could clean it up later. It was a friendly thing. A hug to cure sadness, and she wrapped her arms around him before she could think better of it.

"Az," she whispered into his shirt, trying not to breathe in the scent that undid her resolutions. "I'm so sorry."

He held still, and she wondered if she'd misread, but he moved his lips closer to her ear.

"Atta ghoul, helping me say goodbye."

The tension cracked, and she was giggling now.

For a moment they were both laughing, arms still around each other, and then he was pulling her toward him, hazel eyes shadowed and still a little red. He looked like he might kiss her, but it would be too fucked up to let him do that without clearing the air.

As much as she might want to. For friendship alone, of course.

"Az. I want to tell you something about the time in college." He pulled away, and the chill of their bodies separating brought with it the weight of what she needed to say. She tried not to notice how he flinched and ran a shaky hand through tousled curls.

"I am not honest with myself about how I feel a lot. But you broke my heart that day, when you came back with cold coffee and told me you didn't want anything serious." The words poured out in a deluge of shattering truth. This was the worst time to tell him. She couldn't stop.

Vickie swallowed, eyes watering. He opened his mouth, but she went on, and he shut it.

"Wait, Az. Let me get it out or I might never. I try not to think about it. When you changed your mind, you broke my fucking heart. And I am sorry if that's awkward. I should have told you then how I felt. That's why I kept my distance. That's why I didn't text. Or call."

He stepped closer to her, bracing her with his hands, and she couldn't help it. She leaned forward, pulling toward him. Her heart hammered in her chest.

"I was lying," he said, gripping the counter on either side of her. His forearms flexed, and the dread pooling in her twisted despicably into longing. Hope. "I . . . I panicked and broke the law. Broke my own code. I used gravedirt on your roommate. And Natalie."

"You WHAT?"

It hit her in sharp waves. He hadn't talked to her. They were friends, best friends, and he had tricked her roommate and her ex with magic—the kind that was illegal for him to use on mundanes—instead of talking to her. She dug bitten-down nails into her palms to keep her hands off him; whether to stop pent-up affection or anger, she didn't know.

"They told me you were fucking your way through distractions. Hooking up with your hot neighbor to get it out of your system." He was only a few inches away from her, but the distance was insurmountable.

Her eyes followed the path of his hand running through his hair again, and this time she grabbed the counter behind her. "I said that, but I didn't mean it." Her cheeks were too hot now. "I didn't want her to think I was dumb enough to like someone else so soon after I got out of a messy relationship, but I also didn't want her to think that I was uninterested and you were free for the taking."

Vickie paused, the reality setting in. They had an opportunity two people didn't get twice in one lifetime. Something had stretched between them, beautiful and then cruel, and before she could find out if it was good magic or the sort that cut too deep, they had snapped it in half. Severed it.

It was too late now, six years later. They had been so young.

Azrael reached into his pocket, but then shook his head and drew it out again, empty.

"I didn't want to burden you with attachment you didn't ask for," he whispered. "And I didn't think I could hide how I felt, hide it all, if I was around you. If we talked." She covered her eyes, just to break from the intensity of his gaze, and the maelstrom of conflicting emotions it summoned. He stepped forward, thumbs gentle on her pulse points as he pulled her wrists toward him. He bit his bottom lip for a moment, and his cheeks flushed as he went on.

The years slipped away. She was as breathless for a moment as she had been before.

"Fuck, Victoria, this isn't how I want to tell you that I used to love you since before I could remember. Since before I could name it or make myself tell you. I longed for the way your hair smelled and the way your body felt next to mine and the way our magics sang, *actually sang*, to each other when we touched. I loved you, and I needed you, and lied to you anyway. I used magic to avoid the possibility of rejection. I did not deserve you."

He *loved* her. In the past tense. Which made sense; it had been six years, and what kind of a clinger would hang on to an old love for six whole years?

And wasn't that just fucking perfect.

He had loved her. He had used magic against mundanes rather than talking to her about it.

"Vickie?" His voice cracked. "Vickie, please. I am so sorry. I was a kid. Young."

"Dishonest," she added, grinding her teeth. Not meeting his gaze. His parents were dead. He had just bid them goodbye. He had been her best friend. And in the weeks since his return, in the volleys of text messages, tentative at first and then steadier, the cat pictures, and the tea shop talk, he was something to her again.

Maybe he had never stopped being something to her.

She hadn't exactly been honest either. But the past tense cut her, and she needed to reassure not just Azrael, but herself.

"I wasn't honest either. I should have told you that I loved you then too." Then. She loved him then.

"What if," he began, voice rasping. "What if we tried again?" Hope bloomed, a small burst of wanting in her chest, but she shook her head.

"I—I need time," she whispered. "Time to figure out how I feel, and if that's a good idea. And we've got plenty. We are both older and wiser."

"Of course." His words were clipped. Strained. She felt his hollow response rattle in the equally empty hull of her chest.

"We see what happens. Take it slow. I mean, obviously"—she gestured to the distance between them—"obviously we like each other. We are friends. Just two friends who happen to be attractive, and to have acted on attraction once, a long time ago. I'm sorry I lied about my feelings. You're sorry about the gravedirt. So maybe we leave the past in the past."

"Vickie," he began. His voice was low.

Surely it wasn't wrong to comfort a friend in need. To top off the confessions with a kiss.

Vickie traced a finger down his shoulder. Feeling what it was to touch him now, years later, how he was both different, and in some ways, precisely the same.

Grabbing a fistful of her T-shirt with one hand, Azrael cupped the back of Victoria's neck with the other. It was a desperate pairing of grief and comfort, and maybe part apology, and then it was more. Heart racing, she wound her fingers through his curls, his hands tracing wicked little circles on her back, lower and lower. Their faces were close, paused as they prepared to reacquaint themselves with long-lost sorrows and joys. Lips hovering inches away. Not meeting.

Slipping clever fingers under her shirt, he ran them across the dips in her back, a groan escaping his lips as he murmured, "I remember these. I remember every inch of you, Victoria." His voice was rough, each syllable hitching on a breath, and however lacking she feared his feelings might be, pressed against him like this, it was clear to her that his arousal was not.

What stretched between them now was no longer polite conversation or hedging apologies or friendly joking. The air was thick with the past and the creeping, tempting *almost* of the future. Perhaps there was something to be said for repeating her mistakes.

In the name of comforting a friend in need. Nothing else.

She ran her tongue across her lips, pulling him closer so their bodies lined up, everything hard of his pressed against everything soft of hers. They had crossed an invisible threshold, and she let go of the threat of more heartbreak and rose to her tiptoes to murmur into his ear.

"I missed you, Az. I missed the way you taste." She trailed a finger along his jaw, relishing the way he twitched at her hip as she did it, and how his greedy fingers dug into her sides.

"I feel so useless lately," he muttered into her hair, pressing kisses on her earlobe. "Will you let me be useful for a moment, Victoria? Please? Will you let me make up for all the lies and the ugliness?"

The begging hit different with her full name, the sounds of it dragging against her ears, enticing. Each one a plea that their bodies should slide against each other in a way that she knew would feel so good. Her thighs clenched in anticipation.

"Yes."

In a quick move, his fingers dipped below her sweatpants now, sliding forward so that his thumb brushed the skin just under her waistband. He tapped gently, fingertip sneaking lower on her hip bone. "Just so we are clear, I'm asking to kiss you. And to touch you. Everywhere. Is that all right?"

She was too far gone to pretend to be anything other than slick with desire and impatient with the closeness of him and the yearning of not having his fingers on her.

But he had just said goodbye to his parents. The man was grieving.

It would be taking advantage. And good goddess, she wanted to take advantage.

Stepping back, she shook her head, swallowing. Kicking herself for this already, but she couldn't hurt him.

"Actually, I have an early morning tomorrow. Rain check?"

Azrael frowned, his brows wrinkling together for a moment, looking at her for explanation. Like he was waiting for an out here.

Well, out successfully given.

She was a fool, and she couldn't let him see how desperately she needed him to touch her again, so, ignoring the restless screams of her body—that it was not done, and how very dare she—she grabbed an oversized cardigan from where it was draped over the television and wrapped it around her.

Brownish eyes, flecked with gray and green, clouded. His

mouth tugged downward, but he nodded. "Sure. It's late. I get it. I'll text you."

His face had shifted from muddled by lust to sharpened with hurt.

It was better that way, really. Even if she wanted, again, to push the flirtation of their friendship into something more, it was better to hold this boundary. She didn't want to take advantage, and if she was honest, she was a little bit afraid that Azrael Hart would be something she couldn't have just one more taste of.

CHAPTER 11

Victoria

The week passed in a haze of customers, and on Az's first staff day, Vickie got so busy that she didn't see his text until she was already closing and too tired to reply at great length.

He had sent a picture of his cat, sitting on top of his newspaper, looking disgruntled.

> **Azrael:** Much madness from Emily Lickinson when I don't feed her immediately.
> **Azrael:** She doesn't want to be old news
> **Vickie:** She could never

The next morning, she saw that he had tried again, undeterred by the brevity and delay of her response. His persistence, and his messages, made her smile. This part of the friendship, this unwavering loyalty from him, and the unquestionable desire to talk to him herself, this had once grounded her.

His friendship had been the charm against a cruel world, the right words to murmur, a small, secular prayer to make the more stressful bits of living more bearable.

She had missed him, more than she'd allowed herself to remember.

Azrael: I think my department chair might be, like, a vampire or something.

Azrael: No, not suave enough to be a vampire.

Azrael: But he gives me the heebie jeebies even in the group text, always replying with things like "I shan't be participating in that, Mr. Hart."

Vickie: MY STARS! The Heebie Jeebies? Az, your Uncle Larry called from Sunnyhallow Senior Living, and he said your slang is so old it wouldn't even fly there.

Azrael: It's not me, it's HIM.

Azrael: *I* am a professional wielder of words, a connoisseur of language.

Azrael: so what I'm saying is I'm a nerd, sure. But he's kind of an asshole.

Vickie: hate that. What's up with him?

Azrael: He just—he's so terse. Yesterday was the first day for new teachers, and he showed up and gave us this talk about how adults are too soft on children nowadays. I don't think he likes kids. Or people. In fact I'm kind of confused about why he would want a job interacting with other humans at all.

Vickie: Ew, hate that. Are the other teachers at least nice?

Azrael: They're great! Super helpful, and a good range, so some are fairly new, and then there's the lifers, and the people kind of in the middle of their careers, like Chet.

Vickie: That is an unfortunate name.

Azrael: Yeah I was trying to give him the benefit of the doubt; can't be easy with a name like that, and a stick up his ass, etc. But get this; he got all bent out of shape at the introductory meeting today when they made us do icebreakers with the staff. Said it was beneath him as a professional. And I tried to do a quick tension tamer spell; you know, the shoulders back and relax, deep breath one?

Vickie: I sure do, that saved a lot of asses on standardized test days.

Azrael: It did nothing. Nada. Zip. Zilch. It was like I hadn't even snapped.

Vickie: That's weird. Does that happen?

Azrael: Only when I'm stressed, or once, super high, in college. But the thing is, I've been feeling pretty on top of my anxiety. And I'm definitely not stoned.

Vickie frowned. That was strange. She wondered if it had anything to do with the warnings. They still needed to investigate what the ghosts had said about the town's fake psychic, Madam Cleopatra. Though why Benedict Hart's ghost would have wanted her to look into the local palm reader, who they all knew to be entirely nonmagical, was beyond her.

Her to-do list grew longer, and Vickie was too busy. It would have to wait for a day off. Though she and Azrael kept texting, they never brought up the almost kiss. For the best, she was sure. She had mortal and otherworldly obligations, and three souls to reap. By the time Friday rolled around, she knew Azrael was ready for the day off. The local school system followed the four-day summer workweek, which meant that this was his last free Friday for a while.

And he had spent it all here, in the corner, at the coffin-shaped table—not to be confused with the casket-shaped one—eating muffins and reading a romance novel.

It was hard not to catch feelings for Azrael Hart. Again.

Today, Azrael lingered past closing, lounging at one of the sofa seats with a paperback copy of what appeared to be a romance novel about baseball. She hoped he was here out of longing to see her, but suspected that it was to ask more questions about the investigation, or worse, her soul debt. A thread of worry knotted in her stomach, reminding her of her obligation to the devil. She didn't have time to sort through long-buried feelings for a friend.

Perhaps Lex could be summoned by mere thought, though, for when she locked the door and hung up her apron—black, with cheery little red skulls clustered like cherries, which would have made Persephone Hart proud—she heard a low laugh from the back. Azrael sprang up from his seat and was at her side instantly, hands poised to snap.

"Let me take the lead," she hissed, and he frowned but nodded.

She pushed open the swinging door, and Lex was there, clad in all black, smoke billowing dramatically in his wake as he leaned against her desk. He laughed again and inspected his long, graceful fingers, wisps of gingery, warm air trailing in their wake.

"What is it that you need now, devil?"

"Ah, Victoria, my dearest, can't I just long to see your lovely face?" He was frustratingly handsome, even in his unwarranted intrusion.

"Unlikely," she said, rolling her eyes. Next to her, Azrael tensed.

Lex's smile curled up, a catlike, sensuous thing that shouldn't have been allowed. Vickie supposed it was his right, as a devil, to be charming as hell, but she didn't have to like it.

"Fine, *pet*, if you must know, I do have some business with you, of the sort that all lesser devils do with their debtors. But I *am* additionally pleased to see you. Who is your friend?"

Azrael opened his mouth. "How dare you call—" Az began. Vickie grabbed his arm, shaking her head.

Lex was trying to vex her. He saw it work on Az, and mischief flitted across his face.

"You have no right to spy and sneak up on us." Vickie crossed her arms, not breaking eye contact. Devil or not, she was unafraid. Lex held up a hand, tossing and catching a pear. Hallowcross was known for orchards, but this wasn't just about sampling the local delicacies.

"Don't worry, Victoria, I wasn't sneaking. I just couldn't miss the scent of pining lingering here. I can pick up traces of heartbreak, too, so it must be rough for him, poor chap. You little minx."

"My parents died," Az muttered. Steamy magic lingered at Azrael's fingers. She needed to get control of this.

"His heartbreak is not about me," she cut in. "And he always smells like that. Burnt lemons and wood." He always smelled so good, like home, the kind she'd never had in her parents' house.

Lex sniffed. "Like Pine-Sol?"

"Oh, for fuck's sake," Azrael bit out, but he stopped again at her grip. Lex's eyes flickered down to her hand, narrowing.

"No," said Vickie, unable, as always, to pipe down. "Sweeter. Lemonade. Warm summer evenings and a crackling fire." She needed to tread lightly here.

"Well, in that case, it's a shame he's so cross with you." He winked and bit into the pear once again, but there was an edge to his voice now as his eyes darted between them. Juice dribbled down his chin, and he wiped it with a finger slowly enough that sensation curled in her stomach and lower. This was going beyond sympathy for the devil.

"You must be the Hart boy, then. Sister just won a seat on the Council. Parents just died. Bit of a local tragedy, I hear. Very sorry for your loss, handsome. The Harts were exceedingly good witches." His gaze flitted over Azrael. "And, obviously, exceedingly good-looking." He winked.

"Um. Thank you?" Azrael's brow tensed tightly into the beginnings of a permanent line, though she noticed his eyes dart up and down the devil's body, and the tips of his ears redden.

She glared at Lex, and he wiped pear juice off his lips once more with a look like he'd very much prefer to run those long, pale fingers across anything soft and secret. Her. Azrael. Both of them, maybe at once.

She shoved *that* thought out of her mind.

Azrael was looking between them now, crossing his arms. "And what does a devil care about the Witchery Council?"

"Now, now. Watch your words. We mustn't throw around names. Do call me Lex. There are greater devils than those of us tasked with rounding up souls and keeping them orderly." He turned to Vickie, stepping closer. "Which, by the way, my pet, is why I need you tonight."

"How did you know who Az was?" Vickie asked, trying not to feel his words thrum a little, forbidden and delicious. "And what do you mean about greater devils?"

"Ah, pet, I forget sometimes that you are mortal." He smirked, smile crooked with temptation. "There are three greater devils, who reap body and soul. Lucifer, who you so ignorantly mistook me for when last we met, is one of them. Four lesser devils, like me, who reap souls and can bestow gifts. Our bargains are less…" Lex's mouth ticked up for a moment, and a shiver of fear slipped down her spine. "Consequential." The word was lascivious in her ear, inappropriate as that reaction might be, and she suspected there was more he was not saying. If bargaining with a lesser devil meant she owed three souls, she could only imagine the price of a bargain with a greater one.

"What does that mean?"

Lex rummaged around in his pocket, pointedly ignoring the question.

Sighing, he pulled a star-shaped box the size of a fist from deep within his pocket, which had to be magical. His pants were snug, and he'd reached his hand far enough down that he ought not to have been able to fit it. The box glowed, a cool copper that radiated death.

"A soul prison," said Azrael, snapping his fingers and muttering. Warmth buzzed across her skin, and Vickie knew Az had cast a protective spell over her. Lex's eyes narrowed, and he growled, the rumble of it low in his throat.

Fear gripped her now. She remembered the day she'd taken over the shop.

Three souls, he'd said. Three souls would be the cost of her freedom from the contract her parents had entered into without her consent, and, however accidentally, severed legally. Devils did honor contracts. Her power was hers to keep, but the debt was also hers to pay.

She worried about the catch she had yet to suss out.

"You're here to collect on the first soul," she whispered.

Lex set the pear down and she glared at him. Holding his

hand up in apology, he put it daintily in the trash can. When he saw her scowl at the sticky, juicy spot on the marble, Lex shook his head, but waved his hand and the surface was immediately spotless and pristine.

"Yes, I need you to collect someone, *pet*." His voice drawled across the word indulgently, and she didn't miss the way Azrael frowned at that. Lex's eyes danced between the two of them, his face offering a bemused smile. "Azrael, you handsome doll, you can leave, though I certainly don't mind if we see you later." He paused, eyes tracing Azrael's frame, and as she tracked them, she couldn't help but remember how much broader he was now. Her face felt hot, and Lex caught her in the hunger of the look, winking and waggling his eyebrows. "I'm sorry it couldn't wait longer, Victoria, but I have need of your power. This particular soul has tried to evade me."

"I'm coming with you," said Azrael, crossing his arms.

Lex shrugged. "Have it your way," he drawled. "But I warn you, the soul we go to reap now is unpleasant, to say the least."

He looked uncomfortable. What could be bad enough to discomfort an actual devil?

"Victoria, my luscious treat, do put a jacket on. It's a tad chilly."

Swallowing, she nodded, and slipped her cell phone and her keys into the pocket of her pink puffy coat. Not the best outfit for reaping souls, but then again, there was nothing perfect to wear for the purpose of capturing a being's immortal essence.

"Explain the box." Vickie followed Lex into the night. Azrael never left her side, and the pull of both, the man named for devils and the devil himself, was dizzying. She blushed, hoping the dim night covered it. To one side, Lex radiated devilish temptation; to the other, Azrael called forth a similar lust, with the added jumble of emotion that threatened to distract her from their goal.

"It's an arcane puzzle box. A soul prison, and a rather complicated one too. Typically, as you must have deduced, souls go on to their final plane of existence when you reap them. But when I collect, I get to have my way with them for a few hundred years until they learn a lesson. I trap them. The soul I need to you to collect today has slipped out of my grasp for some time now, and he's a particularly nasty shade of evil."

Lex grinned, but now it was the grimace of a creature tasked with torturing the wicked.

Azrael reached for her hand, but she shook her head. She had a soul to reap, and she wasn't about to do it without being certain that this person deserved such a thing.

"A few hundred years trapped alone in a box will be a good start, and then I will submerge him in the same hell he made for others for all of eternity," said Lex.

"Fuck me, he must have done something terrible. Is this the one you said was a lobbyist?"

A peculiar expression crossed Lex's face.

"You know, I wouldn't mind that first part, should you offer in earnest."

Bristling, Azrael interjected, "Let's just stay on topic here, shall we?"

Lex winked at her and then turned and stared at Azrael. She didn't miss the sharpness in the devil's violet gaze. "And yes, the lobbyist. He's a dreadful soul. The worst of the worst."

They walked past taller trees now, past the well-lit shops and into the more quiet, residential parts of town.

"What did he do? Was he some sort of murderer? A serial killer, maybe?"

Lex shook his head. "Quite worse. Donovan Wagner. He was a gun lobbyist."

Her stomach turned. She knew that name.

"Wait," said Azrael. "The man who said school shootings were not about the guns, but the people?" He looked horrified.

"Precisely," said Lex, a dark glint shining in his eye. "He also said that a few dozen dead children were not that many in the grand scheme of things." Lex stopped and turned to her, the smile curdling into something truly horrific. "I shall enjoy pulling his entrails out with the tip of one of his rifles, and then forcing him to relive the hellscape of pain he created."

That evil smile was unreasonably attractive now, or maybe it was quite reasonable, and what Vickie was attracted to was the justice of it all.

Lex turned to Azrael, and Vickie's stomach soured. "My most illustrious young Hart, perhaps you are not suited for this comeuppance. It won't be pretty."

"He's with us," Vickie said, glaring. "We're friends." She emphasized the last word.

For some reason she couldn't fathom, this made Lex smirk and Azrael frown.

"Indeed, pet, whatever you like. You can bring your *friend*."

Vengeance toward the ghost they sought curled, tempting, sweet, and slick, in her stomach.

"What I would like is to help you capture the bastard. With pleasure."

"That certainly makes it easier. We need to trick him. He has a penchant for younger women, and there are few ghosts not complicated by the same foibles of their mortal lives."

"Wait a minute. What makes you think you can use her as bait?" Azrael's interjections were bordering on dangerous now.

Vickie shuddered. She did not want to play coy temptress to this sort of a man, however dead he might be, but she steeled herself. The cause was important. And a debt was a debt.

"I'll do it," she said, threading her fingers through Azrael's to still his nervous flexing. Emotion flickered across Lex's flawless face. Dark eyes contracting, he waved a hand, and the night snapped out in front of them, whirling in a tumble of air and atmosphere that smelled pleasantly of bergamot.

They stood in the parking lot of the luxury apartment building on the edge of town, overlooking the valley and the mountains. It was a glistening white marble castle of capitalism. The view alone made the price tag for such living far out of Victoria's current range, though she remembered how her parents had suggested it once for when she graduated.

She noticed a cherry-red, souped-up antique Packard. Persephone Hart's old car. Priscilla drove it now.

"Why would Prissy be here?"

"My sister's girlfriend lives here," muttered Azrael, nodding at the car. "Evelyn's subletting one of the condos."

"Not to worry," said Lex cheerily. "Little chance the interim Council president is cordial with the ghost we have business with this evening."

Azrael looked at him suspiciously, and Lex shrugged. "What? I find it makes things easier to stay up to date on witch business from time to time."

Victoria and Azrael followed Lex into the gleaming silver elevator. It was made of glass on the window side, and it dinged as they reached the top floor. Lex held out a hand, indicating to Vickie that she should exit first. She didn't dare look back to see whatever pecking order Azrael and the devil established for who walked out next. Lex strode up to the door and knocked on it casually, as though he were delivering pizza and not damnation. Leaning against the doorframe, Lex dazzled. His eyes shone, purple, dark, and as alluring as a midnight ocean. The kind that tempted foolish mortals to dive into its depths, willing to die for the smooth caress of the current.

Intentionally, she realized.

A sharp, clinically beautiful woman opened the door. Her blue eyes were unfeeling ice, but despite her glower, Vickie noticed the dip of her collarbone and the way the cut of her dress drew the eye downward to where the tips of her bleached hair met her neckline. The woman stood there, looking miffed, until she saw Azrael, and smiled a little at his angsty, stubbled face. He wasn't that pretty for nothing. When she saw Lex, her face softened completely. Vickie wondered if it was the wrong apartment, but Lex flashed a smile that he probably quite literally used to steal souls.

"Good evening, ma'am," Lex began, his drawl slow and velvet. The words tasted like magic and enchantment. Mystery. Sex. They raised goose bumps on Vickie's arms, and from the looks of her, the woman was not unaffected. "I'm from the town newspaper, and my colleagues and I are running a feature on your late husband. I was wondering if we might come in and take some pictures."

Vickie blanched. Donovan Wagner had been over sixty years old, and this woman looked barely old enough to buy a bottle of wine. Biting her lip, the woman pouted, and Vickie wondered if she was going to tell them to get the hell out of there. It's what she would have done if Lex had fed her an invented story like that. He didn't even have a camera.

"Of course," she said, voice breathy. Vickie rolled her eyes, ignoring the roller coaster in her own stomach. "I'm Clarissa," she said. She still sounded as though she had been running vigorously or spending a great deal of time with her hand between those unfairly sculpted legs.

Best not to picture that, though. The idea made it difficult to focus, especially pulled as Vickie was by the musky bergamot of the devil and the woodsy lemon of the witch. She was a veritable bouquet of lustful thoughts at the moment, and so was Clarissa, who looked up at the devil from beneath unnaturally long lashes. She smelled like spun sugar and something sharp. Peppermint, maybe. Vickie shifted, made restless by the three of them.

Lex leaned into her and whispered softly, entrancing command in his voice.

"That's generous of you, Clarissa. It's a shame you have to take a bath." His voice spoke command now. An otherworldly influence that made Vickie desperate to go, and even Azrael looked with interest in the direction Lex gestured. "You'll be so busy with yourself and that bath that you'll forget we were ever here."

Clarissa sighed, running a hand down her neck.

"Come on in. I was just about to get in the bath."

"Lex," Vickie hissed. "We are not getting in the bath with her." *No matter how hot she is.*

His eyebrows shot up. "Victoria, if you wanted to play kinky, all you had to do was ask. But no, not right now, we are not. She'll be out of our way while we get what we came for." He winked. "We can talk about any particular multiplayer bath fantasies you might have later."

Azrael muttered words under his breath that she didn't catch.

"What was that, Hart?"

"Let's just fucking do this," he said, voice clipped and strained.

She cleared her throat. The interaction felt sexy, but uncomfortably empty.

"What does he value the most?" She looked around the sparse apartment, peppered with mirrors and decorated almost entirely in spotless white, from the carpets to the sofa to the walls.

"It's a limited-edition Genesis vinyl."

"Is that—"

"Yes. He doesn't listen to it. Just for show."

"The cliché and the satire of it all lost on him, then?"

"Vickie, darling, men who profit off annihilating other humans are almost always immune to critique. Now let's reap this soul and get out of here before his newest model finishes getting off in the bathtub and realizes she's let three strangers into her house."

Victoria hated the idea of even touching anything that monster had, but there was no way she was letting this slime bag escape, even in death. The bedroom was done in modern linens, a wall of windows, two walls of mirrors, and no other art besides the record. She punched into it. Lex cleared his throat and Azrael snapped, and the glass vanished without puncturing her hand.

She wasn't sure which of them had done it, and she didn't have the time to sort out which one she wanted to have done it at the moment. "Ready?" Her heart was pounding.

"When you are, pet."

"Just tell me what you need," said Azrael softly. Lex glared at him, and she ignored it.

Vickie touched the record with both hands, and a square-jawed man in a suit with thin-rimmed glasses appeared. Gray hair sat limply atop a weak forehead and a face twisted into a grimace that was either an awful attempt at a smile or some sort of intestinal problems. She was fairly certain ghosts didn't get those, so it was most likely the former.

"Donovan," she said.

"Actually, it's Mr.—" His arrogance told her he realized his predicament at once.

"I don't give any fucks what you'd like to be called."

The ghost sniffed. "Well, if you're going to be one of those terrible woke snowflakes about it, I'll be going, then." He fisted his hands and concentrated. "Fuck you and your feelings."

Now he looked even more constipated, but he didn't go anywhere.

"Exactly what is your problem, young lady? And why the devil can't I portal out of here? It's the best part of being dead. Finally, the control I so deserve."

"Ah, Donny, tsk tsk tsk." Lex stepped forward, and the shade paled, which was impressive for a person who was already only a transparent shadow of a being.

Azrael looked around, confused, as he realized he was the only one who could not see the ghosts.

"You," spat the man, pointing. "You can't take me. I have things to do. Unfinished business. You know the rules." Vickie felt cold. Why was it that evil held so much control, even in the afterlife? The shade continued. "You have no power to destroy any object that anchors a soul to this world. I figured that out quick enough, you dumb fucking devil."

"Ah yes, do enjoy that satisfaction. You caught me there." Lex's smile was lazy and slow, and Vickie thought that Donovan Wagner was far too confident in his hand here.

"Unfortunately, my dear Donny, *she* is not so inconveniently limited."

Vickie smiled at him, hoping it came off as cruel as he had been in life. It had only been two minutes. "Should I give him his remaining time?"

"No need, pet. Go ahead and immolate him."

She smiled and held the record in both hands. Concentrating, she willed the flame to build faster than the usual five minutes.

"No! Don't!" The scream was pitiful and hair-raising. "I have information you need. There's something rotten in Hallowcross. You have no idea—"

In her hands, the record had turned scalding, and burst into flames, and with them, the essence of Donovan Wagner flickered like an old television losing reception. Lex opened the box, and Donovan let out a high-pitched screech until the noise cut abruptly and the box slammed shut.

"Hello?" Clarissa called from the bathroom. She sounded breathless. Confused.

"We ought to leave before she breaks from my trance," said Lex. He put the box in his pocket and winked at Vickie, who followed him out of the unit, Az behind them.

"She'll be okay, right?" Azrael asked Lex, and Vickie's heart cracked at his concern.

"Indeed," said Lex, sniffing. "I'm not a monster. She'll sleep it off and wake up hazy, unsure if this was all just a beautiful dream." He turned to Vickie. "Excellent work, pet."

They paused in the hallway outside the apartment.

"Stop calling her that," said Azrael. His eyes glinted, the gold flecks angry in the dark light, like sharp splinters of defensive hurt. Vickie slid her palm around his waist, tucking it into his back pocket and pulling him toward her, as though she could hold him in against the hurt of the moment. Against the cruelty of humans, even in death. The greed. But there was no time to unpack it; next to her, Azrael was stiff, the emotions roiling and radiating off him.

She wasn't sure why he was so angry with Lex. For a moment, she pressed into Azrael, smelling lemon and wood.

"Interesting," said Lex, and there was a dangerous edge to his voice she didn't recognize. The tension between the two had pulled too thin now, and Lex ground his teeth. Her hand in

Azrael's pocket was a promise, and Lex saw it. A decision. His eyes darted, lingering on her hand against the fabric. Against Azrael. Lex waved his hand, now full of something.

"Well then, I see that I may be the devil in name, but neither of you deliciously lovely creatures are quite angelic in honesty, now, are you? Your *friend*, is he?" Violet eyes sparkled, dancing with mischief.

Vickie couldn't quite distinguish what was in the devil's hand, though she had a feeling Azrael could, for he tensed and drew her closer, tucking her under his arm as though he wanted to shield her. Her chest filled with warmth at the gesture, a flicker of hope in the desperate fear burrowing there.

The devil raised his hand and smiled, a treacherous, tempting thing, and blew on the glittering dark dust cupped in his palm.

A cloud of brown enveloped them, settling on Vickie's jacket and face, in her hair. It fell on Azrael, in his dark curls and lingering on his long eyelashes. He blinked, looking at her, and her heart twisted again. She understood now why people were always saying that. It really did feel as though the muscle were contracting and reshaping with her realization. She felt for him, all sorts of confusing things, and it was too late now to tell him on her own terms. Enchantment cut through her denial; she knew her mistake. She had waited too long and there was no time.

Lex smiled again.

"Gravedirt," said Azrael, the word between them an accusation and a revelation.

"Yes," purred Lex. "I am a force of justice. Truth." He paused, drawing his fingers together. "Well. Mostly justice, anyway."

"You're a devil," spat Azrael. "Isn't manipulation in your nature? Isn't it why you're looking at us like that? At *Vickie* like that?" The words came out cruel. She frowned. Azrael knew better. But gravedirt would make him honest, and she realized that if he was jealous of Lex, that would show. In the first few hours of it, emotions would show completely.

Unfettered. Tension froze in delicate strands between them, threatening to snap at the fire in Azrael's eyes, and the coldness mirrored back in Lex's.

Tell him, she thought. *Tell him you could one day love him again, maybe, before something terrible happens.*

"You can't judge us all in one fell swoop, Azrael Ashmedai Hart. Though I suppose I have succumbed to my baser angels in this moment, and I'll admit it, but devils are part human too. And for what it's worth, I'm looking at *both* of you like that." His voice was icy. Piercing. "And now the two of you *will* be honest."

"How dare you," started Azrael. He ran a hand through his hair. It came away dirt-streaked. He looked down at her, swiping a thumb to brush some of it off her cheek. There was warmth in the gesture, and she hoped his feelings would survive what would happen next.

And that hers would.

"I am sorry, Vickie. This is going to hurt us both," Azrael whispered.

"Too much honesty almost always does," she choked out.

CHAPTER 12

Victoria

Azrael wiped her cheek again, the pad of his finger tracing her skin. "I have always loved this constellation of freckles." His voice was reverent as he traced them, the path of his fingers sending little tremors of pleasure licking down her body, lower. He moved his hand to her neck, running a thumb down it and onto her shoulder. It took her a moment to recognize what glinted in his eyes. Fear. He looked afraid.

Like he had not been prepared to be that honest. He was racing time before the devil asked him specific questions.

Lex saw it, and broke the moment, clapping loudly. Desire and dread pooled, threading together in her stomach into a heavy knot.

"Victoria, pet, answer a question for me." Lex's voice was velvet. Sharp. It cut through the almost of Azrael's confession like a sleek, smooth dagger, and she turned to face the demon, not breaking the connection with Az but unable to bring herself to look at his face while it crumpled.

"Don't do this," she begged.

The look in his eyes was calculating. Clever, like he knew how to twist that knife.

"Tell Azrael how attractive you find me. What do you think of my face? My *body*?"

Tears pooled in her eyes, and she heard the sharp intake of

breath beside her. Felt the clench of his fingers digging into her side. She tried to bite back the words.

"I think you're angelically beautiful. Carved from stone, in your features and your physique. I could hold myself against it, against you, and the sensation would be exquisite."

It was true, objectively. She just didn't love him the way she loved Azrael.

The way she had *loved* Azrael, and the way she had fallen back into an easy rhythm of messages and talking, as though no time at all had passed. The way she would now cut his heart wide open. Lex wasn't done.

"It's fine, Vickie," Azrael was saying softly in her ear. He pulled her closer, thumb strumming a reassuring stroke against her skin. "It's totally normal. Even I can see that about him."

"Oh? Tell me, witch. What do you think of me, romantically?"

"I think . . ." Azrael clamped his hand over his mouth, but it was no good. He sighed and dropped it. "I think if my heart weren't elsewhere, I would be very interested in learning more about the magical potential between witches and devils. I think, though, that I am mostly jealous that you and Vickie might try out devils and debtors instead."

He choked a little, trying to swallow back other words, and she remembered that he wouldn't be able to lie. "This decimates my heart in the jealous, scarred part of it, but still, it beats for you, Vickie. It hurts, but I know, I understand. You wouldn't if you didn't have to."

"Az," she whimpered, burying her face in his shirt for a moment, trying to memorize the scent of him in case this ruined everything. Imprinting on her brain the press of his chest against her cheek. They had just rebuilt what had broken between them into a shaky semblance of friendship. She wanted to pause Lex's forceful honesty. To lock out what was happening.

This was a mistake, with Lex watching them like a cat about to pounce.

"Tell me, Vickie, do you desire me, pet?" His voice was not just gentle. It was *hopeful*. Yearning. Like this cosmically powerful creature needed to hear her say that she did.

No matter what that might do to her soul, or to Azrael's.

"I," she started. Blood rushed to her cheeks. *No. No.* She made the mistake of looking at Azrael. His face was ashen. Wrecked. A muscle ticked in his jaw.

"Yes. I desire you. You're attractive and mysterious." The words slipped out unbidden, along with tears tracking down her face. Azrael was pushing them aside with his thumbs, both moved up to her face now, and murmuring words she didn't hear. She couldn't look at him. "I don't feel for him what I feel for you, Az." She whispered it, as though maybe the closeness could shut out the devil at their side. "I don't desire him the way I desire you. I'll never feel for him the way I feel for you, Azrael."

His arms moved down and tightened around her, and she realized what he was muttering.

A protection spell. His fingers snapped at her sides.

Lex threw his head back, laughing. There was a sharp edge to it. He was angry. He'd gotten what he wanted, but her honesty had too many facets. The truth had consequences. And from the looks of it, even if he wasn't an evil creature, he was still jealous enough to do harm in return.

"You'll rue the moment you chose to do that, witch," Lex said, eyes flashing. "This isn't a game. Something magical is afoot here, which means someone else has struck a deal. I can't find a source, and even your Council is worried. This is serious business, and Victoria, pet, you still owe me two more souls. And if you care to save Hallowcross, you'll need to help me find out who's traded with the greater devil. Unchecked, that person's power—well, it's more than a person should have, pet. It would be more devastating than this sad tableau. Have care to remember that, as well as the fine print, the *deadlines*, of our bargain, in what comes next." He looked back and forth between them, as though deciding. "I'm sorry, *pets*." He looked at

Azrael on the sobriquet, pointed. Sharp. "I fear this is the only way to impress upon you the severity of the situation in Hallowcross. Consider this a warning. Me lighting a fire under you to figure out who's behind this mess before it does any more irreparable damage."

Flame stirred at Vickie's fingertips, and at Azrael's, strangely, for a moment, before fading away. Lex vanished, this time in a cloud of black smoke that tasted like regret, and, oddly, she got the feeling that it was Lex's regret, and not her own. Azrael pulled Vickie close until the smoke cleared the hallway. Looking down at Az's hands, she thought she saw a flash of flame illuminating his mother's ring, but she shook her head, and there was nothing.

"I'm so sorry, Az," Vickie breathed. "This is not how I wanted to tell you, but I'm—I feel things for you. Again. What you did in college is still fucked up, and I'm working through how I feel about us then, and now. Everything I said was true, but, goddess, I wish I hadn't been forced to say it."

Azrael pulled away to get a better look at her, hazel eyes wide with pain and wonder.

"I get it, Vickie. Me too. With the old feelings and the confusion. I've made mistakes, and I've missed you. We made no promises to each other, and it's normal to notice physical beauty." He bit his lip, like he didn't want to go on, but his mouth opened again. He didn't say it back. He didn't say he was falling too. Why didn't he say it back?

"There's so much I want to ask you, but I don't want you to *have* to answer now." Az ran a hand over his face. "I wanted us to be honest with each other, but not like this. I wanted us to be able to take the time you asked for. Not with forced honesty, and I wanted it to be perfect. Storybook perfect." The devastation written on his face broke her. She needed to do something. To fix what had shattered there.

"I would not have slept with him, if that's what you're thinking of," Vickie said. Her heart was pulverized. As much ash as the possessions of any of the ghosts she'd laid to rest.

Resolve filled her. "From the moment you came back to town, I would never have touched anyone who wasn't you if there was even the slightest chance that you and I might be more than just friends." Azrael bit his lip.

"You didn't have to do that. I never expected you to wait for me, obviously. You don't owe me anything. But I have to be honest." A muscle twitched in his cheek. He did *have* to, she realized. "I'm glad you did. Every time he calls you *pet*, I want to tear him into pieces. And the thought of you being with someone else, while any possibility of trying again glimmers between us, well, that makes me want to just lie down and die right here."

Vickie felt completely alone as they stood in silence, each ripped wide open and raw from honesty in a hallway outside a stranger's apartment. Her back found a wall, and she slid down to the floor, tucking her head in her hands. It was too terrible, all the truth she'd endured in the last hour, not just about Lex or Azrael, but also from the cruel soul they'd just reaped. Vickie loved sunshine and daisies and happy shows with young love and gay pirates. She wore strawberry perfume as though it was a prescription. She even recovered after that night with Az that had left her curled up in despair, watching weather drip down the window of her dorm room. But thinking of the calm, collected evil of the soul she had reaped, juxtaposed against the sharp, chaotic truth of her feelings for Azrael, her own fallibility, and all the time they'd wasted, the feeling of the spirit lingered. His corruption had persevered even after death.

Vickie's truths crashed over her in waves, too many to process all at once. Her parents and their lingering, impossibly selfish debt. Her powers, and what it felt like to only know how to burn things down. Her feelings for Azrael, and her foolish heart. Vickie chose difficulty every time, rejecting her upbringing and longing for love.

Before she knew it, Vickie was heaving awkward breaths between her fingers, tears streaming over the chipped remains of her pink nail polish. Then Azrael's smell was on her, like warm summer nights and campfire, and his arms were around her, his face close to hers, but not touching, murmuring in her ear. "It's going to be all right, Vickie. It's a lot, and it's okay to be overwhelmed right now, but it's going to be all right."

The elevator dinged, and she didn't look up, hopeful that its occupant would keep walking and leave her to cry pathetically in Azrael's arms.

"Hey." The voice was gentle. Familiar, and then, more accusatory, "Azrael Ashmedai Hart, why the fuck is your girlfriend crying on the floor of my girlfriend's apartment building?"

"She's not—" Az began, at the same time as Vickie blurted, "It's not like that."

Priscilla glared at them, raven-colored hair braided loosely to one side, her fingers intertwined with Evelyn's.

"Hi," Vickie said, hating how small her voice sounded.

"It's been a rough night, Prissy," said Azrael, running a hand down his face. "Evelyn, good to see you, always."

"I'm Vickie," she said, holding up her hand in a weak wave. "Don't let my awkward crying in your hallway fool you. It's very nice to meet you."

"It's good to meet you too. I was sorry to miss last week at your *Star Trek* bar." Her voice trailed off uncertainly, so Vickie coughed but didn't correct her. Evelyn's eyebrows knit together. "Something came up at work; I've been filling in for the Witchery Council president after taking some time off from the European Council to do research in New Haven."

"Evie, perhaps now is not the best time to give them your entire résumé," said Priscilla, and the sharp undertone of her voice was not lost on Vickie. She fixed her gaze on Azrael. "If you've done something dreadful, I don't care if you're my own brother, hell hath no fury like the pranks I will unleash upon you. You better sleep with one eye open, and dream of needles. Big needles."

"Fuck," Azrael muttered, and Vickie shook her head.

"It's not really his fault." She regretted the qualifier immediately at the sight of her friend's face. Still, it was reassuring, knowing that acerbic, highly powerful Priscilla Hart was on her side.

"My apologies, Vickie. Would you like to come inside?" She glared at Azrael. "Not you, not if you're the source of her discomfort." Evelyn rooted around in her bag, pulling out a set of keys.

"That's not quite—" he started, but his sister interrupted.

"Vickie? Are you okay?" Priscilla leaned down to look her in the face.

Shit. There would be no good way to hide that she had been crying. And the gravedirt made it impossible to lie. They had to get out of here.

"Yeah, this isn't what it looks like," she started. "It's *not* Azrael, but it's also not something I can discuss in a public space."

"Oh, good. I thought maybe Azrael was doing that shitty thing where he waffles back and forth about telling you he has feelings for you again," she said.

Azrael's eyebrows shot up, horrified.

"Listen," said Evelyn, sticking out her hand and helping Vickie up. Next to her, Az dusted himself off and got up while Priscilla glared, arms crossed, as though she didn't quite believe that he wasn't the cause of the tears. "I live just down the hall." Evelyn's clipped British accent was comforting. "Priscilla and I would be delighted if you came in and joined us for a moment." She hesitated, looking at Az. "You, too, I suppose."

"Perhaps some tea? I know you like tea," Priscilla added.

Vickie looked at Priscilla. For once, she didn't appear to be orchestrating any sort of romantic setup.

"I don't want to intrude, but I do have a favor to ask," she said, trying to collect herself. "We are stuck without a ride. It's a long story."

Priscilla dug in her purse, sighing. "Take the Packard. Evie can drop me tomorrow. But, Azrael, you have some explaining to do, and Vickie, hexing him is not off the table if I'm not pleased with his explanation, or if you ever just would like me to, on a whim or anything." Priscilla handed Azrael the keys.

"Great. Thank you," said Az, shoving a hand through his curls, which stuck up ridiculously. "We need to pay a visit to Hallowcross's resident fake psychic. Dad, uh, mentioned her to Vickie."

Looking at Vickie, Priscilla said, with a twinge of sadness, "You spoke with Dad?"

"Um," said Vickie, but the gravedirt had other plans.

Azrael cut in. "Yes, we did."

Priscilla scowled at her brother. "You contacted Dad without *me*?"

Vickie lowered her gaze. She hadn't thought of it, but maybe they should have invited her.

"Sorry," Azrael offered, "I didn't realize."

"I bet you didn't," she began, glaring. Her eyebrows furrowed, and she paused. "Wait. You said *psychic*. You know about Madam Cleopatra?" She glanced furtively up and down the hall. "Let's talk about it inside, asshole."

Azrael rolled his eyes, but he nodded to Vickie and they followed her into Evelyn's place.

The apartment was modern and sleek, full of stainless steel and accent pieces selected to be purposefully minimalistic but riveting. A small lamp of a mermaid sculpted in bronze sat on an end table, and behind her stretched a deep turquoise canvas of abstract paint that called to mind the sea.

It was lovely, if a bit cold.

"What can I get you? You can come 'round and see the options if you like." Evie made quick work of filling a kettle and setting it on the stove.

"I'd love an Earl Grey with a splash of milk, if you have it."

"Of course. Az?"

"Surprise me."

Evelyn smiled, a bit wickedly, and winked at Priscilla.

"Not with anything magical, though," he added quickly.

Prissy sat down at the glass-topped table and gestured for Az and Vickie to do the same. "It's nice that you talked to Dad. I thought you might, eventually." She sighed. "What did he have to say? What do you need with Madam Cleopatra?"

A pang of guilt ran through Vickie. "I'm sorry. I should have offered for you to be there too."

Prissy shook her head. "No. It's fine. I mean. I was here when they died, and I had my closure."

Azrael looked ashen. A whistle of the teakettle interrupted them, and Evelyn set two steaming mugs in front of them, returning to the kitchen to get two more.

"Again, I am sorry we didn't ask you."

Prissy rubbed her temples. "Maybe better not to reopen that particular wound at the moment. Not like I could see him again, anyway." She sighed and opened her eyes. "What did he say?"

"He said to be careful of the megachurch. And to warn the Council that there could be consequences for Madam Cleopatra."

"The Council is already watching Madam Cleopatra closely," Prissy said wearily.

Hairs on Vickie's arms raised. "Is she in trouble?"

Evelyn looked at Priscilla, mouth set in a firm line as she placed a mug in front of her. "That's Council business."

"This is *family* business now," said Priscilla. "You're the one who is always saying family is the most important." She looked thunderous, and Vickie suspected she wasn't only talking about a roadside psychic.

"Fine," said Evelyn crisply. The slight blush on her face said otherwise, so Vickie offered more, hoping to iron out the tension.

"When my parents disowned me, the debt they owed for my gift passed over to me. I'm collecting souls, and I just reaped a nasty one down the hall from you. That's why I was so upset. I'll need to collect two more, but the devil I owe them to assured me they were all dreadful in life. And every ghost I've talked to lately has hinted that something is rotten in Hallowcross."

Evelyn sighed. "That awful man. I hate to celebrate a death, but no one here was sad to see him go, not even his wife. I think she married into money and got in over her head with a monster. Go on, then," she said to Priscilla.

"I should have asked for a stronger drink than tea," Priscilla said darkly, snapping her fingers and taking a sip. "Better. So, Madam Cleopatra. Her real name is Connie Witherspoon. She's harmless, one of those fake psychics who makes a decent living telling people what they need and want to hear to believe she's contacted the beyond. It's a hustle, but it's not hurting anyone."

"So why would the Council need to keep an eye on her?" Azrael looked puzzled, but he was also running a finger back and forth across the middle of Vickie's back, over her shirt, and she was having trouble focusing on what Priscilla was telling them.

"Because Connie has been in a coma for a month now, and no one knows why." Az's finger paused on Vickie's back, Prissy's words sending an unexpected shiver down her spine, entirely different from the one incited by Azrael's touch. "She was attacked in her own shop. There was a burst of unsanctioned magic, which we investigated, but its source was not traceable to witches. It was something else. We set up a warding system around the hospital she's in, and it's been tripped twice since then. So far, whatever is trying to get through hasn't been able to, or, if it has, it hasn't caused any changes, but she's not in good shape."

"She's showing signs of an adverse reaction to rudimentary spell work rejection," Evelyn chimed in. "It's odd, because the skill by no means matches the power of it."

"Come again?" Vickie had been around magic her whole life, but she wasn't a witch.

"It's like someone tried to take her soul out with magic, and then stuff it back in, but they were sloppy. Only time will tell if her soul is able to reattach properly."

"But it shouldn't be possible to reap living souls," she said. Soul reaping, she *did* know.

"No," said Prissy darkly. "No, it should not."

Evelyn's mouth was set in a frown now. "I can hold off on bringing your family into it, or mentioning the discussion with Benedict from the beyond, but it's already a strain on my professional obligations. If Connie dies, or anything else goes haywire, my hands are tied."

"I know, I know." Prissy put her hands on her hips. "But you are the one always harping on the importance of family, and helping them when they're in need."

"Let's not right now," said Evelyn, through her teeth.

Azrael looked between his sister and her girlfriend and snapped his fingers covertly under the table. The tea in Vickie's cup vanished, which was a good thing, because the threat of unfettered truth amid a couple fight was a recipe for disaster.

"Well, look at the time! Vickie has a very early morning opening the shop, and I don't want her to be exhausted tomorrow, so I'd better get her back. Thank you for the tea." He looked at Evelyn. "And for giving us a chance to sort this out without the Council breathing down our necks."

"Yes, thank you," Vickie said and smiled. However weak and wobbly her smile might appear, she was earnestly grateful, and it was real enough to convince them.

Prissy took a break from glaring at Evelyn to look up and wink at Vickie.

"Should I expect to see you at home, or are you sticking around to help put things in Vickie's oven?" She paused, letting her brother splutter and blush.

"That's not. No. I'm not," he protested.

Priscilla waggled her eyebrows. "For the shop, of course."

"I'll talk to you tomorrow, Prissy," said Azrael firmly.

By the time they got out to Priscilla's car, it had started to drizzle. Rain always reminded her too much of college. Of the incident. Of what it felt like to be alone, in the pouring rain, crying her fucking eyes out and hoping Azrael would come back and change his mind.

He could have changed his mind. Or she could have changed

hers and run after him. Asked him what had gone wrong. They had come so close to being really, truly happy. All this time. She bit the words out between sobs. "You hurt me once, and part of me still hates you for that." The truth was lonely. It always had been, for her.

But now, Azrael sat with her in his sister's Packard, handing her tissues as the rain fell around them once more, and eventually the patter of the drops calmed her. When she had quieted, he said, "It breaks my heart, too, Vickie. What we could have had but didn't. I understand."

"How could you? You left."

He threaded a hand tentatively in hers. It felt heated, surely from the excitement of the night. "I was there too. In your dorm. After. I know how close we came to having everything I ever wanted. I also know what it is to discover how far out of my reach it ended up being out of sheer misunderstanding and the stupidity of youth. That's worth crying over. I get that."

She squeezed his hand. All the crying had left her hollow. It reminded her of what it had been like to lose him. The bone-deep pain and the withering from the inside out. She could play it safe. Truthful, for she had no other choice, but safe. Honesty didn't mean she had to act on her emotions.

"Thank you."

"For?"

"Just being."

He squeezed back, steering the car around a turn with one hand. "Thank you for just being too."

She bit her lip, the memory of his hands tracing patterns across her back seared into her. Maybe this was the time, though. Maybe gravedirt could be the excuse. There were ways to play it safe emotionally but still take the sort of risks that might be worth it.

"Hey, Az," she said.

"Yes?" His eyes were on the road, so she studied his profile, the dark thick eyebrows and the slope of his nose down to the plush lips she wanted so badly to feel against hers.

What good was a little magical honesty if it didn't come with benefits?

"We're friends, right?"

He chuckled, and the sound of it made her press her thighs together. "Good friends, I'd say."

"What if I wanted to suggest something that might ruin the friendship?"

Azrael sucked in a deep breath. "I don't think anything could ruin the friendship."

"What if I wanted to pretend we were more than just friends?"

He swerved a little, and she was grateful that the road was empty.

"Holy shit, Vickie, you can't just say that when I'm operating four thousand pounds of murder metal hurtling down a highway."

"Sorry, but I'd like to call the first pretend." She traced a finger down his thigh, over the material of his pants. He kept his eyes on the road but swore softly.

"Fuuuck you. Respectfully," he moaned. "Vickie," his voice ground out, hoarse enough to drive her fucking crazy. "Vickie."

"Shh, Azrael," she said, tracing a finger through his hair, and down to play with the collar of his shirt. Her fingertips played along his shoulder bones, and he let out a deep sigh, shifting in his seat.

"You're going to be the death of me," he muttered, but he reached out and slid a hand from her knee to her upper thigh, squeezing tightly before returning his hand to the wheel for a particularly sharp turn.

CHAPTER 13

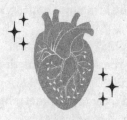

Azrael

The drive home was exquisite and excruciating. Vickie ran a hand along the back of his neck, curling her fingers into the hair at the nape of it, sending jolts of feeling through his spine. Az's left hand twitched, oddly warm. He wanted her with every fiber of his being, every thread of his magic, every bone in his body.

Pretend, she had said. Devil damn him, he'd pretend anything if she'd let him put his hands on her. His heart could break a thousand times over in the morning, but it would be worth it if she let him pretend with her all night.

Vickie placed her left hand on his right, and the ring on his other hand throbbed, along with his heart and, well, other parts of him. He wanted to pull the car over and fuck her right there on the side of the winding road, but it was too dangerous. Until the gravedirt wore off and they figured out what the devil was up to, there were too many unknown factors. And yet the only unknown he cared about was whether Vickie wanted him in this moment as badly as he wanted her. Azrael had to get his shit together and stay focused.

Any thought of control eddied from his mind as Vickie's fingers traced a pattern on his thigh. She had to have noticed how hard that made him, the outline of him straining against his tight jeans. Her fingers snuck closer, and he groaned, unable to recall what had seemed so urgent a moment ago. He felt overheated.

Azrael stole a look at Victoria's face, and the spots of color on her cheeks confirmed it.

She wanted this as much as he did. Well, almost. He wasn't sure anyone could want anything the way he did in this specific moment. She shifted in her seat, removing her fluffy pink jacket.

"What are you thinking?" Her hand drifted to the back of his neck again, and he shuddered. Her fingers felt warm against him. So, so warm.

Shit. There was no lying.

"I'm thinking so much went wrong and we should talk about it, but all I want to do is pull this car over and make you say my name until we can both forget the complications for a moment, and then deal with them later. If you want to pretend, I'm thinking I'll pretend so fucking hard you see stars. I'm thinking about the way you felt all those years ago. I'm trying to remember, and wanting you to refresh my memory."

Her soft gasp undid him, along with the way her hot fingers dug into his neck now. Surely this counted as distracted driving.

"Do it. Now. Pull over."

The command rippled through him, a burning spreading like ink and madness through his chest. He felt too much to possibly express in words, so he pulled onto the shoulder where it was widest, the moon glinting off the concrete. The road was empty at this hour, but he snapped his fingers so that the windows darkened anyway, feeling the shade reach into his soul, carving her name there for the thousandth time.

"Victoria," he said. Each syllable of it was an exhale that took him closer to the height of ecstasy, along with the pain, that the gravedirt had wrenched from him.

"Yes," she breathed, unbuckling her seat belt and sliding over the center of the seat to straddle him. The heat of her was so good, so urgent, that it was almost unbearable.

Both her hands were on his face now, and she laughed at the insistence of the steering wheel behind her, scooting closer to him. When she lowered against him, even with layers between them, grinding her hips down, he thought he might come, hard, just from the hot pressure of her, the way her chest rose rapidly, betraying her thoughts as well as any spell.

"I don't want you to do this for the wrong reasons. Why are you doing this?" he asked, even if the answer might hurt him, as she pressed kisses against his neck, tearing his need from him in breathy groans. Each place her lips touched seared his skin.

Her truth could hurt him now, it could scald him, but he needed it before he dug his fingers into the soft skin of her body and released all that he was feeling and had ever felt into the abyss of wanting.

Her breath hitched. Goddess, she was fucking extraordinary. How had he ever touched anyone else and not thought of her? How had he ever stopped thinking of the smooth slide of her skin against his fingers? She whispered the words on his earlobe, lips grazing against him. "I'm doing this because I want you and I need you, more desperately than I should," she said. He froze, running his tongue over the words carefully to make sure he hadn't imagined them. And she kept going, while magic that could not be undone blossomed in his chest. "Because all of that outweighs all the hurt, and I can't bear the thought of the next few moments in this car without the sweetness of your skin against mine and the feel of you on me and in me."

Damn. The way she moaned when he pulled her against him in response carved his erection in marble.

He reached for her now, kissing her deeply, left hand twisted in her pale pink shirt, almost the color of her skin as he moved his mouth down, lower, tongue stroking across her neck and worshiping her collarbone. Her soft little gasps threatened to undo him. He had to focus.

"I want you," he murmured against skin that tasted like

sweetness and belonging, the only kind he'd ever felt in his soul. "I want you so much, Vickie. I always have. All that I am is yours."

Home was a person and not a place for him. He had to have her, to taste, to touch, and to fill completely.

Whatever might happen next.

Victoria pulled his mouth up to meet hers, and their lips crushed against each other, brutal and unyielding with desire. The kiss was more than claiming; it was branding. Her hips were rolling over him again now, grinding, and he thrust against her as they lined up, aching for each other through too many layers. He wanted to take her somewhere he'd have space and time to worship every inch of her. He wanted to screw it all and take her here and now, limitations of the front seat and all. The dual desires twisted and wound, clouding his ability to think of anything at all other than the gorgeous expanses of rosy, freckled skin he could imagine whenever he shut his eyes.

He didn't have to weigh patience and immediacy much longer, though. Vickie was driving this thing, and she had plans more urgent than his agonizing indecision.

"Azrael, my jeans. Can you take them off?"

Well, that solved that issue. Heat rippled between them.

He smiled and pushed her back. Ran the tip of his right index finger across the seam of her pants and watched as she squirmed, color rising to her cheeks.

"Is this what you want?" Azrael wasn't willing to waste years of practice. This could be nothing less than earth-shattering; he wanted—no, needed—for things to be so phenomenal between them every time that she would maybe understand one fraction of how he felt. He increased the pressure through her pants, feeling the way she bucked against his fingers and drew in a sharp intake of breath.

"Now," Vickie commanded. "Do it now." Her voice was yearning. Desperate. Like his soul.

With his left hand, he gripped between her shoulder blades and pulled her against him. He felt the heat of their most sensitive parts and their secret hearts, almost uncovered and pulsing between them. It was like being consumed by flames, and he was eager to burn.

Azrael shook his head.

"Soon," he said, slipping a finger into her waistband and unbuttoning her pants, pulling them open just a little.

Her underwear was lacy and a delicate pink one shade brighter than her shirt. He moved the hand that was currently unwrapping his deepest desires down between her thighs, pressing the pad of his thumb against the denim.

Vickie rolled her hips, and, fuck, he could finish just from rubbing up against her.

Azrael gritted his teeth. He *would* make this last. He would make it *everything* for her, the way that she was every single damn thing for him.

"Tell me," he said, his words a whisper against her collarbone. "Tell me what you need. Tell me what you want. Anything, Vickie."

"Touch me until I almost can't stand it anymore," she said, breathy with desire. She was digging her hands into the seat behind him now and leveraging it to press herself against him so hard that it almost hurt.

Almost was sometimes the most exquisite word in the English language, and with Vickie it meant stars. It meant fire blooming between them and exploding into a constellation of desire. Devil damn him, she was hot. Under his left hand, her body felt fevered, even through her shirt.

"I want you unraveled. Undone. Falling apart so thoroughly that you can't think, and that the next time you're alone and touching yourself, you can't help but moan my name, and think of this. Of us." It was honest, and dark, and her answering moan intoxicated him. He was fearless now, burning brightly, as powerful as his twice-magicked name. "I want you to feel me, to finish so hard that I am the only person you need like this. So that you can see for a moment what it's like to be me, wanting you every fucking moment of my life."

He circled his thumb slowly along the soft inch of her exposed stomach, relishing the way she writhed and bit out his name. He ignored the heat of his ring, focusing on the more present pleasures of the woman on top of him.

"Azrael," she whimpered. "Touch me everywhere."

He ran a finger down the column of her throat, tracing her collarbone. Slow, languorous brushes, and his fingers were grazing her breast, skimming over the hardened nipple through her flimsy bra and shirt. He brought his other hand up to do the same so that he swiped each one, featherlight, with a thumb, and then pinched gently, relishing her moans. He was uncomfortably hard against the seam of his pants. He was uncomfortably hot under her. Goddess, he'd never pictured it like this, the steering wheel jamming against the back of her and his seat in the way of thrusting the way he wanted, and yet even the idea of it was still enough to turn his blood to honeyed wine, pumping through him, blazing and bold and epic. He was an inferno.

"Touch me," she breathed into his ear, nipping at the lobe and making him groan. He wanted to be in her; he wanted to undress her; he wanted to listen and do absolutely nothing other than what she commanded. He was so swollen with all the wanting that it was hard to think. Was it possible to actually catch fire?

Vickie unleashed was his favorite Vickie. Her bright-wildness was so different from his own simmering, cold loneliness. He growled, shoved a hand deeper into her jeans and yanked her underwear to the side with his hand, dipping his fingers into her as best he could against the stretch of denim. He pulled his hand back out, catching her gasp with his mouth and consuming it, the way he wanted to consume her.

"I want to taste you, Vickie," he gasped against her, but she shook her head. Gravedirt had cleared all pretense between them, or perhaps it was the intensity of what they were doing, but their hearts and their wants were naked now.

"Make me feel so good that I can't stand it," she breathed. "Ruin me for my own hand, without you, next time."

She pressed that hand against the window, leaving a steamy print where it was wet with condensation. The shading magic on the window was unnecessary now, but he left it, the filtered moonlight drifting in casting her in purples and grays that painted her pale skin and her bounty of freckles as little road maps to pleasure that he wanted to trace with his tongue. He couldn't wait to lay her out on an actual bed and take his time worshiping every single fucking inch of her.

But he could follow directions. She had told him what she wanted, and he would give it to her.

He breathed against her neck, sliding his hands down to grip her hips, and then working his fingers over the denim again. He rubbed her center through her pants, and she lifted her body up and then down again, the agony of being so close to where he wanted to be and yet so far pushing against his boxers and his pants. He was throbbing, and his hand was *burning*. He ignored it.

"Az. Please. Stop fucking around."

"Shhh," he said. "I need to do this carefully so I can remember it. I want you to beg. Desperate for me."

He had no shame now, no room to be embarrassed at the bare urgency. He ran his fingers across her back again, trying to cool them. "You feel so good, and I need you so much. I always need you, but it's excruciating. It hurts, Vickie, the way I need you right now."

"Yes," she gasped out, running her hands up his shirt, tracing his stomach and the clenching muscle lower in his abdomen, the waistband, to prove that two could play a game of wanting. Of teasing.

He kissed her neck, increasing the pressure of his lips the way he knew she liked, her soft noises increasing and her body tensing around him, driving him out of his mind. He smiled as he felt her rub against him, the friction between their clothing almost unbearable. Almost.

He was dying to make her scream his name, and then to haul the hot wetness of her down on him. But he had waited so damn long, and he intended to savor this, and to ignore the cramping in his hand. He'd deal with whatever odd injury was paining him later.

"Azrael," she sighed into his mouth, and he met it with his, lips clashing, tongues exploring, swallowing her sounds. He dipped his hand lower, back past her zipper, and slipped his hand between the denim and her panties first, savoring her gasps, and then, tugging them aside, slid his fingers into the hot wetness of her that cleared his mind of every other thought, rubbing for a few moments and then pulling them out.

"What are you doing?" She moaned the question.

He drew his fingers out slowly and licked them, not breaking eye contact.

"You taste so good that I could die to put my mouth on that sweetness," he gasped, thankful, for once, for the gravedirt that meant she would know how serious he was.

"Please, Azrael, fuck me now. Taste me later."

Her fingers were unzipping his pants now, and then scrambling up his chest under his shirt. He ached for her in the dim light streaming into the car.

"Azrael, pretend," she whispered. "Please."

The words were talons ripping his soul a little, that she thought this would end badly, but he didn't care. He would give her exactly what she asked for.

He always had. He always would.

Biting his lip and concentrating to keep from unraveling, he held her hair with the tingling, burning hand and her hip with the other, committing the moment to memory.

She rolled her hips, and he couldn't take it any longer. Moving his hand down and gripping her shirt, he thrust against her, pulling her on top of him and then hauling her off, dry humping like they were teenagers again, whispering dirty nothings into her ear and moaning.

"Tell me," he sighed against her ear, noting how her breath caught as his lips brushed her soft skin. Could they unravel like this? Fabric against fabric, desperate, and in half measures?

Azrael swore to himself that he would always capture every detail of her pleasure. He had failed at so many things, and at telling her so many times, but never at loving Vickie. Never at wanting her, mind, body, and soul.

"Tell me," he said, more insistent this time.

"What?" Vickie asked. Her face was flushed and heated as he trailed kisses along her jawline, moving to finally trace that constellation of freckles down the column of her neck. This was better than every time he'd pictured this moment.

"Tell me you want me. Tell me how much." Azrael surprised himself with the force of his own words, as though they had been building under a façade of caring less. The more she begged him to pretend, the faster his pretense crumbled around him. All his walls. His soul, too, maybe. And his fucking left hand ached now, as though she were undoing the ligaments holding his bones together.

"I," she started. Her breath was ragged, and he kissed her neck, slipping his hand between them once more and continuing the motion with his thumb, harder. Listening for the susurration of her breath to tell him what she liked most. He wanted her undone. Insensible.

"What was that, Vickie?" he growled, snapping his fingers behind her to alleviate the twinge in his back from the angle in the car, and the ache in his hand, and then pushing back up through her shirt, hand skating upward, into her hair, pulling her closer.

He needed her closer. Always.

Her lips were on his now, and then she was whispering, almost into his mouth.

"You don't have to bother trying to make me think of you when I'm all alone in my apartment. I already do. When I touch myself, I always think of you. That's how badly I've wanted this."

Fuck. He wasn't sure how much longer he could hold out before tearing her clothes off and hauling her down on top of him.

"Me, too, Vickie. Me too. I want everything with you."

"I don't think we can have everything. But I want this, at least," she said.

That hurt, but he gritted his teeth, moving his thumb down in relentless circles and snapping his fingers to increase the pressure on her neck, her ears, the rosy buds of her nipples, which he could see peeking through her shirt and her thin bra.

Thank goddess for mesh and lace.

He stroked, with gentle, snapping magic, everywhere he had felt her gasp softly against him. The hand in her pants pressed against her in that panoply of pleasure points he had taken care to memorize in all the times he'd ever touched her. All the moments six years ago, all the breathless stolen glances as teenagers, every word that had ever made her bite her lip in anticipation. The way her hand had paused just below her navel above her hip the time they went skinny-dipping. The way she arched for him now. The soft exhales the times he'd run his fingers over those dimples on her back.

He knew them all. Which was good, because he needed her to finish before he was inside her, and his blood thundered in his head and lower, begging him to let go. His left hand throbbed, but he told himself it was nothing.

She was everything that burned brightly and beautifully in his universe.

Brighter than can be sustained, a small, broken part of him whispered.

He needed to be closer to her. He had to be touching all of her.

Slipping his left hand under her shirt, he let the warmth of her skin seep into it, easing the stabbing pain for a moment. Then, before Azrael knew what was happening, his hand was so hot that it almost burned the metal of his mother's ring as he caught his breath and kissed Victoria. Magic he didn't recognize wreathed them, shifting and snapping into place.

Vickie gasped at the heat of it and pulled back to look him in the eyes. Emotion flickered across her face; the pain in his hand was excruciating now.

Azrael looked down. Flames licked for a moment around his mother's ring as he stared in horror.

"Az," she whispered, voice shaky. "Don't touch me again." She was scrambling away from him, and for a heartbreaking moment, Az wondered what he had done wrong.

He let her go in an instant, but it was an instant too late.

Holding the hand that felt like it was engulfed in flame in front of him, his ring was too hot to bear, and he pulled it off, putting it on the console between them.

The agony in his hand vanished.

"No," whispered Vickie, reaching for him and then stopping herself, suddenly, holding her hands up away from him, and scrambling farther away until she was pressed against the passenger-side door, zipping her pants, pulling back on her coat, and wrapping it around her. "No, no, no. That can't happen. It shouldn't happen if I let go. It can't be happening."

His lust-addled brain tried to process the words and the sensation of them. His hand was still throbbing, and he realized that the back of his neck, where she had been gripping, was raw and scraped. Burned.

Vickie spoke now, but not to him. She was looking at the back seat, and suddenly he knew his parents were there. Azrael's stomach dropped and then heaved, and for a moment, he was afraid he might vomit. It shouldn't be possible. She wasn't touching the ring anymore. How was it possible that the ring was burning between them on the seat of the car, small flames licking up the side of it without so much as a second brush of her skin?

This was the worst thing he could think of—almost having the woman he had loved forever, finally telling her how he felt, and then having the ghosts of his parents immediately appear to her.

Vickie was listening, her face crumbling, and tears gathering at the corners of those beautiful green eyes.

It occurred to him that there might actually be worse things.

"They said I burned you, where I was touching you. That if I touch you again, you'll summon them back. That you're like a departed's precious object now. Like the ring was. If we touch again, you'll die."

The pain of the realization prickled at him gently for a moment. Az breathed through it as the feeling deepened, spiraling out of control, and slicked like oil on top of water, not yet plumbing the depths of despair it would cause when it sank in.

Lex's words echoed in his mind.

You'll rue the moment you chose to do that, witch.

A curse trapped in a ring, and now, in him.

Azrael was a precious object now. Another soul to be collected.

And if she touched him again, he would die.

He buried his face in his hands, barely hearing the sound of Vickie's voice as she spoke in hushed tones with ghosts he could not see.

CHAPTER 14

Victoria

Benedict Hart's gaze felt painful as he focused his golden eyes on her. Victoria resisted the urge to duck and hide as her pulse slowed. Nothing killed a mood like almost immolating the object of her affection in front of his dead parents. Vickie breathed in and out slowly, trying to focus. And to stop the awful, damning blush running up her throat and her cheeks.

"You will kill him if you are not careful," Benedict's ghost was saying, voice sharper than she had ever heard in life.

"It will kill him a little bit if she is," said Persephone, her gentle whisper full of worry, clutching at Benedict's arm. He wrapped a translucent palm around hers, but didn't break eye contact with Vickie.

"Better alive and brokenhearted than dead," Benedict said, and Vickie could feel tears threatening with the rush of emotions swirling in the wake of so many extremes. She swallowed.

"He's right," said Persephone. "I don't think there's any way to undo the curse, though I can't fathom how Olexandre could make your gift function on a person when it is so clearly meant for objects. He must have spelled something to Azrael, something that could transfer on contact."

"An objectification spell," said Benedict gruffly. "Shadow craft. Devils may do it too."

The ghost of Persephone Hart frowned.

"It is impossible for a *witch* to undo, but as long as one is careful with the terms of the contract, it doesn't have to be deadly."

Benedict looked at Persephone now, their shared gaze heavy with meaning.

"Victoria Starnberger," Benedict said, voice heavy. "You must now deal with two devils. The person loose in Hallowcross who has made themselves a worser demon by attempting to steal lives and souls in exchange for corrupt power, and Olexandre, the one who gifted you with your own power, to whom you are indebted."

"There has to be a way to undo this. How do I keep him safe? What can I do?"

The elder Hart smiled sadly. "It won't be easy. You'll have to untangle the corruption here in Hallowcross. The church, and whatever bargain has been struck to cause harm."

"Do you know anything else that could help us?"

The ghost regarded her quietly for a few seconds, precious time slipping away.

"The psychic. I would start with puzzling out what it means. For her to be unreachable like that, in a coma, well, it's some sort of spell blowback. Someone tried to take her soul and then stuff it back in. There will be consequences even if you can revive her." His eyes darkened. "She'll come back different. Don't forget it."

It didn't make sense to her. What would a power-hungry creature linked to Brethren of One Love want with a roadside fake psychic?

"Why her? She's a known fraud. A tourist trap. And what about the church?"

Benedict's shade shook his head. "Everything to do with that church is murky. Shielded. I can only see that Madam Cleopatra is in danger. She was *not* what the evil sought, in the end."

His wife clutched his arm.

"Please," Persephone begged. "Don't let Azrael get caught in the cross fire. He'd die for you. Don't let him."

"I'd sooner die myself," Vickie said, moving her hand to her heart, against her jacket, to stop it from inching toward Azrael's. Az's head was still in his hands, and Vickie wanted so desperately to comfort him, but to touch him would be murder. What if he reached for her in desperation, unthinking, and touched her hand? Her face?

He would never touch her face again.

The thought slammed into Vickie, and she was crying now, slow sobs ramping up, escalating into breathlessness so different from the heady one she'd shared with Azrael only minutes before.

Benedict was looking at the flaming ring.

"The object." He frowned. "It shouldn't burn when you're not touching it." Understanding creased his brow. "Transfer spell and then objectification. An order of operations sequence spell. Very tricky. Highly personal."

Vickie blanched.

"Olexandre must have enchanted it to capture your touch," said Persephone. "Devils are clever, calculating. Whatever it is he needs from you, he must need it more urgently now. Get it to him quickly." Persephone's eyes bored into Vickie's, red mouth set serious. "Be careful. Tell my son the same. And that we love him. Tell Priscilla we love her too. Do not despair, Victoria. All that is made can be unmade, and so long as you are both breathing, you may find a loophole, and a way to each other yet. Have faith in your love, darling."

Their ghosts flickered now.

"Az," Vickie said softly. "Azrael."

Az lifted his head out of his hands. He looked absolutely destroyed, tear tracks on his cheeks and a muscle jumping in his jaw.

"Your parents love you very much. They said we have to deal with two devils now, but they love you. So much." Vickie's voice broke again a little.

Azrael ran a hand down his face. "No one I love can touch me anymore. And it's all my fault." His voice was gravelly.

Broken. It was an exaggeration, of course, but correcting him wouldn't kill the pain, or the fact that it was, in this moment, his truth.

"Tell them I love them." His voice was muffled by his hands, covering his face as he leaned against the steering wheel. "Tell them their memories are a blessing."

Benedict nodded, a muscle in his jaw twitching in a motion so similar to his son's.

His parents' ghosts clutched each other, as though they feared that they, too, could be cursed apart. "We love you, Azrael." Persephone's voice was already fading. "You as well, Victoria. And Priscilla. So long as you have each other, you are never really alone."

The ring turned smoky and then disintegrated, fine ash the last remnant of the protection it once held. The love it symbolized, though, lived on. One didn't need an object to love fully and well.

"Az," she began, but he shook his head.

"I need to drive us home. I need to find the strength to move, knowing how mind-blowing it was to touch you, and also knowing that I can never do it again."

The words were sharp and honest; the pain there left her almost breathless.

Azrael snapped his fingers and the windows cleared of condensation.

Moonlight streamed into the interior of the Packard, a sharp juxtaposition to the heaviness in her soul.

Vickie opened the glove box and found what she was looking for—a pair of expensive-looking leather driving gloves. Thank goddess for Persephone and her glamorous style.

Pulling the gloves on despite the August heat, Vickie slid her covered hand into Azrael's.

"It doesn't fix things, but this way I can at least hold your hand."

Azrael made a choking sound, and his face twisted.

"I would give anything to kiss you right now."

"I know," she said softly.

He dragged her gloved hand up to his mouth and pressed his lips against the leather sheathing it.

Tendrils of longing radiated through the fabric from where they touched, but it could be enough.

It would have to be. What other choice did they have?

The rest of the drive was silent, though Vickie held Az's bare hand in her gloved one the entire time. When he dropped her off at Hopelessly Teavoted, she leaned forward without thinking, and he stilled, frozen, not moving away, even when she only remembered, inches away from his face, that she could never touch her lips to his again.

Vickie had lost her only surefire way to pray, losing the slide of his body against hers in the only religion she knew. Something in her broke.

A shattered glass could not be reassembled.

A curse could not be broken.

And yet here he was, holding still and looking at her, hazel eyes full of love and longing, like he'd kiss her even if he had to burn for it. Even if it was the last thing he ever did. She remembered the terms of the bargain.

There actually was something worse.

Be careful what you touch if you happen to have an object with particular sentimental value.

She had touched the saltshakers, and the ring. And if she touched him again, he would burn.

If she *beheld* him after the terms of her bargain, after October 31, he would die.

Vickie couldn't allow that.

Her heart remained in the car next to his untouchable lips as she pulled away and spoke clearly so there would be no confusion.

"We can't be together. Even with gloves. From now on, to avoid sudden death, we are just friends. Business associates." Vickie looked away, unable to keep contact through the intensity of his gaze.

"What about how I feel, Vickie? What about how *you* feel?" Az's voice was accusatory, as though she had dismissed an essential detail. He ran a hand through his hair, and the way it stuck to the side made her think he had pulled at it. Harder than she would like.

"My heart will break every day. I expect yours might as well. But it's a better option than you dying," Vickie said. "If you died, my heart would crumble entirely. And the terms of my contract mean touching you will kill you, but if I don't collect as promised, if I don't pay off my debt, even *looking* at you will kill you after Halloween."

"There has to be another way." Agony lined his face, creasing between his eyebrows. "We have two months to figure it out. That's plenty of time. Between you, me, Priscilla, and the Council, if we have to get them involved. Plenty of time."

Vickie opened the door.

"I have to go," she said.

Azrael nodded and snapped his fingers, and her disheveled hair and mussed clothing smoothed back to perfection.

It was as though the night had never even happened.

The thought of it broke her even more than the knowledge that everything between them had changed for good.

CHAPTER 15

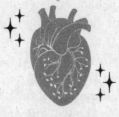

Azrael

Two months was definitely enough time to fix this.

The drive home gave Azrael time to think. He would give Vickie some space. Spend a weekend stroking himself in the shower to get the image of her squirming in his lap out of his brain, if such a thing was even possible.

Get his shit together. Focus on the start of the school year.

Az pulled up to Hart Manor glad, for once, that Prissy wasn't home, though he'd realized after moving back that he was glad to live with his adult sister in a creepy old mansion, even if people thought that was weird.

The house welcomed him home as it always did, the haunted knocker moaning at him pleasantly, the door swinging open to Emily Lickinson, who yowled around his feet, hungry as always, and left a puff of little white hairs in her wake. He fed her, and sat down to put the polishing touches on his syllabus before passing out, exhausted, in his four-poster bed, the curtains drawing around him, and the comforting weight of the cat at his feet.

The worst of the gravedirt wore down somewhat after the first day, but still left him emotional and moody. He spent all of Saturday bingeing a steamy regency romance show to avoid his sister's interrogations and distract himself from thoughts of Vickie.

By Sunday, he was going out of his mind with longing, but he had promised himself he would focus on work.

Azrael: School starts tomorrow for students, so I might be a little scarce for a bit. Maybe we can have dinner on a Tuesday in a few weeks, once things slow down? At my place? Since you're closed Wednesdays?

Azrael: If you want. Goddess, I hope I don't make a fool of myself in front of 200 10th graders with my lingering honesty.

Vickie: Kids love honesty. You're going to be great. And no worries, I'll be scarce too. I'm backed up on Hopelessly stuff for this week already.

It was brief enough that he threw the phone onto his bed, and snapped to change into workout clothes, storming downstairs to the gym.

Thwap. The pain of his fist against a punching bag radiated outward. He was hitting too hard, and he didn't care.

Thwap. Thwap. He one-two punched, moving to double time like the old Billy Blanks Tae Bo videos his dad used to tease his mom about loving in the early aughts.

Thwap. For his parents dying and not being around to help him untangle his shit. *Thwap. Thwap.* For his asshole boss, who rubbed him the wrong way. *Thwap. Thwap. Thwap.* For the curse that kept him from touching Vickie, and threatened to do worse. *Thwap.* For stupid early August Azrael, who squandered the chance to fuck her senseless immediately, while he still could.

"Hullo, Azrael? Are you well?"

It was Evelyn, clad in exercise gear so fancy that he doubted she'd be too out of place if she stepped onto the Council floor like that.

It was long enough after the gravedirt that he might have been able to at least obfuscate, but emotions always made him more susceptible to magic, and here he was, traces of the gravedirt still in his system, caught unawares, and unable to answer falsely.

"No. I'm the least well I have ever been. The furthest possible from wellness."

He sat down on the mat, and leaned his head into his knees, crying softly.

Evelyn patted him gingerly on the back—a commitment, given the sheen of perspiration leaking through his shirt. It calmed him down a little. She must not hate him, or she must really love his sister; he was *disgustingly* sweaty.

"Here," she said, voice gentle. She handed him a very nice moisture-wicking towel, which he took gratefully and used to dry his eyes.

"Thanks."

"Hey, Ev, do you want to spot me ..." His sister stopped short, seeing her girlfriend crouched next to him, trying to console him. He must have looked completely wrecked, because the next thing he knew, his sister was by his side, wrapping an arm around him.

"Azrael, you smell *so bad*. What's going on? How long have you been in here?"

His eyes flickered to the wall. Too long. He needed to get his things together for the week. For his first day.

And yet, he also really, really needed his sister.

Before he could stop himself, the words slipped out like smooth shards of glass.

"My heart is broken, my soul is crushed, and I doubt if I can ever be happy and whole again."

"All right," said Priscilla, frowning. "All right. Start at the beginning."

"We talked to Mom and Dad. Again. Because that insufferable Olexandre object transfer cursed me."

"I'm sorry, I don't follow," said Priscilla.

"I think he means that the devil transferred the essence of an object to him, thus rendering him subject to Vickie's gift," Evelyn explained.

Prissy's eyes widened. "Sweet baby Beelzebub. Do you mean that if she touches you—"

"I burn," he said miserably.

"Shit," said Priscilla. She snapped.

"What did you just do?" He eyed her with suspicion.

"What did I undo, you mean. It was a prank that even I am not mean enough to spring on you in your condition." Priscilla traced a hand down her braid.

He smiled weakly. "It gets worse."

"Go on."

"We still haven't checked in on Madam Cleopatra, or made any progress on the church situation. Mom and Dad are still dead, and my boss is an ass. And Vickie wants space to think about what will happen when our time runs out."

"Ah," said Evelyn. "Of course. A curse with fine print. Go on, then, out with it. You might feel better."

"Let us carry some of the weight, Az." Prissy snapped her fingers again, looking sheepish. "Sorry. Forgot about the guillotine."

"She has until Halloween to pay the devil her debt." He cracked his knuckles, but it did little to relieve the stress.

"And?"

"And if she doesn't, she can't *behold* me without immolating me."

"Clever magic," mused Evelyn. Priscilla elbowed her, which knocked her off the mat she had been perched on the corner of. She caught herself on the floor, wrist behind her.

"Ouch. Awful, but also awfully clever." Suddenly, Evelyn smiled, which was an odd reaction to being sprawled across the exercise room floor. "There is a solution, you know. A workaround that would prohibit her from reaping your soul, and yours alone."

"Is there?" Priscilla's eyebrows wrinkled and shot up. "Oh!

That would be very, very serious, though. Permanent. The soul tattoo of magic, really."

"What?" Azrael frowned. What would be the most permanent magic between two powerful creatures?

Then the answer hit him like a punching bag.

"A soul binding. You want me to magically marry my childhood sweetheart, the same girl whose heart I accidentally broke in college, who I have only just barely reestablished a friendship with for a month. Prissy, no. That's insane. We did talk about having feelings for each other, big feelings, even, but under the duress of gravedirt, not, like, naturally in the course of a relationship. She wants to still pretend the feelings between us aren't real. You're suggesting an unbreakable, undoable thing that most witch couples don't even do."

"Well," began Priscilla. "I'm not saying to do it, just that it's an option. Mom and Dad did."

He grimaced. "Would you soul-bind with Evelyn?"

Both women stiffened.

"No," said Prissy softly. "I would not. I'm not opposed to marriage, mundane or even witch, but I don't ever want to be bound. I don't need to tattoo my soul onto someone else's on top of it. I don't think I'd like to bind myself to anyone like that. Ever."

Evelyn looked sad but not surprised.

"As for the other things. Mom and Dad are dead, but we also can keep their memories alive. Like, do you remember the time we came home early from school and caught them tangoing in the hall?"

He smiled. "In formal wear and all, every sconce in the place lit, and a full orchestra of instruments enchanted to play for them. Yeah, I do."

His heart still felt heavy, but the telling of the story felt right. Like sitting shiva, which he had missed in lockdown. He thought about what he would have wanted to share, had he been there. "Uncle Larry once told me that in college, they were rivals. That one time, Mom hexed Dad's hair short and he hexed her nails and lipstick pink for an entire month."

"Mom with pink lipstick?" Priscilla laughed.

"It must have been something," he said.

"Yeah," she said softly. "They really were."

"Thanks, Priscilla."

"You're welcome. And I tell you what. Out of courtesy, I won't prank you at all this week."

"Thanks for that," he said darkly. "Maybe you could extend that no-prank rule for a few weeks? I invited Vickie over for dinner some Tuesday. In a few weeks, when I've got a good rhythm going with school."

Priscilla's eyes lit up. "Hart family dinner! I'll cook, and I'll refrain from pranking for it and all, I swear." She winced a little at the thought of it. "But after that, all bets are off."

"I would expect nothing less."

"Hey, Az?"

"Yeah?"

"Take a shower. You smell like self-pity and ass."

He sighed. There was the sister he knew and loved.

By the time he climbed the stairs, the banister rising to meet his hand like a dog leaning in to be petted, his thoughts had drifted to Victoria.

The house must have known; it drew the curtains and ran a shower that smelled like the lemon soap he favored and steamed the mirror up immediately, stopping him from having to stare down the echoes of his own lust.

He showered, trying not to think about the way Vickie had tasted on his fingers what felt like lifetimes ago, and the soft sounds she had made. The other sounds he had wanted her to make. He knew how to kill the thoughts, though. All he had to do was shut his eyes and picture his mother's ring turning to ash. And the realization that both his parents were gone, out of his reach to talk to, and that he could never touch Vickie again.

He snapped his fingers and the water turned cold, which also helped.

On Monday morning, he stood in front of a mirror, running a hand through curly hair, and he suddenly couldn't stand it. He snapped his fingers a few times, and then a few more. A simple suave barber spell, one that Priscilla had perfected years ago and taught him as an alternative to spending hundreds of dollars at the salon.

The trick was to think of a few sensations you loved while you did it, and the magic did the rest to craft the art of the haircut.

He had tasted strawberries and felt the soft fuzz of that pink jacket, and smelled the lemon scent of his own soap, the kind he'd used since his mom started ordering it from a witch a few counties over and stocking it in her shop when he was a teen. A few blinks later, and the haircut was good enough that he felt camera ready, the sides of it trimmed close to his head, and the top an inch or so longer. He smiled as he shrugged on a dress shirt, chinos, and a blazer.

Azrael had a bit of a chip on his shoulder about teachers who boasted that they were unapproachable, especially if they were white men like him. They always seemed to be assholes, and he didn't think there was any merit to pretending to be what he was not. Teaching was not sitting at the front of the classroom; it was active motion, and it required authentic attire. He'd known plenty of people who rocked pantsuits naturally, but he was not one of them. Casual professor chic, he decided, looking in the mirror.

If he knew anything about teaching, it would be such a busy, exhausting day that he would not have time to consider Victoria and his longing.

The redbrick exterior of the high school looked drabber than he remembered from the week of staff orientation, but he swallowed the thought and walked through the double glass doors, swiping his badge to get through the secure outer door. Tan linoleum stretched out in front of him. Dust bordered the floors and the crumbling corners, and he felt overwhelmed at the prospect of doing this for the next thirty years until he retired. Alone and dreaming of her. Remembering the squandered years they could have been together. Would it be better or worse if she paid her debt and the curse couldn't kill him by Halloween, and he ended up watching her, from afar, never being able to touch her, for years, stretching into decades? He pushed the thought aside and focused on the present.

Out of courtesy alone, he said hello to Chet. Devil damn him, Azrael already hated his department chair. Chet Thornington was an absurd man, shirt buttoned up all the way to his neck, shoulders slumped downward. He was always wearing a formal shirt, a thick tie, and a Fabio haircut that hung past his ears. He was even worse here than he was yelling at coffee shop employees and clinging to a dead aesthetic, with his hair slicked back in a futile attempt to mirror a trend that hadn't been popular for a decade. He looked like a has-been, a rejected regency romance cover model out of work and left with nothing better to do than talk smack about current authors. It was Prufrockian, really.

Chet was arguing with a younger woman Az recognized from orientation as another teacher in his department. Aurora. She had to be no more than twenty-one. Maybe twenty-two.

Far too young for the way Chet was looking at her.

Yeah, judgmental, or not, Azrael hated this guy already.

"It's the first student day, Aurora. You won't have grading yet. We'll be done early. Are you sure?" Chet was stepping toward her, and her body turned toward him, but she flinched a little as he drew closer.

Whatever was between them danced on a line of attraction and pain, and Azrael cleared his throat, not wanting to intrude but also not comfortable walking away.

"No, I'm busy. I can't." With a small wave to Azrael, she grabbed a stack of papers off a copier that was still spitting a few of them out, leaving him alone in the room with the man.

"Chet Thornington," he said, holding out a hand. "Just got back from the leadership retreat."

Azrael considered refusing the man's hand after what he had seen. This was the third time he'd met Chet, but being cold would be a bad start to the year.

"Azrael Hart. We met briefly last week at the first day of orientation. And via video call when you hired me." The man's hand was just a trace clammy, and Az resisted the urge to recoil.

"Right. Right. My new teacher. The same Harts as the weirdo family with the manor on the hill?"

"Yes," said Azrael, keeping his anger and magic in check. He was good at it, after so many years of denying himself.

"Sorry about your parents. That was unfortunate."

"Thank you," Az said, unsure of how else to respond. He stood awkwardly for a moment.

"Hey, your sister is hot, though. Is she single?"

Azrael glared at the man, who five minutes earlier had been clearly intimidating a much younger woman who, if he was a betting man, Az would be willing to guess Chet was fucking.

"No. And you're not her type either."

"What precisely are you trying to imply?"

Azrael stared. This was getting out of hand. "Just that it looks, from an outsider's perspective, like you, a man old enough to have a specific and clear memory of the Challenger explosion, are messing with a girl young enough to have been your student, if not your kid." Az ground his teeth. There was the lingering effect of gravedirt, days later, threatening his job already.

Or maybe Chet was just too much of a tool to ignore.

"I don't pretend to know what you're talking about. But watch it," said Chet, glancing around nervously. "She's from Scarsdale, not here, and she was never my student."

Azrael snorted. "Does saying that make you feel better about it?"

"Look. We won't have to like each other, Hart, but I've been teaching English here almost the longest. Which means I am the most experienced, and therefore the best at it. From what I hear, you're taking some of the most crowded class sections. So you need me. You'd do well to keep that in mind."

The logic didn't even make sense. Azrael ground his teeth,

resolving to cool Chet's temperature a little, maybe make his shoes more supportive. Something that should make the man just a little kinder. He snapped, but it did nothing. Azrael frowned and looked at his fingers. Was there such a thing as being too big of an asshole for magic?

Azrael knew it was a low blow, but as Chet stormed out, he snapped his fingers again in the empty staff room, and the stack of sticky notes next to him was one shorter. The missing note slipped itself onto the back of Chet Thornington's shirt, with the word *asshole* scrawled on it.

He grabbed Aurora's papers off the copy machine. He sure as hell wasn't going to let a human monster ruin this poor woman's life.

This close to a dosing of gravedirt, anger still pushed him over into abject honesty, and he was certain that the effect of his anger toward Chet would last a few more days.

Fortunately, he knew better than to be angry at any children he taught. He'd been a substitute long enough to know that drama and rudeness from teenagers was about what they were going through more than what the person instructing them was going through, and that it would pass if he waited patiently and checked in about what they needed.

No, he would not be angry at the children, but Chet was another story.

When he walked into Aurora's classroom, the first thing he noticed was her last name, Schumacher, stenciled across the wall in glittering rainbow, she/her pronouns underneath. A giant Black Lives Matter Pride fist hung on her wall, reminding him of his mom and the posters and flags decorating Hopelessly Teavoted, which of course reminded him of Victoria.

"You left these on the copier," Az said, and she looked up, sniffling a little like she had been crying, quietly, alone in her classroom on the first day of school.

"I—thank you. Dust got caught in my contact." Her expression was defiant, and he nodded wordlessly. "Welcome to Hallowcross High," she said. "Sorry your first interaction was with Chet. He's not exactly our most pleasant department member."

"No," Azrael said slowly. "I imagine not. Listen. It may not be my business, but anyone who is going to talk to you like that is not worth your time. You don't deserve that."

Aurora stared at him, and Az wondered if he had overstepped. They had only spoken briefly at orientation, but he hated the idea of the first friendly face he'd seen here being trampled by the first unfriendly one.

Aurora's eyes snapped shut, though, and she sighed. "I know. We aren't even a thing anymore, but he keeps texting and calling."

"Don't pick up."

"It would be rude. We're colleagues. He's kind of my boss."

"*He's* rude. I'm telling you. Don't pick up. Don't answer his text messages. Don't argue with him, just stop responding. Block his number if you have to."

"Why do you even care?"

Her words were more curious than accusatory, but Az was angry.

"Because I have a person I love, who loves me, and we wasted years—almost a decade, in fact—dancing around instead of being honest with ourselves and each other. And now things are complicated, but I would still do anything, *anything*, to fix my relationship. You clearly know Chet is not that person for you. Go find your person. Don't waste any more time. There could be thirty perfect partners out there for you, in fact. Thirty not-Chets, or even thirty fun flings. Just, life is short. Don't waste it on the Chets of it all."

Aurora's mouth opened in surprise.

"Wow, new guy. Out the cut with the serious opinions." Aurora paused for a moment, and he was pretty sure she was going to laugh at him. Then she said, "That's cool, though. Do you want to tell me about your partner at lunch? I eat with some of the other teachers. I'm the disaster youth who keeps them entertained with my bad choices." She looked at him and smiled. His first real work friend. "They're about your age, too, so you'll have things in common. There aren't any other people in our department my age, but I sometimes hang with the math teachers. There's one, Kelley—she's really nice. Her husband died when she was like three months pregnant, and she has the most adorable little baby."

Az noticed that Aurora blushed when she mentioned the math teacher, and he smiled.

He'd accidentally adopted a cat *and* a work friend now.

At least it would keep him distracted from Vickie while they figured shit out.

CHAPTER 16

Victoria

Vickie told herself she was giving him space during the busiest month of the school year, but part of her also needed the time to process the gravity of it all. So she had insisted on visiting Madam Cleopatra in the hospital on her own, telling the orderlies she was a niece and touching everything she could get her hands on in the room to see if she could rustle up a spirit to talk. There was nothing, which made sense. Madam Cleopatra wasn't dead, and hospital rooms didn't generally hold objects of significance. All she'd found was a chart that said Connie Witherspoon had no changes since she'd been admitted in July. *Persistent vegetative state*, it read, but the cause was still unknown. She'd have to look for leads elsewhere.

When she brought Azrael a basket of muffins, she left them with Priscilla on her day off while he was at school. She didn't trust herself not to ask him to pretend with her again, creatively and from a distance this time, and she wanted to think it through without the temptation of his fingers, snapping and so dexterous.

The trill of the phone a week and a half later reverberated through her. The clock said it was barely still Saturday, and she was bone tired after the day at the shop plus the evening's preparation for tomorrow. There was only one person who would be calling her. And the thought of his lips made her thighs clench.

Remembering that her kiss would kill him sobered her up from her own longing immediately. He never called, usually. Goddess, she hoped he wasn't hurt. It had to be serious for him to call in the middle of the night. No one was more considerate than Azrael Hart, especially now that he was two weeks into a lifetime of early wake-up alarms.

"What is it? Is someone sick?" Vickie asked. Az couldn't possibly be expected to withstand much more heartbreak. She'd make her own deal with a devil to avoid any more loss in Azrael's life. However ill-advised such an arrangement would be.

"No, no one is sick or dead. Priscilla and I are fine, but someone broke into the house. It shouldn't have been possible to trip the magic alarms, but they were delayed, somehow. It didn't wake us up until after. Someone stole some plants from my mom's garden. Pretty powerful stuff, things you would use to immobilize people or build dangerously impenetrable wards." He stopped, his voice intense enough that she wanted to murder whoever was responsible. "They painted a giant cross with a circle around it on one of the broken panes of glass. That's the logo for the Brethren of One Love church. I think someone there wants us to know they did this."

"Are you sure you're all right?"

"I'm fine. I swear."

"Then I need to tell you. Az, I stopped by the hospital to see Madam Cleopatra. It was a dead end, and she was just there, roots growing out a little blond, looking unassuming. There were no objects I could find, no traces of anything. But what if someone knows? That was Wednesday. What if someone did this because I got too nosy?"

"This isn't your fault. Listen. In witchcraft, and in my mom's people—well, my people, too—we're certainly no stranger to this kind of thing. It's never your fault if a bad person takes issue with a thing you did that you needed to do."

"Still. I should come over," Vickie said. She needed to see that he was, in fact, as fine as he claimed.

"It's late. You don't have to." He sighed. "I know I've been busy with work, and we haven't had the space I wanted to talk it out. Later, at another time, I do need to tell you about something Prissy and Evelyn figured out about the curse."

"Friends don't let their friends put their fingers in each other's pants, sustain epic curses, and then just walk alone into danger." She said it firmly, ignoring the fact that she had done just that with the hospital. "And besides. I am thinking about it. A lot. I miss you. I want to be there if you're in trouble."

Vickie heard the sharp intake of his breath on the line.

"Friends. Right. Okay. Evelyn is here too. I think more eyes on what happened here is better, short of involving the Council. And I've got my reasons for avoiding them; once they get involved, they'll cut us out entirely."

"Understandable. That would make paying my soul debt difficult. Evelyn is fierce, and so is Prissy. But don't worry, Az, I'll come over and protect you."

Az laughed. It was rasping and loud on the line. It wasn't hurtful, and it wasn't mean, but it sounded rusty, like it had been too long since someone had made him actually laugh.

She should have called him this week. Or the one before it. Or maybe every day. Maybe she wanted to call him every day from now on, and if she couldn't, maybe she wanted to pretend that she could.

"Thanks. My knight in glittering hairspray."

"Don't you own an actual suit of armor? So theoretically, I could just be a knight in shining armor."

"Obviously, I do. But it's my size, so it's much too tall for you. I can pick you up in about twenty minutes, if that works."

"Az, have you actually tried it on? And I can drive myself."

"No comment on the suit. We have a break-in to solve. Let me come get you. This has all been a lot, and driving clears my mind."

"That sounds like an excuse for *you* to be a knight in shining armor. How do I know you're not going to show up in a metal suit, driving a car?"

"Well, for one thing, it would be much too hard to drive in. I'll be there in fifteen."

"Fine. But no armor."

"Suit yourself," he said, hanging up before he could hear her cackle at the silliness of it.

CHAPTER 17

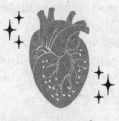

Azrael

Driving helped distract Azrael from his desperation to pull more of those soft gasping noises from Vickie. It was terribly bad form to be fantasizing about her thighs while he should be focusing on figuring out who was responsible for the break-in at the manor.

Vickie was sunshine and butterflies and soft, soft kisses. But she was also burning fire and a hidden, tender heart that he had once glimpsed for long enough to be willing to shatter his own to protect it. He shoved those feelings out of the way and concentrated on the task at hand.

He cleared his throat.

"So, uh, how's business? Picking up?"

"Ah." Vickie paused after the nonanswer, and he wondered if it would be better to sit in silence than to endure the weirdness of the stilted conversation. "It's improving, but you could say that I have the *boos* about the whole thing. I'm getting there, but it's tough. Your mom was a force of nature."

Good. This was good.

He drummed his finger on the steering wheel. "Well. I guess you have some *soul*-searching to do, then."

Vickie laughed, and when he glanced over, she was staring out the window.

Azrael let her have the space. He wanted to tell her that he wasn't entirely sure that his survival instinct could outweigh his need to touch her now that he was seeing her again.

"Vickie, I know we said pretend, and I know pretend is safer, but I want you to know that if things were different—"

"I know," she said softly.

"Can I tell you anyway?" His knuckles were white against the wheel now.

"Of course," she said. He could see her knitting her fingers together in her lap.

"I would want to give it an honest shot, if things were different."

"Me, too, Az. I would want to see where it goes. But things are what they are."

"Right. So, without any expectations, then, let me just put this out there. Anytime you want to call pretend, we can. Short of actually touching, we can pretend things *are* different."

She blushed. "You, too, Az. Anytime you want to call pretend."

He thought about the soul binding. He was all in, as quick as that was, but it was too much pressure for her, especially now, when she'd only just agreed to be pretends-with-benefits.

Running his hand along the imprint of his wallet against his thigh, he thought of the note. The one he should have given her before they left for college. Before any of this madness. Before he became so heavy with grief that he feared his heart would weigh her down, just like her parents had. It was better to keep it to himself. The note, and any words that might come out if he opened his mouth, which was desperate to confess again.

No. He would leave it at the possibility of pretend. Pining silently was better, anyway. Now he could focus totally on whatever was going on in that megachurch and the slight panic of knowing that his dead parents had warned him of sinister activities. The creeping knowledge that the Brethren of One Love had something to do with whoever had broken into their home. He could ignore the obvious, soul-crushing fact that he couldn't do more than pretend with Vickie unless she allowed him to bind her life and soul to him permanently. That he had to pause any plans to woo her in earnest in pursuit of answers to his immediate suspicions. This kind of coincidence could not be ignored, especially not after Kyle George had warned Vickie. And Donovan Wagner had tried to warn them. Sure, Priscilla was a more powerful witch than he was, and Evelyn even more so. They were more than capable of fending off any threat, but it involved Vickie. He needed to help. Then there was the looming approach of October, which gave them only a little more than a month to figure it all out.

It was fine. He would just be sure to refill his Zoloft prescription on time. The last thing he wanted to do was lose track of managing his anxiety. He could find time to make peace with family tragedy, untangle his impossible attachment to the person he'd loved forever, solve a magical mystery, and write meaningful feedback on hundreds of diagnostic essays for junior English.

So, no pressure.

Beside him, Vickie squirmed in her seat, and he wondered if she was as inappropriately distracted as he was by just the idea of steering wheels near her now. She had to be. Azrael had felt her, not just in the way she had moved against his hand, in the brief, stolen seconds before calamity struck, but in the way that he had forgotten she made him feel when they touched years before.

It was, every time, once again, like the magic in him sang to her, and hers responded.

Now that he could no longer touch her, Azrael couldn't tell her again that it still felt that way. He had to tell her. Was there a way to tell her and not tell her?

He wanted her to be able to choose. He knew few witches who did the soul seal, even among happily married couples. His parents had been two of them.

"I once asked my dad how he knew my mom was the one," Az said, staring straight ahead at the road.

He could feel her eyes on him, but he didn't dare look over. For safety, of course.

"What did he say?" Vickie's voice was soft, and he could hear the click of a zipper sliding as she opened her bag. He forced himself not to look, but he smelled that berry-scented lotion that made her skin glisten. His senses were full of her. She brushed her hair, and he smelled lavender as it fell back around her shoulders in waves. He tore his eyes away and back to the road, swerving to avoid a pothole, and swore to himself that he wouldn't steal any more glances to his right.

"He said that when he was with her, a sad world seemed brighter. That when he touched her hand, their magic knew, and even though he favored shadow craft and she plant witchery, the two different strains of enchantment warmed each other."

"Their bodies knew," whispered Vickie.

"He said their bodies sang to each other." Az paused. "I was super embarrassed when he said that. It was right after we, you know."

"Found their sex dungeon?"

Azrael frowned. He *hated* to refer to it that way. *Dungeon* had such negative connotations. "You know I prefer to call it an extra basement bedroom."

"Fine. Is the extra bedroom still around?" Vickie's voice softened, and he snuck a look, eyes lingering longer than was safe on her parted lips. Az swallowed, remembering her voice in the dark all those years ago after, asking if he had ever thought about spanking anyone.

"No. Priscilla cleaned it out, thank goddess. We decided it would be a little too much to keep that particular memory of our parents around. It's a home gym now."

"You mean you work out where your parents . . . you know, worked out?"

Azrael smiled. Say what people might about Benedict and Persephone Hart, but they had never wasted a moment of their married years pretending they didn't love each other passionately. There was something beautiful about that, as much as he also didn't need to know the precise details of their sex life. "You know, I think if we wanted to avoid rooms where they . . . worked out, we might just have to burn the whole house down."

"Yeah, that tracks," Vickie said. "Happy for them, though." He wondered if *she* ever thought about the spanking conversation. If that was something that she wanted. But spanking generally led to touching, and touching was off the table. Though if he was honest, he could imagine any number of non-touching activities that could be exquisitely arousing. Especially in a sex dungeon. Forcing himself back to the conversation now, he went on. He would keep this casual. For now. They could have been knee deep in the passenger seat if things were different.

"I used to be embarrassed to know that about them. Not just the sex, but the depth of emotion. Witches have this rare ceremony called soul sealing. Most witches, even married ones, don't do it. But my parents did, and it means their souls are together forever. By choice. I used to think that was so corny. But now that they're gone, honestly, I'm just happy that they loved each other that much. That what time they had was completely honest, and that in the end, they were together."

"Definitely," said Vickie. She sounded quiet. Broken. "They never took each other for granted. That sounds like a sweet life. And it's nice that they got to choose that."

"It was," Az said. Some of the guilt of not being here was gone now, he realized. Because of her. Vickie was the girl he used to know, but stronger. More capable.

A woman who had finally struck out on her own and left behind her cruel family and the weight of their emotional baggage.

"Vickie. I know I said I was sorry for, you know, the lies and misery–slash–unfortunate no-touching situation, but I should have also said thank you. I want to thank you for helping me say goodbye. That meant everything. I mean, I was trying to thank you that night." He blushed. She was so put together now, working on her own business. He wanted her to know how grateful he was. Even if the possibility of a normal romantic relationship was over now, by necessity.

Shit. Az hoped she didn't think he had almost finger-fucked her in the Packard as a thank-you. Or was it better if she did think of it like that? He dragged a hand down his face, lingering for a second on his fingers, which he swore still smelled ever so slightly of her. Obviously that was wishful thinking. It was just his memory, infused with magic and longing. He could almost taste the sweet salt slick of her. The thought tormented him.

"Oh," Vickie said. "Is that what you were trying to do before the curse?"

"No," he said, against his better judgment. "No. I did that because I wanted to. Because of how I feel about you."

They had reached the gates now, and Az rolled down the window to key in the code. The iron teeth lifted from above and receded into the ground, and then snapped shut after the car passed through. He began again, reaching for his pocket. "I know it's a lot. But it wasn't—"

But Vickie cut him off. "Don't."

He sighed, but he was too tense to argue, so instead he wound the car carefully down the dark cobblestone driveway and parked out front behind the hearse.

Priscilla waved to them from the porch, where she sat, a cigarette in her right hand.

That was a bad sign. She'd quit after college, and then she had said she quit again for good two years ago.

"Listen," said Vickie as he unbuckled his seat belt. He looked over at her. She had put on some sort of shimmering lip gloss on the ride over, and her hair fell in soft curls, a few gold specks, probably lingering from the last Sultry Sunday, bouncing off her natural brown. He wondered what she had dressed as this time. It was her armor. The makeup. The hair. The clothes. She'd dyed it back to brown, no highlights, he realized. It suited her, and even better, it would suit the places between his fingers where he wanted so badly to feel it. To tug it hard enough to make her pant.

Fuck, he was such a mess for her.

Again.

"Clearly, we are attracted to each other, and clearly the circumstances are less than ideal as of late. But it doesn't have to be awkward." She said it firmly, voice clear. "We have a lot to think about. And no rush. Grief does weird things to people."

Az bit his lip. Willed himself to come clean. To tell her he'd rather be with her and never touch another soul again than give her up. What was better, now that the gravedirt had worn off? Harsh truth that hurt, or a tiny lie to smooth away the wrinkles of complication?

"If that's what you want."

"Yeah." Vickie stared out the window, the dullness to her eyes disappearing as she saw his sister. Priscilla approached the car, looking thunderous, and banged on the hood of it.

"Evelyn's inside, taking pictures of everything. You coming out of there or do I need to threaten you with gravedirt again?" she bellowed, though Azrael knew her anger was more fear and frustration than rage.

"Too soon, Prissy, too soon. You forget you're not the only creature who favors it."

"It *was* my specialty, and I resent that Sexy Lexy took that away from me."

"Ugh. Please don't call him that," Az yelped, climbing out of the car. "I've had enough of gravedirt truth to last a lifetime."

Az ran to his sister, and when he hugged her, she returned the gesture. Even after the drive, he was shaken. He rarely sought out hugs. Growing up, they had all called him Prickly Azrael. The little cactus. But he needed a hug now.

"Thanks for coming, Vickie." Prissy released him, pulling ahead to walk with Vickie.

"We're hoping you can give it all a nonwitch perspective."

Goddess, he hoped that Vickie had never had reason to tell his sister about that mistake he'd made in college. He didn't need anyone, particularly his sister, to point out the irony of someone using gravedirt on him.

Az had once, drunk at Uncle Larry's retirement party, mentioned his undying love for a girl who, according to her illegally spelled roommate, had *absolutely no interest in him romantically whatsoever.*

He had never told Priscilla the girl was Vickie. His sister would have little patience if he made things awkward with their neighbor and friend. She had always been too enthusiastic in her support of their romance. Like the time right after he graduated when Priscilla ditched him for her girlfriend on a midnight hike. When he was alone with Vickie, she had dared him to help her cross skinny-dipping off her bucket list. To get naked. In the water.

He'd missed his chance then too. He had gone home the next day fuzzy, but the memory of watching her body from a few feet away in starlight had been burned onto his eyes. That's when he had written the bloody letter, and then failed to give it to her before they both left for college at the end of the summer.

Az had texted Vickie awkwardly, and they'd FaceTimed occasionally for a few years, reliving every single word for weeks afterward. Then he'd flown to see her. And fucked everything up. How he had managed to unfuck it and then have it refucked while not being able to *actually* fuck was beyond him.

And now his sister was plotting. He could see it on her face, in the twist of her lip. She was not spooked enough by their predicament to give up meddling.

If only he had turned around and talked to Vickie six years ago. If only he had been there, maybe things would have played out differently, and she wouldn't be indebted to a handsome, jealous devil. He could have been her handsome, jealous devil.

Az remembered what it was like six years ago.

The morning after was cold and desolate precipitation, lonelier than he had ever been as water streamed from the clouds, matting his hair and echoing his loss. Magic sizzled and extinguished, unused at his fingertips, which he kept apart to avoid misfires. He had forced his legs to keep walking, one foot in front of the other, moving forward when what he wanted to do was drop everything and stand there in the rain holding her, pressing kisses to her cheeks, and begging her to love him back even a tiny fraction of the amount he loved her.

He hadn't looked back once as he'd walked away. He couldn't bring himself to look.

And now here they were, back to the same holding pattern, but with his sister glaring at him, her arm through Vickie's the way he wanted his to be as they walked through the door.

Priscilla had never been patient, and there was a distinct possibility that she might unleash the house's charming swinging axes or wall nail traps on him if he stepped out of line. At the very least, he could count on the ghouls rattling walls at him. They always noticed when he came home with complicated feelings. He'd better take down any fragile art, just to be safe.

The door nudged him toward her a little, the house agreeing with his sister that he should brave the threat of death to be with Victoria Starnberger.

Az sighed, running a hand through his hair. Even the doorframe groaned at him, as though it was deeply disappointed, as he ignored its unsubtle gesture and entered. When he walked in last, the door shut sharply, nearly missing his head. The drawback of a semi-sentient house was that, like everyone else, it had *opinions* on how his life should go.

And honestly, damn if he didn't share its disappointment in this moment.

CHAPTER 18

Victoria

Mint and sage from the herb patch next to the crop of Venus flytraps wafted past Vickie, calming her despite the jarring sight of the shattered glass from the green panels missing from the side of the conservatory. The one with the cross and the circle drawn on it sat in the middle.

"Definitely the symbol of the megachurch," she murmured. "Can we be sure it's them? Isn't it a bit obvious to leave their own symbol?"

"I did a spell to check if it was done in authenticity or faked. It's authentic, so whatever it means, whoever drew it did it in earnest." Priscilla snapped her fingers, and a broom and a roll of duct tape appeared in each hand. She tossed the broom at Azrael, who caught it in such a way that Vickie couldn't help but look at those very talented fingers for an extra moment.

Stop it, she told herself. Home break-ins were not the place to feel frisky about Azrael Hart, witch extraordinaire, and his magical hands.

"Patch this up with plastic sheeting until we can get a new pane of glass in?" he asked his sister. There was no need to sweep, Vickie realized, but she remembered Azrael explaining why witches also had to clean up. It was one of the first rules of magic their parents had taught them, he had said.

The act of cleaning could be as important as the cleanliness, and with stress running high, it was Hart family protocol to fetch the broom with magic but do the sweeping by hand. She smiled as she watched him, thinking of how his parents would be happy to know their small lessons lived on.

"That sounds right," said Priscilla, as though echoing her thoughts. "A good, old-fashioned, do-it-yourself Benedict Hart cleanup, and then, once we buy the new panes, we snap to replace the glass, obviously, since that's not a skill set either of us possesses. Do we have any plastic drop cloths in the house? I don't want to summon the closest and risk accidentally stealing it from somewhere if I'm not sure."

"I'll go look," Vickie volunteered. She needed a moment to collect herself, and to stop thinking of how Azrael's breath felt against her collarbone and how his hard-on had pressed against her hip before the world had gone and turned upside down. To focus on the task at hand and not on the fingers now gripping a broom.

The door to the small wooden shed attached to the greenhouse was past the hemlock and the poison oak. Along the path, glorious roses sprang up in all shades of red and purple, blooming like gorgeous bruises against the pale green of the glass. Between the bloodred and the crimson sprouted shiny black roses, the kind only witches could grow, which Azrael's mother had used in healing potions and other small tinctures. Persephone had once explained that her son was a rose: sharp in some ways, soft in others, and too easy to wither under a harsh stare.

Vickie traced a finger across the tops of them, the petals so much softer than the thorns Persephone had treasured. Thorns, her neighbor had explained, were the truly precious part of roses, the things that made plant craft work perfectly. *People always try to use the petals*, she'd said, *but it's their loss, for the things that are most difficult to see the beauty in can sometimes be the most essential.* The memory made Vickie smile, though she wished that she had realized earlier that, under his thorny exterior, Azrael always could have loved her as more than a friend. Maybe they could be in love without ever touching, at least until Halloween. They could pretend there was no soul-crushing deadline on the possibility of their love.

They had more pressing issues now, though.

Next to the shed's brown door, and between the wood and the roses, was a gray three-tiered stone fountain carved with snakes and cherubs and filled with sparkling blue water that she dipped her hand into. She drew her fingers back before the tiny, razor-sharp jaws of miniature snapping turtles could close around them.

The shed was dark, and she couldn't see the light switch, but she heard Az call from outside the greenhouse. Part of her wished he would join her here without the glaring truth of light, but the other part wished he would stay away long enough for her to remember how she'd immolate him if she wasn't careful. To protect him, she needed to reconstruct the guards around her heart that he had sliced through so seamlessly when he returned to town.

"I can get the lights for you, Vickie." The sound of Az's voice from across the greenhouse slid against her like rain on smooth pebbles. There was no hiding the effect he had on her from herself.

She had admitted to herself too late that she had feelings for Azrael Hart, after all these years. Strong feelings. And she was going to have to deal with them eventually.

Ornate sconces on each wall lit up with flame, and the shed, as though sensing her presence, slammed its door shut. This dramatic, haunted house had always loved her. It hadn't frightened her, even as a small child. She could picture Benedict Hart, in his fancy suit, explaining that the house showed affection by shutting the door to the room, like it was giving you a hug.

Hart Manor was old and ornery and full of sharp things and spires that twisted into the clouded sky, but the house knew Vickie, and she knew it, and it would always be a safe space for anyone who cared for the family. She had stared into the darkest corners of the house long enough to know that the dark not only stared back but did so with kindness. There was a love in the sentience of Hart Manor that was more than her parents had ever offered her. The dark wood panels of the house were a home and a friend to Victoria, along with the Harts, and as a child, it was adaptable to what she needed.

All she needed, then and now, was to fit into a family full of affection. A family so different from her own.

Azrael was her oldest friend, and there might not be anyone she cared for more. For a time, she'd thought she might care more for Natalie, or Robbie, or even her best friend, Claire, but Claire had drifted away after Vickie dropped out. Besides Priscilla, and by default, Evelyn, Vickie didn't have close friends anymore. Her parents had cut her off from one social circle and leaving school had cut her off from another.

Her friends and family were here, in this house, and she was more than willing to dig through a dusty ancient shed to help them. There were no plastic sheets in the organized stacks of material on metal shelves, but she found a box of extra-large garden garbage bags that would do nicely.

On a whim, Vickie passed the racks to the sturdy wooden desk in the back. A row of serious-looking knives hung above it, but she knew from the chips and shavings that they were for carving wood and not bodies. This was where Benedict had practiced his shadow craft, the brand of witchery where the practitioner could construct a magical token out of whatever medium spoke to them, and then cast the shadow of that thing's essence for a time. A gargoyle for protection, a dragon to do battle. A cupid to mend hearts. She could have made good use of any one of those.

But instead, sitting on the table was a roughly hewn wooden angel. An archangel. *For Azrael*, she thought. Occasionally, the fire that brewed in Vickie's veins pulled her toward objects, telling her that they would help her behold a spirit. Her pulse beat faster, half fear and half curiosity, as she picked up the carving with both hands.

It heated up, and Benedict Hart appeared, sitting in the chair. Alone. His golden eyes softened, and he spoke swiftly, as though he had been waiting for her to summon him.

"Victoria. How is Azrael?"

"Mr. Hart." She paused; it was strange to see him without his wife. "Grieving, but other than that, doing well. Azrael just started teaching. I think he's going to be extraordinary. That he already is, really."

Benedict nodded, his white hair shaking back and forth, and let out a little grunt of satisfaction.

"Good. That suits him. But we have other things to speak of. Your gift."

Vickie was glad he'd called it a gift. She hated when her parents, the very people who had stuck her with it, used the word *curse*.

"You're not the only one with bargained-for power. Yours allows you to see souls and burn the thing that bound them to this world as sacrifice. There are others with gifts like this, gifts that allow kindnesses. You can summon the dead. Some can persuade them. Others walk in dreams, or enchant with beauty in any craft. These are the gifts of the lesser devils. Of your devil. And he might be tricky and haunt you with his caveats. Still, he does follow a code."

"But?"

"Someone has made a worse bargain with a much more terrible prince of Hell. A greater devil. Their bargains are rarer even than yours. And more deadly. The ability to reap bodies and souls. Sometimes the ability to see the future or the past. Gifts humans shouldn't have. It complicates things too much. It may not have been a bargain that greater devil made willingly, which means it may not be limited in scope and power the way it should be." Benedict's transparent brow wrinkled. He cracked his knuckles and tapped them on the table.

"Who?"

"I'm not sure. It's unclear, and things are . . . a bit murkier on this side of life. Time, existence, identity . . . they all stretch and contract, blur, and blend together. I know that I love Persephone, and that she is my world. I know that I care about my children. Dying is letting go, and there's deep sadness there, but also a fading connection to the living world. I'm losing small parts of the life I used to have—names, faces, memories, they're all slipping away, to ultimately make it easier when I slip away too."

"It's a gradual process, then?" Vickie had long suspected this, for the ghosts could always be summoned until their most beloved objects from their earthly lives were gone from the world. Then they burned, whether to the more lush and lovely parts of a great beyond or to a cool and torturous damnation. When they were ash, she always sensed they were gone, from this plane, at least.

Benedict flickered, and the wooden angel, carved in enough detail to show a craftsman's face, trembled in her hands, growing hot. She was sad that Azrael wouldn't get to see it. He would have loved the memento of his father.

"Have care, Vickie. Be ready when you go to the church. For now, what Azrael needs is in the family grimoire. Find out who has dealt with the devil with baser intentions than yours. And be honest with Azrael. Even when it is difficult. He puts on a good front, my son, but he needs—"

The figurine flamed out, cutting Benedict off.

Vickie wasn't sure how long she'd stood staring at the empty desk and chair when a knock at the shed door startled her out of her reverie. The door was refusing to open unless she allowed it. Hart Manor could be downright loyal when it wanted to. The walls tucked in protectively around her, bending ever so slightly to the middle.

"Dammit, let me in, you pile of brittle bricks." Fists slammed against the door again. "Victoria! Vickie?!" Azrael's voice was muffled with concern and the weight of the wood between them.

Vickie pulled open the door, and his face relaxed into relief.

"I thought I heard you talking," Az said.

"I accidentally summoned your dad."

"That tracks." His hand came up, reaching for her, but he shoved it into his pocket. "Guess I'll have to learn to curb that habit," he said, smiling wryly.

"I mean, only if you want to live." She smiled up at him and reached for the plastic bags that would do in the place of glass. "Come on." She gestured to the door, and to Evelyn and Priscilla waiting for them.

"I've submitted a formal report of the stolen plants," Evelyn announced. "But all of the things together, well, it will take some time to process, since there's no immediate threat. I can only keep the Council from this for a little while longer. You have until the end of October, but once the veil thins, it's too dangerous."

Prissy glared at her. "Fine. We need to find out who else cut a deal in Hallowcross. Is there anything unusual?" Priscilla tapped a finger on her chin. "Any instances of magic gone awry, or working weirdly? It could be something small."

A sinking feeling in the pit of her stomach told her that she almost knew what Azrael was going to say before he said it.

"My asshole boss."

"Being an asshole is not a crime," said Priscilla with a sigh. "Though if it were, things sure would go a lot more smoothly."

"He's not just an asshole. He seems immune to the little world-healing spells." Azrael ran his hand through his hair, shook it out, and cracked his knuckles. So many nervous tics in a row for her handsome, angsty witch.

Prissy's face softened. "Mom's spells?"

"Mom's spells. I thought maybe he would be less angry, and nicer to my colleagues. To the kids. But the only thing that worked was a very childish bit to stick a Post-it note to his back."

"Magic didn't work on him at all, save for attaching a note to his jacket?" Evelyn's voice was sharp. "But still, nothing's tripped my alarm at the school," she mused. "I suppose it could be possible that he has some sort of protective spell work, but if that's the case, then if it is him, he's already powerful enough that we ought to tread lightly. You're certain the magic didn't work on him directly?"

"It did not." She looked at him the same way he had looked at a student last week who had sworn up and down that he had turned in his paper, only to discover it in his own backpack later and turn it in sheepishly.

"We need to keep an eye on him. A close eye, Azrael. But be careful. He sounds like the sort we don't want to find out any of our secrets regardless."

"Agreed," Azrael said. "It's possible he's not the person, but even so, I wouldn't want him knowing I'm a witch."

"Precisely," said Evelyn. "We think we know the motives behind the fake psychic attack," she continued, glancing at Priscilla. "I shouldn't be telling you until the Council rules officially, but they are dragging their feet on account of the woman still being in a coma. They think the perpetrator believed she was a real medium. A witch. They're looking for who did it."

Tension gathered in Vickie's chest. She really hoped this wasn't about Chet. If it was, goddess, based on what Az had said, she couldn't think of anyone who would be worse to add to the fray of their magical problems.

"I'll go back to the hospital one more time. I had no luck summoning anything, but who knows. Maybe something will jump out at me."

Evelyn sighed, dragging a hand across her face. "The Council's been over it a hundred times, but it can't hurt to have a nonwitch take a look."

"I'll go Wednesday," she said.

"Be careful." Priscilla looked meaningfully at her, and at Azrael.

"I'm always careful."

Azrael coughed but said nothing. She glared at him. "You

just focus on telling me everything you can think of about this. The more I know, the more likely I am to spot anything that I should be noticing."

"There are few reasons to try to take the soul of a witch," Az said, and Vickie knew it was for her benefit. Priscilla and Evelyn looked significantly horrified, and whatever he was going to reveal had to be something they had already considered. She needed to know, though.

Vickie stepped toward Az, stopping short of deadly distance. "What are they?"

"One is to trap it, to force a favor. Usually magic craft of some sort, potion work, or shadow craft. There's old-fashioned bigotry and hate, of course—taking for the sake of killing. Either of those are better than the third."

"Those are the *good* options?"

"There's a reason we don't tell people we're witches," said Prissy quietly.

"The third reason is to eat the soul. To consume it, and with it, its power. Soul eaters are the worst kind of monsters. They're human, so shackled by their biases, but able to do magic undeterred. Undetected. It's why we sometimes wonder how an evil man in power could get so much power. How evil could manifest in such awful ways, and how money and status can prevent human justice. Usually, if the person is really bad, it's a soul eater. The loss of compassion is what kills the humanity in people."

"We may have time," said Evelyn. "Not much, but some."

"How do you figure?" Vickie was winding her hair around her finger, nervous.

"Because those sorts of ceremonies, even by a human, only take if the veil is thin between the worlds. It's a time for the resolution of bargains. Culmination. A harvest, often physical and spiritual. A guiding bonfire directing spirits home."

"Halloween," she said. "Why is it always my favorite holiday?"

Evelyn nodded. "Samhain is the closest one, yes."

"Az, can we talk about what your dad said?"

"When I was talking to your dad . . ." Vickie picked at chipping nail polish on her thumb, reassuring herself with the repetitive motion that she hadn't failed Az in this. "I didn't realize what I'd find in here or I would have come to get you and Prissy before . . ."

Azrael swallowed and stepped toward her in the shed, pausing a safe distance away. The torchlight illuminated his curls, and the gold speckles in his eyes were tiny flames now.

But it was Priscilla who spoke, her voice cracking just a little. "What did he say?"

"To make sure you and Azrael are okay, but also what we know: that someone else has cut a deal with the devil for a slightly different gift. And that you need to check the family grimoire for what you need." Vickie bit back the part where Benedict had beseeched her to be honest, but it lingered, heavy on her tongue.

The truth wanted out as much as her body wanted Az. But there was no gravedirt now, and she didn't have to give in to either.

"This is exhausting." Priscilla gave Evelyn a lingering look.

"Absolutely. Perhaps a trip to the home gym could do you wonders? We could work off the stress." Evelyn threaded a hand through Priscilla's, and she nodded. The two of them slipped out of the greenhouse.

"Well, fuck." Azrael ran a hand through his hair. "We'd better check to see if there are any tracing spells for that sort of thing. Come on, we can feed Emily Lickinson on the way."

"I guess I was hoping for wild nights, huh?" she quipped, waiting to see if he would remember their entire month on Dickinson in high school poetry class together, and how she secretly loved it, though her parents drove her college admissions goals in other directions.

A smile snuck up the side of his face. Crooked and unfairly handsome.

"Who would have guessed a business major would take enough lit classes to whisper sweet poetry?"

Vickie smiled back at him. "I contain multitudes," she said, smirking now.

This earned her a chuckle, and he shoved his hands into his pockets, cocking his head toward the door.

"Let's head to the library. Emily's unofficially taken up the role of book guardian."

CHAPTER 19

Azrael

The fluffy white cat meowed loudly at him, making her presence known as he pushed open the double doors to the library. As soon as he stepped inside, the earthy scent of old books and amber wood shelves alleviated the tension in his shoulders as the cozy room welcomed him. He'd always loved it here.

Vickie knelt down and smiled, holding her palm out to Emily, and to Azrael's utter surprise, the indomitably aloof Emily Lickinson purred and rubbed her head against Vickie's outstretched fingers. It had taken months for Emily to warm up to him in California, but she'd welcomed Vickie from the start.

"You are the bustle in this house after death." Vickie said it softly, almost to herself.

Az tried not to lose his mind. It wasn't fair that she was beautiful and kind and smart, and that they quoted poetry at each other but couldn't touch. Emily Dickinson herself would have rolled over in her grave to know it; she was certainly no stranger to pining. Sometimes Az lost himself in obsessive details from his memory, like the feeling of sliding his fingers along Vickie's skin or the deep dimple behind her knee where her plump flesh gathered under his fingers. The sort of touch he'd only know in dreams now.

Emily hissed at Az a little as he gestured for Vickie to get up.

"Come on, Vickie," he said, reaching for her, and trying not to cry at the way she shook her head and took a step back, reminding him. His hand dropped, flexing in agony instead of tingling, as it had before the curse, when their fingers could lace together.

Just because they couldn't feel their magic hum on contact now didn't make it any less real for him.

The library was a sweeping, two-story affair with bookshelves stretching up to the top of the grand ceiling and a cutaway loft furnished with couches he and Priscilla had turned into the bows of pirate ships and hangman's stands as children. On the first floor, near the back, there was a set of magnificent high-back chairs facing a fireplace, which he snapped his fingers to light. Another snap and the temperature set so that the roaring fire warmed them comfortably.

"It's a bit risky, isn't it, a fireplace in a library?" Vickie asked, smile stretching wide as she moved closer to it.

"Well, you know what they say."

She looked at him suspiciously. "What do they say?"

Azrael grinned and winked. "I just can't help my shelf."

Vickie groaned. It was reminiscent enough of other moans to heat his skin.

He walked over to the grate and lifted it, setting the pewter cauldron directly into the flames.

"It's enchanted so that it can't burn outside of the fireplace, and it's better for spell work like what we will need for the tracing. I just need to look it up." He snapped his fingers. Books shuddered out of the way, and pages ruffled from the highest shelf. The familiar heft of the family grimoire landed in his hands, and Emily Lickinson made her way back to them along with the book. She purred once, circled his feet, and padded away to sit watchful at the door. A few strands of long white hair lingered at his pant cuffs, tickling his nose. A smile tugged at the corners of his mouth.

"She's a mortal cat familiar," said Vickie, and her laughter made his chest warm. Her eyes glinted. "She's a *fur*midable guardian."

Devil damn him, it was sweet agony to be around her. Finding someone the exact brand of weird he was, well, that was rare.

The leather cover of the Hart family grimoire was worn with time, but the carving of their name and crest was still clearly visible in the flourishing lines of an anatomically correct heart with magic eyes and runes encircling it. Leaves patterned the inside of the heart, and in the flickering firelight, it almost looked like it could genuinely be beating. Only a Hart witch could summon this book in this library, and Az relaxed knowing this was one way he would always be connected to his parents, even in their death.

Witches had ancestral magic. Bone magic, passed down from parent to child, whether by blood or by choice. When predecessors died, their magic seeped into the grimoire and into the next generation, strengthening their inheritors, so long as those children did not take the powers by force.

It's how Az had known, heartbreakingly, the moment it was too late to come home. When his parents died, it had felt like the time he went on vacation in Costa Rica, and dove into a beautiful pool after a long hike, resurfacing refreshed, like he could do anything. The cool wash of power and then emergence into a different self, an Azrael who could no longer avoid his magic, had told him that his parents were gone. One after the other, like diving in twice.

Az already felt the pages flip with greater ease than they ever had, and he knew, as though a reassuring hand rested on his shoulder, that part of Benedict and Persephone that would never leave him. The passing of that magic was never intended to be a burden that reminded the younger generations of the dead, but rather a nudge, that the shock of grief was a gift. That it was the thing that allowed the memory of his parents to persist.

"Witches know that our dead loved ones are never really

gone," Az said. "They live on in our memories. In our spells, and in every decision we make. In our magic, and in our bones. Every step."

"That's lovely," said Vickie, stepping closer, though not close enough. Az could smell her again—berries and lavender, and, he thought, with his hand deep in the ancestral magic of the grimoire that sharpened his senses, lust. He had so much power, touching this book. He could read her, and he knew, *knew*, that she wanted him as much as he did her. The knowledge of it burned through him, tautening his entire body like a rubber band pulled back and stretched too thin, ready to snap.

"Here," Az said, feeling the warmth of her next to him and of the fire, and fighting the uncomfortable instinct to go completely rigid against the zipper of his jeans just knowing what Vickie was feeling.

Az pointed at the book to distract himself from the blood rushing to his lower body.

"The tracing spell is simple." He snapped his fingers, summoning the necessary herbs from the garden, and a speck of gravedirt from the pot that Priscilla used to ferment it, mixing in the ashes of a gravedigger, willingly given, every so often to ensure that it was potent enough to provoke truth.

At the behest of his snapping fingers, the ingredients stirred themselves in the cauldron with a long metal spoon.

"Now what?"

Az shut the grimoire, stroking the cover once, lovingly, and then snapped his fingers, making the book disappear again.

"Now we wait, and in an hour, you offer something of yours to it, and we hope that it's enough to trace a similar gift."

"The question is . . ." she started, stepping closer to him, close enough that it was hard to ignore all the tiny moments of her perfection.

So.

Hard.

"What should we do in the meantime?" Vickie's eyes were wide, her cheeks flushed.

The house shuddered a little, and the doors to the library slammed shut, the large wooden bolt sliding closed. Velvety drapes swished shut with care. Soft flame jumped up in chandeliers, and the record player popped on; a vinyl recording of a passionate tango flooded the air.

"I think the house has some ideas for us," Az said, and he wondered if maybe the house was right. Perhaps he could let himself be wild and untethered with her for just a little while. They almost certainly were approaching dangerous territory, and who knew how long any of their lives were, in the end? "There's something I need to tell you, but how could we deny the house? The Hart Manor wants what it wants, Vickie. Let's pretend. We can be normal, for a moment."

The smile she gave him in return for his foolishness dazzled him. His heart could hurt for this later; he didn't care. He closed the distance between them, as far as he could without dying, and snapped his fingers. The recording switched to Hozier, she was his darling, and Azrael was starving.

He snapped his fingers, donning gloves to avoid catastrophe. Eight years too late, his traitorous fingers finally listened, running across her cheek and tucking her messy brown hair behind her ear. Vickie sucked in a sharp breath at his touch.

"Shall we dance?" She asked it so solemnly that it almost broke him.

Az swallowed. His clothes felt too tight, and the tension building against his zipper pressed an outline into his jeans he definitely could not pretend away.

"What did you have in mind in terms of avoiding death?" Everything was too much for him now: the memories, the chemistry, and the clothes. There were far too many clothes. He smiled at her. "Or would you like me to die holding you? I'd be willing. It would be worth it."

It would, he realized, and he thought his heart might beat out of his chest, or explode entirely with all the things he wanted from her.

"Don't die. We can think of something." Vickie's mouth tugged a little. "How hard can it be for two people who can't touch to dance?"

"How much do you want to pretend?" Az reached up to trace the side of her arm, a glove's fabric between him and the utter annihilation that he longed for. She stepped closer.

This was such a bad idea.

"Pretend that this isn't just one stolen moment in a very romantic wingman of a library. That things are easier. No curse. No restrictions. No misunderstandings."

"I can do that," he bit out. Goddess, his heart would shatter for this later. But he was weak, and he wanted her, and the fire crackled, highlighting remnants of glitter in her soft brown waves. There always seemed to be a little bit of glitter in Vickie's hair.

Vickie smiled, plush pink lips stretching wide, and then stepped back again to safety.

"Look," she said, pointing to the corner.

"My knight in bejeweled armor," Az said softly, looking at the suit of armor. Unlike the set in the entryway, this one was hollow, uninhabited by spirits. Though he didn't try it on often, a man with a full suit of armor at home can't resist the occasional summer renaissance festival while home from college. Or, if he was honest, the occasional drunken sword fight with imaginary foes.

And now it was what he needed, a romantic homage to knights and ladies of storybooks.

The suit of armor was a perfect solution; he was witch enough to have already tailored it so that he could move easily, and his drunken antics in years prior had suddenly put him in a position to be perfectly prepared for this very occasion.

Vickie smiled at him wickedly, and for a moment he couldn't understand what it was that had her looking so pleased with herself.

Until she traced her fingers along the hem of her shirt, pulling it off over her head, and then sliding her sweatpants down to her knees and wriggling a little, stepping out of them to reveal the fancy underthings he now suspected she favored. The unexpected lack of clothing, paired with a lavender see-through bra and the neon pink lace thong against her smooth, freckled skin, made Az's heart throb. Among other things.

He could get used to that sort of a predilection.

"Magic me into something elegant enough to dance with you in a suit of armor." Her face was earnest, green eyes wide in a challenge.

"It would be my pleasure. Just don't move for a second."

Vickie paused, one arm holding the elbow of the other, skin prickling in the air.

Az flicked his fingers, and Vickie was wearing a long-sleeved, high-necked, pink floral-patterned gown he remembered from the costumes in the attic, complete with gloves and boots. It was fitted, but it covered her securely enough to help prevent actually burning for her.

"Is this your mother's?"

He shook his head. "No. I don't know whose it was, but Persephone Hart would never have been caught dead in anything so festive."

She smiled, picking up the heavy, finely stitched fabric.

"I look like an extra in a Jane Austen movie. And I can't walk in these shoes."

"Yeah, but an attractive extra. At least as attractive as any rendition of Darcy moving through the misty moors, and that's saying something." He snapped his fingers, and the shoes were gone, replaced with her worn green Chucks. "I was really, really into him in that moment. My very own pansexual awakening."

"I remember." She bit her lip. "I think we left off in an unfair advantage for me," she whispered. "I showed you mine . . ."

"My lady." Az gave a mock bow and pulled his shirt over his head. "Your wish is my command."

"Fuck me, Azrael. I thought I felt them in the Packard, but fuck, when did those abs happen?"

"It was a long lockdown, and I was bored and lonely. We need to work on this *fuck me* expression," he said, shifting his weight to prevent his blood from going straight south.

"Never," she said solemnly. "Now take off your pants, and let's dance."

"You're missing a step there," he said wryly, pulling off his pants and tossing them at her. He stood in front of her in his boxers for a minute longer than he needed to, not mentioning that he would magic light sweatpants and a shirt on under the suit of armor because, frankly, it was not comfortable to wear a suit of armor naked. If she wanted him to strip, he'd do it, gladly, old rumors from high school and all.

A few snaps later, and he was suited up, peering at her through the visor. Holding out a hand.

Vickie stepped into his arms, sliding one around his metal waist and shivering.

"Cold?"

"No," she said. "I'm just glad you're willing to do all this, Az. It's— It means a lot."

He took her gloved hand in his and pressed it against the breastplate of the armor.

"I would do more for you without batting an eye, Victoria."

Quietly, she pulled him closer, and he wrapped her waist with his other arm.

"Sometimes I pretend that everything that could go right did, instead of the opposite. I pretend that it has just been me and you, since we were kids." He was glad for the armor to hide whatever emotional tornado wrecked his face as he admitted that one.

"I think things like that too," she said, pressing a hand against the metal. "Sometimes."

It was a little more clunky than he'd imagined dancing with her to be, because, of course, in his dreams he wore a different sort of suit. But the smile on her face, stretching from ear to ear, and the laughter gently nudging him into a whimsical happiness, made it worth it. A thousand times over, he would do things strangely if it meant being with her. He hoped he wasn't about to ruin it with honesty.

"Vickie, about what Priscilla and Evelyn figured out," he said.

She tensed in his arms at the words. "What?"

"It would be a very serious solution, but a soul-sealing ceremony is an option for us, to get around the curse. Not that we would have to. And not assuming you would want to."

"Like what your parents did? The seal?"

"Yes," he said, looking at her through the visor. "The soul seal."

And because he wanted so much for what they were pretending to be real, he told her.

"If I'm honest, all pretending aside, I would turn to ash for you. I'd burn if you touch me. And, if you wanted to, though I have zero expectation that you do, I'd absolutely fix this by making it permanent between us. I'd seal my soul to yours, if you'd have me."

"I'm not sure I completely understand the soul seal, or how it would fix the curse." She looked up at him, a wrinkle between her eyebrows. "Can you explain it?"

"It's permanent binding. Like my parents did. It's a bit like tattooing your soul onto another person, but they're marking the soul on yours too. The two branded together. Prissy thinks it's a way to get around the curse. If my soul is tied to yours, then you can't reap it."

Her eyebrows raised. "Because you can't reap your own soul, and if our souls were bound together, then I couldn't. Oh . . ." She trailed off, chewing on her lip. It was a lot, but he was in it now, so he went on.

"I'd still rather break my own heart than tether you to do something you're not sure you want. I would never chain you in that way. I would want you to be free, rather than with me, if that makes you happy."

Vickie remained silent, but she pressed herself closer to him, as close as two people separated by old-fashioned cloth and a suit of armor could be.

The music rose and fell.

"Is it too much, Vickie?" He murmured the question. He wished he could brush her hair back from her forehead. Cradle her face in his hands.

She shook her head. "No," she whispered. "It's a lot, but it's good to hear all our options, Az. And it means a lot to know how you feel. I'm thinking. Let's just stay here for a moment. Don't stop."

That was *something*. A hope flared in his chest. He would never stop.

They turned in slow circles, over and over across the dance floor, until his feet grew sore from dancing in heavy metal and his heart grew sore from holding her but not really pressing against her skin.

When the house slowed the music to a low background noise, she sighed.

"I'll think about what you're asking me," she said. Her voice sounded careful, but not, thank goddess, scared. "Can we sit down for a little?"

"Anything you want." He meant it. His heart was on a platter. His whole self was laid bare for her to burn. Everything he owned, which was only half a haunted manor and a cranky yet affectionate cat.

"I've always loved those armchairs," she said, and he snapped his fingers. The chairs slid close to them, one directly behind her.

"Are you going to change, or do you want me to do it for you?" Az was honest with himself enough to know that he was motivated not just by knightly chivalry, but also by a keen interest in seeing her in her underwear, however briefly, once more.

"Take off the dress for me. I know you want to. And I wouldn't mind another glimpse of everything you've got going on under that suit of armor either." She gestured toward him, and he magicked them out of dress and armor. They stood there, underwear and space between them, before he shut his eyes and forced himself to snap his fingers and put them both back in their clothes.

She pulled her sweatpant-clad legs underneath her, settling into the velvet armchair, and he returned the armor to its rightful place in the corner.

He smiled, sinking into his chair.

"Azrael," Vickie said breathily. "I know this complicates everything. But I'm going to think it over, the soul sealing and all the what-ifs. I have to admit that I might not be ready to brand our souls together in this moment, but I want to be honest. It's not as scary as I thought hearing something like that would be. And I, I love all the little charming bits of you. The abs. The parental puns. The neurotic worrying. Everything about you is for me."

Azrael took a few deep breaths and tried to remember his name—she had just said it—and wondered what he was doing here. Gave himself a moment to calm down, snapping his fingers to brush her hair gently, and then again to magic a stick of lip balm into her hand when she rubbed her lips together.

"Everything about you is for me, too, Vickie," he said, his voice quiet. Solemn, like he was vowing it to her. Like it was a promise. "No matter what you decide you want. You can pretend or not."

She smiled and looked at him, applying the ChapStick in an impossibly sexy glide that he would definitely think about later.

Among other things. So many other things. Some lavender, some pink.

"What would you do if you could do anything at all? Not for pretend, but if you could for real?"

"I'd kiss you," he said, his voice coming out low and laced with longing.

She waggled her eyebrows.

"Where?"

"There would be many delicious places to choose from, but

for right now, I think I'd choose the press of your lips against mine. The way I miss already."

She bit her lip. "I have an idea."

"I love ideas."

"From a show."

"What do you know, I also *love* shows."

Vickie giggled and propped her head onto her elbow. "Can you get us plastic wrap?"

"Your wish is my command." He snapped his fingers, and the roll appeared on the arm of her chair.

"It's an old trick, but a good one." She stood up. "Face me." Her voice was thick, honeyed. He wanted to taste it. He needed to taste it.

She stretched the plastic wrap out, carefully tearing an arm's length of it off on the perforated edge. "You hit me like a hurricane tonight," she murmured, and she leaned down to where he sat, raising the wrap between them.

"Is that bad?"

"No." She leaned closer. "It's just big."

It wasn't quite a kiss, lips against thin plastic, but it wasn't quite not, either, with the plushness of hers against his, and the desperate, deadly desire to bite her bottom lip unspooling in his stomach. He wanted to reach up and touch her face; he had everything he needed already in this one lingering, chaste kiss.

"I think I could lose myself in this," he said.

She pulled back and lowered the barrier. "Don't." Her face was drawn. "You mean too much to me to lose."

He swallowed, unable to collect his emotions completely. "I won't."

"The tracing spell, then?" She stepped back and toward the fire.

"Yes, it's ready." He joined her, snapping to still the spoon in the cauldron for a moment.

"What do I need to do?"

"A strand of hair, lit on fire and dropped into the cauldron, should do the trick," he said, and Vickie, cheeks still flushed with the almost kiss and all the emotion that he had wrung from her, nodded and complied.

Her scent, lavender and strawberry, brushed his nose as she stepped back from the fire.

This pretending was going to hurt in the morning when he woke up without her.

Az wasn't sure he cared, though.

CHAPTER 20

Victoria

Vickie would have to go home as soon as they were done with the spell. There was no way she could stay the night. She had to work in a few hours. And if she didn't get some sleep after the enormity of finding out about the soul seal, and then actually considering the soul seal, of the emotions and longing tied up in that plastic-wrap kiss, of all of it on top of not being able to touch, on top of their fuckup six years ago, she might lose herself in real feelings. Lose the friendship and the only family she had now. She wasn't willing to let him go, even if they were just friends, now that she finally had him back. And the idea of being eternally bound to him at some point, well, it wasn't as terrifying as it maybe should have been.

But it was awfully soon for that kind of decision.

He deserved her certainty, and if she moved forward and acted on the sneaking feelings that were about now, and more than sex, and not just history, and a delicate dance of never touching, she had to be absofuckinglutely sure. That type of certainty should take her time.

It was fine to fuck around and brainstorm creative ways to get off without fully touching until her legs shook and she screamed his name, but she didn't want to play the part of the game where she fell asleep next to the familiar form of Azrael, on a separate bed or from the other side of a wall. That was too close to always.

Vickie didn't want to know how much she could pretend not to be tempted to kill him just to feel his lips on hers, without anything between them, the moment before he died, for it felt earnest, and it felt like they could love each other, really love each other. A part of her crumbled at the fear of that it was *loved*, and not *love*. Could love go on without touch? Would it wither in disuse? The fear that what he had done in the library—what they had done when they danced into more than just friendship—had been some sort of twisted blip, pounded into her in thigh-clenching enthusiastic rhythm from the record player. That same part had blossomed again when he admitted that it was now too. Fear and hope, past and present, things were complicated.

Always just a friend, though, and wasn't it better that way? What would happen if she let herself feel for him fully, if she bound herself to him and then he found her wanting later? How would he feel, waking up ten years from now, or twenty, or thirty, if she agreed to solve the problem with the sort of magic that would take away their future choices to look elsewhere if it didn't work out? Vickie feared that choosing him, in that way, might mean losing him if they forced something neither of them was ready for.

The way she had lost him, for years, after that ill-advised incident. Which it turned out, had been even more foolish than she'd realized.

These problems were for later Vickie.

Azrael was pouring the contents of the potion over a map he'd set on a carpet near the hearth. A few droplets hit it and disappeared; the thick shag seemed magically resistant. The liquid settled and swirled, and drifted in giant blue and gray waves to the northern corner of the map. Havenwall. She frowned. She had been expecting the church, or the high school. Something to lead them directly to Chet.

Not this, which suggested that maybe Azrael's boss was just

a jackass, after all. It meant a three-hour drive, and there was no way they could do it tonight. Maybe Hazel could handle the shop, or she could open late. Close for the day if she had to. It wasn't ideal, but it would be all right.

"I'll scry again later, but I think what we need is in the graveyard there. You can stay here, and we can leave first thing in the morning," he said. His pupils were blown wide, but under his eyes, shadows lingered, purple and blue traces of restless nights.

Grief had hit Azrael Hart, and she ought to respect that too. Give him time to process. To protect her own heart by leaving. To avoid taking advantage, as much as she wanted to see if he still had those velvet curtains around his bed, and if they could be magicked to be the only things between them.

He pulled her hand away when she went to touch. Like he didn't need her the way she needed him. Before she remembered that what he rejected, with her touch, was sudden death.

Vickie shook her head. "I can't. I have to work in like four hours, Az. I need to go home and change. Can I borrow your bike?"

"I can drive you again, or put you up in a guest room and take you early. I wouldn't assume anything, and the house made you welcome here before."

She shook her head. "I need some time to process. This has been a lot, with the break-in and the scrying. And the news about our options. Good 'a lot,' too, with the dancing and what not. But I need to clear my head and I need to sleep on my own pillow."

Azrael's eyes clouded and he opened his mouth, but then shut it again, whatever words he had in response dying on his lips. He shook his head.

"I get it. Maybe another time. Wednesday? When you're closed? I can call in sick. We could stop by the hospital too. Check on Madam Cleopatra."

She nodded, unable to find the right words to bridge the gap between the past, the impossibility, and what was now reality.

"I'll drive you back. Seriously," he said. The shadows under his eyes were deeper than she remembered.

"No thanks, Az. I'm good on the bike. Really."

"Are you sure?" He sounded uncertain.

"Please." She needed solitude and the chill of the night air against her face. The space to think outside of the spell of his nearness.

Az's face softened. "Of course." He snapped his fingers twice. "The bike is sitting out front with a helmet. There are jackets in the hall closet if you need. Text me when you get home, though?"

"Always." It had become an unspoken tradition, sometime in early September. They texted when they went places. When they woke up. Before they went to bed.

He snapped his fingers and the remaining potion vanished. Rubbing his temples, Az said, "I'll pick you up early Wednesday. Maybe seven?"

She nodded. "Text before you leave. I'll be ready by the time you're outside the shop."

"Vickie." Az looked at her, searching her face for something, and settled on a gesture instead. "I don't want to give up just because it's complicated. I want you. I want to be with you. Whatever this looks like. I'm all in."

She sighed. He deserved her certainty. "I want to be with you too. But we need to be reasonable and think it through here. I don't want to slip up and kill you. And I don't want to jump into something permanent just because our choices are limited. We're friends first, always. We have things to do. Feelings, for sure, but also a mystery to unravel. Jobs to think about. Death to avoid. We can take a beat. See where it takes us. While we figure it out, whenever either of us needs to, we call a pretend."

I can't afford to lose my best friend again, she thought to herself. To heartache, or worse, to murder caused by her own hands. She didn't want to rush into forever with the person she loved most, not when the consequences of one stumble, one misstep, were too great. She held her tears. She held them long enough to hug Azrael—a careful, chaste, gloved-riddled, arms-only affair of a goodbye—before stepping away. She moved quickly, the physical distance between them an effective barrier for her sneaking feelings.

"Vickie," he said, scrubbing a hand over his face and striding toward her.

"Don't." She held up a hand. "I just need a few moments on my way out to collect myself. Please. Stay here." She stopped hard on the last word, and he opened his mouth as if to argue, but then closed it again, shoving hands into his pockets.

Good. It was better this way. It gave her a moment to clear her head if he didn't fight her on it.

He mumbled about cross-referencing the location with a few other maps in the library, and she let the door slide shut behind her, shoving it back closed when it tried to reopen and invite her in once more.

Faking nonchalance, Vickie darted through the foyer to say goodbye to Priscilla and Evelyn. The pair sat at the dining room table, a magical whiteboard between them with numbers and words and symbols spinning in Priscilla's looping, thin script, and Evelyn's near-perfect round letters. The were splitting several bottles of wine over the Council business on the board.

"Hey, one of these days, you and Az should take a midnight hike," said Priscilla, winking and not even attempting to hide it. "Like we did in high school, remember?"

"I remember you ditching us to go run off with your girlfriend."

"That sounds like you," said Evelyn fondly. She appeared much more relaxed after a glass of wine. Vickie wondered how much of her apparent coolness was really nerves.

"We'll all go hiking another time, Priscilla. Azrael's got witching to do." She hoped Prissy wouldn't push her on it.

"Come and have a drink, then?" Priscilla held the wine up and waved her hand so that the giant polar bear rug on the steps roared slightly in agreement. "See? Even Franklin wants you to join us."

"Next time, Prissy. I promise. I have an early morning. Az and I are going to the hospital and then Havenwall on Wednesday. I think we can figure out what we're missing here. See if there's a link between the attempted soul stealing and the megachurch and whatever the scrying found in Havenwall. The tracing spell says what we need is there."

Evelyn raised a sculpted eyebrow. From what Azrael had told Vickie, Evelyn had not been pleased about any of this. Something about foolhardy actions without Council approval, but he said Priscilla had brushed it off—for now, anyway. "Anything the Council should be aware of?"

"Just buy us a little more time before they get involved. We'll keep you posted." She paused. "Havenwall will help us put together all of these pieces."

Prissy fixed her with a brown-eyed stare, and though her eyes had a sleepy drunk sheen to them and her signature braid was coming loose, her severe expression made Vickie want to confess everything.

"Put a pin in that, killer. What's going on with you and Azrael?" Priscilla squinted at Vickie; she hoped the younger Hart didn't have any gravedirt on her. Evelyn grabbed Priscilla's hands, rubbing each one separately in one of her own in a romantic gesture that, it did not escape Vickie, also prevented her old neighbor from snapping her fingers.

"Nothing," squeaked Vickie. "We're friends." Whatever was going on between her and Az, it was *not* ready for a family inquisition.

"Really?" Priscilla's face was emotionless, but the set of it reminded her of the way Emily Lickinson stalked Az when she was about to pounce.

"Truly. I'll see you two later. Can't wait to take that hike sometime." If Vickie's voice had shifted up an octave on one of those words, it wouldn't be enough for them to notice.

She hoped.

"Drive safe," said Evelyn. "And do let us know if you need the Council for anything at all."

Vickie could feel Priscilla's eyes on her back the entire way out.

"Your shirt is on inside out," Prissy called as she shut the door behind her.

Vickie looked down. It was.

Fuck Azrael and his quick-snapping fingers.

CHAPTER 21

Azrael

Thank goddess Priscilla had agreed to let him take the Packard. Arriving at a haunted old New England church that had historically been the site of everything from hangings to burnings was creepy enough without showing up in a hearse.

He and Prissy had thought about getting rid of it, but Uncle Larry would roll over in the bed of his retirement home if they sold the old clunker before he was dead. He always insisted they pick him up in it for a monthly lunch out. Said it felt like home more than anything, though when his health failed him enough to move out of his own place years ago, he had also insisted on Sunnyhallow Senior Living instead of coming to stay with them like Persephone and Benedict had suggested.

The old man had winked, leaned in, and whispered conspiratorially, "Much more strange ass at the retirement community. Folks are like vampires there, around too long to be picky about who they're shacking up with. It's all love and none of this foolish normie discrimination about the bits of the ones we love. It's basically Woodstock, but with pudding."

Azrael had recoiled at this particularly gelatinous imagery, and tried to object, but Priscilla magicked an axe at his head, narrowly missing his ear, and insisted that his being a stuck-up prude who kept quiet about his sex life didn't mean the rest of them had to be.

"Priscilla," his mother had reprimanded. "Don't make Azrael uncomfortable. And Azrael, sex is a normal and healthy part of life. If your uncle wants to live in a retirement community to procure it, he has our full support."

Larry smiled wide, and Benedict slipped an arm around Persephone's shoulders. "Ah, my darling, you always say the loveliest things." He kissed her cheek.

The memory was hauntingly honest. That kind of love was eternal. Maybe he should tell Vickie again. That even if he couldn't, he wanted to kiss her from her fingers to the top of her head. Tell her it was more than the magic of their bodies; it was that his skin sang when she touched him. He pulled up next to the shop.

Fuck. The reality of the woman was almost too much. Vickie was standing outside of Hopelessly Teavoted, the sign turned to closed.

Azrael snapped his fingers, summoning a few leaves from his mother's ginkgo tree. He rubbed them between his hands, murmured a word for dreams, and snapped both fingers. There. Now any human who stopped by the store on the days it was closed would remember the next morning, and with any luck, return when it was open. It was harder to work on witches, but it had been one of his mother's favorites for aiding the struggling mundane students who sometimes sat studying and leaking stress.

Vickie was texting someone, and the right corner of her bottom lip was tucked ever so slightly under her teeth. She was wearing high-waisted bleached jeans, a snug peach-colored top that fell just above the sparkling rhinestone charm in her belly button. That fuzzy hot-pink coat stood out against the bustling street. Even her rose-colored hiking boots matched, and her hair was pulled up into a messy bun. Stray strands were held back by rhinestone sunglasses.

Azrael was utterly and hopelessly in love with Vickie in this moment. He didn't want to break it by telling her he had arrived. It didn't matter that he could never touch her. He had been down bad, crying, for so many years, and he'd shoved it aside, tried his best with other people. Each more lovely than the next. All potentially well suited for him.

None of them Victoria.

He'd moped through a parade of paramours intent on cracking that distant, heartbroken demeanor. He'd run through countless hookups, none of them quite right, his friends telling him he was just too picky and that he would have to settle eventually.

Looking at Vickie now, Az decided he'd tell her the full extent of what he felt, that he was still into her. He'd hinted at it, talked circles around it, but there were three more words he had been holding back. As soon as they solved this nasty business, they could pretend until it was over, until they solved all this magical mayhem, and then he would let her decide if she wanted to stop pretending.

If he ever bound his soul to Victoria Starnberger, it would be because she wanted to, not because she needed to outsmart a curse. In that instance, the missing his parents was a little easier to bear. The atoms in him, still reeling from their loss, still rearranged strangely by a world without them, settled down, soothed by the realization that being with someone he chose for himself who also chose him, wholeheartedly, was what they would want for him. He felt as though his blood pumped less chaotically through his veins, as though he'd finally caught his breath after the panicked, laborious breathing of grief.

He knew what he wanted. What he would choose to do when she asked him. He would let her decide if she ever wanted it to be for real, but he was done pretending.

Azrael was picking her. Choosing her, whatever complications that entailed.

Her finger slid against the phone screen, scrolling something now.

He would tell her how every beat of his heart was for her. How he hadn't been able to fall asleep at night without thinking about the soft gasp of her breath when they had danced or the way he wanted to make her scream in ecstasy when he finished her, a thousand times over. How complete he would feel, having accomplished it, and showing her, more openly than he had with anyone, what it was to be with him, body and mind and magic and soul. He had magic, and he could fuck her senseless without touching her. And he wanted to, he really did. He wanted to bury himself in her, even from a safe distance. To give her the best version of his whole heart, from afar.

After all, it had been hers, always.

Years of torment and longing and thinking it would never happen again had built to a tremendous crescendo of almost happening and then never being able to happen the way he had imagined it would. He could figure this out before all hell came crashing down on him and Hallowcross on Halloween.

Finally looking up from her screen, Vickie smiled, and Azrael was certain that the very heavens above them parted and glinted off her shiny rhinestone heart earrings. She shoved the phone in her pocket, slung a tote bag over her shoulder, and opened the passenger door.

"Hey, Az," she said.

Normal. Casual. Like he didn't want to spend the rest of his day, dick in hand, stroking himself to the memory of the shape of her mouth, the way he had in the shower this morning. Slamming his hand onto the shower wall, considering the way the fire flicked behind her, illuminating her freckles in licks of pleasure on her cheeks. Last Saturday was the best night of his life, and he'd spent it cleaning up a home break-in, horny, frustrated, and dancing in a giant metal container.

"Morning, Vickie. You look nice."

She patted the coat. "Thank goddess I love my Swiftie wardrobe. I didn't want to take more than I needed, and when my parents threw me out, I got a few staples I wear most, a suitcase full of underwear, and a suitcase of clothes. My mother sent me a certified letter to tell me she'd donated everything I didn't take with me as soon as the paperwork went through."

The callousness of Amelie Starnberger.

"I'm sorry to hear she did that." He pulled the car away from the curb, turning onto the winding road that would take them to Hallowcross General Hospital.

Vickie shrugged. "I gave up long ago on the hope that they would be what I needed them to be." She flipped down her cat-eye rhinestone sunglasses.

It was sunny enough that he pulled aviators out of the cupholder, thankful for Prissy's good taste. Next to him, Vickie tapped her own glasses, smiling wide in a way that made his heart want to split right open.

"You really got the whole outfit from the video, huh?" he quipped.

"Listen. I was bored, rich, and slow-rolling business school in twice the recommended years while telling myself I wasn't good enough to stop clinging to my parents and their money." She gestured at the jacket and the jeans. "Think of this as both art and armor, Azrael, like your clothes. There's a message there."

"Really? What is my message?"

She paused for a moment. "It's broodingly handsome with a sour exterior but a heart of gold. It's wealthy enough to own many solid T-shirts that fit in a way to make your arms look godlike, but are still down-to-earth enough to tell us that you're not *that* wealthy, because they're fraying a little bit at the seams."

"That's a lot first thing in the morning." He couldn't hold back a goofy smile; she had called his arms godlike. Thank goddess for the lonely nights in he'd spent with nothing but free weights and an exercise bike in the height of the lockdown.

Vickie drummed her fingers on the dashboard and dug around in her tote bag, pulling out a bag that smelled like apples and cinnamon. It reminded him of solstice cider and the new year. The scent stoked a feeling of home absent in him for a long, long time.

"Apple pie donuts," she said, handing him one wrapped in

a napkin with little bats printed on it. She was careful not to touch him.

He bit in and wasn't even embarrassed at the moan that escaped him.

"This is the best fucking donut of my life." He paused. "It's a thing of beauty."

"I know, right? I couldn't sleep after all last night. I found your mom's recipe for cherry pie donuts. This is a riff on that. I'm going to offer it with a whipped vanilla latte and call it pie à la mode."

"Vickie, this is genius. I'd marry you on the spot if you had coffee with this."

Her cheeks pinkened a little and she coughed.

"Well, I do have a thermos and some cups." Now he was blushing, too, and trying not to think of the way her mouth had tasted last month, like mint and the tail end of berry lip gloss rubbing off between their lips and bodies.

Of how normal he felt at the casual offer to spend forever with her just for a donut. He'd offered more for less.

"How far is the drive?" Vickie's eyes were bright and her smile wide, cheeks still red from his faux pas of a proposal joke. In light of the soul-sealing option, it seemed more serious than he had intended.

Or exactly as serious, depending on how he looked at it.

"After the hospital, it should be three hours if we can avoid the traffic. Which we can, of course, because Evelyn and Prissy helped me charm the GPS."

"Have I told you lately that I love your family?" She said it offhandedly. Casually, he was sure, but it froze his tongue.

What if he dropped it on her now? What if he told her right here what he felt? There was so much love and memory, the two twined together.

Azrael shut his eyes and remembered his mother in her midnight rose garden. She wore that black velvet dress with the cap sleeves and the breezy sheer gray cardigan over it, deadheading the roses because they made excellent potions for easing everything from stomachaches to heartaches with the petals, and the thorns. She mixed magic with the ordinary at the tea shop to make the world a little brighter.

Never enough to violate the code, the way he had with Vickie's friends in college. He was pretty sure that it was only Priscilla keeping Evelyn from retroactively reporting him to the Council, which would definitely slap him with some sort of community service at the least.

The hospital was only a twenty-minute drive from Hopelessly Teavoted, and he couldn't help but spend most of that time thinking of his mother, and how she and his father had died there, in the end.

Witches were allowed small magics to make things easier for mundanes. It was difficult. Humans were cranky and ill-tempered and often made decisions that could not be righted with simple spell work. But his parents had believed in healing the world. Making it better. As a Jewitch, Persephone's craft was mixed with the practice of healing the world. Her spells were for kindness and her potions for health. She had brewed and distributed, for free, an effective gender-neutral birth control Az had been on since he was thirteen. She also made a useful tincture that magicked a temporary thread tattoo around your finger if you were sick and needed to seek medical care or a heart on your palm if you could rest at home to recover.

Persephone would have known from the thread that she should go to the hospital and would have gone right away. Neither medicine nor magic could have saved her or his father from death in the end.

When they pulled into the parking lot, Vickie's hand on his arm, far up enough to touch only fabric, for just a moment, pulled him from his reverie.

"I know you miss them. And I know it hurts to talk about them and that you'd rather sulk and brood, because that's your brand and you're entitled to it, but Az, you have to talk to me about it sometime." Her voice cracked a little, and with it, his resolve. "I need to know you're okay," she finished softly.

"Let's talk after this." He didn't tell her that if he didn't go into this hospital, the place that had seen the end of half his family without him, right now, he might never go in at all.

She nodded, leading the way inside. He watched her put on the armor she had talked about, rolling her shoulders back. Standing a little bit taller. Grinning cheerfully and greeting the receptionist.

"Hi, I'm Connie Witherspoon's niece, here to visit her again."

The nurse looked up from her clipboard and tucked a pencil behind short gray hair, skeptical.

"Sign in here." She pointed to a visitor's log. "And wait just a moment."

The skin on the back of Azrael's neck prickled.

"Something's off," he murmured to Vickie.

"I know. Just be calm." Her voice was barely a whisper, the lines of her smile still intact, and when she picked up the pen, she froze.

"Az." The sudden pallor of her face was almost enough to have him press his hand to her forehead, death wish and all.

"Excuse me," a stern voice interrupted. "I'm Dr. Words-worth, the attending on duty, and I don't care how many more of you charlatans come in here, Ms. Witherspoon has no siblings. First that insufferable man claiming to be her son, now a mystery niece. Whatever you're selling, get out of here."

"We'll just go." Azrael gestured to the door.

The woman crossed her arms. "Get out before I call security."

He hustled Vickie out the door, careful to only touch her coat.

"That was a bust," he muttered, half running to the car.

"No," said Vickie breathlessly. "Not entirely."

"What?" He turned to her.

"What did you say your boss's name was? Chet something?"

"Chet Thornington."

She smiled, satisfaction creeping across her face. "I thought so. Azrael. I saw the log. Chet Thornington was the last person to sign in."

"The insufferable man. Of course. That's a spot-on description."

"Now why would Chet be sniffing around Madam Cleopatra?" She picked at the polish on her fingernails. "I guess it's also possible that he was visiting someone else. It's a big hospital."

"That's true. Being an asshole isn't a crime on its own." He pulled out of the lot, and within minutes, he was on the freeway.

"I'll keep an eye out at school, though he does seem to be all business, even when the business is cruelty to children for some sort of twisted fun."

Vickie shook her head. For a few minutes, he thought that maybe they would drive silently. It was kind of nice, just being here in the car with her.

"Before we went in. About your parents. You were saying."

"You want honesty?" He gripped the steering wheel.

"Yes."

"No pretending, then," he started, voice hoarse. "I was an ass to them." Focusing on the road, he told himself he was avoiding looking at her because of the winding curves and not because of the shame rattling around his rib cage. He felt hollow. Small.

Vickie's hand pressed against his shoulder, thumb to clavicle, and the risk of the inch of fabric separating life from death made him swallow. That and the unbearable closeness of her.

"Hey. You were who you were. They knew you, and they never expected you to pretend to be anything you were not. They accepted you. They love you, Azrael."

"I wish I could tell them," he said. Her face lit up.

"You can." She rummaged around in her bag, pulling out a velvet box. She opened it to a shiny pair of cuff links shaped like skeletal ravens. They were a gift from his mother to his father for their twentieth anniversary. "I found these last night, along with a rather ominous noose, when I was looking for extra donut molds. I figured we could ask them what more they know about the situation, and that maybe you could talk with them. I could help. It could be good for you."

He inhaled deeply, holding it for four counts and releasing it for eight. Letting the anxiety and the self-loathing roll off him. He tried not to linger on how much it meant to him that she saw him, really saw him, for all he was.

Azrael wanted to dance with her in libraries or swoon over her while sipping on coffee and tea.

Though a small, angry part of Az's brain told him he should let Vickie go so that she could find someone who could really be with her, the larger part of it, the rational part, told him that this was the anxiety, and the depression, fucking with him. He had made his choice about not pretending. And he would let her make her own choice, too, rather than deciding for her.

"Is it too weird to summon them in a car? After last time?" She bit her lip, and he wondered if she was also thinking of the way she'd writhed in his lap. The way they'd burned for each other before he, well, almost actually burned for her.

He shook his head to clear the cobwebs of lust. "What the hell. We have hours. Yes, let's do it." He swallowed, hoping he didn't regret this decision.

CHAPTER 22

Victoria

The cuff links heated in Vickie's hands, and she turned in her seat, catching Azrael's eye before he returned his glance to the road. He was searching for the things only she could see.

"Victoria, please tell Azrael that we are with him when he needs us. Always." From the back seat, Benedict spoke in that rough, stony voice, and his gold eyes flickered over his son. Persephone, ethereal arm linked through her husband's, as though she couldn't bear to part with him, even in the afterlife, nodded and met Vickie's gaze.

Vickie tried not to blush at this, and she *hoped* they had not been haunting the library yesterday and watching the strip-tease that had accompanied the dancing. Vickie reassured herself that she would have sensed that.

Probably.

"I saw what he keeps in his wallet, still," said Persephone softly. "Tell my son that I understand. He thinks reserve can shield him from the harsher parts of reality, but he deserves everything. Even if it is difficult. Tell him that it is worth the risk. All of it. He deserves every single moment of joy that his father and I had, and will continue to share in whatever awaits us. We chose this life together, and death won't stop us from choosing each other. Always."

Vickie cleared her throat, her chest twisting at the pain in the shade's voice.

"They are with you, always." Vickie glanced back at Benedict and added, "And they both love you very much."

Benedict's ghost raised an eyebrow, but the corners of his mouth quirked up. It was not untrue.

A person wearing a pink puffy coat and rhinestone sunglasses, after all, knew how embellishments could sometimes make a message even more honest.

Azrael's face was tight, and he swallowed.

"Your mom said that she knows what you have in your wallet, which I personally hope is a condom, because as you know, safe sex is very important."

And because she was wondering if it would be possible, very cautiously, to use barriers to master the logistics of sex with a person she couldn't touch. Especially given that after Halloween, if things didn't go as planned, she wouldn't even be able to see him, let alone fuck him without touching. But she didn't think she wanted to bring that up at this particular moment.

Azrael let out a stunted laugh at that, an anemic thing, but still enough to make her smile. He was grieving in a way that was healthy. Like the pain wasn't gone, but he was allowing it in. Learning to move forward with it. Vickie wanted to make him laugh a thousand times, until it felt hearty, and she had other ideas. Ideas that could blend magic and latex for the kind of sex that could be safe for them. Some people were worth trying new things for, especially if it meant touching and not dying.

Azrael's mouth quirked up. "I guess you could say that right now my parents are two spirits with the best *sheets* in the house back there."

Vickie couldn't help smiling. The joke was *so* bad. She had forgotten, because he still looked so devastatingly cool, what an enormous dork Azrael Hart was sometimes.

Good grief, it was those moments that made her certain she was doing more than pretending.

Az was fantastic. And touchable or not, part of her already knew he was hers.

In the mirror, she could see the ghost of his parents exchange a look. Good goddess, one couldn't even count on death to halt parental scheming. She ignored it pointedly.

"Your mom said you deserve everything. She said you deserve what she had with your father." Vickie paused to make sure she didn't miss anything. "No, what she *has* with your father. You deserve everything, Az, everything you could possibly want."

Even if what we have shatters, and it gets too intense. Even if I have to cut you loose so I don't kill you, and even if that person isn't me.

But Vickie didn't have time to linger on more thoughts of self-loathing.

"Ask them what they know about where we are going. Ask about the historic church in Havenwall." Az's face was clouded, and she couldn't tell if it was irritation at the message or concern about their mission.

Vickie didn't need to repeat Az's words; his parents could hear him just fine. Persephone wound the train of her long gray sleeve around the opposite fingernail. Even in death, it was polished to a lovely wine-red point that looked as though it could draw blood.

"We know a few things," Persephone said. "For whoever it is to go undetected, they had to have made a deal with a greater devil. It would be all-consuming. When the dealmaker uses their power, it doesn't just call forth a person, living or dead. It absorbs that person's soul. It kills them in body and in spirit. We think the particular devil who made this trade either miscalculated or was tricked. But every bargain, even the ones made in trickery, has rules. Fine print. The power still has to be linked to something, probably a greater sacrifice. Someone who was important to the person making the deal."

"Lex didn't mention the trick part," breathed Vickie, anger curling in her stomach. The devil hadn't clarified that they were looking for someone sharp enough to trick a greater devil.

Persephone's and Azrael's heads snapped up, asking the same question. Azrael was scowling, though the tips of his ears were red enough that she knew he thought of the devil in a way that made him at least a little bit hot to go.

"Lex?" The chorus of their voices made her smile, but both the shade and her son stared at him with the same intense expression that for some reason made her inclined to confess to having once stolen lip gloss from the local corner store and to more than once having thought about Az at inconveniently intimate times.

Az gripped the steering wheel hard enough that the car jerked a little.

"I know it's a sore subject," Vickie said, not meeting Azrael's eyes. It wasn't entirely the bad sort of sore, either, for either of them, she suspected. Anyone with a pulse could see what a smoke show Lex was. "But we need to know."

Azrael cleared his throat and looked in the rearview again. "Before he strolled in, distractingly charming, and did this"—he gestured between the two of them—"Lex helped Vickie capture the first of the three souls she owes him."

"Humph," grunted Benedict. He and Persephone exchanged another look, and holy hell, these two had endgame-level romance to keep holding these silent conversations that were half eye-fucking, half imparting of essential details.

"We know you would never harm Azrael," said Benedict. "Not if you could help it."

Vickie nodded. "Of course, I would never hurt him. I've already collected one soul. The other two will be deserving of capture, I swear. I won't reap Azrael. We agreed they would be wretched souls. The first was a gun lobbyist."

Persephone smiled, and her eyes and teeth glinted in a way that was otherworldly.

"Good riddance to bad men," Persephone said, her voice scraping like cold sandstone. "We need to talk about what to do when you find the villain. You'll need to be careful not to—"

In Vickie's hands, the cuff links smoked, cutting her off. "I've got another object," she said. Benedict and Persephone burst into flames and dissolved into ash. "We have one last chance to finish this." She reached into her bag for the odd noose she had found in her apartment's storage; it had beckoned to her strongly enough that she had put on gloves and stashed it with the other precious objects. She had wrapped it carefully in an old scarf.

"I once worked with a devil out of a film studio in LA. *The* Lucifer. Called himself Frankie," Az said.

"Wait, Az. The alleged *king* of the greater devils goes by Frankie?"

"I know, right? But it's pretty typical for devils to take on names that fit more easily into the current age. The two I am named for, Azazael and Ashmedrea, go by Al and Ashley. Anyway, we need to be careful here. We can't afford to accuse the wrong person, but whoever we're dealing with, they managed to trick a greater devil. They're dangerous." Azrael's voice was sharp. Laced with fear.

He was right to be scared. She'd been talking to dead people her entire life, and it scared her.

"We need to know what else your mother had to say. She was telling me about how to stop the person who tricked the devil. She said that even if he tricked Lucifer himself, there would be rules to it, still. We need to know as much about those as we can, and we need to ask your parents about the church in Havenwall. See what else they know."

"Wait, did she say it was a man? Do we know it was a him? We can't just assume a name on a hospital visitation sheet is an admission of guilt."

Vickie snorted. "Even if it's not *him*, it's always a him. I'm taking a wild guess. For safety, anyone could be our suspect. But until I know otherwise, I'm using 'him.'"

She reached for the creepy rope, unspooling the scarf around it carefully.

"I only have this one left, so this is also it, Az. The final goodbye," she started. She left out the reminder that he was the true final goodbye, should she mess up and touch him. No need to say it. They both knew.

"Let me think of what I want to say," he said.

They drove in silence for a few minutes before he spoke again. "Got it. I'll talk first, be really quick, I promise, and then you ask about Havenwall."

She nodded, pushing the rhinestone sunglasses up into her hair.

The rope warmed, and she sensed Benedict and Persephone before she could even see them in the rearview mirror. In the back seat, Benedict and Persephone appeared once more, and this time, before speaking, Benedict wound a hand around the back of Persephone's neck, kissing her passionately and murmuring words Vickie couldn't hear, before turning to the front. Even in death, they were truly, madly in love.

Az looked at her, and she nodded.

"Mom. Dad," he started, and his voice cracked a little.

She watched his lips, trying to focus on the words coming out and not the soft slope of them and the way they had felt against her skin. These were inappropriate thoughts to have while he grieved the loss of his parents. After all, to kiss him would be to send him to an untimely end.

"I wanted to say I am sorry. I wanted to say I love you. There are a thousand things I wanted you to see happen for me: I wanted you to see me be more successful, and find love, and have a family, and be happy, whatever that looked like, and I'm sorry. So, so sorry, for how embarrassed I was of our family. I don't feel that way anymore. I really don't."

Persephone smiled.

"First, Vickie, you must be careful not to overlook whatever objects anchor the devil dealer to not only his power but also his protection. He would have made a sacrifice, probably human, to remain undetected. You're looking for someone who would have wished to keep him safe in life. Something that did that to someone. And, Azrael, you could never disappoint us. Never," Persephone said. "We love you so much.

And even when we are gone, we will be with you. Your sister already knows the same thing. When you are sad, when you struggle, remember that I have never found a heartache that wasn't at least somewhat healed by a nice cup of tea and dessert."

Vickie committed the words to memory as carefully as she could.

Persephone paused, looking between Az and Vickie. "Things were complicated for your father and me at the start too. Love each other. Be happy, darling."

Vickie choked on the last few words, both on the boldness of Persephone announcing her most secret emotions, the ones that she had been attempting to pretend away, and at the thought that she would now have to recount them.

"What did she say?"

"That she's always near, even when she's not right here. That she lives in your heart, and that there is nothing bad enough that a cup of tea and a pastry can't fix it. I'll tell you the rest later," she said, avoiding Persephone's stern look. "We needed to ask you about Havenwall. We traced the devil dealer to the old, haunted church there. Do you have any idea where we should look? And once we're back in Hallowcross, does the name Chet Thornington mean anything to you?"

Persephone's forehead wrinkled, and she frowned.

"I've never heard that name. Havenwall is dangerous, though. Don't bother with the church itself; one never knows what sort of horror you'll find in one of those. Go to the Rosehill Mausoleum in the graveyard behind it. You'll need to take an object from a dead Rosehill witch to summon their ghost. Azrael can cast a spell to secure the spot, and to counter the bad luck of grave desecration. Be careful. Whatever evil has traded with the devil probably seeks a witch soul."

Vickie nodded. The knot in her hands grew warmer.

"Ah. My darling," grumbled Benedict, his voice thick with emotion as he looked at his wife. "It is our hangman's knot. From Jan Mydlář."

"Jan Mydlář?" Vickie asked.

"The Prague Punisher. I'll tell you about him later." Azrael's knuckles gripped the steering wheel so tightly now that they looked white. In her hands, the cord grew more heated. He was right. Time was running out.

"Make sure we don't see you again," Persephone said softly. She meant that there were no other remaining objects. To see her again would be to kill Azrael, but the warning hung unspoken in the air. They all knew. "Tell my children to be proud of who we are. Harts. Capable of love and magic, and so deserving of both, no matter how people may at times mistreat our people, and mistreat others in our names. Remind them that we have a duty to help mundanes. To mend the world."

Persephone gave Vickie a stern look and continued, "Protect Azrael. Don't let him burn."

Hand to her mouth, Vickie was unable to stop the gasp. Persephone didn't really think her capable of making such a mistake, did she?

Vickie's fingers flamed a little now, leaving ash prints on the rope. It wasn't just her magic working; it was her magic *warning*. Warning that she could kill him if she touched him now, and warning that if she even so much as looked at him after Halloween, she would.

Persephone looked sympathetic as the noose burst into flames. She and Benedict were saying something more, but it was too late. All Vickie could do was relay Persephone's final warning. "They said this is the last you should see them." She left out the obvious, that if they did again, he would die. "They said you deserve love. And magic."

Azrael's eyes were dark now. Angry.

"I want those things. I also want to wring the neck of the devil that did this to us. That made it so that we can't touch without destruction."

"We should be more concerned with the greater devil that traded with a human. Your mom said he will be looking for a witch soul. To anchor his power."

"He would want that by Halloween." Azrael's knuckles clutched the wheel even tighter.

"So if we don't figure out who it is by Halloween?"

"Not only do we never get to see each other again, but also he gets the kind of power that serves as a shield. That protects him from repercussions from any sort of crimes."

"Why would someone do that?" She pushed her sunglasses up and pressed her palms over her eyes for a moment.

A muscle in his jaw twitched. "Think about it, Vickie. I think you're right that this is a man. The sort of man who would grab for power, in the world and the workplace, and then brag that he was infallible. It's usually a politician, sometimes a businessman. Think about the men we hear of who walk away from assault with community service, with positions in the land's highest courts. In the land's highest offices. More often than not, they've traded for that kind of shielding, whether in spells, or in human riches."

"Fuck," she swore. "So this could be bigger than Hallowcross. Bigger than us."

"Right. If we don't stop this person before the veil thins, this is power that poisons the world."

She didn't know what to say. He needed her reassurance, but she couldn't think of anything that would make him feel better about it all. So she reminded him of the only thing that she could control.

"Your mother said she loves you, and she's proud of you. She meant it, Az. I've seen you with her mending spells. You're just like her, making the world better, bit by bit."

"Does it even matter when the people on the other side are making it worse in such drastic leaps and bounds?" He sounded tired. Defeated.

"It *matters*, Az. Kindness always matters. Small instances of it add up."

They spent the rest of the drive in silence, neither one able or willing to go on with words. It was enough to sit together to the sound of the radio, to know that they sped toward danger and could try to stop it.

And maybe she could consider moving forward in how she felt too.

Vickie could stop pretending. She could tell Az she loved him still. That it wasn't just the incident, or the longing, but all of him, then and now, the way he cared so deeply, the way he wanted to heal sadness and sorrow when he saw it, all blended into higher love and magic than she'd ever known. She loved him enough to sacrifice ever touching him again. And when she was ready, if they survived this, maybe she could seal their love in a way that would fix things between them for good.

CHAPTER 23

Azrael

Az hated that Lex was out there somewhere knowing how he and Vickie were suffering. But he had bigger problems to solve; whoever was behind the Brethren of One Love had made a deal so evil it was ironic that they would masquerade as angelic while hunting witches and humans to fuel their power. It crossed over from the order and organized chaos of devils. This was how demons could be made. Even greater devils were lawful; Az had met Frankie out in California. He was one of the execs at a firm Azrael had interviewed at, and he had told Az they could only hire him if he was willing to use minor witchery to prepare ready-to-use spells for executives. He'd absolutely despised that guy, and yet he still had rules. Give and take. Trade of power for power. He wasn't half as bad as what was going to happen in Hallowcross if they let the church seize control.

Just like angels weren't necessarily kind, devils weren't inherently cruel creatures. They were often charming and well-to-do, and *always* strikingly good-looking. They embodied a wide range of good and evil intentions. They just had more power than most to act upon them.

Azrael wasn't sure how he'd fare matched against one in combat, and as they pulled up to the old church, he hoped he would never have to find out. The thought of fighting something worse than the devils made him a bit sick to his stomach, so he pushed that thought away. That was a problem for later Azrael. For now, he had a grave to rob.

Gray mist wreathed the top of the stone spires, cut through with gorgeous designs in dark stained glass in some places and iron bars with jagged scraps of what once must have been lovely panes in others. Right away, they set off for the mausoleum, Vickie's pink jacket in sharp contrast with the muted greens of weeping willows and the overgrown gray path in the graveyard.

Here and there, trees sprouted from graves and vines leeched the stone monuments away from humans and back to nature.

"Who was the Prague Punisher?" Vickie whispered.

"Seriously? You want me to tell you about a murderer in a graveyard? While we prepare for maybe our most dangerous magical encounter yet?"

"Sounds like he was an executioner, Mr. Hart." That title hit so differently from her than it did at work. Her smile dazzled him, and when she pulled her bottom lip between her teeth for a moment, he wondered if she was being hot on purpose to distract him from the anxiety coiling in his gut.

"Stop it. You know that's the same." He sighed.

"Fair. Tell me about the murderer, then." She was twirling a few strands of her hair absentmindedly. It was actually helpful to concentrate on something other than potential impending doom.

"Well, legend has it that he lost his love. She was executed when he was a young medical student, and he exacted his revenge on the world in his red hood, chopping down those sentenced to execution with vigor and enthusiasm. He was a hangman with a tragic past."

"Now, that is both creepy as fuck and kind of romantic."

Az snorted. She would think that.

"Listen. Vickie. We need to be careful. This place is old. Powerful. More than my witchery and your gift combined. Stay close."

"Az, you have to be so careful, too, if this person is hunting a witch soul. You're my favorite witch soul. Just don't let yourself be hunted. Promise?"

Fuck. His heart pounded, and his face felt flushed. How was everything she did always so inappropriately, effortlessly hot?

"I promise. Just stay close."

Vickie stepped closer and slipped a hand into his back pocket, holding herself far away enough to avoid touching his skin.

"Is this what you had in mind by *close*?" The question—a dare, he recognized—rolled off her tongue easily, but the moment stretched between them like a soap bubble he was unwilling to pop.

"It works," Az said, hoping he sounded more casual than strained. "Just try not to trip and fall on my mouth."

Casual, because that had to be the right reaction, and strained because, well, his dick was trying to escape his pants through the very unmovable wall of his jeans, and the zipper hurt. Even through boxers.

Az hoped Vickie wouldn't notice, but maybe she did, because she squeezed his ass through the denim fabric. Hard enough that he bit back a moan.

"This is helping, right?" Her voice was barely a whisper. "This is helping you? It's keeping me from panicking about what we're about to do."

"It's helping something, all right," he muttered.

They reached the biggest mausoleum, with columns grand enough to be someone's actual house and not just a glorified coffin holder.

"Shall we?" Vickie removed her hand—he instantly felt the chill of her absence—and darted ahead to pull open the stone door by the iron handle.

The inside of the mausoleum stretched out into an abyss of artificial midnight.

Az snapped his fingers, and the flashlights he had tucked into the trunk of the Packard appeared in their hands.

"What, no fancy torches?"

"I'm a modern man," he said.

"You're a witch," Vickie teased, smiling at him.

"Fine, I'm a modern witch." Az angled the beam inside, unable to restrain the lopsided, besotted grin creeping across his face. Goddess, she made him wild.

He stepped inside and she followed, the stone door scraping shut behind them.

"Az. You promised you would be careful. Please be careful. Your mom said to set up wards. For safety."

He nodded. Whispering and snapping, Az summoned herbs from the clippings he and Priscilla kept in the car emergency kit—lavender and rosemary and rue—and cast a bucketful of salt around the perimeter.

"There," he said, snapping his fingers one last time to tuck a sprig of lavender behind Vickie's ear. "We should be safe now."

She fingered the bloom.

"What does this do?" She breathed the words, a genuine question, but also like she knew everything in his skipping, cowardly heart.

"Jewitches believe it can be cleansing and promote peace." He paused for a moment to commit the sight of her to memory, here in the dimly lit house of death. "Also, you're beautiful, and you smell like lavender sometimes." His words were slipping, along with his control, as though the emotions he'd kept locked below the surface would soon burst forward. He would tell her. That he could easily sacrifice ever really touching. He wanted to profess his love, even here in the cemetery. He'd gladly risk death to make it official. To be her partner, whatever she wanted that to look like. He had to tell her. "I'd keep your heart warm, Vickie."

"I." She paused and a blush rose to her cheek, pinkening skin under whorls of freckles. "It's just my conditioner."

Az wanted to take her chin between his thumb and forefinger and show her just how beautiful he thought she was, but they had a coffin to desecrate, an object to steal, and a witch's soul to summon. Also, it would kill him, so it would have to wait. He couldn't just lick her fucking face until he died when they were supposed to be raising the dead.

"Here," Vickie said, pointing to the most recent entry into the house of death. " 'Tina Rosehill, daughter of Mordecai and Leeara, beloved cousin of Cal and Sienna. 1995–2021.' "

"Shit, she died young."

"Yeah," said Vickie. "That's the nightmare. Die before you have a chance to do things in life." Her fingernails dug into her hands, kept firmly at her sides, hard enough that he could see the muscle in her wrist clenching where the sleeve of her coat ended.

His heart cracked for her. They were two imperfect, broken people.

Why couldn't they just reassemble the shards of themselves together?

"So," Vickie began, patting around the edges of the stone blocking Tina Rosehill's final resting place. "What did your mother mean when she said she knows what's in your wallet?"

Panicking a little, Az pushed his hand against his thigh to check for the bulge of his wallet. It was there, and his pants were tight enough to keep it close.

"Nothing, really. A condom."

"That's *not* what she meant. Though, do you really carry a condom in your wallet?"

"No. And to be honest, it's been months since I even needed one. Before my birthday. And putting them in a wallet wears down condoms, by the way. It's not safe. As long as there's one nearby, I can summon it."

"Wait, you haven't had sex since *June*?" She was attempting to wedge the stone lid off, and it gave slightly, but didn't come loose. "I want to see if we can get this off without breaking it," she explained.

"I mean, yeah, it's been a while." He rubbed the back of his neck. "I definitely haven't been interested in anyone else since we . . . you know. Got to know each other again recently."

"Yeah. Me too." She stepped back, examining the mausoleum wall. The metal handle had bled a little, staining the pale stone a greenish hue, as though it had been there much longer than Tina had been interred. Vickie cleared her throat. "I think you're going to have to use magic. It's not budging." She paused, the corners of her mouth quirking upward. "Have you ever stolen a condom in summoning?"

He shoved a hand into his pocket, absentmindedly snapping with the other to continue spelling extra wards around them for the violation of Tina Rosehill's peaceful resting place.

"Well?" She was staring at him again, her eyes wide and her nose scrunched up a little bit, and he wanted to pepper those freckles with kisses until he got to her pouty mouth, now twisted slightly in disappointment.

"Yes. Fine. I did steal a condom—once—and I feel terrible about it." He snapped twice, gradually loosening the stone before trying it again.

"When?" Mischief sparkled in her eyes.

"You want to know this right now?" He jiggled the stone, and then tried again. Still nothing.

"I do, yes," said Vickie, brushing a little bit of dust off her fluffy pink coat.

He sighed, running a hand over his face, and then regretting the nervous tic when his fingers smelled of stone and metal. He paused for a second, collecting himself with the story.

"It was senior year. Alison Price."

"Alison Price? When did you hook up with Alison Price?"

"You remember the ill-fated Halloween party?"

"Ah yes, Anya Stein threw up in my hair while I was going down on them," said Vickie, brushing at her hair now and grimacing.

"Yeah. That one. Anyway, before shit got out of control and it shut down, I was all emo."

"Typical," said Vickie solemnly, hands on the hips of her high-waisted jeans. Her little rhinestone belly button ring glistened in the stream from the flashlight, which she was spinning in one hand.

"Shut up," Az said. "Yes, okay, I stormed out after some slight or another."

He avoided mentioning that it was because he had lost courage, again, and hadn't told Vickie how he felt. And then, the next thing he knew, they were switching beer pong partners and Vickie was slipping her arm around Anya, picking them, even though he'd been magicking her balls into the cups that night, hoping that he could at least get a congratulatory hug.

Like the lame creep that he was.

Before he knew it, he had been sulking off behind Danny Nguyen's house and away from the bright lights of the party, up toward the gazebo on the edge of the property.

"I went for a walk and Alison followed me. We were both a little tipsy, and she kept telling me I was like Mr. Darcy because I was cranky, and we were in a fancy garden."

"Oh my goddess. How did I never know this? Did you *Bridgerton*-style fuck Alison Price in the Nguyen's fairy garden?"

"It was a gazebo, and no, I, at age seventeen, was not doing anything with the finesse of a reformed rake. I had very awkward sex with her in a gazebo, and the sex involved stealing a condom because I didn't bring one. When she wasn't looking, I magicked it from someone else in the house. I truly hope it was from a box and one of many, or else I ruined someone's night."

"I'm sure you weren't half-bad."

"That's actually very similar to what Alison said afterward," he deadpanned, and Vickie's laughter pealed across the mausoleum.

Az had forgotten he was even in a house of the dead. It was so easy to forget everything else when he was with her.

Vickie stepped closer, though still at arm's length, and he could smell her now—strawberries and lavender.

"Don't worry, Az. I'm not sure if you're not giving yourself enough credit, or if you've learned a lot in the years between, but everything we have ever done, or almost done, has been fucking fantastic."

Her cheeks colored, the heat stretching tightly between them. He wanted all sorts of totally inappropriate things now. To distract himself, he snapped a final time, and the stone loosened enough that he should be able to pull it off. He tried, but it was still stuck. Must be screwed in.

"That was years ago, and you may be remembering things as better than they were. Or better than I was, at least. Besides. We have a coffin to break into," he said, not proud of how strained his voice came out. It was bad form to be slightly erect while discussing grave robbery.

"Did you know that most American burials use caskets, not coffins?"

He nodded. "I did. Witches prefer coffins. Most magical creatures do, really."

"Right," she said, shaking her head. "Based on the vampire romances I've read, that tracks."

Azrael shook his head, forcing himself to think of the body they were about to disturb instead of Victoria, hot and heavy, reading steamy paranormal novels.

The necessary evil of grave robbery chilled him enough to sober the way he felt.

With a snap of his fingers, the stone finally loosened. A second snap would pull it free completely.

The coffin itself would be trickier.

"Better hope this is a burping coffin, or that it was propped open."

"Excuse me, a *what*?" Vickie's eyes widened at this.

"I did some work for one of those detective procedurals. I'm not proud of it, but I was broke, and screenwriting can be a tough game. I had to learn all about coffin types."

Vickie's eyes were glittering now, and the corners of her mouth pulled up.

"Go on," she said, rubbing her arm through the pink fluffy coat.

"Bodies emit gases as they decompose," Az said.

She wrinkled her nose. "Damn, and I thought my deep dive into caskets versus coffins was a lot. I am so glad I deal with the noncorporeal part of death."

A chuckle escaped his mouth. She was fucking adorable. How was he supposed to *not* be completely in love with her?

Six years of silence between them, a college degree, plenty of failing at screenwriting and substitute teaching high school, and he had learned absolutely nothing about how to stop loving Victoria Elaine Starnberger. It wasn't his fault. He studied and taught literature, and that shit was chock-full of unrequited infatuation. It was a dangerous business to be in.

"So, coffins, or caskets, if you seal them too tightly, explode. If you prop them open, it can cause a smell, which is why proper ventilation and drainage are so important. Some companies design them to let puffs of gas out."

"That's disgusting, but cool that you know it. And here I was thinking you were nowhere as morbid as good old Benedict and Persephone."

"You know, I wish I could have been even half as authentic as they were."

"Yeah," she said, sounding wistful. "I get that." She set the flashlight down on a ledge, balancing it on its base so that it shone upward and cast the room in a wide, eerie glow. "Okay, Mr. Hart, let's ruin Tina Rosehill's death."

Azrael scoffed at the nickname, but his heart wasn't in it. He reached for the metal handle and pulled, snaking an arm under the stone to catch it, and it came away easily. He set it aside. He snapped a few times to pepper the area under the coffin—which, thankfully, was unexploded and intact—with ball bearings, and together they slid it out and placed it on the ground.

"Stand back," Vickie said, and he stepped closer to her. Almost close enough to burn, but he could be careful.

Az snapped his fingers, and the wooden lid groaned, springing open. Instinctively, he held his breath, as though the air from the sealed death box might release a sinister creature. Vickie tensed beside him, too, but all that remained in the coffin was a decaying body. A discarded, but mortal, coil.

Witch or not, there was nothing otherworldly about the remains of Tina.

Vickie pointed to a necklace on the putrefying remains.

"There. That should work. Can you, I don't know, magic it to get rid of the corpse goop?"

"Yes," he said, trying not to retch at the sight of it. To his deep embarrassment, Az had thrown up while working on the very script he had mentioned to Vickie earlier.

Thank goddess for magic; it was all well and good for him to gag, but he didn't want Vickie to watch him be sick. He snapped his fingers and the necklace, sans fluid and decay, was in his hands. For good measure, he snapped them again, and the lid closed.

"Rest in peace, Tina," he whispered, though they were about to disturb that very slumber. "Ready?"

Vickie nodded, holding out her hand for the gold. He snapped his fingers, and gloves covered both their hands.

Az placed the locket in Vickie's fabric-covered palm, missing the spark of connection that always came with touching her skin, even for an instant. There was no denying it was real magic now.

And unless they fixed things, he would never feel that particular sensation again. Or, if he did, it would be the last thing he ever felt.

The thought of it was more sobering even than robbing a grave to summon a ghost.

CHAPTER 24

Victoria

When Vickie took off her gloves to touch the locket, the shade appeared at once, along with a winding sensation of dread in her stomach. Tina's ghost was cruelly beautiful, with sleek blond hair and sharp, angular features. Even in death, her nails were filed to sharp points and red enough to shine bright without a corporeal form.

"Well?" she drawled lazily, inspecting those deadly digits. "Have you robbed my grave to stare at me, or is there something I can do for you?" Her cold eyes ran up and down Vickie's cheerful attire, and she sighed, as if to express her disbelief that a person wearing rhinestone sunglasses and a pink coat could have summoned her.

"Yes, there is. Sorry to disturb you, but it's urgent. We need to track someone who made a deal with a devil."

Tina's eyes widened into ominous ice pools and her face twisted into a gruesome snarl, teeth slightly larger and mouth stretching wider than should be possible.

"Who sent you?" Tina's head whipped around so quickly that Vickie feared it would detach from her body. The angle was severe enough to remind her that ghosts were *not* human. A shiver ran down her spine.

This was not the vibe she usually got when summoning.

There was something *off* about Tina, something Azrael's

parents must not have known. It couldn't be simply that she was a witch; this was nothing like summoning the Harts. Vickie's fire licked at her fingers, raising hairs on her arms in a way it never had before. The only thing that came close was summoning Donovan Wagner, and Tina reminding her most of a highly evil lobbyist could not be a good sign.

"Az," she said softly. "Tina seems worried someone's after her. Any chance anyone terrible could get through your wards?"

"I don't think so," he said, looking around furiously, and then removing his gloves and rubbing his fingers together, as though preparing for the worst.

The ghost relaxed a little, but still looked wary.

"As long as he has those bad boys ready to fire." She nodded toward his fingers. "Who sent you?" Her eyes narrowed toward Vickie. "Who made you?"

"Listen, Olexandre might be a little eclectic, but he's fair. There's nothing to be afraid of." That wasn't exactly true, as she was fairly sure she'd need to reap Tina's soul for Lex. Was there a way to call him? She shut her eyes and concentrated hard on the fire she felt touching the necklace.

Tina laughed, a short bark more intimidating than it was reassuring.

"Ah, thank goodness. Lex is practically harmless. I thought you meant Frankie had sent you himself, after that bad business with the normie." Tina sighed, and her eyes returned to their normal size; her teeth looked less pointed than they had a moment earlier, but the sinking pit in Vickie's stomach only grew.

This was all wrong.

"She thought Frankie sent us."

Azrael bristled. "Shit. I knew it. Someone's tricked Lucifer into something. Someone from the megachurch."

"What bad business with a normie?" Vickie asked, but the ghost ignored her. "Who? Who was it?"

She had never been afraid of a spirit she had raised before.

Tina stepped closer to Azrael now, and the wrongness

spread upward from Vickie's hands, the skin on her neck prickling despite her coat. She clenched nails in her palm around the necklace to keep from reaching out and stopping the spirit.

Lex, if there was ever a time to let yourself be summoned by one of your bargainers, please let this be it.

She didn't have an actual way to summon him, but she hoped he'd stay true to his promise to be there for soul reaping. If she was right, he would have intended to collect Tina Rosehill anyway. She could feel it in her bones that this was the second soul. He'd warned her about this feeling. She just had to keep the ghost talking long enough for Lex to stop fucking around in another dimension, or whatever it was that devils did in their downtime.

Her nose inches from Azrael's chin, Tina looked up, mouth twisting, and ran a long, red fingernail over Azrael's arm.

"You must be a Hart, undoubtedly. Oh, he looks like the one with that tall, broad, *fuck me* body." Tina ran a shimmering hand over Azrael's chest, and he shivered, eyes darting, the gold and green specks in the brown reflecting oddly through Tina's shade. "But you can see his mother's pouty, pouty mouth here." A sharp bloodred nail traced the bow of his lip, and Vickie couldn't hold herself back anymore.

"Stop it." Vickie's voice came out angry. Scolding. Even this horrible dead woman could touch him. Tina flinched and froze. Vickie squeezed the locket, its heat momentarily flaring in her hands.

"Tell me what you know about the Brethren of One Love church. Who dealt with a devil there? Whose soul should I be reaping?"

It was a mistake to say that, because Tina looked at her, understanding and anger brewing on her face. Furious now, the ghost's eyes widened to saucers and threatened to swallow her whole, mouth stretching in a way that was more than a little unsettling. Tina's teeth sharpened again, and when she opened her mouth, Vickie shuddered.

Az stepped closer, carefully slipping a hand around Vickie's waist over her coat. The ghost's gaze darted to the shrinking space between them. To the way he touched her, careful not to really touch her. Her eyes were magnetic, yawning chasms now, expanding steadily and just brushing the edge of natural. Vickie's heart pounded.

"Well, isn't that pleasant? Why don't you two just get to it now? You better make sure the devil who gave you this awesome little party trick doesn't see that closeness. Devils are a jealous bunch. Just like you, princess, unable to even watch me touch this delicious morsel of a witch." Tina's voice cut across the mausoleum.

Vickie closed her palm tighter around the locket, burning now as the ghost went on, unknowingly exacerbating her greatest wound.

"Someone at the church was dangerous, and more than human. I distributed north of the county line. High-end clients only. I got sloppy, though, and started off-loading the job onto other people. A desperate fake fortune teller, too scared to sell anything other than weed. A youth pastor with an eye for the big drugs. *That* was a mistake. Soon after, a college kid, some lacrosse player, died of an overdose. I never met the boss in person—the one who must have dealt with the greater devil—he always sent someone to deliver for him, but I sold a wide range of things. Coke. Adderall. Fentanyl." She grinned, maw gaping wide now. "Roofies."

Her chest tightened. Kyle George had mentioned the dead lacrosse captain whose mother he had been involved with, and she wrote it off as just a dead man bragging about his conquests. Maybe part of what she needed had been there, under her nose the entire time.

"Did he kill you? The boss?"

"No. I told you, I got sloppy." She examined her fingernails. "I took the money and fled. Wrapped my car around a tree. It was a stupid, mundane way to die."

"Az, it's a drug ring. Tina was a dealer for bougie country clubbers. Sounds like she branched out, dealt to Madam Cleopatra and a youth pastor. She said that's why that college student overdosed, so she fled."

Az's mouth turned down in a frown, and his brow furrowed. Goddess, she just wanted to make it easier, but there was no undoing destiny, and she and Azrael, try as he might have to escape it, were not normal.

Not in the slightest.

Neither was Tina, who was stalking toward them now, mouth growing larger.

"Stop," said Vickie, voice stern. Where the fuck was Lex?

"No," said Tina, snarling. "I don't think I will, not when I'm so close to disappearing." She nodded to Vickie's hand. Her hand reached toward Azrael, shimmering and sheer, the nails elongating into cold spikes.

"Az," breathed Vickie, fear spreading in her stomach and up to her chest, where the air was coming with less and less ease. "We have to get out of here." His eyes darted around, frantic to find the threat he could not see, and she stepped away to protect him from self-immolation in his jerky movements.

"Don't worry, pet." The velvety, luxurious baritone licked the air around them.

Vickie watched Azrael whip his head around at the same time the ghost did, one face earnest and handsome and soul-crushing and the other terrifying and breath-stopping.

"You," growled Azrael, but she could hear the relief beneath the anger. She could feel it herself.

"Me," said the devil, the air around him shimmering.

Lex was leaning against a column, his black hair in stark contrast with the pale marble of the stone and his face. Preternaturally violet eyes burned into Vickie. He might not be for her, but damn, he was handsome.

Lex was equal parts threat and delicacy, wrapped in silky, expensive black clothing and a magic Vickie didn't quite understand that had become the root of all that she was. She imagined this was the way vampires felt about the creatures that sired them. It was a longing about creation.

It was not the same as love.

Azrael frowned and moved toward the devil, but Lex drew a soul prison from his pocket.

"NO," screeched Tina, and Vickie felt the necklace heat to burning, and then ash, but the macabre ghost was already being sucked into the trinket.

"That's better," purred Lex, waving a hand, and the box disappeared.

"What the fuck," started Vickie. "Where were you? I thought you said you'd be here when I needed to reap souls."

Lex flicked a speck of dust off the lapel of his jacket. "It's not like we arranged to do this one," he said. "And besides, I was here. I just got a little distracted. You're not the only person I've cut deals with."

Vickie rolled her eyes. He looked ever so slightly disheveled, as though he'd cleaned up quickly and missed a few spots of hair left angled a few degrees away from perfect.

"You owed me three souls, Victoria, darling. That's two." The timbre of his voice stroked velvet against her ear, a sensory overload as grating as it was seductive. He was trying to distract her from asking about what had delayed him.

"Fine. Thanks for showing up, I guess." Vickie glared at Lex, who closed his eyes for a moment, cocked his head as though listening, and then straightened and nodded.

Victoria couldn't bear to look at Azrael now. She could feel his anger simmering even without touching.

"Ah yes, beautiful. It seems she supplied the greater Vermont area with drugs. Her dealing led to five overdose deaths, one dreadful beating, two executions—at her own hands, I might add—and several assaults. She was *not* a nice woman, pet. But she didn't know who her boss was. Some volunteer youth pastor, maybe?"

"That's what she said," Vickie started.

"I'll fucking kill you," began Azrael, lunging unwisely. "Cursing me. Literally objectifying me, and then waltzing in here late and throwing around sobriquets."

"Objectifying would be so hard to resist when you look like that." Lex blew him a kiss and smiled wickedly. "As for killing me, you could try, handsome. I'd wager you can't do it, but I might enjoy the attempt." He winked.

Looking between them, Lex smiled widely now.

"Oh, come now, nothing's permanent. Victoria could still find the third soul in time to meet the terms of the bargain, and I'm sure a pair of clever witches like you and your sister can figure out a way around the teeny-tiny complication of turning to ashes on Halloween."

Azrael swallowed and didn't meet Vickie's eyes.

"Oh," said Lex, running a finger across Azrael's jawline. "But you've already figured it out, I surmise." He winked, grinning evilly. "What's the holdup, then, lovers?"

"Stop it," said Az, but he was blushing.

"What does that mean?" She looked from Lex to Az.

"He means the soul seal. The soul seal could circumvent the curse."

"Bingo," said Lex, reaching for Az again. This time he was quick enough to duck.

"My dearest pets, it seems the two of you have more truthtelling to do, on top of a villain to catch. I'll pop back in if I can find anything helpful. In the meantime, be good."

He winked again and withdrew a closed fist from his pocket.

"No!" Azrael moved to snap, but before his fingers connected, Lex vanished in a flash of musky smoke that smelled of bergamot and ginger, and covered them, once more, in brown dust.

Vickie turned to Azrael and sighed.

"More gravedirt."

"Vickie," he began, the bags under his pleading eyes heavier than before.

"We're in a fucking mausoleum," she said. "With the corpse

of a soulless killer. Let's clean up and get out of here. Help me with the coffin."

Az swallowed, eyebrows furrowing, but he complied, snapping to lighten the weight. A few sweaty moments of lifting later, the last remains of Tina Rosehill on this earthly plane rested back in her crypt.

Azrael raised his hands—those big, strong hands that she had loved the feel of so much on her body and her face and wound between her own fingers—and snapped. The plate sealed back on, and another snap replaced the bolts holding it in.

"Come on," he said. "We need to go."

"Do you want to talk about it now, or wait until you have the option to dissemble?" It didn't fit the perfect story they had wanted to pretend. But there was no such thing as perfect, only real. And her reality was that she wanted to talk about it.

"I do want to talk about it." He looked at her, expression weary. Ash and dirt lingered in his hair and streaked down his left cheek, and yet, he was still impossibly good-looking.

"About the soul seal." He hesitated. "I know it's soon. But I want to do it. And I'm done pretending."

"I'd still like to be able to call a pretend, in the meantime," she whispered. "But it's not off the table. Forever, I mean. Forever is not off the table."

"It's just a lot," he offered. "I know."

"A thing I'd want to do, but maybe later, unforced." She paused, shutting her eyes. She did want to be honest, though. "If it were later. If we had more time."

"Yeah," he said. "I get that."

She held her arms together, hugging herself. "How are you feeling?"

"Like I love you more than I ever have. Like my heart is shattering into a million glass fragments that can't ever be put back together." Az frowned. "Devil dammit. I don't want to pretend, Vickie, gravedirt or not."

He threw his head in his hands. He loved her. Still.

"I feel everything, Azrael. But I'm not ready to give up pretending. Things are complicated, right? I want more, but I'm afraid. That's my truth. I'm afraid of getting hurt again. Do you understand? You haven't even been back more than a few months."

"I'm trying to," Az said slowly. "I'd wait forever if that was an option, but if we let Halloween pass, well, there's no sealing a dead man. But I think we can figure it out. Maybe we should go home."

"Oh, shit," she said.

"What?"

"You work at a high school, Az."

"Yeah." He did not sound thrilled. "Yeah. I am really not looking forward to another uber-honest week with teenagers. It will wear off a little bit by tomorrow, but I'm absolutely going to be planning a film study for tomorrow and Friday now. As little talking as possible. Fucking devils, always meddling."

"Az," said Vickie, her voice small. "This could get worse before it gets better. We still have no idea who we are even looking for. And if you have to talk to Chet, if he turns out to just be an asshole, unconnected, but you're stuck being honest . . ."

"Right. Avoid my boss when I get back. Noted."

Vickie hoped she was wrong, but the fiery doubt swirled, along with the betrayal. The pieces weren't fitting, and now that they had destroyed the last relic she was willing to use to talk to the Harts, she had no one to advise her. Lex had toyed with them both. But Azrael had broken her heart back in college, using that same gravedirt trick. She was pretty sure, as terrifying as it was, that she would be interested in binding their fates together for good. She just wished she had more time to think about it.

And most of all, she wished she could do what she wanted without it killing him.

CHAPTER 25

Azrael

The macabre staccato of the doorbell cut through his reverie in front of the mirror.

As though staring at his reflection could change the reality that he could not touch the woman he loved.

Or, rather, Az could touch her, but it would be his last living act. It wouldn't be a bad way to go. Even if she did still want to pretend when he wanted to go all in.

Azrael pulled open the heavy door, and there stood Vickie, an anchor in the cold early October night, trepidation on her face, eyes wide with concern as they flicked from him to the door. She had to be doing the same mental calculations about how safe it would be to walk close to him. It had been two weeks since they had reaped the soul of Tina Rosehill, and it was already October, but Priscilla had finally bullied him into inviting her for dinner.

He was tempted to pull her in for a hug, to risk it all in the hopes that fabric could save them from fate. Instead, he stepped back. "Come on in, Victoria."

Vickie flinched a little at her full name. It had been a devotion earlier, but it was a wall between them now.

It was also a confession, an explosion of syllables admitting his ardent affection. He wanted to fist his fingers in her hair and pull her mouth close to him in greeting.

But he also wanted not to die, so instead he raised his hand awkwardly. The motion was painfully familiar.

"It's good to see you, Az," she said weakly. "Prissy insisted that I needed to come early to keep you company while she and Evelyn cooked."

"I know," he said, his gut twisting at the thought that she would be reluctant to come tonight. Even after his efforts toward friendship. Goddess, he understood, but it didn't make it hurt any less. He paused, hesitating. It hurt him, but he didn't want to cut her with his pain. "I'm glad you're here, Vickie." He snapped his fingers, pushing the strand of hair caught on her cheek back behind her ear. Her hand flew to her face, as though she might hold the magic there, to touch him without ever making contact.

"I've been thinking, Azrael. You have magic. We are both creative. Flexible. Willing to try new things." She picked at her cuticles for a moment, hesitating. "Maybe we could try this without touching? Have you thought about it?"

"I have considered it in depth, yes." In enough depth to yearn for her, pitifully.

He swallowed and cleared his throat. Was it tempting fate? Asking for too much? The curve of her neck was so tempting, and he was a snap away from touching it, if not with his fingers on her, then indirectly, with his magic.

A yowl at his feet broke the tension, and Emily Lickinson protested loudly until he petted her, and she prowled back over to Vickie, purring against her legs.

"Great timing, Emily," Vickie said. "Give him time to *paws* and think it over."

Dammit. She was perfection.

Az sneezed a little—he'd forgotten his allergy medicine again—but the cat was worth it. A snap of his fingers put a pill and a cup of water in his hands.

"Can I offer you a drink?"

"Yes, but something stronger than water, please."

He winked at her, determined to focus on the fact that she

was here. Tossing the allergy medicine back with the water, he snapped his fingers, and the glass disappeared back to the kitchen. The bar cart had been set up for exactly such things, and three snaps later, a dark and stormy for each of them appeared directly on the end table on either side of the lamp shaped like a warrior mermaid, her trident pulled back in defiance.

"You remembered," she said, reaching for the glass. His arm itched to reach for her, but instead he snapped his fingers again, and a pair of leather driving gloves appeared on his hands. It felt formal in a way that reminded him of his father, and she smiled, stepping toward him.

"I know your favorites. It's either that or margaritas, and the night is too young for vomiting or nudity." His tone was jesting, but his jaw twitched at the last one.

"Az," Vickie breathed, so quietly that he blinked, unsure if it was a real syllable spoken or simply the product of his wishful imagination.

He stepped back, carefully unrolling the sleeves of his crew-neck sweater so there was no exposed skin.

Her eyes flashed with hurt. Dammit, he was an asshole, making the woman he loved think he didn't feel safe enough to know she would not accidentally immolate him.

"I trust you, Vickie. I just feel fucking awkward. Fancy gloves and then what, a merino wool sweater? I'm a mixture of Target casual and old Hollywood glam."

"I know," she said softly. "It doesn't have to be weird. I have an idea. Prissy did say that we should dress up for dinner. Do you have a suit?"

"You think the son of Benedict Hart doesn't have many, many suits?"

"Magic one on. The nicest one you have. Put those clever fingers to good use."

Devil damn him, there were other good uses he wanted to put them to, but this was the option he had, so he slid one glove off his hand, trying not to lose his mind at the slight bite of her lower lip as his fingers rubbed together, and the exhale, barely audible, which reminded him so much of the soft, whispery sounds he wanted to pull from her.

He wanted her, and the suit he had just magicked himself into was cut snugly enough in the legs that he knew it would be apparent. A flush crept up his cheeks despite his best attempts to play it cool.

"Now do me," she said, voice breathy. Eyes caught low enough on him that he wondered how bad it would be, really, to burn for her in earnest.

"Pardon?"

"There's a corseted, off-white gown. It's hanging in my bedroom closet, the farthest against the wall, pushed against an old cauldron. Do me. Put me in it."

He counted backward for a moment, trying unsuccessfully to tame the lust inspired by her words. He closed his eyes, focusing. The magic to transport her outfit from there to here was trickier than reaching for a costume in the attic, but younger Vickie had made him watch the music video enough times that he could call up the image of it easily. With a snap of his fingers, he swapped out her jean shorts, tank top, and sweater for the champagne-tinted dress.

Opening his eyes, he took her in.

She looked like she was going to her own wedding in that thing.

Our wedding. The thought popped into his head, unbidden, and he blanched.

Azrael had always told himself that he didn't need to get married. That it was for old-fashioned folks like his parents, tangoing in their elegant living room and partaking in whatever activities he wanted to forget took place in what was now a very nice home gym.

But he would marry Vickie if he could. Soul-seal with her, marry her, carry her heart in his heart. Carve it there, even. Maybe not today or not even this year, but it was what he wanted, one day. He wanted every single thing with her.

The thought twisted painfully in his chest now that it was impossible to even fuck her the way he had once imagined that he could, skin to skin, and with his hands and mouth.

"Vickie," he said, "I want to—"

She lifted a finger and shook her head, stopping him. "Az. Gloves."

He nodded. Those he knew they had in the house, and a few snaps later he'd put her hair up and added elbow-length gloves.

She looked so good that it burned. Az slid the glove back onto his hand and brushed a finger across her cheek. Her loveliness was bright enough that he could almost feel her through the fabric.

Almost was such agony now.

"I missed you," Vickie said. It pained Azrael that he couldn't kiss her face. In the yearning fashion of his Victorian forefathers—on his father's side, at least; his mother's family were Ashkenazi—Az raised Vickie's hand to his mouth and pressed his lips against the glove sheathing it.

The way her mouth parted and the hand in the other glove clenched, he knew she was as desperate as he was. Victoria's cleavage heaved over the top of the corset, and Az longed to run his tongue down the curve of each breast, to palm them and feel the press of her skin on his lips.

Fuck.

"Azrael," she whispered, and then he was taking her gloved hand in his, pulling her behind him into a drawing room, their drinks sweating, abandoned, side by side, on the table.

He couldn't throw her on the sofa the way he wanted, not without dying. He could only sit down and gesture for her to sit next to him.

He opened his mouth to tell her everything, but she stopped him, a gloved finger to his lips, her pupils blown wide and cheeks flushed with excitement.

"Now that I've got you in formal dinner wear, can I try something a little scandalous?" If he thought her words might end him, her gloved touch threatened total annihilation. She moved his hands down, pulling them toward her waist. His hands gripped her sides, digging in to keep from moving them upward and touching her where it would kill him.

At the door, the house slid the lock shut, the echo of it reverberating through his thick, sluggish longing. He'd die if he touched her. But he might die if he didn't touch her too.

"Yes. Touch me—with your gloves on." The words fell from her mouth, and he wanted—no, needed—nothing more in the world. "Put your hands on me," she whispered.

"I . . ." He faltered for a moment, biting his lip. "Fuck."

"I was hoping to try to, yes. With gloves and with magic." Her throat flushed, she nodded, the words still in her mouth. "If you want, that is. I'm going to need an enthusiastic *yes*, Azrael."

"Fuck yes. Tell me what you need. Tell me how much you need it." He wanted all of her, but he could do this. He would take whatever she would give him. If he couldn't touch her, he at least needed her words, all her emotions.

"Yes. Please. Make me feel good. For fuck's sake, don't die, but make me feel something again. Let's pretend we're not cursed. Let's pretend there's not a good chance we're the kind of tragic play where they both die at the end."

Az's chest was a hollowed-out drum where his heart used to beat, and the misery of not being able to *actually* touch her and have her again was searing. He pushed the pain away. He didn't want it to be pretend, but he did want Vickie to have what she needed, even if it hurt. That was true. He focused on the truth that he could give her, and the more embarrassing one, that he would take whatever he could get, even if it hurt later. He could pretend for her, if that was what she needed. For now, at least.

"Close your eyes, Vickie. Close your eyes and *pretend*."

CHAPTER 26

Victoria

There was that word again, languid with memory and anticipation and dripping from his lips like honey. She wanted to
press her own against his body in a special kind of murder that
would feel so, so right.

Until it actually killed him, that is.

Azrael reached for her, a gloved finger sliding across her
cheek. Vickie gasped and shut her eyes for a moment, pretending it was skin on skin.

When she opened her eyes again, Az was a safe distance
away, sliding the glove off his left hand.

His fingers would need to connect, at least with each other,
for magic. She remembered what those fingers had felt like in
the car, for a brief moment, and desire, mixed with caution,
pooled in her stomach.

"Is this still okay?" The tenderness of his voice undid her
further, and when he brought his gloved hand to hers, circling
her wrist, she wriggled a little, breath catching in the corseted
gown, feeling the press of the boning at the top of the dress
and the slickness between her thighs.

"Yes. I need you. I wish I could touch you," she whispered.

"Shhh," he said. "Close your eyes, Vickie. Pretend."

They had gotten good at pretending, and then good at admitting that it hadn't been pretending at all, and now it felt circular. An endless cycle, the touching and the wanting, but not admitting, then the admitting, and now the not touching. Maybe she was cursed to do this dance with Azrael forever, always almost, never always.

His gloved fingers were still stroking at her wrist, and his other hand, held cautiously away, was moving.

A few finger snaps later, and licks of magic skirted her lips, her neck, her chest. It was like feeling his hands and his mouth, but cooler shadows of the real feeling, and the closeness of it was exquisite agony.

She moaned when the tendrils of magic slipped under the neckline of her dress.

"Please touch me—be careful, but please, touch me." It was an unfair bargain, but it was all they had. She opened her eyes, and took him in, pupils blown wide with desire, worrying his bottom lip with his teeth. He caught her eye and smiled reassuringly.

Azrael was unfairly beautiful in front of her. And unfairly far away.

He must have felt the injustice of it too. Groaning, he ran his ungloved hand down his face. Then, sliding close enough to push the long skirt of the gown up, up, and up with a gloved hand, he snapped his fingers with the other. She was bare now under the skirt, her panties gone goddess knows where, her center exposed and close to his glove.

"Touch me," she moaned, searching for confirmation in his eyes that this wasn't only agony for her.

Azrael's lips curled upward, and his gloved hand reached for her, gently at first, and then harder, circling the sensitive bud of nerves until she was making soft noises of desperation that might have embarrassed her, if she were with anyone other than Azrael.

"I want so badly to devour those little sounds you make," he murmured, leaning in dangerously close. The hairs rose on her arm with anticipation, and fear that a slight loss of control might burn him. She could feel his breath against her now as he spoke.

"Do you want just my hand here, or . . ." He let his voice trail off, tweaking at her nipples gently with two snaps of his fingers. The gloved hand at her center palmed her, rubbing steadily, and she threw her head back, an echo of a time when she would have insisted that he brush kisses along the column of her neck. A time when she would have moved her own mouth lower, down his body, hungry to feel that what they were doing was reciprocal. That he was with her completely.

"I want everything you can give me," she said, suddenly not caring how demanding her words were. "I want you alive at the end, but short of dying, give me everything. Make me forget this mess we've got ourselves into."

"Vickie," Az groaned, sliding a finger inside her, and moaning a little at the way she gasped. "Like this?"

She'd never been fingered with leather gloves before. It was not terrible.

"Yes," she said, and he snapped his fingers with his other hand, increasing pressure on her breasts while moving his gloved thumb back and forth over her clit. She tried not to move up and down on him too much, to ride his hand with the kind of unrestrained lust she felt, and the effort made her even more breathless.

"I'm going to err on the side of caution here, and since I can't check too closely for fear I might lose control and die happy with my face between your knees, I'm going to use lube, and just lean into ruining these gloves entirely. Is that all right?"

The hint of possibility made her tighten a little against his hand, and she nodded her head, biting her bottom lip. Az smiled down at her, snapping once, the tweaks in pressure just this side of painful, just the way she liked. Her nipples, peaked, ached for more than what he could give her without direct contact. Snap, and a bottle of lubricant appeared on the tea table in front of them. Snap, and she could feel his gloved thumb glide more easily along her clit, and the way one finger, and then another, slid silkily into her. Vickie braced herself on her elbows, leaning back against the cushions, and rolled her hips, but Az shook his head.

"Be a good girl and hold still and take it for me, Vickie."

The gravel in his voice rendered all that lube less necessary. Still, she didn't mind the slick, exquisite excess of it.

Watching as two of his gloved fingers slipped in and out of her, Vickie groaned loud enough that the old grandfather clock groaned back and the walls of the house contracted a little while the locked door rattled in support.

She was filthy levels of wet.

"I need to see your face come apart the way I've missed so much for fucking years." Azrael's eyes were serious, lush mouth half-open. He adjusted himself, sitting up so that she was far enough away to avoid danger. Snap, and the magical pressure increased all over her body. "You can let go now, Vickie. Let go."

They had been fools to pretend a death curse could stop whatever this was between them.

Pressing against his hand, Vickie rode Azrael's gloved fingers, tentatively at first, then, glancing down to make sure he wasn't close enough to accidentally kill, again, with the full force of her want—her need—for him. One of Azrael's hands was lost in her skirts, and she drove down onto it as the other snapped rhythmically to pull at her nipples, her neck, and the soft gathering of nerves at the center of her until she could feel her walls closing around his fingers, the ratcheting tension enough to make her whimper his name. Goddess, she wanted it to be his tongue, too, or other bits of him, but fuck it, she'd take whatever she could get at this point.

"That's it, Vickie," he answered. "Show me how badly you've wanted this. How much you've missed me. Show me how wild I make you."

She could see and hear how unhinged he was now, his breath heavy and the outline of his erection clear through his suit pants.

Her eyes were open now, and she stared, heat creeping up her cheeks, but neither of them slowed down.

"You can be honest, Vickie. Tell me what you want."

"More," she panted, and he slipped a third gloved finger inside her. Snap, and invisible kisses traced a path down her décolletage. Vickie felt each one linger, and if she closed her eyes, she could pretend. Covered in the cool glove, his hand wasn't quite as warm, but it was better than her own tired digits. The magic licked like the stroke of his tongue, down, down, exactly where she needed it to be.

"Fuck, Azrael," she ground out as her core pulsed, a squeezing, clamping fist claiming his gloved fingers. Azrael rubbed them in and out a few times before pulling them out completely, and holding them up for her to see.

"Well. This is ruined." A crooked smile snaked up his face. "And so am I, frankly."

He yanked the leather glove off and tossed it aside, snapping his fingers to replace it with a clean one.

Vickie stared up at him as her breath slowed to a normal rhythm.

"Az, what can I do? . . ." His pupils were still blown wide, and she wanted to touch him, to press against him through his pants and gloves, or to watch while he came on her tits, or into his hand, anywhere, really, but his eyebrows knitted together, and a feeling—worry, maybe?—flickered across his face.

It was all too much. Or perhaps not enough? Vickie wasn't sure what he needed.

"We should wash up and have dinner," Az said, adjusting himself in his pants and turning to the door. The house did not oblige, and he had to give the bolt on the door a few raps before it let up. He turned back to her for a moment.

"Fuck," he said softly. "How is it that good without even laying a single ungloved hand on each other?"

"Right," said Vickie, standing up from the couch, a slight wobble to her stance. "Dinner," she said. Her voice sounded weak.

Holding out a fully covered arm, Azrael cleared his throat.

"The four of us have a lot to talk about." It was an abrupt transition, but it was true.

Vickie didn't respond, but did the only thing she could think to do while clad in formal wear with a man who'd just thoroughly finger-fucked her in gloves. She threaded an arm in his, and they walked, as far apart as two people who were in love and definitely in lust could walk.

After all, to get any closer would be to risk a different kind of sparks flying, and she wasn't about to relinquish his soul to a devil.

CHAPTER 27

Azrael

Azrael couldn't shake her, both the scent of her strawberry perfume that wafted off her and the salty-sweet slick of her that lingered somewhere on his person, even though he had washed his hands and changed into new gloves.

Fuck. Blood rushed away from his head. It was October now, and they only had a month to sort things out. They needed to talk about the case.

He pictured baseball, but that never worked. Hot guys in tight pants did it for him too. Gritting his teeth, Azrael thought about the moment when Vickie had rejected him, or when he thought she had. At the party, long ago, when Vickie went upstairs with Anya. When Vickie left for school, taking his whole heart with her. When he realized he couldn't touch her, moments before he would have finally fucked her again and the ghosts of his parents had showed up in the back seat of the Packard.

There. That was better. Now he could focus on solving the mystery.

"So, Priscilla and I put a tracking spell on the metal detector at the front entrance of the school, tracing for someone stepping through it who had close contact with a greater devil," Azrael said. "It was a tricky piece of spell work, but we ran it by the Council. It should have worked. Whoever the big bad guy is, they're not at the school."

"Or they're not using that entrance. Have you talked to Chet at all?" Vickie's grip tightened on his arm.

He shook his head. "He's hard to pin down these days. I've been trying to keep an ear out for anyone who might work as a volunteer youth pastor, but honestly, most of us are too underwater on grading and planning to take on anything else for free."

"Az, I'm sorry. That can't be easy, starting a new job."

"We knew the students were innocent. The Council detected traces of greater devil work near the building, so Evelyn helped to enchant and run the tracking program to prove that no children were involved on the metal detectors. It would catch anyone who came through that way, just in case there was some sort of accidental summoning by a minor they were picking up with those traces. She's got a program running everywhere there's a scanner in town now, so, at the courtroom and the police station, a few of the clothing stores with compatible sensors. So far, nothing."

"That's super smart," said Vickie. "She must really love your sister."

"I think she does, yes."

"But?"

"Never mind." It wasn't for him to share, but he had overheard Priscilla and Evelyn arguing a lot lately. Evelyn wanted to settle down.

Priscilla liked kids, but was happy to like them from afar. He was pretty sure—though it wasn't his business to know for certain—that she didn't want to have her own, and that Evelyn maybe did. But tonight, they all had a common goal, and Prissy wouldn't want to mourn a good relationship before it was over. Sometimes things kept people apart, even when there was also love to hold them together.

Vickie squeezed his arm, pausing for a moment at the end of the long hall and looking down at the polished wooden floors.

"It's still a shame you have to suspect your coworkers. Does anyone besides Chet seem competent enough to pull something like this off?"

"I don't know. I mean, we have a few real assholes on staff, but I'm not sure being an asshole means you are also a murderer. It seems unfair to make that leap, even if there are too many coincidences to ignore completely."

Vickie remained quiet, tilting her chin down.

"I know that look. Whatever it is you have to say, say it."

"Fine. I want you to know this is true whether Chet is suspicious or not. Sometimes men let other men off for being 'just assholes' or 'just creepy' too easily. Like, sometimes those are the folks we should be looking into, who might be up to so much worse."

Azrael opened his mouth to protest, then closed it.

"I hadn't thought of it like that," he said. The guilt over his gut reaction tripped him up, and he stumbled a little, lost in the thought that he had been about to justify other men's bad behavior. And for what? Unwarranted loyalty to people he didn't even know very well?

Vickie steadied him with a gloved hand, turning to face him.

"I've got you," she said. "But you're better than that, you know? *Be* better."

He nodded.

"We think we've narrowed down a more specific tracking spell. One that might work to help us pinpoint who our person is. And if that doesn't work, you and I can go through a staff directory and start investigating one by one."

It wouldn't be fun, sleuthing on his new coworkers. But he'd do it for Victoria.

He'd do just about anything for her.

CHAPTER 28

Victoria

Priscilla sat at the head of the table, her plunging, gold V-neck dress shimmering with sequins that would have made a flapper jealous, a roast chicken on an ornate red cast-iron platter in front of her. To her right sat Evelyn, wearing a stunning crimson gown fit for a queen. The flowing sleeves of it tapered into lace at the tips, and the back dipped low under a gold linked necklace that hung glittering against her skin.

It was hard not to notice the constant refrain of Priscilla's fingers strumming at the chain down Evelyn's back, especially when all Vickie wanted, all she could not have, was for Azrael to touch her like that. Skin to skin.

Emily Lickinson, that prescient ball of fuzz, curled sympathetically around Vickie's feet, rustling through the skirt of her gown, as the chair nudged itself under her where she sat to Prissy's left.

Azrael, hair still a little rumpled from their abandoned cocktail hour even after washing up, sat a safe distance away on the other side of the table, though Vickie noticed that the mahogany rippled every so often, sliding her place setting toward Azrael with the soft *plink* of her fork and wineglass against the table.

"That's quite enough," said Priscilla, rapping at the table sharply with her knuckles, and it stopped.

"Why is it that the furniture always likes you better?" Azrael muttered from down the table, which seemed to have snuck its way around the reprimand by shortening and pulling Azrael's chair closer. He was still farther away than Vickie would like, but if she reached out, her gloved hand could have touched his now.

Priscilla shook her head.

"Our dining room always has been hopelessly romantic."

As if on cue, candles lit in the corners and the chandelier dimmed, spools of diamond-shaped light reflecting off the tiny crystals onto their faces. Everything seemed warmer in low lighting. More magical.

Evelyn smiled at Priscilla and placed her hand on top of the other woman's. They exchanged a look that made Vickie's insides twist.

Vickie refused to look at Azrael. If she didn't look at him, she didn't have to think about the empty longing of not being able to touch.

"Victoria, we are so glad you could join us." A dangerously large knife moved with alarming speed to cut the chicken, and four successive snaps of Priscilla's long, white fingers had fresh bread and salad in front of each of them.

"Thank you for having me. I didn't realize we were going to be so formal. I thought Az and I had dressed up too much."

Evelyn smiled. "When witchery makes clothes so easy to exchange, why not dine with the magnificence the house deserves?" She rubbed her hands together in her own brand of magic, and the sound system kicked on.

Calypso drums and horns picked up the sounds of Harry Belafonte, and it was a sight to see the elegant witch councilwoman dancing a little in her seat, the carving knife beside her swaying dangerously from side to side, and the black velvet curtains picking up the tempo at the windows. Priscilla snapped her fingers, and flowers streamed in from the door closest to the garden, bright red hibiscus blooms tapping in time with purple violets and lush pink lilies.

Vickie melted at the sight of a smile that twitched up Azrael's cheek, and the hard lines of his unfairly symmetrical face softened ever so slightly as he watched his sister and Evelyn. It made Vickie perfectly happy, surrounded by dancing flowers and music drifting through the air.

Even Az, closer and closer to being right beside her, could not stop his head from bopping. An errant crystal cocktail glass danced along to the tune, tapping lightly against his cheek and begging to be picked up.

She watched his broad shoulders and arms as he brushed it aside for a moment, snapping his fingers. Digging the fingers of his gloved hand into his palm and flexing a nervous fist. Vickie tried not to think of all that those hands were capable of as she watched an identical fine crystal glass, the cut lovely enough to reflect even the low candlelight, appear with a fresh dark and stormy in front of her.

"To solving complicated problems with good company and good drink," Az said.

Sloshing wineglasses danced into Priscilla's hand and then Evelyn's, the magic keeping wild droplets from spilling. The toast spread warm in Vickie's mouth, rum and ginger blanketing her tongue with comfort.

She might not be able to touch Azrael directly, but she was happy here in this odd, dancing dining room, the furniture lightly haunted and the glasses insistent that they be drunk from enthusiastically.

It was the only place she had ever really felt home, after all.

He was the only place she had ever felt home.

Priscilla cleared her throat.

"Speaking of complicated problems, we need to discuss our options here." The two looked at each other and then at Azrael, the tips of his ears blushing red.

"We have been talking about the way around the curse," said Evelyn.

Vickie reached her hand out to hold his, glove in glove.

They were close enough that she suspected the chairs and

table had been in cahoots, for now the table stretched not even half the distance of the majestic room, and the red-and-black patterned carpet sprawled out behind Azrael. She could have sworn he had started at the edge.

"Setting a soul seal is an old spell," explained Priscilla. "You'll have to take some time to think it over. To be sure." Beside her, Vickie saw Azrael's jaw clench.

"Are you sure we should even bring it up again?" His eyes were wild.

"It's fine, Az. I don't mind." Vickie bit her lip, thinking of the armchairs. Of the day he spent reading in the tea shop. The way he remembered her favorite table at Kessel Run.

Priscilla looked at her brother with sympathy, of all things. "It's the sort of thing Mom and Dad would have done, Az. Actually, it's exactly what Mom and Dad did."

"Yeah," he said, running a hand through his hair. "Yeah, I know."

Prissy's face softened into an expression that Vickie hadn't ever seen before, and it struck her that they were all grieving for Benedict and Persephone in that moment. Every single one of them in their own way. Az, for the parents he had not reached out to until it was too late. Prissy, for the role models she had always adored. Evelyn, for the people who made the person she was with happy.

And she, Victoria Elaine Starnberger, mourned the family she had both always and never had. The eclectic and lovely Harts, who had taken her in. Who had treated her as one of their own, and who had never judged her for the gift.

They had brought her Azrael, and now they were gone, and she was determined to make sure that she didn't lose him. To make sure that she loved him wholeheartedly, even if that was a little bit terrifying. No matter what, she would make good on that promise to his parents. She had been thinking about the soul binding for long enough, and here, at the dinner table where she'd enjoyed the only loving family meals she'd ever known, she realized she belonged.

She also realized that everyone was staring at her, waiting for a reaction.

"So, how do you do this love spell?"

Az shook his head. "Not a love spell. A binding. A fastening of souls."

"Those are all serious words," she said, hoping she sounded calmer than she felt.

From the eager expression on Priscilla's face, Vickie knew what her old friend was rooting for.

"You don't have to," said Azrael, looking embarrassed. "She's not suggesting we have to."

"Azrael," she said. "I *am* serious about you. I want to hear what it would be like. How it would work."

He pressed his lips together, emotions at war on his face. "Would you really want to bind yourself to me? A soul-binding is forever. Do you realize what it would mean?"

Vickie turned to Priscilla. "Explain it so he knows I understand."

"There is some spell work, and some plant craft. Nothing simple, but also nothing beyond what we have in the greenhouse. Myrtle. Rue. Honey, harvested yourself from a wild beehive. You work the spell, clear whatever lingers between you untold. You set a magical seal, with Az. A permanent magical seal."

"It cannot be undone," he added. His eyes clouded.

"What does that mean, exactly?" Vickie's voice sounded reedy and desperate, and for a moment Priscilla's eyebrows furrowed, her head tilting to the side, mouth drawing into a tight line.

"It means that there can be no lies between you, first of all, and then, you set the seal upon your heart. Upon your souls." Prissy looked at her brother. "It's serious enough that most witches don't do it."

"How does the seal work? Literally, I mean. What do we do to set the spell?" She hoped it wouldn't be painful or bloody. It didn't sound like it.

"We kiss," he explained, a muscle in his cheek twitching. "But it's a . . . significant kiss. A soul binding. It means we will always be bound to each other." Az looked at Vickie, and then looked away.

"Az. We are bound to each other already, with or without a spell." Vickie hoped he would hear the honesty of her words and take heart, but the weight of the attempt was terrifying. She knew they were tied to each other now, again, even with a curse keeping them physically apart, but they hadn't been back in each other's lives for long at all. She wasn't sure how things would turn out this time around. And she had other concerns too.

"If we did it, and I'm not saying we should do it, just that I want to know all our options. If we did it wrong, or if it didn't take. What would happen if it doesn't work?" Vickie whispered, though part of her already knew the answer.

He shrugged, snapping his ungloved fingers, on the hand opposite the one touching hers. The music picked up again, louder, and their drinks refilled. Wreaths of flowers settled around them on the table and danced into the air. He scattered a few purple lilies around her table setting and drink with another snap, as though sensing how nervous she was about this new information.

"If it doesn't work," he said, running a gloved thumb over her own, "then I die."

"Oh." Vickie bit her lip. "So, no pressure, then."

"It will work," said Evelyn, confident. All business. "If you decide to do it. If you love each other completely, and without reserve, it will work."

That was the catch, then. There could be no reservations. And just as she was finally sure she didn't have any, she had the awful sensation that maybe, just maybe, he did.

Azrael didn't meet Vickie's eyes, and her stomach lurched.

What reserve was he hiding behind that sculpted face? She could keep going as they were, pretending when she needed, until she was sure that reserve wasn't, well, deadly.

"Take some time," said Priscilla, snapping her fingers so

that the chicken appeared on their plates, garnished with fingerling potatoes and fresh herbs. "You two should talk about it after dinner. For now, let's all go around the table and say things we like about one another."

Azrael's smile curled up, his eyes still crinkled in slight distress.

"Hart family grace. Like Mom and Dad used to do."

"Yep. I'll start. Evelyn, *ma chérie*, I love that you are as exquisite in the Council room as you are in my foyer. Fucking perfect, everywhere." Prissy winked, her hand resting on Evelyn's back and the necklace there. She and Evelyn smiled at each other, unspoken words passing between them. "Az, I love that you are a good brother, despite never being as enthusiastic about my pranks as I want. And now that you're back here, you always show up. It means a lot. I know I could count on you to drive a getaway car if I ever needed it. Vickie, I love that you bought Hopelessly Teavoted and stopped it from becoming bougie and boring."

Evelyn leaned in and brushed a kiss along Priscilla's jaw that would have been too much for most dinner tables.

Not the Harts', though.

"Priscilla, lovey, I worship that thing you do—you know which one. We'll go to my place tonight." Evelyn winked, and Vickie was startled to see unflappable Priscilla blush, actually blush, and Azrael look like he did not want any further information. "Azrael, I love that you are both a powerful witch and a high school teacher. You're exactly the sort of absurdly noble combination I want in my chosen family." He smiled at this, clearly relieved she had shifted the subject. "And Victoria, I simply love that gown. The corset is giving me Swiftie."

"Thank you." She *loved* Hart grace, and it was the perfect relief from the tension of discussing forevers. "Well, Evelyn, I love your entire vibe. The outfit, your condo's decor, the fact that you're the president of the Witchery Council. All of it. And Priscilla, I love that you don't take any crap from anyone, including Azrael."

Vickie swallowed, looking across the table. Deciding between the smutty and the silly, the absurd and the thigh-clenching.

"Azrael Ashmedai Hart," Vickie began. "I love that you're willing to raise the dead with me if that's what it takes to solve a mystery."

"That's what you're going with? Not my stunning eyes, or all of this?" He gestured to his torso, and lower, and Priscilla snapped her fingers, magically throwing a bunch of bananas at him, from goddess knows where. They hit his shoulder with a thump, and she shook her head sternly.

"No judging, Az. Your turn."

"Fine," he said, his hazel eyes flashing, specks of green glinting against the brown. "Evelyn, I love that you're such a fierce leader, and your commitment to uniting the European Council with NACoW." Evelyn smiled. "Priscilla, I love that you took care of Mom and Dad when I couldn't be here." His voice cracked, and Vickie squeezed his gloved hand, glad for the interfering table and its shortening shenanigans.

"Vickie," he breathed, and the flowers paused for a moment, hovering in the air. "I love that you wear shoes that are too tall even though you are, by all means, very clumsy, and end up stumbling. Honestly, it's a wonder you don't fall into a ditch. You're very lucky I'm here to catch you."

Priscilla pelted him with plums now, each finger snap a barrage of purple fruit.

"Az, I thought you were going to be serious."

"I will be," he deadpanned. "I intend to be completely serious with Vickie in the future. But the things I want to be serious about are best said once we figure all of this out. And we all have business to attend to before that happens. Best not to start a thing until I can finish it."

He winked, and to Vickie's embarrassment, Evelyn and Priscilla exchanged a knowing smile.

CHAPTER 29

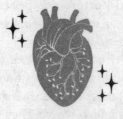

Azrael

The rush of the school year picked up, and without help from her high school employees during the week, Vickie was stretched so thin catching up at the store that Az felt like he had blinked and they were halfway through October without talking in more than passing and text messages.

People weren't kidding about the exhaustion of first-year teaching, or of running a whole business, it seemed.

Still, there was something nice about having a person to text message with a picture of his cat at 7 a.m. before he left for work. Something reassuring about seeing that she had texted him back right before he crashed on his couch Thursday, falling asleep at 6 p.m. only to wake up at half past one and stumble up to bed. The year was hard. The case seemed to be stalling, waiting for him to either find something on Chet or find another lead. And as far as he knew, Thornington had been up to nothing more nefarious than terrorizing senior literature students. But he had the possibility of Vickie, so he would hold on to hope.

By the time the early dismissal day rolled around Friday, he was desperate to see her.

They needed to figure out who the greater devil had bargained with, and it was less than a month until the veil thinned.

Only the little skull bells jangling at the door of Hopelessly Teavoted could soothe his anxious, roiling soul.

This late on a Friday afternoon the shop was mostly clear, and Hank's plate was already empty as he read his newspaper at a high-top in the back.

Azrael smiled. Hank's presence felt like another sign from the universe that he should follow in the footsteps of great loves like Hank's, and his parents'.

Touching be damned. You didn't have to touch to love a person, did you?

"Mr. Hart!" Hazel's cheery voice called from the cash register. He'd been in every morning under the guise of picking up coffee and donuts, and every day, she asked him the same thing. "Do you know when you'll be done grading essays?"

"I wrapped up my penultimate set this afternoon. Your class is next. Not to worry, you'll get feedback and the next glorious writing lesson soon."

Hazel smiled. "I was hoping that my all-time favorite teacher might be able to tell me how I did on mine, since, you know, he's in love with my boss and all."

Azrael rolled his eyes at this, trying to keep his face impassive, though he felt a blush creep up, and there was absolutely no way Hazel would let it slide.

"Awwwww yeah, VICKIE. MR. HART IS HERE, eager to see you."

Dammit, Hazel. There went his plan for a cool, nonchalant entrance.

"Mr. Hart, do you want a drink?"

"Yeah, coffee. Black, with a little room."

"As though I don't already know your order. Just wasn't sure if you were going with your coffee or your tea since it's close to closing time. Banana bread?"

"When do I ever not want banana bread?" Azrael said jokingly. He loved that Hazel was his student. She kept discussion time sharp and engaging, and her thoughts on Mary Shelley were downright inspiring.

"Coming right up." She beamed at him, and then mock-whispered, "I have been putting in a good word. We all have."

From behind the counter, Hank nodded and set down his paper.

"Hazel!" his jolly voice boomed. "Weren't you saying you had to get home to watch your baby brother?"

"Yes, Hank, thank you so much for reminding me. I'm in such a hurry, and I almost completely forgot. Vickie! Can you close without me?"

Hank tapped the side of his nose with a chubby finger, glee stamped across his face, and Hazel winked at them, as though the pair actually thought they were being subtle.

"You know, it's been so long since I've seen your mother; I could give you a ride home so you're not late for that very urgent babysitting job that you have to get to." Hank made a dramatic gesture of checking his wristwatch.

Vickie appeared in the doorway from the back, glaring at the two of them, who ignored her withering gaze.

"Well, since it sounds like you have an important family obligation that for some reason Hank wants to remind you of, you'd better get going." Her gaze fell on Az, bright green eyes more tired than he wanted to see, stress written across her forehead. "Azrael," she said.

"Bye, boss! Bye, Mr. Hart! Don't do anything Mary Shelley wouldn't do. See you Monday!"

Hank and Hazel hustled out of the door, locking up, and not even bothering to complete their ruse when Hank turned left toward the parking lot and Hazel right to her bike on the stand out front.

Azrael couldn't help but chuckle.

"Well, they could not have been any more obvious, could they?" Vickie grabbed a rag and did a final wipe down of the counter, though it was clear that Hazel had planned this and cleaned up before taking off. "I'll be out in a moment if you want to sit down and drink that. I just need to dump the rest of the coffee."

The kitchen door swung behind her, harder than he wanted it to, and he thought about following her. Hazel and Hank had to have been plotting daily, hoping he'd show up at the right time. That made him smile. Hallowcross felt like home in more than just Vickie.

So he could sit here and wait and breathe in the rightness of it all.

Home was in the warm smell of mint and rooibos drifting from the drying sink, where Vickie had dumped the teapots. In the lingering sweetness of baked goods and, always, the strawberry scent of Vickie. The way the shop was both old and new, part of his family growing up and his love—his new family—now.

He pulled the coffee cup Hazel had given him closer. It was patterned with small bats on the inside that changed colors with the heat of the coffee. In sprinkling his sugar, he'd missed a little bit, and the dusting of it clung around the rim in a spot he'd hit with liquid. It reminded him of years ago with Vickie.

Azrael remembered the burn of the margaritas they'd made, rimmed with sugar like this, but coarser. Vickie hated salt, even for margaritas. She had been sweetness and deviance rolled into one glittery sunshine girl stealing liquor from the cabinets of her parents' posh barroom. The Starnbergers never noticed it was missing. Or if they did, they never cared.

That night with the margarita had been one of many nights in high school when Azrael almost told her how he felt. He recalled the pads of his fingers grazing those soft, soft spaces on the backs of her legs that he now missed so torturously as he carried her to the bathroom after one too many blender margaritas. He hated vomit, but he didn't care quite as much if it was Vickie's.

Any amount of grossness was worth the song that thrummed in his blood when she had been near, and he'd been a fool in his love for her. Consumed.

He'd peppered the walls of his gothic bedroom with posters of old movies. His parents had left them there, and the memories made him ache, for the tragedy, but most of all, for Victoria. Before school started, he had finally taken down the matte images of a retro space opera he adored, and the poster of the much-older-than-he-was seventies band fronted by a free-spirited woman Vickie loved. He'd rolled up the posters of the fictional British prince who loved an American president's son, the first movie, and then the second, and the print she'd given him once of two old-fashioned movie starlets kissing passionately. Taking the art down made him ache, the thought of the fairy tale of one couple, and the tragic ending of the other, but most of all, Victoria. The girl he worshiped more than his first kiss, Mike Starnes, and his perfect blond hair with the little swoop that had made Azrael's heart skip a beat when he kissed him. More than Nella Caruthers, who had been the person he'd had awkward sex with for the first time. More than gorgeous Alison Price in the gazebo that mildly embarrassing time senior year.

He even had a Kinks poster, an homage to Vickie's name that he wondered if she had figured out. He always thought of her when he looked at it. But the posters were better suited to hang in his classroom now, relics of who he had been as a child paired next to iconic poets and authors, a jumping-off point to understanding the children who would walk through his doors. When he'd taken the parts of himself into the blank walls of his classroom back in August, hanging them carefully with a pride flag and his heart, he was happy. Hopeful that he could be the person that they came to when they needed help with writing, with reading, and with thinking critically about the world. That they could add posters too.

Every day he was tired, and every day he worried about the looming deadline, but that didn't change how he felt about Victoria. He'd messed up before, waded through the heartache of misunderstanding. He could handle the threat of potential immolation.

Vickie was still rustling around in the back, but Az had waited long enough.

He strode through the door, confident in his ability to keep his distance. He'd win her heart, even if it was from afar. He wasn't just done pretending away the way that he loved her. He was ready for her to be done pretending too. But he could wait until she decided that on her own. Being patient was awful, itchy almost, but it was feeling something real.

"Hey, Vickie," he said, stilling the swinging door with his hand.

She was standing at the back counter, cleaning up from measuring ingredients for tomorrow's pastries.

Her shoulders tensed a little, but she tossed the rag to the side and wiped a stray spot.

"What?" When she turned, he saw it on her face. The pinched lips. The wrinkled forehead. She rolled her neck, and he must not have hidden the cracking of his heart at her tone well because her face softened. "Has there been news? With the psychic? Your asshole boss?"

He shook his head. "No change with Madam Cleopatra. Not even so much as someone trying to break past the wards around the hospital again."

"That's strange. And your asshole boss?"

"He's still an asshole, but I can't prove any other wrongdoing. I'm tempted to start following him after school, but what if he catches me and we're wrong?"

"I think, if there are no other leads, it may be time to sacrifice yourself on the altar of dignity."

"Yeah, I get that." He wasn't looking forward to it, especially not with how snappish the man was about sharing a copy machine. He could only imagine how grumpy Chet would be if wrongly accused of villainy. "I do need to do that. I will. Monday."

"Do it, but be careful. Text me if you need anything. Promise?"

"I do."

She bit her lip, and he leaned against the closest wall to keep from giving in to the pull that was her body, beckoning him always to come closer, even if it would mean sudden death. "Az, I've been thinking about everything. About forever. But in the meantime, what if I called one more pretend?"

How bad was dying, really?

Fuck. Two minutes and his resolve to avoid a fiery death was already at an all-time low. He had to cut the tension between them, and he couldn't do it with his tongue the way he'd most prefer to. Tongues, though, had other uses.

"I accept *your* pretend, though I told you, I'm not pretending anymore. I want you to know that everything I say, everything I do, isn't pretending anymore. It's all real."

"Oh yeah? Want to come upstairs and talk about it? I can't promise anything fancy, but I do have several packages of ramen that could have your name on them. From across the table, of course."

"Obviously," he said, smile faltering. She bit her lip, and he pushed on. "Is it the chicken flavor?"

"The best one. Yes. Come on, you can help me." She stood up, fishing in her pocket, and took out a pair of long silk gloves. She rolled the sleeves of her turtleneck up, pulled the gloves on, rolled the sleeves back down so that the fabric overlapped, and reached for his hand.

The warmth of it hit him through the fabric, and he wondered for a moment if he was burning, heart bursting at the almost of touching her, his joy drowned once again.

Az focused instead on watching the shape of her as she walked up the stairs slowly, not dropping his hand, though stretching back to hold it must have been awkward. Vickie's jeans were tight enough that he could see the outlines of her hips, her thighs, and the spot where they met and the fabric had worn almost bare. Damn. That was his favorite spot, but he'd have to be careful about touching her, even through clothes.

One little hole, one ripped seam, one tiny mistake would be all it took to kill him.

Half-hard by the time they reached the top of the stairs, he wondered if his dick had a death wish. He'd have to be very, very careful around Vickie.

The size of the apartment didn't help. Five minutes in and he'd resorted to standing across the kitchen from her, snapping his help from afar.

Leaning against the refrigerator, he watched her at the stove.

"Tell me you at least have a vegetable to add to that."

"I'm not sure. Can you spell one for me?"

"Vickie. Is there anything relatively healthy we could add? Tofu?"

"I have jam," she offered, gesturing to the refrigerator.

"Jam is not a vegetable, and it does not go with ramen."

"Well, help yourself to the fridge. I was going to get fancy and put eggs on top."

"I could run to the store."

Vickie whirled around. "And pass up on the urgency of pretending?"

"No, you're right. Who needs vegetables? Vegetables are the worst." The slow curl of her lip gave her away. He'd never deny her this pretend. Never.

"Yeah. You know, I was going to have a few drinks anyway, and I shouldn't drive home." He flicked his fingers together, and a dark and stormy appeared on the counter next to her, matching the one he held, both in plastic pirate-shaped cups that his mother had left over from some sort of event in the storage area.

"Nice," said Vickie, smiling at the cup, and taking a sip.

He took a long drink, set his glass down, and opened the fridge to see if there was actually anything that could help them eat like people who were approaching thirty and occasionally required nutrients. She had cheese, coffee creamer, and eggs, but there was an unopened bag of baby carrots he could work with. He snapped his fingers, and the carrots cut themselves with a knife, folding into neat matchstick piles.

"Quick thinking, Mr. Hart," she said, her tone playful enough to force him to down the rest of the drink.

"Don't—" he bit off, shifting uncomfortably in his jeans. "Don't call me that."

"Fine."

She took out a pan and glanced over her shoulder at him.

Goddess, what he would give to brace her over the counter and rail her until she screamed his whole name and dropped the smirk. It was impossible, of course, or if it was possible—and he wasn't saying he *hadn't* considered the logistics of, say, a full latex suit—it would be different enough that they would need to talk about it more than just a little bit of banter over vegetables, or the lack thereof.

"Can you crack the eggs?"

He snapped his fingers, and music drifted from the speaker of his phone as the eggs flew through the air and cracked gracefully against each other to the rhythm before dropping into the pan.

"Would it be so bad, Vickie? To live like this? Together, at a small distance, touching carefully? Protected."

"Azrael." Her voice was a warning. "I can't cook distracted, especially when you're smoldering like that."

"You're making instant noodles."

"Exactly. They require precise timing. Can we just pretend it's a normal dinner date, between two people who aren't cursed not to touch?"

Shit. She'd meant that kind of pretending. Which he could do. He swallowed. "I'll drop it. I promise. Listen, let's eat, and then we can plot out everything we know about the Big Bad and have a few more drinks." Her eyes narrowed for a moment, and he held up his hands in an offering of peace. "A few more safely distanced drinks, and then maybe I can take the couch." He gestured to the couch, pressed up against the wall shared by her bedroom.

"That couch is not comfortable enough to sleep on."

He snapped his fingers, and it extended. The cushions fluffed and moved outward. It was big enough now to stick out into the edges of the hall.

"Fine." She stared at him. "But we stay far enough away from each other to avoid any temptation. And you put my couch back to fitting in my living room when you're done."

Swallowing, he nodded. He wasn't sure there was any distance long enough to do that, but he'd take what he could get.

By the time they were done with the instant noodles, he couldn't believe they were from a package.

"You're impressive," he said, digging in.

"I aim to please." She swirled a fork around in her bowl, catching noodles and eating for a few minutes before pausing. "So, asshole boss?"

"I'll follow him this week. I should have done it earlier, but I got caught up in grading and anxiety, and since we knew whoever it is won't really make a move until Halloween, it kind of kept sliding down my to-do list."

"I get that. Even the end of the world feels like it could get pushed back when things get hectic at work."

"Shop busy?"

She sighed.

"I'm running myself ragged. I need to hire more help now that Hazel's only weekends and early dismissal days. I just worry about money, and I told myself if I work hard enough, I can handle working all day and baking and prepping late into the night. Doing the bulk of everything else on Wednesdays when I close the store."

"Vickie," he started. He couldn't reach for her hand, so he snapped instead, warming the apartment to the perfect temperature. "It's okay to ask for help sometimes."

"I know," she said, biting her lip. "Do you think you could maybe set up some of the baking prep work with magic? I suspect that's how your mom made things run so smoothly."

"Shit," he said. "Yes, of course. That would be so easy. I can take care of it tonight, and set it up so the prep work happens up here, so Hazel doesn't notice anything amiss. But you have to look for more help in the shop too. You deserve rest."

"While we are on the subject of burnout," she began. "I think you could ease up on the weekend-long grading stretches."

He frowned. "Won't students—or their parents—be upset if they don't get work back right away?"

Vickie shrugged. "Probably some will. But most will probably understand, and even the ones who don't, I bet they'd be more upset to lose you as a teacher if you keep up this kind of unsustainable hustle to return every assignment so quickly."

"Fine," he said. "It's a deal, but only if we both agree to set aside some time for solving magical mysteries."

"And for personal pursuits." She pushed the empty bowl away from her, and he smiled, snapping his fingers to take care of the dishes. "Can you get the ones I left in the shop too?"

He winked and snapped twice. "Washed and dried. It's done. Did you have any other specific personal pursuits in mind?"

"Actually, yes, but it's not going to be what you think." Her eyes glinted.

"I'm happy if you're happy, Vickie." He meant it too.

"In the spirit of pretending we are a totally normal couple, want to watch a movie?"

"Yes. Do I get to pick?" He sat down on the edge of the couch, and she shook her head, laughing at him.

"No. My choice."

"Fair enough."

"I think you'll like it, though. It involves a character storming through a misty moor in a see-through white shirt."

Azrael smiled widely. "Excellent, excellent choice."

And when he fell asleep, several hours, several drinks, and very little progress on identifying any suspects later, he raised his hand to the wall next to him, pressing it as though he could feel her on the other side, where her bed was.

The magic thrumming under his fingernails and in his wrists told him where she was, and he fell asleep like that, half reassured by her presence and half agonizing over his inability to get any closer than two hands pressed against opposite sides of a wall.

It was something, though. And something, with love, could be better than nothing.

He hoped.

CHAPTER 30

Victoria

In high school once, Vickie had woken up to this same feeling of longing and *almost* that burrowed in her bones and rushed to both her heart and between her thighs. She wanted him not just for sex but for the closeness, and the smell of burnt amber and lemon.

For the home of him.

When she'd woken up, ten years earlier, the pit in her stomach had been from overindulgence, but this felt very much the same.

She'd had too much to drink at a party and Az had driven her home and put her to bed across the king-size mattress from him. The slide of those silk sheets, absurd for a sixteen-year-old to have, had been a cool relief on her sweaty skin. She'd woken up to velvet curtains drawn tight so no sunlight could get in, and to Azrael still sleeping on his side of the bed, but with one hand thrown over her. She'd thought, for a moment, that if she didn't move at all they could stay there forever in the embrace of the room and the bed. Azrael's eyes had fluttered and her stomach had twisted. She had wanted to crawl toward him and touch him, but unfortunately, the twisting had not been due to desire alone. She had heaved, and his eyes shot open, fingers snapping a bucket under her head, while the other hand moved to pull her hair back from her face.

Az had shushed her and rubbed circles on her back. He'd gotten her water and reassured her in soft words that the magic had gotten rid of the vomit and the bucket fast enough to avoid any lingering smells, though she had still cried in the bathroom adjacent to his massive room while brushing her teeth.

Vickie hadn't spent the night again after that, but on more than one occasion, she'd had sweaty, frustrating dreams starring Azrael Hart and those curtains. They turned to nightmares at times, and to something else entirely in the darkest part of the night, when she lay there, guilty over touching herself and thinking of him, trying to think of other things—breasts, whoever she was dating, the best sex scenes in books she had read. Nothing was quite Azrael then, and nothing was quite Azrael now, and it made her fucking furious that she couldn't touch him.

And when she woke up, before her alarm, body throbbing from the nearness of him, the warmth of her comforter a hug, it was too easy to shut her eyes against the nascent slivers of sunlight drifting through the slatted blinds. To slide into memory and longing, and slip her hand beneath the waistband of her pajamas, and pretend, for a few agonizing moments, that it was his.

The pretending was good enough for now; it would have to be. If she closed her eyes and concentrated, it was almost like being with him, close enough to touch through the wall, and with the door cracked open to the bedroom, breathing the same air. Her fingertips picked up speed, racing against the alarm that would inevitably sound and dictate that she should start her morning. Her hand slipped in and out easily now, and she brought the other upward to her breast, her nipple, thinking of him, wishing it were his, burning for him until she was so close that she swore she could feel him.

A shattering sound tore her eyes open.

Azrael was standing in the doorway, lips parted, coffee splattering his front, the shards of her favorite mug at his feet.

She withdrew her hand, and he swallowed.

"Don't," he croaked, and then tried again. "Don't stop on my account. Sorry, Vickie, I was going to bring you coffee, but I thought you were still asleep. I was going to leave it on your nightstand to wake up to." A ferocious blush covered him, from the tips of his ears to his cheeks.

She nodded to the puddle of porcelain shards and liquid. "Clean that up. I have an idea."

Az snapped his fingers, and it wasn't lost on her that they were shaky, his eyes darkened by desire. They couldn't touch, sure, but she didn't get through undergrad and three-quarters of a master's degree without some ability to improvise.

"I want you to watch me, and then I want you to follow me into the shower."

"I—yes. Okay. Anything."

Standing up, she let her fingers slide under the edge of her T-shirt. Azrael braced an arm against the doorway, biting his lower lip.

As slowly as she could, she drew the shirt over her head. The delay was agonizing; each inch of fabric set her ablaze, and the rough scrape of it against her nipples made her breath catch.

"Victoria." He sounded strangled. "You are the most beautiful creature I have ever laid eyes on. Fuck." He scrubbed a hand down his face and shook his fingers out for a moment.

She tossed the shirt at him, and he caught it, setting it down on a chair.

"You're not so bad yourself, Mr. Hart," she purred, cupping each breast with a hand against the chill of the early morning. "Can I get by?"

"You can have literally any fucking thing you want, Vickie." He flattened himself against the doorway and she ducked beside him, narrowly avoiding calamity, the danger of it thrumming through her veins.

"I'm going to take a shower," she said, stopping halfway through the living room, and bending over slowly to slide her sweatpants down, and then step out of them and toward the bathroom. "Care to join me?"

"Yes," he said, voice solemn and eyes blazing as he strode toward her, stopping an arm's length away. "I have never wanted anything in my life so much."

"Good," she said, walking to the bathroom door and pausing in the entryway to slide her panties off and toss them at him.

He caught them with little effort, running them through his fingers. He groaned. "Damn, these are so wet. You must have been close."

"I was thinking of you."

"You know what, how bad can dying be, really? Death comes to us all. I'm ready."

Vickie laughed. "No dying today, Az. I have a walk-in shower with a corner bench and a particularly strong showerhead that I had to install after a leak."

"Holy shit," he breathed, running a hand through his hair, face flickering with understanding of what she meant. "You won't be late for work?"

"I have to shower anyway, and I know someone who offered to help me cheat and make the baked goods more quickly from now on."

"Devil damn me, yes, you do."

Walking into the bathroom, she slid the glass door of the shower back and stepped over the rim of it to turn on the water, running it until it was warm.

"Get in here and take your clothes off, Azrael." The tension stretched between them, agonizing. Between her thighs, her body throbbed for her to finish what she'd started.

"Tell me what you want me to do." His eyes bored into her.

"Take your shirt off first. Slowly." He complied, pulling it over his head. She wanted to lick his stomach, the way the muscles moved when he tossed the shirt to the side.

She sat down on the corner bench of the shower, closest to the water, and reached for her breasts, one in each hand.

"Now strip. Slowly. So I can see every inch of you while I do this."

He bit his lip.

"Can I—with magic—can I help?"

Shit. She'd forgotten about the magic.

"Yes," she breathed. "Please."

Pulling his pants down, Az stumbled a little, and she watched him as he struggled to get the tight jeans down over his socks. Brow furrowed, he snapped his fingers, and the pants and socks were off, leaving only boxers, patterned with little cats, straining to contain an erection that she wanted so badly to run her hand across.

"Vickie, where can I touch you?" He snapped his fingers, and the magic brushed against her throat. "Here?"

She shook her head.

"Here?" Under her fingers, invisible wisps of power grazed, hardening her nipples. She shifted, and he swore. "Devil dammit, you are so fucking beautiful." He tweaked them again. "Here?"

"Mmm. Almost," she said. "Take your boxers off and get in here. Touch yourself the way I want to touch you."

"How do you want to touch me?" He snapped his fingers, staring at her from under hooded eyes, and his underwear was on the floor, one hand hovering above his erection, the tip of it beading and glistening in the cool morning light drifting through the narrow horizontal window above her.

"I want to touch you so hard you can't stand it. Like, literally so hard you have to brace yourself. Come here and do it, Azrael."

Carefully, he walked toward her, and for a moment she thought he wouldn't stop. That he would take her in his arms and burn for it, the exquisite feeling of skin against skin. But he stopped and leaned against the wall of the shower across from her, the water from the larger, fixed showerhead streaming in rivulets down his hard body.

"Use both hands for a moment, Az. Stroke it for me until you're desperate, and don't you dare stop watching."

He slid a hand down the length of himself, groaning a little, adding a second hand, and then leaning against the cream-colored tile. "You first."

Vickie bit her lip, and stood up, sliding the mounted shower-head out of its holder. Water teased her now from the head, splattering across her body and onto his, almost like touching. At her thigh, the showerhead sprayed a steadier stream.

"Both of us together," she insisted, sitting back down on the corner seat. Spreading her thighs all the way, and fumbling with the stream adjuster so that the water began to pulse.

Azrael moaned, slapping a hand against the tile. "Dammit, Vickie, you're going to be the death of me."

Moving fingers to her nipples and holding the showerhead at a distance for a moment, Vickie shook her head. "No dying. Watch. Do it the way I would, slow and slick and sweet at first, and then harder, rougher, until you can't stand it."

"Fuck," he swore, his face flushed, but he complied, sliding his hand down his dick once more and cupping his balls with the other.

"This definitely counts as fucking," she said, turning the showerhead on herself so that the spray pushed against her folds, her center. She sighed a little, running a hand through her wet hair to keep it out of her eyes, and then down her shoulder, her neck, her nipple, tweaking, before sliding her fingers down, to bracket where the water hit, slipping in and out of herself, angling her hips up to meet the water, forcing herself not to tear her gaze away from Azrael.

He was bracing himself against the wall of the shower now, teeth buried in his bottom lip, hand moving furiously up and down, panting, chest heaving.

"Vickie, this is not going to be an all-day affair," he moaned.

She was too keyed up to answer, though: starting in bed and then stopping before the agony of almost touching had set her on fire, and the water was pounding, pulsing, just the way she liked it when she was alone. It was a thousand times dirtier with Azrael standing there, muscles straining in the corded forearm that braced against the wall, the slap of his other arm against his body as he drew it back and forth and back and forth driving her toward madness.

This was more than pretending. This was the kind of love, the kind of lust, that undid people.

And Vickie was coming undone, one hand scrambling at the slick wall, the other pushing the showerhead closer and closer to her body, the intensity of the pressure building in her and against her, until sparks rose, gathering at her core, and heat coiled to a withering crescendo, and she finished, screaming his name.

Azrael watched her, eyes greedy, grip firm, for a few seconds in the aftermath as she writhed on the small shower bench, pounding on the wall once more as he spilled, steady spurts onto the taupe tile of the floor, the water washing the traces of both their pleasures away.

"Damn," he whispered.

"Right? It wouldn't be such a bad setup. Living like this."

"No," said Azrael, voice reverent. "No, it would not."

Somehow in the postshower haze, while he was helping her prepare the shop in record time, Vickie agreed to join Azrael after work for that long-promised midnight hike. Which was how she ended up, water bottle in hand, at 11 p.m., dressed for the outdoors, and facing the haunted knocker of Hart Manor.

It groaned a little when she lifted it, and to her surprise, it was Priscilla who answered the door, dressed in hiking gear next to Azrael, a long dark braid hanging down over her left shoulder.

"Vickie! I thought I owed you an actual hike this time, since, you know, I bailed on yours last time."

"That was years ago," said Vickie, looking at Priscilla with suspicion.

A smile quirked up Azrael's face.

"Where's Evelyn?" Vickie asked as Azrael shook his head emphatically behind her.

"She went back to England. She'll be here tomorrow for a few weeks before flying back permanently." Priscilla stared at Vickie, eyes defiant.

"Oh no! She isn't coming back after that?" Azrael was shaking his head again, and Vickie realized, a moment too late, what he meant.

"She's thinking about it," said Priscilla, and her voice was an octave too high and brighter than it ought to be. "We're working through some things. The Council president is back from paternity leave, but only temporarily, and she's trying to decide if she wants the job when he leaves, but meeting his new baby has made her . . . a little more urgent about some of the things we don't see eye to eye on."

"Sorry, Prissy." The distance between Vickie and Azrael seemed smaller now, compared to an ocean.

"I'll fly out and work it out as soon as we get things cleared up here, but I don't want to leave before we solve this business."

"Oh, good," said Vickie, though the look on Priscilla's face suggested there might be more to the story than that. Az shook his head again when his sister turned to pick up a water bottle, and Vickie got the message loud and clear.

This was a friend thing. Which was good. They were friends.

And besides, a mid-October night hike in Vermont was cold enough to warrant gloves and outerwear that would keep them protected. It was the perfect activity, even if it was the opposite of what she would rather be doing with him.

Which involved less clothing, but more danger. And the possibility of death.

The hike was better. Even if the trail narrowed the farther they climbed, and as they had gotten to the tricky part, they weren't talking to save breath, so when Azrael moved to walk single file behind her, he'd brushed his hand against hers.

She had flexed without meaning to in the glove, a tiny spasm of emotion at being so close to touching, and yet so far away.

"Sorry," Az said, the gravel of his voice seeping through her layers. Fuck, why did he have to be so hot?

"Hey, guys, I'm going to go pee," yelled Priscilla unceremoniously.

They paused, Vickie sitting on a rock. She knew this trail like the back of her hand, and they were ten minutes away from the falls. Around this corner, they'd make a steep descent, and then the path would level off. It was always harder coming than it was going.

"Vickie," Azrael began. "I'll follow Chet, and then maybe we can reconvene. Go over everything."

"I see you started the important conversations without me," said Prissy, emerging from the bushes and rubbing hand sanitizer in. "The Council still has the wards up around the hospital, and we did determine that if we can figure out who tried to take Connie's soul out of her body, we have a better chance of setting her right. The Council thinks that the person may have inadvertently been successful with just a miniscule fraction of it."

"Someone stole part of her soul?"

"It isn't technically possible, because she's nonmagic, but the thing is, one of our research assistants found this old tome about how most mundanes have small threads of magic in them, so inconsequential that they'd almost never come into play, unless something really weird happened."

"Really weird like an unknown villain attempting to reap a soul, finding it to be boring and human, and then stuffing it back in?"

"Yep, just like that. Anyway, if the person were to be apprehended, we could probably figure out how to release that scrap of soul without killing them. Probably." Her smile widened. "And if that person—a villain, obviously—did end up dying, well, it should solve the problem completely. That would make my life much easier, actually, paperwork and all. Whatever does happen to Madam Cleopatra is my jurisdiction, so it will be my problem."

"Is there a point at which we can ask the Council to step in and help us find them?"

Prissy frowned. "Maybe. They are already trying, is the thing. So it would be stepping in and saying you don't think they—well, *we*, really—are doing a good enough job. It would be a little messy. I'd give it till the full moon, run a tracking spell then." She paused. "The concern is that if they become . . . irate . . . with you, the retribution could involve looking into all of your past." Vickie winced at that. "If you don't come up with anything, that gives you two weeks to get the Council involved."

Azrael shook his head. "And once they're involved, they won't want *us* involved unless they say so."

"Exactly," said Priscilla darkly. "That's why it would be better if we had new leadership to steer it back in the direction Dad was taking it. A more collaborative community, and less of a hierarchy modeled after the human shenanigans that pass as politics."

"Until the end of the month," Vickie said. They were missing something, and she wasn't sure if they should force the puzzle if it meant shoving their lives under the microscope of the Council's scrutiny. Beside her, Azrael sighed, pushing a curl out of his eyes. His hair was getting long, and she wanted to catch it in her fingers, to weave it around her hands.

To push her mouth against his and feel with her lips, her tongue, her teeth, what it was to love Azrael Hart. When she looked at him she wanted, she realized, with a start, to bind her soul to his.

Probably. And it was too big of a thing to admit just yet.

For now, Vickie settled for rummaging in her backpack and pulling out a few baggies of homemade snacks.

"Trail mix?"

He took the bag, his shoulders relaxing slightly and the corners of his mouth twitching.

"This is a bag of chocolate candies with a few walnuts on top."

"What? Trail mix is just chocolate candies with obstacles. Everyone knows that."

Laughing, Azrael pushed her shoulder gently. Like they were bros. Like he hadn't stared her in the eye and told her that he was done pretending. And then fucked his hand watching her writhe under her showerhead until he came all over her bathroom tiles. They could always settle on the easy way out. Be friends at a distance after Halloween. Phone calls only, sight unseen. Something in her chest twisted painfully at the thought.

"All right, come on, lovebirds," said Priscilla. "Let's go see a waterfall."

This time, Vickie took the rear, and it was all she could do not to watch the back pockets of Azrael's jeans like the miserable, frustrated creature that she was.

She thought she had known what it was to pine, but this, this was what it meant to burn for someone.

CHAPTER 31

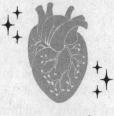

Azrael

The alarm rang, and for a brief moment, Azrael remembered only what it was like to watch Vickie in the shower. To hold her hand, even if gloved, on the trail.

That he loved her.

Then sleep cleared from his eyes, and he rolled over to empty silk sheets, dark underneath him in the canopy bed, and the torturous dream, the one where they were together and he was curled around her like a cat, slipped away.

He sighed, and a low purr beside him told him that at least he was not completely alone. Threads of white fur speckled the otherwise spotless fabric beneath him, and he smiled.

"That it will never come again is what makes life so sweet," Az murmured to Emily Lickinson. There was despair in losing the ability to touch Vickie, but sweetness, too, in at least knowing that there had existed moments in which he'd had a place in the universe. A home without loneliness.

The cat, too, though he had protested adopting her, was a comfort to him.

Emily rubbed her white fur against his arm. She was a contrary, ornery creature, but she had a knack for knowing when he was in pain. She surprised him by curling up next to him when things were at their worst.

He'd been following Chet home since Monday, and nothing. The man had gone home to his apartment and emerged only to go to the gym Tuesday and Wednesday. Az had been busy setting up Vickie's baking to happen via magic even when he was not there, and between that and getting off together from a safe distance, he had been working himself to the bone.

He'd fallen asleep not sure if he was swollen and stretched taut with the despair of losing the ability to have her the way he used to imagine just as they were finally ready to come together, or if it was desire lingering from the way her hands had gripped his neck before the curse had ignited. Or the way his name had sounded on her lips on that shower bench, across her couch from him, or on her bed while he leaned in the doorway. So close and yet so far away.

He'd been a wreck. And since then, Emily had wound about his ankles. Prowling. Waïting.

Staring at the pictures the house had plastered on the walls for him now, he recognized melancholy watercolors it must have dug up from the basement to match his mood.

Could cats appreciate paintings? The sorrowful brushstrokes made him feel for Vickie, an achy longing that he wasn't sure was healthy but wasn't willing to give up.

He loved her. And he was pretty sure Vickie loved him. Sitting up, he snapped his fingers, magicking allergy pills and a glass of water into his hands.

Would it be enough to live loving her from afar, at least with a pet now to keep him company? Could they spend moonlit nights like that hike, at arm's length, and sleeping with walls between them, always only almost touching? Mornings in the shower, watching each other get off, slick with finishing but also with longing, not able to finish the other the way they each wanted to? Could they do it without seeing each other, phone sex only, conversations separated by never beholding each other so that he wouldn't immolate? Wondering if she would eventually move on, or if he would, or both of them, knowing they might always be a little bit wistful, and yet finding solace in the wideness of a world sure to hold other people who could make them at least somewhat happy.

Or would she decide to choose him completely? Solve the problem of her curse's deadline with a seal that bound them forever.

Either way, he couldn't decide for her. After the shower, he had almost asked her to be his. Asked her to go through all the ways they could be together. They could use gloves and great caution, or continue to kiss through plastic wrap like that old show with the pie maker who could reanimate the dead. It had seemed so cute and kitschy on television, as though it was charming and inconvenient but possible. Not deadly, like in real life, when the looming expiration date of Halloween in a little less than a week put a damper on all the possibilities. He had almost offered on the hike to touch her with clothes on, but his sister was there, and that was, quite frankly, an important safeguard that Priscilla was maybe aware of. She had insisted on coming along, even though she tended to curl up in designer pajamas and drink expensive sauvignon blanc when Evelyn flew back to England.

He had wondered if maybe it would be a good way to go— burning to death to touch Vickie. Priscilla had coolly reminded him that this would be much more injurious to Vickie than it would to him, since she would have to live on to deal with the guilt and repercussions.

No, his self-immolation would involve Vickie facing a Witchery Council investigation, on top of the terrible heartache of killing the person she loved.

No one should have to do that.

The best thing—the only thing, really—was to get up and go on with his life and keep it friendly unless she decided she was ready to stop pretending too. They could be friends. Colleagues in supernatural investigations, even. Occasional partners in shower fantasies, though that wouldn't stop him from loving her forever.

He had driven back to the old church with Priscilla the

previous weekend, but they had found nothing but broken stained glass and the remnants of a few wild break-in parties.

That left Chet. Az was so tired, but he resolved to follow the man, one last time, after school today. After all, the full moon had been last week, and the month was dwindling.

CHAPTER 32

Victoria

It had been Az the whole time. It hadn't ever been Natalie, or Robbie, or any of the other people she had dated who were terrible for her in the end. They had all been distractions.

The universe had a sick sense of humor, and she'd known when he texted her last night about tailing Chet. They were close enough to the deadline for this to be dangerous, and when he said he saw Chet go into the Brethren of One Love building Friday night, she realized, with a whisper of intuition, that none of them should confront him alone. She made him promise not to go in without them. They needed Evelyn, who returned this afternoon, and Priscilla, and now she needed to get through this Sultry Sunday.

Vickie knew, the second she realized how close Az could have been to death, tailing Chet, that she did not want to just pretend anymore. And this morning, having admitted it to herself, she realized she had never actually been pretending.

The day before they left for college, words had hung unspoken from her lips that it wasn't right. For them to be apart.

Vickie wanted to dive into the memory of what it had been like to feel Azrael's magic, and to watch him lose control in the shower, but she had a shop to open. And then a makeshift coven to assemble, and a soul to reap.

With a ding, the baking timer disrupted her fantasy, and she pulled the muffins out of the oven, checking her watch and silently thanking Azrael for the spell work that had made this a thousand times easier. Sultry Sunday started in twenty minutes, and she still had to make coffee. Hazel wouldn't be here until nine, which meant Vickie would handle the first hour on her own.

She adjusted the belt on her jean shorts, re-tucking her skintight cantaloupe-colored tank top. She was aiming to look like Baby from *Dirty Dancing*, and she'd curled her hair carefully for this. The white tennis shoes would not make it through the day in pristine condition, but that was all right. She could talk Azrael into spelling them clean again. This week's Sultry Sunday was iconic movie outfit themed, and she hoped her customers came out in style.

Worry made Vickie bake, and so there were more muffins than she needed, but at least the kitchen smelled like her blends: blueberry and lavender, festive October chocolate and pumpkin, and banana nut vanilla. She'd arranged them in mahogany wicker baskets lined with orange-and-black cloth and carried them through the swinging doors to the front.

From outside the glass window, Hank waved. Today, the retired postman was wearing the exact red outfit Chi-Chi wore in *To Wong Foo, Thanks for Everything! Julie Newmar*, and Vickie had to admit that he made a striking, albeit slightly larger-scale, John Leguizamo.

She flicked open the locks, and the little skull bells jingled.

"Morning, Victoria, or should I say, Baby? Get out of the corner with those coffees," Hank joked.

"Morning, Chi Chi!" Vickie fired a smile, quite possibly her first authentic one in days. It was impossible not to smile at this man, dressed as he was.

Hank did a little twirl and a sashay.

"I brought my camera," he said. "If you want to document this."

"Yes, those will make for good pictures. What can I get you?"

He slid into the high-back velvet booth with the coffin-shaped table.

"One of those heavenly-scented muffins and a cup of Earl Grey, please."

"Coming right up. What kind of muffin?"

"Whichever one smells like pumpkin, darling." Hank's face fell for a moment. "It was always Edwyn's favorite."

She smiled softly. "That's nice. The people we love live on in our memories, Hank."

Hank fiddled with his wedding ring, and she wished for an easier world, where magic didn't have to be hidden and she could offer to bring Edwyn back for a few minutes, to say goodbye.

But the world was as it was, and sometimes that meant the best people were gone and the worst still with us. Vickie had seen her mother slink by in the back seat of the chauffeured town car behind shaded windows last week, likely sniffing at the little shop Vickie held so dear. Probably looking to see if Vickie had failed, and then driving away, disgruntled at the obvious success, but trying not to show any emotion on her face at all to avoid wrinkles. Reality wasn't fair, but it existed.

"Yeah, that makes sense. This place always makes me feel better. Persephone Hart was so kind to us. We used to come here every Sunday. When Edwyn died, that first Sunday, she stopped by our condo with muffins and tea. The neighbors were aghast; you know how some people felt about the Harts, but damn if it wasn't the only thing that made me feel better. Like Persephone's kindness was what Ed would do. Started coming back here since you reopened. You do her memory justice too."

Spots of color rose to Vickie's cheeks. She was going to do it, to do what Persephone would have wanted, to love Azrael and watch over him. She knew the Harts worried; she knew how Azrael struggled to be normal, that silly concept that doesn't really exist, and that results so often in squashing down individuality in favor of empty conformity.

Vickie poured boiling water over a rose hip and hyacinth blend in a teapot with glittering skulls, serving Mrs. Weatherby, who was clad in full *Breakfast at Tiffany's* regalia, complete with sunglasses and what might have been authentic jewels.

As soon as the nonagenarian walked away, Hazel leaned onto the counter and turned to Vickie, smiling at her like a cat about to pounce.

"So, Vickie. Mr. Hart has been brooding a little more than usual. We have all noticed in class."

Oh lord. If there was one thing Hazel loved, it was meddling.

"That's nice, Hazel."

"Don't act like I don't remember him coming in here all the time in the summer, and like I haven't seen him lingering when we close on weekends. The tension between the two of you was epic."

Vickie rolled her eyes. Hazel and her friends were all over the spicy romance novels on video social media platforms, which was funny, because she'd heard more than a few adults argue that teenagers shouldn't read romance novels. That made her snort. Hazel, like all teenagers, was an actual human person who did, in fact, know that sex existed. Books were a safe and healthy way to explore that.

"It's complicated, Hazel."

"Omigosh. I cannot wait to see whatever drama the two of you have play out here, like my very own book. Maybe I'll tell him in class that he should come by the shop more often."

"I can see the wheels turning in your head, Hazel, and no. Do not tell him any such thing." Vickie said it a little more firmly than she meant to, but Hazel's eyes glinted, undeterred. Time for a subject change. "Listen, things are picking up enough that I need to hire a few more people to work weekend shifts, and maybe some of the busier nights."

"That's cool. I'll let people know."

"I was thinking of designing a flyer and sending it to the school's counselor's office, in addition to printing some out for our bulletin board." She gestured to the black corkboard, which held an old invitation to a ballroom-themed Halloween party the town had held a few years earlier, and a smattering of advertisements for tutors and babysitting.

"Vickie," squealed Hazel. Vickie winced a little at the volume. "Can I make it? I can post it all over. You can put it on all those old-person social medias too."

"It would be great if you made it, since, according to you, I might need the time to hobble over to AARP for some brochures at the ripe old age of, I don't know, not even thirty." She smiled at Hazel, who scoffed.

"You're old enough to buy beer legally and I think maybe also old enough to know which beer doesn't taste like ass? I'm not 100 percent sure, but in my book, that means you're relatively mature."

Vickie smiled. Hazel was great.

The girl gasped a little. "Speaking of old hotties, isn't that Mr. Hart's sister, with the Kate Sharma look-alike? Sapphic Kanthony goals there—my heart."

"Hazel, what have I told you about writing fanfic about customers?"

Hazel giggled and waggled her eyebrows.

"That you support young people writing things?"

Vickie sighed.

Priscilla and Evelyn swooped into the shop, hands entwined, though not standing quite so close together as they had when Vickie had first met the councilwoman.

"Two honey cinnamon lattes and one of each of the muffins to go, please, Victoria." Evelyn pretended to be interested in an advertisement on the corkboard, and Prissy leaned in.

Clearly, this had been orchestrated.

"Come to dinner at the house tonight, Vickie." Priscilla's brown eyes bore into her. Her dark hair was in a single braid, over the white collar of a black dress shirt tucked into jeans that looked more expensive than the entirety of Hopelessly Teavoted and all the real estate on Main Street combined. "We need to talk about what Azrael found."

"I, ah . . ." Vickie blushed, hoping Hazel wasn't listening too closely. "Yes. I can do that."

Prissy's matte red lips pulled into a tight line across her pale face, and in a full pantsuit, Evelyn looked all business.

"He misses you," Evelyn said, and then leaned in, speaking quietly enough that no one would overhear. "And, as a NACoW representative, I must remind you that at this point, I'll have to file a report if we can't wrap this up. But I do think we can solve this together, the four of us." Evelyn's phone buzzed, and she stepped away from the counter again. Priscilla glared at her, crossed her arms, and frowned.

"Sorry, she does that a lot. Council business. But I convinced her to hold off on reporting just a little bit longer, so we do this tonight. If the Council finds out about it before we can, they'll want to isolate and protect anyone involved that could be tempting to the megachurch." She looked meaningfully at Vickie. "As a Hart, Azrael is already high profile, but if they connect the dots and realize he's close to the perp? They'd isolate him for his own safety. And that would likely take until *after* the end of the month."

Which meant they'd quarantine him until after Halloween. Prissy, too, probably, although she didn't have any time-sensitive curses riding on her, at least not that Vickie was aware of.

The tension hung heavy in the air.

"I'm closing up at eight. I'll be by after." Vickie was trying to speak quietly, but there were few whispers soft enough to evade Hazel's curiosity.

"Ah, boss, we are never busy Sunday evenings. I'll close. You head out at six. I can use the extra cash anyway." Hazel butted in, looking all too eager, and Priscilla's smile curled upward. "All those romance novels aren't going to buy themselves," the girl said, her eyes wide with feigned innocence.

"I'll be there as soon as I can," she said.

The house welcomed her more eagerly this time, and she wondered if it could sense that something had shifted.

Azrael's eyes had circles under them, but he looked happy to see her, as though he, too, knew that something had changed. "Vickie," he said. "I think it's Chet. He's got no other reason to be going into that church. I have heard him brag to several other department members about how he's a deist, like Benjamin Franklin. Why would he be going into that church otherwise? The whole time, it's been Chet. We can go tonight, with Prissy and Evelyn. Pay off your debt to Lex. You can be free to do whatever you want, or whatever you don't want."

He snapped his fingers, and a pair of cocktails appeared on the end table.

She pressed a hand against the door behind her, smiling at the warmth of it, the relief of finally knowing.

Not just about who the real villain was, but about what she wanted.

"Az," she said. "That's wonderful. But I want to talk about us."

"Over drinks?" He gestured and she took hers, a perfect dark and stormy. "I have a nice selection of cheese and crackers. Prissy reminded me that it's not a good idea to have a huge meal before big magic." She walked past him to the kitchen, and saw the counter festooned with plates of crackers and charcuterie spreads. She turned to smile at him.

"Azrael Hart, did you make me girl dinner to snack on before we have to go save the town?"

He leaned against the entryway, laughing. "Evelyn said we leave at eight, promptly, and then retired to take what sounded like a very important phone call."

"That's plenty of time for us to have the conversation I want to have."

Azrael's eyebrows shot up. "Oh yeah?" He walked toward her, leaning against the counter. Close enough that he could reach out and touch her; far enough not to die from doing so. "Do you want to fool around and pretend it's only pretend again, Vickie?" His voice was a growl. "I told you it's real for me, but I *never* mind pretending."

She shook her head. Goddess, he smelled so good. Lemon and warm, woodsy echoes. They were so close to being able to do what she wanted.

"I don't want to pretend anymore, Azrael," she said. Being

careful and moving slowly so he saw what she was doing, she reached a hand toward his sweater. Az froze, his eyes tracking her movement the entire time.

"Vickie." His voice was strangled now. "Victoria. Do you mean . . ."

She ran the hand down the sweater, all the way to his belt loops, running a finger across the button of his pants. He sucked in an audible breath, and she stepped back, to make sure she didn't do anything foolish in the heat of the moment.

"I mean I don't want to pretend anymore either." She felt the emotion of it, welling up in her chest. His eyes were wide, a smile pulling up his cheek. She had to get the rest of it out. "I choose you. Even after we break the curse, repay my debt, save the world . . . Even if we don't have to. I want us. For always."

Vickie couldn't hold Azrael's hand, so she held her own, and he must have understood, because he snapped twice, grinning from ear to ear, and two pairs of gloves appeared on the counter next to the untouched spread. He looked at her, waiting to watch the slow slip of the fabric across her skin.

"It must be true love if you haven't even touched the cheeses," he murmured.

"It is," she said, sliding the glove on and reaching for his hand after he had done the same. He watched her, and his face felt flushed with hunger. She knitted her fingers into his.

"I love you, Azrael. For real, not pretend. We should do it. The sealing spell. The soul binding."

Azrael squeezed her hand, at a loss for words for a moment.

"Are you sure?" His words sounded reverent, and she couldn't help but grin.

"More than I've ever been about anything," she said.

"Promise?"

"I swear it on everything I love most. The shop, on Hart Manor, and every breath in my body. I'm yours. I always have been, Azrael."

"It's nice to see you here, finally," he said quietly.

"At your house?"

"No." He shook his head, and grinned, leaning against the counter, their arms still stretched between them. "I mean here." He pressed a hand to his heart. "Absolutely, hopelessly, and desperately in it. You know, like I have been, with you. I love you, Victoria. Everything I am, and everything I have, is yours. Always."

He smiled, that same smile, a little crooked, and absolutely heart-shattering in intensity. It was the same way he'd looked at her in high school when she threw up margaritas in his bed; in college when they'd giggled, knocking knees and elbows against the dorm room wall, too much for one twin bed. His eyes lit up across tables dancing with magic and across laminate mundane ones too. It was the same way he'd looked at her in a fancy gown and in sweatpants and writhing on a bench in her shower.

"You're sure, Vickie." He said it like a benediction, not a question, but she answered anyway, because she could. Because she wanted to hear herself say it, again, out loud.

"I am," she said, and she laughed, because it was funny, really, that she'd been so worried about being too clingy, and as a result, had almost ended up clinging to doubt for long enough to miss this.

"What do we need to do next?"

"Don't worry." He nibbled on his bottom lip, unable to stop another smile from stretching across his face. "I started preparing for this moment as soon as I knew it was a possibility. We can take what we need from my mother's garden, and then we'll set up the spell. It takes hours, so we should start it now. Come on." He led her, gloved hand in gloved hand, through the house, its floral wallpaper blooming, roses expanding and contracting around them as they hurried down the hallway. The bearskin rug roared in approval, and Vickie smiled as they stepped out into the conservatory.

Azrael snapped, and fairy lights appeared, threaded through hanging trellises and tinting the room in more than just moonlight.

"Do we have time for all of this?" Above her, the garlands twinkled and swayed, tiny stars dancing in pale greenhouse moonlight.

He winked. "Benedict Hart rule. We always have time for mood setting."

"He said that?"

"He sure did. Used to embarrass the hell out of me, but I kind of get what he was talking about now."

He moved from plant to plant, and she followed.

"Lavender, for protection, and because you love it." She smiled and watched him with the shears, cutting as carefully as Persephone ever had. "Myrtle, for love." She held out a gloved hand to hold the sprig as they moved on. "Sage. We write our names on it with wild honey." He gestured to a little jar sitting next to the plant.

"You already got the honey."

"Of course I did, sweetheart." The nickname struck a chord in her heart that made her wonder if it would be fine not to make it out of the excursion tonight. She could die happy knowing that this moment had existed, when she and Az had finally dropped all pretense between them.

"A few more things here, if you want to meet me in the library with those?"

She nodded, picking up the jar and the other clippings.

"Don't be too long," she said. Azrael winked at her, smiling crookedly and making her knees a bit weak before she hurried from the room.

"I'll be there. And, Vickie, when it's time, I'll tell you what's in my wallet."

Desire pooled in her stomach, her core clenching. An illadvised longing, for the soul-binding magic would take time, and it wasn't like they could really *be* together until it was done. They had a trip to take, and then, upon their return, a seal to set.

There was a promise in Azrael's voice, though, a reverence. Yearning.

She had a feeling that his confession would untether her, body and soul.

CHAPTER 33

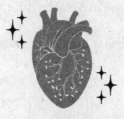

Azrael

Preparing the potion had been the easy part; waiting for it to brew would be difficult. How he'd longed for the slip of his fingers against each other so that he could touch her, even if only with magic and not with his actual hands.

But longing looks from the back seat of the car would have to suffice. Evelyn was driving, and to avoid potential death, Priscilla shared the back seat with him like they were small children pranking each other with real snakes in cans again.

"Remember the time you almost killed me when I was ten?" Azrael asked fondly, though the recollection was har-rowing.

"Ah, you were fine. You know how I love a classic copperhead-in-a-can trick," said Priscilla, examining her black fingernails.

Once the venomous thing had bit him in fear, his mother had to snap her fingers to remove the poison quickly while his dad magicked the snake out of the car.

"Yeah, Prissy, almost killing your only brother. You're hisssssterical," Az teased.

Priscilla rolled her eyes, but Vickie laughed so hard that she snorted a little bit in the front seat, and the sound of it filled him with the sort of warm fuzzy feelings that he recognized from so many books. He may as well have stretched out his arm toward a light, or declared how ardently he loved her, or compared her to the sun.

He was hopelessly devoted to her.

And somehow, in a moment more magical than anything he had ever wielded, she loved him too. She chose him, and had agreed to the binding. To set the seal. Their eyes locked as she turned back to look at him, pupils dilated.

"How long again until the spell work is ready?" Vickie asked.

"Seven hours precisely from when you began brewing it," answered Evelyn.

They had five hours, then, to investigate, get to the megachurch, and stop Chet. It was this or go through the staff directory at the church, asking intrusive questions or tricking people into magical scans until someone allowed them in, and he didn't relish the thought of doing that, so they had agreed to break into the church.

A mundane crime, he supposed, was justifiable in this situation.

"Explain to me again why we can't just portal in," Az said, scrubbing a hand across his face. "Can't Evelyn get a special exception to the portaling suspension?" He was tired, and he wanted to talk to Victoria again in private.

Well. Maybe he wanted to do more than talk.

"No special treatment. Especially since we don't want them to know *why* we need it," Prissy said pointedly. "Besides, it would be detectable by anyone halfway decent at witchery, and it would give us away if we meet nonwitches. Chet's been sniffing around enough as it is. No need to appear out of thin air and confirm his suspicions if there's a possibility that we can catch him unawares. The car is much more sensible."

"Sure, sure. Totally normal to drive an enormous vintage Packard to a church in the middle of the night."

Priscilla shrugged. "I'm a beautiful, eccentric lesbian, Azrael, and none of that is out of the ordinary for me, to tell the truth." Evelyn glanced at her in the rearview mirror, winking.

The corners of Azrael's mouth pulled up as he watched

them flirt, without words or shame, in the little reflective glass. He was glad his sister was happy, even if it was only for now. Prissy reminded him so much of his parents, always knowing that she was perfectly normal and acceptable the way she was. Never caring—relishing it, even—when people disliked her.

It had been true the whole time, and he had been too fucking foolish to acknowledge it.

Just like he had been too scared to tell Vickie how he felt that time in college, or before that when they'd parted ways after high school, and how he'd wasted so much time wallowing in his own agony. Just like when he'd let her tell him it was just pretending. All the pretending in the shower, and the library, and the car. All the pretending that it was pretending, until it was crystal clear to him that it was anything but. He patted his thigh for his wallet, thinking again of what he kept there, wrinkled and full of heartache and history. It was the last thing between them, and he needed to be honest before they set the seal.

After this, he would.

The car stopped, and Evelyn parked it under the partial cover of enormous oak trees at one end of the parking lot. From the street, it was barely noticeable in the dark.

The clean modern lines of the building glinted in the moonlight, a sharp contrast to the graveyard that had housed Hallowcross's dead for almost two hundred years. The building had been destroyed in a fire in the late nineties and rebuilt in modern splendor on the dimes of the congregants, as such things usually went, while the wealthy pastors reaped the benefits and spilled their corruptions into fancy accommodations bought with tithing.

The hypocrisy of religion could be chilling, and Azrael, a witch named twice for devils, didn't use that assessment lightly.

They broke in with little difficulty, Evelyn muttering about detection spells not being clever enough. But the desolate, empty aura of the building plunged them further into the cold.

Vickie shivered, and he snapped his fingers, adding, atop her jeans and shirt, a heavy cable-knit sweater he kept in the trunk of the car.

Evelyn and Priscilla, unsurprisingly, hadn't bothered with jackets. Probably a warmth spell, which he didn't care for himself; Azrael preferred the weight of actual layers. And the flexibility they afforded him in touching Victoria.

"Thanks, Az," she whispered, sniffing it, and he wondered how he could have deluded himself into thinking she didn't care. It was so clear to him, not just in what she said, but in how he felt around her. Home. He wanted to move to stand next to her, but it was too risky. He would need to keep his fingers bare for any magic casting.

They walked, feet spelled against sound, disturbingly quiet on marble floors that stretched on forever. Finally, they reached a staircase that must lead to offices on the second floor.

A light at the end of the hallway upstairs and a cracked door let them know that someone was there, beyond the extravagant door marking the head pastor's office.

Azrael gestured for them to go ahead, and Priscilla took the lead with Evelyn close behind, Vickie hugging the left wall of the hallway while Azrael stuck to the right, careful not to comply with the gravitational pull of their bodies toward each other.

They turned a corner, and Azrael stopped; Vickie stepped backward.

Priscilla snapped her fingers and the air turned bluish in a simple spell for detecting intentions. She blew at it, and waved her hand, the color seeping into the gap of the door that stood ajar. They watched as it turned purple.

"What the . . ." sounded the familiar voice, the one Azrael had expected to come from inside the room, as Priscilla kicked the door the rest of the way open. She was a sight to behold in a sleek black pantsuit that he suspected had more give to it than it appeared to. His sister always had been good at magicking her clothes to look like business but feel like loungewear.

Azrael would recognize that voice, and the middle-aged, gelled receding hairline of a man behind the desk that it belonged to, anywhere. Part of him had hoped it wasn't his boss. That the man was just an asshole, no magic involved, who happened to also be a youth pastor.

But it was, and apparently the man's assholery didn't stop at terrorizing his coworker.

"Chet."

"What the fuck are you doing here, Hart?" The man smiled, and there was something sinister to it. As though he wasn't upset at all to see them.

Chet's lecherous eyes raked up and down Priscilla, and he raised his eyebrows. "Did you finally decide to introduce me to your hot sister after all?"

Priscilla's snaps should have restrained him with something quite horrific, but a greenish hue shimmered around Chet Thornington, at the invisible barrier where the intention spell had been blocked. A physical protection spell, with what looked like a four-foot diameter. Object-based, then.

Chet pulled a lighter from his pocket, tossing it in his hand, and laughed.

"I *knew* it. I couldn't afford to act on it until I was sure, not after that fiasco with the fake psychic, but I knew you were witches."

Azrael snapped furiously, but the barrier held, his magic having no effect.

"My preparations should have worked for this," muttered Evelyn. "I was careful. It should have been enough to break his shield."

Azrael snapped again, but to no avail.

"Ah, Hart, you couldn't have thought it was that easy. Now I suppose I'll be eating three souls tonight. I'll save the fourth for Halloween, of course. Seal in the kind of beautiful power that I have always deserved. God, I wish I could savor each one of you, make it last. But I'm not fool enough to let more than I need live, not when things are lining up so nicely. That's a fucking shame; I'll be bloated for days after that much consumption. Nothing to be done about it, though, and I can't say I'll mind the power upgrade. I haven't had witches—yet. I was so cross when that psychic turned out to be a fraud, but no matter. I have you now. Shame you'll all have to die before you can find out what kind of powers I might be able to manifest once I've absorbed your souls."

Chet moved quicker than lightning. Before Azrael knew it, his hands were on Priscilla's, cleverly keeping her fingers from connecting, just in case. She struggled and kicked at him with her pointed heel, and then headbutted him hard enough that Chet looked dazed before shaking it off.

"I'm afraid I've traded quite a bit to the king of the devils to be able to withstand physical attacks," he said. "And I guess I should say thank you for the plants. They helped me trick old Frankie into granting me this protection spell in exchange for my dear old dad's soul."

Evelyn pushed angrily toward him, but the invisible barrier was impenetrable, and they stood there, magic jumping and flaring as they tried to free Priscilla, who was attempting to bite Chet with some success, though not enough to free herself.

"You cut a deal with Lucifer," breathed Azrael.

"The one and only. I cut two deals with him, as a matter of fact. Did you know he goes by Frankie these days? A bit less intimidating than the original name, if you ask me, but hey, it works. I met him on a trip to Vegas this summer. My family was clever enough to be born wealthy, and I'm clever enough to gamble with more than just that money, it turns out. Challenged him to a game of pool, drunk off my ass, but joke was on him—he had no idea how much time I've spent in bars all my life, and to be honest, I think he was drinking too. By the time he sobered up, it was too late. I had bargained to eat living souls, not just to reap the dead. And I'd gotten him to throw in a personal protection sacrifice, which made the plant-based magic extending the spell that much easier to weasel out of him." Chet smiled, a sickly, scheming thing. "He wasn't too happy when I trapped him into more than he wanted to bargain for, but you get what you get, and sometimes it's unfortunate."

"I'll be devil damned," said Azrael softly. He had to keep this man talking until they could figure out a plan. Whatever deal he had made must have been a wretched one, to grant a mundane power against a witch as mighty as Priscilla.

"I turned down a job from Frankie once," Azrael said, as casually as he could while a monster gripped his sister by her hands.

The snapping wasn't working, and Azrael couldn't get around the barrier. He had to think, and he had to keep Chet talking.

Chet scoffed. "You're exactly the kind of maudlin weirdo who would do that. Just think, you could be collecting souls just like your pretty little girlfriend there." He winked at Vickie. "I like you better in the lingerie from your whorish tea shop." He smirked, and Azrael lunged toward him, but the protection spell held, blocking any of them from going farther. "Who knows, though, Hart? The night is still young." He leered at Vickie, and Azrael knew then that it would not be enough to just defeat the man. He needed to destroy this kind of evil, to rip it from the world.

But Chet wasn't done. With the aura around him still intact, Chet whipped Priscilla's head against a bookshelf, knocking her unconscious so that she slumped to the floor, still out of Azrael's reach. Azrael snapped with all his might, but his magic, like Evelyn's, bounced back harmlessly.

"You beast," screamed Evelyn. "I'll kill you for that."

Chet smiled and shook his head slowly. His terrible, product-laden hair barely even moved.

"Ah, darling, that's what they all say. Before they die."

CHAPTER 34

Victoria

The cream-colored sweater smelled like Azrael so much that Vickie wondered if this was the most she'd ever been in love with him, desperate to stop him from losing another family member while the scents of lemon and burnt amber crept into her nose and around her like a hug, reminding her of what was just out of her reach.

If Chet killed Prissy, Azrael wouldn't just be out of Vickie's reach. He would also have to grieve another unbearable loss. He didn't deserve this.

The thought made Vickie absolutely furious.

On the desk behind Chet, now far enough away from the protection spell to reach if she moved cautiously, lay the lighter he had tossed, and suddenly, Vickie understood.

Azrael's magic was out of play, and he could do nothing against the protection. But her gift should be intact. She needed his objects.

Chet Thornington had flicked that lighter there as though it was a token of protection in symbolism only, but she had grown up summoning the dead from what they had loved most. Trinkets like that were almost always the most precious objects.

Vickie slid slowly over toward the desk while Chet focused

on taunting Azrael and keeping Evelyn at bay, Vickie's movements going unnoticed.

People always underestimated Vickie, thinking she was just the bubbly girl next door. But Vickie was more than just champagne problems in a fuzzy pink coat bottle, and by the time she was done, she'd be willing to bet that Chet would think about her.

Well, for as long as he still had the capacity to think, that was.

The edge of her smile twisted as her fingers touched the lighter and warmed. The familiar sensation confirmed her suspicion. An old man with thinning hair, a thick white mustache, and a jean shirt appeared, looking confused for a moment. His eyes grew wide when his gaze landed on the battle in front of him.

"Ah, my foolish son," the specter said, sadness reverberating through his ghostly form in his last earthly minutes. "What have you done now?"

Vickie looked at the shadow of the man expectantly.

"Can he not see me?" he asked Vickie. "Hear me?"

Vickie shook her head, unwilling to betray what she was doing. The lighter grew warmer against her palm. Chet ate souls. He didn't collect them, usher them the way she did.

The ghost looked from her to the fight again and nodded. She angled her body to block the flame.

"Very well. Perhaps it is better this way. Chet is arrogant. Greedy and overly privileged, but completely unwilling to acknowledge it. I paid his way in everything, but he still gloated like he'd earned it all. I am sad to say that I allowed him to go unchecked for far too long. I indulged him. Vouched for his goodness. Protected him. Excused his behavior."

Vickie cocked her head slightly to the side, trying to ask the question without alerting Chet to her subterfuge or the presence of his father's spirit.

"He's a teacher, but a cruel one. A youth pastor, for the control, with nefarious intentions in his heart. Malice lies in the heart of the head pastor here too. They live for the power and money afforded to them by their congregation, oblivious to the horrors their tithes and ignorance support. My son here"—the ghost gestured to him—"he preys on younger women. Legal, but young enough not to know better. Lonely and insecure enough not to see his red flags. Chet always makes sure they are willing, at least at first, but pushes them beyond what they feel comfortable with. It is a pattern I excused in life, but what excuse shall I make for the boy who killed me, who sacrificed his soul and his own father for the power to devour other souls? He plans to kill all of you, and to make himself untouchable, to sow even more discord in the world. He plans to force souls from people. He's never understood consent."

"How do I defeat him?" Vickie whispered. She could only hope that in death, the man would be more inclined to stop his offspring than he had been in life.

Azrael's head turned slightly toward her, and he glanced at her hand, eyes opening wide with realization. Azrael lunged toward his colleague with renewed zeal, drawing the man's attention and ire further away from Vickie.

"I'll kill you, you fucking monster," Az screamed at Chet, who threw his head back and laughed, his forehead glistening and red. His laugh was maniacal and cold, and he was oblivious to the imminent threat.

It was the laugh of a man who had never been met with the consequences of his own actions, and who had failed up for so long that he knew no other way to succeed. He was the sort of person who would tell you he could have been a millionaire, or a surgeon, or a jet pilot, if he had only applied himself. The sort of man who would meet any accomplishment in another with an excuse for why he himself hadn't achieved such a thing. A pedantic, modern-day Mr. Collins in the flesh, but with far too much bite for Austen.

"When I'm gone, along with this lighter, Chet's protection will fade. He traded my life for that shield, and used his own soul as collateral in exchange for the power to consume others' souls. There's a fancy pen in his pocket, which may be the only thing he loves. He considers himself god's gift to creation, slicing necessary prose with a red pen, yet incapable of creating anything real. He's a disgrace to good teachers, and to good people everywhere."

The lighter burned now, and the ghost was fading.

"The pen. Get the pen. He signed his soul away with it. He's bound to it, same as his protection is to this lighter."

Vickie nodded, and with a startling crackle, the lighter disintegrated.

Well, fuck, that didn't usually happen.

"WHAT HAVE YOU DONE?" Chet screamed, moving toward Vickie and dropping Prissy. "I sold my father, his body and soul, for that thing."

The broken spell work of the lighter caught fire as it snapped, and Chet's protective shield shattered, taking with it the secrecy of what Vickie was doing.

"And that makes you a coward," she said, scowling at him. "You traded your *father's* soul instead of your own for the protection spell work. That still leaves your soul. *You* still have a soul to take. And I? I'm capable of taking it."

Evelyn scooped up Priscilla's limp form. Vickie tried not to focus on the other woman's frantic casting as her posh voice lilted in soft magical whispers, her hands rubbing together in bursts of healing magic. Chet lunged toward Victoria, hands closing around her throat, squeezing and constricting. Vickie gasped in shock as her air ran out, her vision darkening at the edges as the world started to go static around her ears.

She felt a wave of magic, like nothing she'd known, push her backward. It was cold and empty, and it left a brassy taste in her mouth. Chet's body fell on top of her, winding her further, fingers squeezing around her throat. Then she heard a loud crack, followed by the gasping relief of Chet's hands releasing her and the rush of gulps of air she could pull in again.

"Vickie," she heard Azrael mutter, blood covering the cross-shaped paperweight he held in a white-knuckle grip in his hand, kept at a careful distance away from her. Azrael kicked at Chet, whose body slumped off Vickie. Chet was breathing but unconscious, a fresh lump on the side of his head bleeding.

"I'm fine," Vickie said; she could tell Az was scrambling, desperately wanting to comfort her, to make sure there wasn't a scratch on her, but unable to touch her.

Vickie wrapped her arms around herself, taking comfort in the sweater she wore as she hugged herself instead. She wished for the cradle of his arms now more than ever.

"There's a pen in Chet's pocket that I need," Vickie said.

Azrael grimaced, clearly not happy about needing to reach into the man's chinos, still pressed into a sharp pleat at the front of each leg. After a small, uncomfortable moment of searching, Az pulled out a golden pen, making the man stir. Chet sat up, scrambling to his feet. They were running out of time.

"Throw it to me?" Victoria asked.

Az nodded, and she caught the pen.

"What the devil—" Chet began.

Then, with a *pop*, they were no longer the only ones in the room.

Lex shook glittering gold dust from goddess knew what from his hair and took in the room. His black hair was mussed, his lips swollen. He strutted toward Az and Vickie, looking even more self-satisfied than usual, and clapped his hands together. Chet froze, mid-scowl.

"Very nicely done, pet!" Lex said, smiling at her in a way that made her furious. "You've caught one of Lucifer's projects gone wrong." He shook his head. "This is why I don't care to take him up on any golfing invites, the ass." His brows furrowed at that, as though their harrowing encounter in this youth pastor's office was only a small inconvenience to the otherwise glorious day he was having. He smiled, as though noticing something else. He sniffed at the air once, and then again, wrinkling his nose and then nodding. "Yes, he's the person who attacked the psychic. And the villain behind the ills of the megachurch. Ah, well done, Vickie. You're so close to finalizing our contract, just as soon as you serve this fool his comeuppance. Bravo, pet."

"Fuck you, Lex," Vickie hissed, but she only meant it half-way. She was, after all, glad he had come to help dispose of this particular villain.

"Ah, pet, I have offered that, but you did decline, and I respect your autonomy, however shortsighted you might be for depriving yourself of such godlike pleasure." The anger that had previously raged in Lex's eyes was gone. Devils ran hot but were capricious, indecisive, and, occasionally, flighty.

"Where were you ten minutes ago? We could have used you."

Lex smiled again. "I've moved on. But I do so appreciate you catching this particular menace. Once you reap him, I'll have both my third soul *and* a favor Lucifer will owe me, which simply could not have come at a better time for me." Brushing some more of the curious gold dust from his shoulder, he did not offer any further response. It was an odd, knowing, smug expression, and Vickie suspected that wherever Lex had come from, he had not been alone.

A small part of Vickie might have considered burning for Lex once, but that was before she knew that Azrael was hers. It was all real. Azrael was the most honest part of her life.

No amount of devilish pleasure could be worth trading the only person in the world who saw her, *really* saw her, for who she was and loved every bit of her.

"I hope you're here to collect this monster's soul," Vickie said firmly, and Lex shrugged, nodding.

"One small issue," Lex said, examining his nails and looking sheepish. "I can't collect living souls without working a rather intricate curse."

"Are you kidding me right now, Lex? You used 'a rather intricate curse' on Azrael."

"With an object and some motivation of a, ah, personal nature, darling. I do apologize for acting on impulse there. Very wrong of me. Angelic, almost. I'm ashamed, and like I said, I've moved on. This will go faster if someone is willing to kill the fellow."

Nodding, Azrael stepped forward, expression deadly serious. He snapped his fingers, and a pair of rapiers, which Vickie recognized from the Hart family vault, appeared in his right hand.

"It doesn't seem fair to kill an incapacitated man," Azrael said.

"Azrael, no," Vickie warned. He couldn't be serious.

Lex regarded Az with begrudging respect. "Azrael Ashmedai Hart, though you be named for greater devils, I do think we could be friends."

Az's eyes turned thunderous, but he shook his head. "Might still be too soon for that. Still, if you could make this a fair fight?"

Cocking his head, Lex blinked. "You're certain? Fair as in both armed with swords, no magic?"

"Azrael . . ." Vickie began.

"No," Az said. "I want to do this right. I want him to know that it was me who ended him, for all the harm he's caused. For hurting the fortune teller. For breaking into my *home*. For the lives he's claimed by tricking people into an obsessive, cruel religion, and for generally being an absolute asshole. You were right, Vickie. I didn't see that people like him are sometimes guilty of worse crimes than making others uncomfortable. I want to be the one to end him."

Azrael met her eyes. "Vickie, please."

She nodded, taking a step back.

Lex clapped, and a shadow of purple, ginger-scented smoke surrounded them for a moment, and then Chet and Azrael were standing in the center of the room, several arm widths apart, each holding one of the antique Hart family rapiers.

"You're a fool," snapped Chet, his scowl remaining, even though he'd been unfrozen.

"I am," said Azrael, eyes flitting to Vickie. "But not about this." He whirled, thrusting the rapier toward his opponent.

It must have been years since the last time Az had fenced,

but Vickie remembered that Priscilla had often bullied him into dueling with her with the family heirloom he wielded now, and Azrael had been a fierce combatant.

Their swords clashed, sparks flying off gleaming metal as each desperate lunge and parry made the whole scene feel more and more surreal.

Vickie was going to fucking murder Azrael Hart if he went and got himself killed in a sword fight, of all things.

Chet managed to get in a slash across Azrael's cheek, but Az parried, twirled, and, with a grunt of exertion from cutting through skin and muscle, plunged his blade deep into Chet's chest. He'd aimed with precision between Chet's ribs, and blossoming blood framed the silver of the sword at once. Chet crumpled to the floor, gasping for a moment before his body went limp.

Lex clapped again, and all evidence of the fight, the blood, the struggle around them, was gone in another puff of smoke that smelled far too nice to be murder cleanup. All that was left was the body. Part of her wanted to know where the rest had gone, but she decided it would be best not to ask, and focused instead on clenching her fists to avoid going to Azrael and attempting to tend to the wound on his cheek.

Azrael leaned against a bookshelf, panting, and wiped at the cut with the back of his sleeve, turning to look at Lex. Evelyn was still hovering over Priscilla, muttering and pulling things from her pocket, but it looked like Priscilla was stirring, and the incantations were less frantic than they had been.

The devil pulled another strange box out of his pocket.

"Soul prison," Lex said, holding it up, and nodding at Vickie. She picked up the pen, and the ghost of Chet appeared, took one look at her, and then let out a high-pitched shriek of agony. As Vickie gripped the pen, it began to burn, leeching Chet's essence—starting with his shiny shoes, moving up to his starched chinos and dress shirt, and finally, his crunchy-looking, gel-slicked hair, until the pen was glowing and painfully hot in her palm.

"Nooooo," screamed the fading specter that had been Chet Thornington. "How dare you, you fucking b—"

Before he could finish, Chet disappeared completely, dissolving into the box. Lex snapped it shut and clapped again. The body and the box disappeared. The pen turned to ash, which trickled through her fingers until it disappeared.

The devil laughed once, and then clapped.

"Very well. Good show, my pets. A murderer, a manipulator, and an abuser. Three souls neatly caught. Victoria, your parents' debt is paid, and I am sorry that you had to pay it. Unfortunately for them, because they did not repay the debt themselves, they will lose much of what they gained financially as a result of your powers—which you now get to keep, having paid the debt in full."

"They'll be broke?"

"Ah," said Lex, "not exactly. They're from enough money that they will have plenty to live off, I expect. That's the thing about wealth: very difficult to take away once the grubby rich get their hands on it."

"Not like your parents, pet," Lex said and ruffled Azrael's hair. Az reeled back as if to punch the devil, but Lex was on the other side of the room in the blink of an eye.

Undeterred, Lex continued, "Your parents were truly special people. They never hoarded more money than they needed. Funny, isn't it, that the founding family was stingy and cruel, and it was outsiders who came here to escape oppression who invested in the community quietly and steadily, for all those same years they were ridiculed for their differences. Benedict and Persephone Hart left goodness everywhere they went, pets. And for that, I shall grant you all a favor." Lex winked, and the drastic change in attitude since the last time Vickie had seen him gave her whiplash. He winked. "Since I no longer need a third soul, and you paid in full early, I'll undo my previous mischief." His smile was genuine now. "As of close of business, midnight tonight, you can touch again. Azrael, you are a man, and an honorable one, not an object."

"Even if we don't cast the sealing spell?" Vickie asked. Azrael looked at her. "And even if we do?"

"If you'd like to, of course, go ahead and set a seal upon your hearts, but either way, you'll be able to touch again."

"What about the fake psychic?"

"Who?"

"Madam Cleopatra."

"Oh." Lex looked pleased. "I suppose that will be your sister's problem, but yes, she will wake up, with caveats, of course."

"What does that mean?"

He looked altogether too pleased for this to be anything good. "It means that she won't have to fake psychic abilities anymore. Surprise! Her soul scrap will have been released with that insufferable fellow's demise, and she'll wake up in time, horribly shocked by the ability to be jolted into the future on occasion, and maybe even into the past!" He cackled. "What a treat for Priscilla Hart to sort out! Every Council member loves an exciting challenge, it has to be said."

"That's— Is it reversible?" Azrael looked concerned.

"Not at all, but not to worry. It will make her grift significantly easier, I'm sure. And your sister is in charge of accidental mundane mutations and happenstances. Once she's on the mend, you can tell her. Or not! I'm quite certain the Council will let her know."

"That will be a headache," Azrael said.

Lex nodded, smiled even wider in a lazy, sensual, insouciant expression, and disappeared. It was a devilish move indeed, to catch them beating his game, drop a few bombs, and take credit for the winning move.

But better, she decided, than drawing his ire again in earnest. She had a sneaking feeling this would not be the last they saw of Sexy Lexy.

The unsaid words about what this meant for them together hung between her and Azrael, but they had other things to check on first.

"Priscilla?" Azrael spun, but his sister was already sitting up and scowling.

"I'm fine, thanks to all of you. Though I'm not particularly looking forward to dealing with a fraud-turned-real psychic. An exciting challenge, my left tit." She frowned, crossing her arms.

Evelyn cleared her throat, and Priscilla sighed and continued more civilly, "But particularly thanks to Evelyn. Darling, would you be so kind as to take me to your place? I need your private attentions."

"Of course. I'll finish the spell work to fix you up." Relief palpable in her voice, Evelyn pulled keys out of the air and tossed them at Azrael. "I trust you two can drop us, and then handle everything else on your own?"

"Yes," said Azrael. "It's unlimited what we can handle on our own."

The words curled warm and catlike, a comfortable flame in Vickie's stomach.

Once outside, Priscilla and Evelyn climbed into the back seat, and Az stood for a moment, face serious in the moonlight.

"Would you want to drive?" He pulled his hand through the length of the curls at the top of his head.

"Really?" Vickie had, in fact, always wanted to drive the Packard.

"Yes." His smile was wide, and all for her.

"I would very much like that."

Pulling open the driver's-side door, he gestured and held out the keys. She took them gingerly to avoid any more deaths.

Vickie slid in, buckled her seat belt, and tried not to notice how Priscilla and her brother exchanged a knowing look. Priscilla would carry on her parents' tradition, the next generation of Harts prepared to meddle and encourage her relationship. It softened the blow of losing Persephone and Benedict, knowing that Priscilla and Azrael would look after each other always. Azrael snapped his fingers, covering his hands in formal wear, and threaded a gloved set of fingers between Vickie's for a moment.

As Vickie turned the key in the ignition, the Packard hummed to life, and she relished the smooth ride, punctuated by faint whispers from the back seat that she couldn't quite make out—probably for the best—and occasional squeezes from Azrael's gloved hand—definitely for the best.

By the time Vickie dropped off Evelyn and Priscilla at Evelyn's condo, the magic of anticipation thrummed between her body and Azrael's in that wide front seat. If they were to seal things between them, she needed to come clean.

"Vickie," Az started. "If you've changed your mind . . . I haven't. I meant it all, and I still mean it, but if you have—"

"I haven't. I love you. I still want to do this." Vickie smiled, continuing, "There's something I need to tell you, though." Holding the steering wheel and guiding the behemoth of a car toward Hart Manor made her bold. Like she could direct her own sails.

Like it was time to stop fearing the possibility of loss, in the face of actual loss. To stop fearing clinginess, in the face of a love worth holding on to.

"The night in high school with the sugar-rimmed margaritas."

"I remember," Az said softly.

"I drank too much, and it was hazy, but when I woke up across that king bed from you, I thought for a moment that maybe I loved you. I reached for you, and I was about to tell you."

"Vickie." His voice was a question. "I need to tell you—"

"Hold on, Az. There's more. I'm sorry I threw up instead of telling you how I felt. I'm sorry I didn't have the courage. I was so afraid of losing everything we had, and then I lost it anyway. I want to tell you now. I don't want to wait a second longer to tell you again. I love you."

His gloved hand gripped her thigh now.

"You *never* lost me, Vickie. And you're not the only one who faltered in pivotal moments. Do you remember the time we went hiking?"

"When Priscilla bailed for her girlfriend and I dared you to go skinny-dipping, but you made me turn around until we were waist deep?"

"Yeah. That time." Az's voice was rough now, the words scraping out.

"I was sure you weren't interested. Because you insisted that we could only swim if neither of us looked getting in."

"Vickie. I was a teenage boy terrified of showing you my dick in the freezing mountain air."

She snorted. "You don't need my validation, but I will reassure you that all of you is perfectly magical."

Good goddess, she wanted to touch him now. Not enough to kill him, but still.

It was taking all Vickie's resolve to pay attention to the road, but she snuck a glance to her right and saw that he was blushing.

"I was not thinking straight," Az muttered. "I was so into you, Vickie. I loved you. I still love you, so much. This whole time. I always have."

Had she known the whole time, and just been too afraid to act on it? She bit her lip, uncertain which part of her immaturity of youth had prevented them from being together.

"Okay, then. If you weren't disinterested, how did you really feel?"

"Vickie," Az groaned. "I'm the worst. I . . . I snuck a look when you got out."

"You absolute *dog*," Vickie said, delighted at the admission. "Go on."

Azrael covered his face for a moment with a gloved hand.

"You were standing in the starlight, and I could see all your freckles, water dripping in rivulets I so desperately wanted to trace down the sides of you. Honestly, I almost told you then, but I didn't even know how to put it into words. I went home and wrote angsty poems about it for a while."

Vickie smiled.

"You used to write sad poetry about me? Instead of jacking off? Really?" Vickie teased.

Azrael looked serious now, eyes glancing to hers as they pulled up to the gate.

"As serious as the devils I'm named for. And, fine, I did also fuck my hand afterward. I was weak." Even the tips of his ears were red from embarrassment now.

"Aw, Mr. Hart, you know devils are tricksters. And that I *love* watching you fuck your hand."

"Fine, Vickie, I'm as serious as the grave. As serious as you were when you swore me to secrecy after we found the sex dungeon and you told me you didn't think you minded the idea of whips and spanking."

Vickie coughed a little. The memory made her bite her lip, but his word choice caught her off guard, and she smirked. "I thought you said it was a home gym."

"Yeah, well. Semantics."

Vickie parked the car in front of the house, got out, and shoved her hands into her pockets to keep from reaching for Azrael and tempting death.

They had a vow to make, and she wasn't about to accidentally kill this man just when they'd finally started to get things right.

CHAPTER 35

Azrael

The bedroom door had clicked shut and locked itself, the lights dipped low, as if the room warmed to embrace them. Whatever happened between them, the house approved, and it shifted to make a cat door appear and disappear for Emily Lickinson to escape out of, yowling in judgment as though she was slightly offended that they were kicking her out.

It was warm enough that Vickie's cheeks were spotted with color, and she moved to tug off the thick sweater while Azrael checked the door.

"You take the bed, and I'll sleep on the couch while we wait." He watched, mesmerized, as she slipped her pants off and slid, in a T-shirt and underwear, in between black satin sheets.

He snapped to add blankets and pillows, and then lay down, face up, on his couch. "Vickie?"

"What?"

"When do you think you knew? That you loved me?"

She laughed from between his sheets, and goddess, he wanted to be there too. "I think I knew for sure when you walked away in the rain. Though I definitely suspected the night with the margaritas, and I was too scared then and for years later to admit it to myself." She paused. "When did you know?"

"I think the moment you moved in next door, if I'm totally honest," he said.

"Az," she whispered. "I love you. We should try to get some sleep until after midnight."

For the next hour, he pretended to sleep on the couch, yards apart from the bed to keep from accidentally immolating himself. By the time he heard Vickie wake up, the couch was practically touching the bed, as though his furniture understood that he hadn't been able to bear the distance. He pushed his hand against the velvet of the curtains, safely in the middle and away from the edges, and he felt her hand through the other side, pushing back.

He hoped she had slept while he'd tossed and turned on the couch, counting down the minutes until the spell would be ready and they could fix this thing between them for good. The curse would be gone, and to go through with the soul-binding, even though they didn't have to, well, that meant something to him. Something big, and life defining, and he had spent the better part of the past few hours up thinking about it.

Judging from the shadows under her eyes, though, and the sound of his bedsheets rustling at her every movement, he doubted she'd slept more than he had.

They made their way back down to the library, where a fire rose in the hearth as though to greet them, the warm contained flames of the house licking at the grate.

"Victoria," Az said, turning to her while fishing in his pocket. He pulled out his wallet, and from it the small, crumpled sheet of paper, once fine with newness and hope, now wrinkled by age and time that had defeated even its elegant weight. "I wrote you this."

"You wrote me a letter? Today?"

"No." He bit his lip. It was embarrassing, but it was a secret he'd kept from her. And for the seal to work, he would need to make sure there were no secrets between them. He would need to tell her. To show her. "I wrote it eight years ago."

Her eyebrows raised, and she blushed and whispered, "It's the thing your mother said was in your wallet. You've carried it with you all this time?"

Azrael swallowed. His whole heart was on the line now,

and he had waited too long to give it to her. The note and his heart.

"I wanted to give it to you before you left for college."

"Azrael," Vickie pleaded, and she held her hand out. Part of him resisted, too afraid to show her everything. But he had waited long enough.

Azrael tossed it gently over to her, releasing the weight of all those years of folding and unfolding it.

She read it aloud, voice just above a whisper, and he squeezed his eyes shut, feeling each word, unwilling to watch her as she tasted the emotion he had held for her.

Victoria,

I know things are not always easy. I'm a witch and you're my beautiful, human neighbor, gifted with an impossibly cool power beyond anything I've ever known. But the truth is, I'm in love with you. I have been for as long as I can remember, and maybe it's silly, but I wanted you to know.

I love you for now and always. I love you in a way that unmakes me and then brings me back together. I love you an impossible amount, Vickie, the way you brighten a room, and the way you sing into your hairbrush with abandon. The times you've slept in my bed, I have wanted so badly to wake you and ask you if you could ever love me, too, but I've never had the courage.

So now it's time. I love you with the fire of a thousand universes racing across time and space and being reborn constantly into something new and burning. I love you amounts holding the stars apart. I love you.

-Azrael

P.S. I also want to touch your body. If that's creepy, burn this, and we will never speak of it again.

P.P.S. Here is a poem. Devil damn me, I might never be able to look at you again when you read it, but I have to give it to you. It's how I feel, and besides, I'm about to be an English major.

the light of your dark house shimmers
a blinking beacon harking, heralding
gold light freezing within your flaming eyes
your face when all else crumbles into clay
hearing your voice when my mind starts to stray
feeling your hands on all my stolen days
holding my still heart close and shut away
hopelessly keeping feelings locked away
devoted, golden light across the bay

He cleared his throat. "Do keep in mind that I was eighteen when I wrote it. It's so cringey. But it's honest."

Vickie's eyes flashed.

"It's perfect. Is it time?" she asked in a voice breathy enough that he wanted to taste it. He *needed* to taste it. They had to be only a few short steps away from touching, but it felt infinite, stretching taut between them so that he feared he might snap. "Is it time for the spell? Or midnight, at least? Because I might kiss you anyway, even if it kills you. You're perfection. Everything. Even in teenage poetry. If my mind had known then what my heart has probably known always, Azrael Hart, it would have sung right back to you after this note. This poem."

Azrael's voice caught in his throat, and for a moment he was unsure of whether he could actually form words anymore.

"It's time," he said. His voice shook. "For the spell, anyway."

He snapped his hand over the cauldron, and two goblets rose up from its depths, shimmering with pinkish-red liquid. A double snap and the goblets rested on the table in front of them, cooling.

"What's next?"

"Fire," he said, and he swore for a moment that flame roared in her hands, as though she wielded witchery, too, but it was only the reflection of the fireplace. He put a box of matches on the table and slid it toward her, careful not to let their fingers graze. "Can you light the flames while I work the spell?"

"Yes, I'll light your fire, Azrael."

"Oh yeah?"

"Yeah. In truth, I already burn for you."

"Fuck. That makes it really fucking hard to remember the spell work."

"I bet," she said, smirking. "Tell me how hard it is."

He swore softly, digging his hands into the table to stop himself from tossing caution to the wind and touching her.

"You know how hard, Vickie," he growled, and he trailed his eyes along her neck, snapping so the magic traced the threads of his vision.

"Do the spell. Please."

Clearing his throat and swallowing, he reminded himself to focus.

"First, fire burned between us, with the warmth of desire."

A few finger snaps and a trace of his essence whirled, gold and green, and shimmered in the flame of the candle closest to his goblet. He did the same for Vickie; hers was pinkish and shot through with a similar gold hue. The scent of strawberries and longing, ever-present.

"Victoria," he breathed, and she didn't admonish him for using her full name. Maybe she heard it for the prayer that it was, the brush of devotion against his unworthy lips.

"Azrael," she replied. "Tell me what to do next."

"Hold out your hand," he instructed. "Next, glass—sand forged in the fire."

Rolling his shoulders, he breathed deeply and summoned it from the sea, a handful for each of them. The reach of magic was a strain, but it felt *good*, like running a fast mile or lifting enough at the gym to be pleasantly sore the next day. Magic was as much a part of him as Vickie was.

It was time to let both in.

Snapping his fingers, he moved the sand from each palm to above the flames, and coaxed them to flicker higher and hotter, glistening and forging with enough searing, contained pressure to make glittering glass torches where fresh New England sand had hung suspended before. He lowered them to the table with care, and wrapped them in a heavy cloth napkin.

"Finally, we shatter the glass, to bind us together for as long as it would take to build it again, higher."

"For an eternity," she whispered, and the weight of her words was a pleasure. He needed to run his hand along her face and feel her.

Close. So close.

Vickie was breathing faster now, and he pointed to a dragon-shaped paperweight on a bookshelf behind her. Tried not to watch those dimples above her low-waisted jeans as she stretched up on tiptoes to reach it, smiling back at him in a way that lit fires beyond just the candle and the hearth.

"Smash it."

The weight of the carved brass dragon rocked through the table, shaking them the way he wanted to, and she handed it to him to do the same.

Shards and dust inside the napkin now, fire in the candle, and goblets cool enough to drink, he nodded at her.

"Now repeat after me.

"I set you in my soul, Victoria Elaine Starnberger."

"Exactly after you?"

His mouth twitched, and she blew him a kiss. Always stubborn. Always going her own way. And he always loved her.

"I set you in my soul, Azrael Ashmedai Hart."

"As a seal upon my heart."

"As a seal upon my heart."

He picked up his goblet, and she hers. Tipping it carefully not to spill, he toasted her, the vibration of the goblets reverberating as the table had, deep in his core.

"Now we toast and drink until it's drained," he said. His voice was straining, and his fingers were desperate to have her, his tongue to taste her.

"Prost," she said, clinking the goblet against his and then tipping it back. He would give anything to be the thing her lips wrapped around like that.

He raised his own to his mouth, and the liquid tasted sweet and tart, like berries and lemon. Earthen and heady, with a sharp edge.

Slamming the goblet down on the table, he felt the warmth of the spell spreading through him, like tiny invisible fairy lights burst through his veins and wrapped his heart in the gilded glow of a late porch night full of fireflies and soft music.

"Az," Vickie said, and he got up and crossed the distance between them. "What if it doesn't work? What if Lex was lying and the spell doesn't work?"

"He wasn't, and it will," he murmured, kneeling, and she dropped next to him so that they were both on their knees. "I'm more certain of you than I am of my own name. I've loved you since before I could remember, I love you now, and I'll love you always. Our magics have always known, really." Only inches lingered between them, and the corners of her beautiful mouth tugged upward. "And if by some off chance it doesn't, I'll die happy in your arms."

Vickie swatted the shoulder of his sweater, but she was smiling widely now, nose scrunching into the freckles he loved so much.

"Can I kiss you now?" Azrael asked, wanting to hear the exquisite pleasure of her enthusiasm.

"Kiss me now and always," she whispered.

Azrael raised his hands to Vickie's face, his palms hovering a few inches away from each side, feeling the warmth of her.

Of just her, no damning fire.

Touching nothing else, his mouth grazed hers.

Her lips parted for him, soft and molten, and she sucked in a sharp breath.

He pulled back, closing his hands on her temples, and looked at her, drinking her in.

She exhaled, relief washing away into darker pink that pulled across her cheeks, spotting them with color.

The pad of his thumb traced her jaw, running over her bottom lip and then down her neck, farther, to her collarbone and the top of her breast, over her T-shirt. He reached for her face again, brushing against the freckles. He'd count every one of them. Again.

"Kiss me. Now." The repeated command was edged with sharp need, and, fuck, he couldn't leave her hanging.

Their lips met, and Azrael couldn't help himself. He pulled Vickie's head toward him farther, crushing her moan between their mouths. Vickie threaded her hands in his hair and returned the sentiment. Tongues clashed, hungry, desperate, devouring. He bit at her bottom lip, and she moaned, words indecipherable but so, so sweet.

Moving lower, he pressed kisses along her neck, relishing more of those soft, explosive little gasps of longing as he reached her breasts, and she yanked up her shirt, over her head and off, to give him better access.

He slid his fingers down the sides of her bra, hooking them under the cups of it so that her breasts were free, nipples hardening even in the cozily warm air of the library. Unclasping it with a snap.

"It's your turn," she said, shrugging out of the bra. Pushing him and clawing his sweater off, and then the buckle of his belt and his zipper. "Let me taste how hard you are."

"Fuck, well, I obviously want that, and we should definitely come back to it later, but there is no way I'd last long enough to do what I want with you now if you got these pretty lips"—he ran a finger against the bottom one—"around me."

She flushed and nodded, but didn't let go, pushing his pants down. He was helping her now, stumbling slightly, pushing her jeans down, and sucking in too sharp a breath. He felt naked in a way he hadn't in years, like this meant something that all the other times had not.

"Do you have a condom?" she asked, splotches of desire coloring in the space between her freckles.

"I can get one. I'm also on birth control." Witches, unlike humans, had options for such things. His mother had taught him to make gender-neutral birth control pills when he was thirteen.

"I haven't been with anyone else since Robbie, and I have a breakup ritual of an STI test."

"Nothing more romantic than reproductive health care," he murmured, tugging at her lip with his teeth and running a hand down her arm, relishing the goose bumps that raised in the wake of his fingers. "I am also good. I've been tested since my last partner. But, Vickie, if at any point you change your mind, about the condom, or any of it, just say so."

"I won't," she said. "But noted. I trust you. Only if you want to, though." The uncertainty in her eyes made Azrael want to murder this Robbie person if they ever met, but he let it go, promising himself that their love would not be the jealous sort.

"I want nothing more than that, sweetheart." The word rolled off his tongue and rippled across her, a wave of a smile that told him he had found the sweet spot for what she would be to him. It was the modern version of Benedict's *my darling*. Of Persephone's *handsome*. A new sobriquet for a new generation of passionate, wildly-in-love Harts.

Vickie shuddered against him now.

Maybe he'd even renovate the home gym.

"Sweetheart," he murmured, pulling her closer, gently, by the arms, and tracing his hands up her shoulders to her neck, kissing her softly on the mouth before lowering her carefully to the ground and bracketing her body with his knees and hands on either side of her.

Trailing adorations down the center of her, he rubbed his hands down her sides as he slid down, tracing circles onto her thighs and moving them slowly inward. He pressed kisses against her belly button, her hips, the crease where each thigh met the center of her, his thumbs sliding upward and circling.

Vickie was gasping now, and he wanted to consume her. Her every sound of pleasure, her soft skin, all of her, but he settled for pressing languid kisses on each thigh, closer and closer to where she wanted him, as her legs trembled and she moaned. Azrael drew back for a moment, kissing the crooks of her knees, and then trailing his mouth up, up, up her thigh.

"Sweetheart," he whispered again. He let the letters of it brush against her lower lips and parted her with his tongue. Azrael pressed his tongue flat against her clit for a moment before lapping and circling, pumping a finger in and out, and watching her, the susurrations of her breath, so that he could learn, as always, more closely what pushed her closer and what made her dig her nails into his hair and yank.

Once he could feel her tensing, he moved his head up, smiling at her.

"Take me," she breathed. Her face was open. Flushed. It made his heart ache with joy and longing. "Take all of me," she said.

Pressing a palm against her stomach, he slid it around and under her to tilt her pelvis up toward him, and moved his hand back to circle his thumb around her bundle of nerves once more.

"Now, Az, please." The begging was more than he could withstand, and he moved up her body and nudged at her, relishing the way her mouth opened and she breathed, eyelashes fluttering. He pushed a little harder at the center of her with his thumb as he slid in and felt her adjust to him, her inner walls tight and close, so close.

Azrael drew out inch by inch and then back in, forcing himself to go slow enough to feel every part of her. To commit every exquisite second to memory.

"Faster," she commanded, and then he was gone, reckless and unable to stop himself from pounding so hard that she slipped a little bit and dug her hands into the carpet to stabilize herself, his thumb working at her, and he was so close that if she didn't finish soon, well, he wasn't sure he'd be able to go on.

"Vickie," he groaned. "You feel so fucking good. Come for me before I completely lose control. Let go."

Moving his thumb gently, he pushed into her, finding the

rhythm she'd once lunged toward on his fingers, and then she was arching her back and moaning loudly enough that the flame in the fireplace roared higher in approval. "Good girl," he whispered, "you're so close," and "yes, let me," and everything clenched around him, and he couldn't stop himself; his orgasm and his emotions exploded.

"I love you." His breathing was ragged around the words as they both came down from the high of ecstasy pooling between them.

"I love you too," she murmured into his ear as he collapsed, rolling onto his side and pulling her in to tuck her underneath his arm.

He could die a happy man right now. He snapped his fingers so that a pillow and throw blankets arranged themselves in a makeshift bed on the library floor. The house dimmed the lights, and he drifted, peacefully, into sleep, with Vickie curled around him.

Azrael Hart had come home.

At last.

CHAPTER 36

Victoria

They had woken up to stumble upstairs to his bedroom, the house lighting chandeliers in a soft romantic glow along their path. She tripped up a stair, nearly losing the fluffy blanket she'd thrown around her shoulders rather than get dressed. Azrael, who had pulled on just his underwear, snapped his fingers and two tall tumblers of water and a plate full of snacks materialized, floating in the air beside them.

His chest looked sculpted in the low lighting, and she bit her lip, reaching up to ruffle the dark curls snaking across his forehead. His brownish eyes darkened now, the gold and green almost completely snuffed out, as she pushed her hands against the bare skin of his shoulders and leaned up to kiss him. Hard.

"On the stairs?" he asked, tracing patterns that raised goose bumps on her arm with one hand.

"Another time," she said between panting breaths. "Your bed. The silk sheets. I've always wanted to."

"As you wish," he murmured, grabbing for her hand, and increasing their pace up the stairs. The pictures rattled a little on the walls, as though they, too, were eager, and from the main room, Franklin the polar bear rug roared in support.

They reached his room and the food and water landed neatly on his desk, but there would be time for that later. The curtains of the four-poster bed were drawn back, Emily Lickinson perched atop the sheets. One look at them and she yowled, stretched, and hopped off the bed.

Vickie slid toward the bed, but Az held his hands up.

"Hold on, sweetheart."

He snapped his fingers a few times, and tufts of white cat hair lifted from the sheets and sprinkled themselves into a trash can.

Azrael sneezed. "Cat hair," he said apologetically.

Emily was nowhere to be found now, though, and the clicking noises behind Vickie said that the house, once more, was locking them into privacy.

She walked over to the now shining, clean sheets, the obsidian silk almost glowing in candlelight that had dimmed, it seemed, as she approached the platform. With the practice of a thousand childhood moments, she hoisted herself onto the bed, tossing the blanket to the side.

"I used to dream of being naked in these sheets," she said softly.

"Tell me," said Azrael, moving toward the chair at his desk. Gripping the back of it so tightly his knuckles turned white. "Tell me exactly what you did when you thought of being in my bed."

"I," she started, flush creeping up her cheeks. Good goddess, if she was going to do this thing, she was going to do it completely. Uninhibited. With all her heart.

It was Azrael, for fuck's sake.

"I would picture the way the fabric would slide, soft against my skin." She ran a palm across the cool expanse of it, and a muscle ticked in his jaw. "When I was really wound up, I could always pretend it was your hand, not mine."

"Tell me," Az ordered again, his voice edged with urgency.

"I'd rather show you," she said, not believing her own boldness. But then again, she had been the one to tell him, even in her youth, about how the idea of spanking and whips was exciting. And they had done this before, in the shower, though it felt different now that she knew they could touch. She could do this.

Vickie lay down, settling her head in the pillows.

"Come here," she said, crooking a finger in the air. He walked slowly toward her, excitement clear and visibly defined in the blue plaid print of his boxers. "There. Stop at the edge of the bed."

She slid a fearless hand down her stomach, lower, and snuck the other up toward her breasts, stopping before she got there.

"Vickie," he pleaded. The strain in his voice was delicious.

"Yes?" she breathed.

"Let me touch you," he begged.

"When I'm ready." Sliding her hand lower, she dipped it between her thighs and felt, rather than heard, his groan on the air, in unison with her own. She squeezed at her nipple with her other hand, and sat up, staring at him. Memorizing the way his eyes darkened with need and anticipation. "Do you want to see how I would picture it? When I was by myself and pretending it was you?"

Azrael swore softly.

"Do you, Az?"

"Yes," he moaned. "Fuck. I'll give you anything you want, sweetheart. Show me."

Flipping over onto her knees, she looked back, and winked at him.

"Just like this," she said, reaching a hand between her thighs. Reminding herself at the twinge of nerves about exposing this much of her body to him that this was Az.

And that the prospect had her so turned on that she was soaking wet, glistening against her own fingers as she drew them in and out.

"Fuck, Vickie, I could die happy just watching you do that."

"The sheets are just as silky on my knees as I had imagined," she purred. "Now come over here and fuck me until my face is pressed into them too."

Azrael was beside her on the bed in an instant, but his resolve must have been stronger than hers, because he held back for a moment, tracing the backs of her thighs with a careful thumb. His voice was low, and she felt as though she were stretched too tight with wanting.

"How badly do you want me, Vickie?"

Reaching back, she grabbed his hand, dragging it over her. Into her.

"This much. Please?"

Azrael groaned, dipping his fingers in and snapping his other hand so that his boxers lay in a pile next to the bed.

"Anything," he said, sliding into her. He reached a hand around, covering her fingers with his own, sliding down them and slightly to the left, finding a spot that had taken her years to pinpoint on her own, but apparently was second nature to him. He dragged a finger outside of her as he took her from behind, not releasing her own hand so that she was working not quite at the same angle but at the same rhythm with her fingers. "Anything at all you want. Anything you need, Victoria, say the word, and it's yours."

The sensation of Azrael, of his hands and her own, and the filthy thoughts full of possibility, all pooled in her core. She moaned his name as he picked up speed. Felt everything tremble as he gripped her hips, and rode her to the edges of her pleasure before hauling her torso up, one hand at a hip still and the other at a shoulder. He snapped his fingers, and she felt his magic answer, curling low around her belly, nudging lower as he drove into her from behind.

Removing the hand from her shoulder, he snapped again, this time pinching a nipple, and she was surprised by the burst of pleasure as a twinge of light pain stoked in her. "You're so fucking sexy. Do you like that?" Az breathed, against her earlobe.

"Yes," she whimpered. "More."

Moaning into her ear, Azrael snapped again, and both the physical contact and the magic tugged at her breasts, kneading them; pushed between her thighs like an extra pair of hands; pushed down on the spot behind where he entered her, slick and snug, and suddenly she needed to feel him so closely that it hurt.

"Spank me," she moaned. The sound he made was guttural.
He paused. "Yeah?"

"Yeah."

He paused to bend her gently down back onto all fours, and then smacked the flat of his palm against her hip, the stinging pleasure of it burning across her.

"Harder, Az."

His fingers snapped, and the pressure increased everywhere, his other hand reeling back this time to connect with her ass cheek in a sharp crack that sent sizzling, impossible desire through her.

"Yes," she breathed, an exhale of relief. A torrent of emotion at finally being able to trust someone enough to communicate exactly what she wanted. It washed over her and pushed her over the edge. Everything was clamping, clenching, skyrocketing into pleasure as he gritted his teeth and finished, her name on his lips and his hands gripping her hips as she whined and pushed up against him again. Magic it turned out, was an incredibly useful toy in the bedroom.

"Damn," she panted. "What the fuck is wrong with us to have missed out on that for so long?"

"I don't know," he said, collapsing onto the bed and dragging her with him. "But you're here now, so I vote we have a snack and some water, and see where the rest of the night takes us."

She trailed a finger down his chest, past the line of hair under his belly button.

"I know *exactly* where I want it to take us next," Vickie said, running her tongue across her lips, her eyes flicking lower.

He raised an eyebrow and repeated, "As you wish, Vickie. As you wish."

One Year Later

The fishnet bodysuit under a leotard and the thigh-high boots were a little unwieldy to serve apple hand pies in, but she figured it was worth it both to invest in her business by leaning into Sultry Sunday and to be able to smirk as she told Azrael about it later.

She snapped a picture and texted it to Az. The best part of being with him, besides the obvious, was that she knew she could send him a chain of text messages in a row, and he would relish them all. He would never think of her as clingy.

> **Vickie:** check out my Sultry Sunday fit
> **Vickie:** Look what you made me do.
> **Vickie:** Get it? Because of the video, and also because you inspire me to wear, you know, leather and fishnets?

Typing bubbles popped up immediately, and he shot back a picture of a baby playing with a life-sized human skull. His dimpled cheeks were crinkled into a smile.

> **Vickie:** Azrael, is Milo playing with a human skull? Is that appropriate for a baby??
> **Az:** Relax. It's a toy. I cleaned off a box of old baby things I found in the attic.
> **Vickie:** Just make sure it's not secretly magical, Az. I don't want to have to explain to Kelley Watson that you magicked her baby while she was on a date. Because, you know, the whole NACoW convention laws about not telling humans there's magic and whatnot. But also, babysitting standards.
> **Az:** Got it. Send me more pictures of those boots later. I'll be tired after Kelley picks Milo up, but never too tired for you.

Vickie smiled and set her phone on the counter. There really was nowhere to put it in this outfit. Nowhere she wanted to reach into while working, anyway.

The scent of cinnamon whirled through the air as Hazel and Cole, the college freshman she'd hired in the spring to help staff more flexible hours, refilled coffees and teas. Now that October was in full swing, the scent of spiced pumpkin and apples lingered in the air for Sultry Sunday.

She waved at Hank, whose plate was empty, and pointed in the wordless exchange she and her favorite patron enjoyed. He nodded enthusiastically, and she strode back to the ovens to grab the last batch of pumpkin spice donuts.

Azrael had helped her magic the dough into perfect heart and skull shapes this morning before he left to go back home and babysit as a favor to Aurora, the charming coworker who was currently in the shop, knees brushing her date's in a booth in the corner.

She delivered a plate of the donuts to Kelley and Aurora after Hank for good measure. They looked like a pair who would want a set of hearts and skulls, especially after Aurora's terrible experience with Chet—who, rumor had it, had run away to Florida to escape gambling debts, leaving the English department in the care of one Mr. Azrael Hart. Azrael deserved this opportunity, and he'd earned it, interview and all. And Aurora deserved the kind of wholesome goodness of the young widow Watson. Goddess knew Kelley Watson deserved a little sweetness after losing her husband at age twenty-three, and with a brand-new baby too.

Even if babysitting Milo *might* be making Azrael a little too keen on babies. This was the fifth Milo pic he'd sent her, and she could feel how much he loved kids.

Not that she was ready to have any anytime soon, especially while she was just finally getting the shop into a good rhythm, but she was surprised by how nice the idea sounded.

The past year with Az had felt like coming home, but to the kind of home she had never really known. The kind of home she hadn't expected, that was lined with the wrought-iron snapping gates and shadowy, misty willows of Hart Manor. For now, she wanted her own space in the apartment, which Azrael had helped her clean out, magicking the old boxes of trinkets to the home gym formerly known as a sex dungeon so that he could go through them.

One day, she wanted to move into Hart Manor, and she knew the house wanted her to, as well, for Azrael's bedroom had expanded and sprouted a pink jetted soaking tub next to the shower in his black marble bathroom, and an entire extra walk-in closet. Every time she was there, it snuck in a bouquet of flowers or a piece of art that seemed selected just for her, until she was not terribly certain if it was Az or the house or both, welcoming her at her own pace, showing she had a place there, whether it was tomorrow, five years from now, or just on weekends for the rest of their lives.

Behind the counter, Cole was leaning close to Hazel, whose pink curls bobbed around her like a halo and picked up the warm tones of her dark brown skin. Cole raised a pale, freckled hand in front of their face to hide whatever they were saying, and Hazel shook with laughter.

When Vickie walked toward them, the two went quiet, blissfully unaware that she could overhear most of what they had been saying about what sounded like an extremely nice girl with a crush on Hazel. Cole, apparently, was that ship's biggest stan.

Good. She *loved* young love. She'd seen this type of film before, and she liked the ending.

"Hey, Vickie. So, are things pretty serious with Mr. Hart?" Brown eyes bored innocently into hers, mischief pulling the girl's lips upward.

Shaking her head, Vickie smiled at Hazel.

"Never mind, Hazel. Did you refill the sugars?"

"I got it, boss," said Cole, walking away and abandoning her to Hazel's inquisition.

"Come on, he's not my teacher this semester. You can tell me."

"Listen. Hazel, I've known Azrael Hart for longer than you've been alive. I'm too old to be sharing business like that, and you've got far more interesting things to think about than a high school English teacher's girlfriend."

Hazel grinned and threaded her fingers together.

"See, that's where you're wrong. He's not my teacher this year, but still. There is literally nothing more interesting to me in this moment. And you just admitted you're his girlfriend."

Vickie shrugged and shook her head again.

"Tell me how you guys met."

"He was my neighbor for as long as I can remember. I've been dancing in his bedroom with a hairbrush as a microphone since before I knew that men or women could give me fuzzy feelings."

"That's pretty dope," said Hazel. "I bet you're great at hairbrush karaoke."

"Oh, absolutely. Firstly, I am always willing to dress the part." Vickie gestured at the music video–inspired outfit she was wearing now. "And secondly, I'm goddess awful at singing, but I don't care, and Azrael never has either."

"Yeah," said Hazel, smiling. "He seems like the type to take you just as you are. Relationship goals."

Vickie smiled. She thought Azrael would appreciate modeling healthy love for his students.

Life was messy and complicated, and there was plenty of grief and loss that lingered in her heart, and in his.

But he had still picked the perfect time to drop into her life, full of complications and rejections—the parents who had disowned her, the power that had almost consumed him. And yet, despite it all, she knew he loved her fully just as she was. There would be moments of doubt, of course, but no more self-loathing about clinginess. No more fear of losing her most important friendship.

Azrael Hart had picked the *perfect* time to make himself hers. And she would do as much work as it took to make sure he was as blissfully happy as he had always deserved to be.

CHAPTER 37

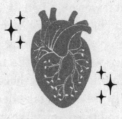

Azrael

Kelley had picked up Milo a few hours earlier, and devil damn him if he wasn't enamored with that adorable little dude, with his wispy baby hair, his enthusiastic cuddling, and his deep dimples. He'd always loved babies.

Someday, he wanted to be just like his parents. As much as they had embarrassed him for his entire life, and as long as he had tried to become *normal*, and carve out a path for himself elsewhere, this was where he belonged. He wanted the world with Vickie. She made everything a little brighter, even when work was stressful or, on occasion, when parents yelled at him. He wanted the touch of her hand to reassure him that she was there, sealed upon his heart. That even though he was a witch, and she was a ray of sunshine who happened to be gifted like a death goddess, their magics knew that they were meant for each other, his might and her fire, each warming the other and winding into something beautiful.

He wanted to have her by his side and in the house and under him and on top of him and with him always. He wanted her to be blissfully happy and to do what she wanted, and to be with him, and have so much love that they wanted other people to share it with too. Even if it didn't go perfectly, and even if one day their kids found their sex dungeon, or if they died too early. He wanted to take a chance on loss with her, because to live without knowing what it was like to have that exhilarating feeling of home, of oneness, that he had with Vickie, well, he knew all too well that it was merely half a life.

No, Azrael would cherish every second of the time they had together, and pray to the stars that it lasted a long, long time. He would dance with her in the moonlit conservatory and bicker with her in the foyer and share meals at that dining room table as a family. He would take her to the silk sheets of his four-poster bed and make love to her every night the way he'd always wanted to, and then some. He'd reach for her in the morning unafraid, without pretending that he was anything less than completely in love with her. He'd fight off a thousand Halloween curses, and solve a thousand mysteries, just to say her name.

What bliss.

He would keep giving Victoria Elaine Starnberger his heart, because, after all, she'd already held it long before he'd written her that letter nine years ago. His heart would always beat for her anyway.

So he stood outside the house, exhausted from babysitting but unwilling to wait even a second longer before seeing her face and reminding himself that she existed, real in the flesh, overwhelming and extraordinary and all that he had ever wanted.

He could see her freckles through the windshield, and the shiny lengths of her polished black fingernails as she pulled the little yellow bug up to the driveway behind the hearse. If anyone could commit completely to a costume, it was Vickie. By the time she parked, Azrael was halfway down the drive to her, and they ran to each other, the way they always did after a long day of work, unwilling to walk slowly to bridge the gap of the day's distance that stretched each morning and closed each night.

"Victoria," he whispered into her hair, breathing in lavender and strawberries and contentment as her arms wound around his neck and he dug his fingers into the fishnet bodysuit in the space between her top and the shorts. "What do you call an animal that steals all the soap from your bath?"

"I don't know. What?"

"A robber duck."

She laughed, groaning a little. "You're absolutely hopeless. It's lucky you're also hot as hell."

"Mmm," he said. "I'm lucky to be with you." He pulled back for a moment, drinking her in. "You've nailed that particular look, but I know you love this music video. Let me put you in a bathtub of diamonds with nothing but red lipstick on."

She giggled against his neck, and warm licks of magic shot through him, the familiar way his body always recognized her.

"You know just what to say to a girl, Az. But a bubble bath might be more comfortable than a diamond bath."

He grinned. "Why not just try one? I can't steal diamonds without violating a dozen Witchery Council codes, but I'm sure we at least have a chest full of imitation gemstones somewhere in the basement that I could borrow. I think the house wants you to use that new tub it got you."

"Well," she drawled, running her lips along his neck until he shivered. "The house wants what it wants, right?"

"It does, Vick, and it's such a good house. I wouldn't want to let it down."

"No," she mused, slipping an arm around him, and walking toward the door, which screeched at her gently. "But I still vote bubbles over baubles." She patted the knocker, and it sighed a little, relenting and swinging open. "I always liked this haunted door."

"It's just fussy," he said. "But it means well." The door still made him jumpy, but like everything else in the house, it recognized Vickie and loved her.

Maybe he had never missed his chance at all. Maybe chances were like his magic, always waiting, buzzing, under his skin, until he got his life together and let them in.

He pulled her in, pressing a kiss on the top of her head as the door shut gently behind them and they stood in the hallway.

Tracing a thumb along her jaw and pulling her in, he slipped his other hand around her waist and kissed her, dipping her low into the sort of extravagant gesture that the house hadn't seen since his parents died.

The blinds shuddered, and the lights dimmed for them, casting everything in a warm, romantic glow.

"Vickie," he whispered. "I love you, sweetheart."

"I love you, too, Az," she said, pulling his face down to hers, and the world around them faded, though he could tell that the runner of the rug was tugging them gently toward the stairs.

"Thank you, house," Az murmured, scooping his hands underneath Vickie and lifting her so she could wind her legs around him. His strides were faster than she could have gone in those boots up the stairs and down the hall to the bedroom that had conveniently grown into a space perfect for them both.

Vickie smiled up at Azrael, and he finally understood.

Their bodies sang to each other. Two strands of enchantment, beating, stretching, like an invisible string that had spanned a distance between them that had been thousands of miles and misunderstandings long.

With all the love in his heart and the power in his veins, he leaned down and kissed her.

Again.

The End

Acknowledgments

First, thank you to my grandmother, who lived to see me sell this book, but not to see it published. I don't have words to describe how devastated I am that she can't read this. Still, her memory is a blessing, woven into these pages in the grand, epic love story of the Harts. She and my grandfather are part of every book I write.

Mel, working with you has been leveling up in word magic. Your notes have made me feel seen as a human and a lover of books and language. And Elizabeth, your enthusiasm and support have been lovely. To the entire team at Atria, thank you for making this dream come true. Camila Gray for bringing Vickie and Az to life in the cover illustration even better than I could have ever imagined. Kelli McAdams for the vision and design that match this book's vibe. Zakiya Jamal, for gorgeous graphics. Camila Araujo for publicity genius. Thank you also to everyone in copy editing, marketing, production, and all of the other behind-the-scenes roles that make this book possible, including the people I meet after this note is set: I am so grateful for your work on this book of my heart too.

To Alex, again, always; you have given me endless grief about long sentences, but also endless support in the form of little snacks, many beverages, and more than half of kid bedtimes by a lot. Here is a concise sentence for you, for once. Happy New Year. To my children, who were three and five when I started writing this, and who told me from the beginning that they loved every book I wrote. Love you more than anything, baby bunnies. Follow your dreams, and know that you will always be welcome home, no matter how far you wander. Anyone who tells you love interests are only great in books is NOT someone worth settling for. You deserve a love that sees all of you and loves every bit of it. Also, don't read this book until you're older.

To Alison and Kristi, I am glad to have lived through so many eras with you two. Best believe we will stay bejeweled because HERE WE ARE, BESTIES. Love you both with the intensity of a random American dude on a Swedish metro raving about bad pizza.

To my sisters: Abi, the first person to read everything I have ever written, and Vera, who pointed out when I inadvertently wounded characters beyond medical help. To all of my family, especially my cousins, all of whom are unfairly charming and funny, thank you. To my dad, for the love of words and books.

To Eva, thank you for your work on this book.

To Missy, Zoe, Winnie, and Alison: I'm going to immortalize the intentions we set here: Hold space for yourself, and don't be a people pleaser. Let go of what doesn't serve you and try to avoid FOMO. Be kinder to yourself and spend time with loved ones. For the environment and for political reasons, don't buy unnecessary things. Erase uncertainty and move forward.

Jordan, my original critique partner, and the only way I survived the absolute hell of writing rejections and drama. DeAndra, who right away felt like a kindred spirit in teaching, writing, and juggling it all. To Faith, and her beautiful writing and her chickens. To Megan Oliver, for really going through it all with me. To the crones, for always being just the right amount of wild and wicked. To hell, to TTPD, to 2025, to the Atrium, and to every chat I've been in and will ever be in that has supported me. To Dallas, for listening and reading and just in general understanding my vibe. I feel like there's a song reference I should use, but all I'm coming up with is a movie quote instead, so "You listen to me! You're so special and you're so talented and you have everything it takes." To Lindsay, RIP Luna, the OG white fluffy cat and the inspiration for Emily Lickinson. To Annemarie & Erin & Rob & Matt, for so many things. To my community in the parent lounge of TS; I appreciate you all so much.

To Jess, thank you for taking a chance on me. To all the early readers who lovingly guided this one forward: Hannah, Lauren, Megan, Christina, Marietta, and everyone else who read. To Laura, who has cheered for me in every career path, even when we were just a silly little Jessica Rabbit and Slutty Care Bear. To Brigid and Kami, for advising me and encouraging me, and for endless patience with my newbie questions. To Erin, the creator of the dental mayhem publishing news plan. To every wonderful writer who has helped me when I'm going through it: Mallory, Maria, Shannon, Noreen, Amy, Lenora, and more. To Amber for always listening, and to Caitlin, for your friendship. And thank you to all the writing friends who have taught me something, even the hard way. I appreciate what you have added to my craft. To Kat, for being an amazing teacher, and then always making time to talk about books with me. You're wonderful.

A lot of people step into your life for a little bit of time and then gracefully out, and that's beautiful. So many beloved friends fall into this category; we may have fallen out of touch, but I still appreciate you so much. Those of you still here across years: love you bunches. Old friends and old colleagues: whether or not we are still close, I hope for joy for all of you. Unless you were bigoted or cruel, in which case, well, I hope you have the life you deserve.

Thank you to every teacher and professor, especially the English teachers who believed in my writing even when I was very dramatically burning my fiction at home in a trash can (do not do this—it's a fire hazard). Truly, thank you. You are amazing. I would not be here without you. To all my former students: I believed in you then, and I believe in you now. Especially if you are queer, or feeling alone and struggling to find a place: I see you.

And finally, I am so happy to be alive and able to see a book I wrote published. That's a big deal for a person with debilitating depression; I hurt my own feelings a lot, and sometimes my brain tries to trick me into NOT being here. So especially if you are writing through depression and anxiety, I hope you keep going too.

About the Author

Audrey Goldberg Ruoff is a former high school English and journalism teacher who taught with the enthusiasm of Valerie Frizzle, but for secondary education. She lives in a suburb of Washington, DC, with her spouse, her kids, a scrappy but loyal little dog, and a witchy black cat. *Hopelessly Teavoted* is her debut novel. Visit audreyruoff.com and follow her on Instagram and TikTok @audreygoldbergruoff.

ATRIA BOOKS, an imprint of Simon & Schuster, fosters an open environment where ideas flourish, bestselling authors soar to new heights, and tomorrow's finest voices are discovered and nurtured. Since its launch in 2002, Atria has published hundreds of bestsellers and extraordinary books, which would not have been possible without the invaluable support and expertise of its team and publishing partners. Thank you to the Atria Books colleagues who collaborated on *Hopelessly Teavoted* as well as to the hundreds of professionals in the Simon & Schuster advertising, audio, communications, design, ebook, finance, human resources, legal, marketing, operations, production, sales, supply chain, subsidiary rights, and warehouse departments who help Atria bring great books to light.

EDITORIAL
Melanie Iglesias Pérez
Elizabeth Hitti

JACKET DESIGN
Kelli McAdams
Camila Gray

MARKETING
Zakiya Jamal
Morgan Pager

MANAGING EDITORIAL
Paige Lytle
Shelby Pumphrey
Lacee Burr
Sofia Echeverry

PRODUCTION
Annette Pagliaro Sweeney
Vanessa Silverio
Janet Robbins Rosenberg
Esther Paradelo
Hannah Lustyik

PUBLICITY
Camila Araujo

PUBLISHING OFFICE
Suzanne Donahue
Abby Velasco

SUBSIDIARY RIGHTS
Nicole Bond
Sara Bowne
Rebecca Justiniano